EMPIRE
OF SIN

EMPIRE

RINA KENT

To writer block
Fuck you, bitch
I win. You lose.

AUTHOR NOTE

Hello reader friend,

This book isn't dark as the rest of my books, but it's filled with a lot of angst and an epic clash of many characters.

Empire of Sin is a complete STANDALONE.

Sign up to Rina Kent's Newsletter for news about future releases and an exclusive gift.

My boss. My sin.

I'm not the type who has one night stands.

It wasn't supposed to happen, okay?

A couple of drinks and a sinful British accent later and I'm in bed with a stranger.

Of course, I left first thing in the morning because I'm a responsible adult.

An adult who has a new job that I need in order to keep my double life a secret.

Little did I know I'm not, in fact, responsible.

Because the stranger I left in bed? Yeah, he's not a stranger after all.

He's my new boss.

Knox Van Doren might have a charming smile, but a true villain lurks beneath it all.

And like any villain, he'll use my sin against me…

PLAYLIST

"Anastasia" – Slash & Myles Kennedy & The Conspirators
"Nothing Else Matters" – Metallica
"Smells Like Teen Spirit" – Nirvana
"Lonely Nights" – Scorpions
"She's Gone" – STEELHEART
"The Unforgiven" – Metallica
"Turn The Page" – Metallica
'This I Love" – Guns N' Roses
"Hey You" – Pink Floyd

EMPIRE

OF SIN

ONE

Anastasia

TONIGHT, I'M GOING TO FUCK SOMEONE.

I don't care who.

I don't care where.

I just need to cross it off my bucket list before I disappear.

Good girls like me don't think about fucking or doing it with a complete stranger. We're taught to always keep our legs closed, our hearts sealed, and our brains dormant.

Oh, and we don't get to curse.

We don't get to live either.

We're just valuable stock to be used when the opportunity arises.

Good girls like me definitely don't dress in provocative red dresses that show more cleavage than it hides. We're not even allowed to buy such things.

But I did. Secretly. When no one was looking.

I'm wearing it now, the red dress that falls amply to mid-thigh and bares half of my back. I improvised and used a dainty chain to attach the straps together at the back and hooking my lucky butterfly motif to it—the only thing my mom left me before she also disappeared to a different place than the one I'll be going to.

With each move, I feel the soothing coldness of the pendent against my bare back. Normal people hate the cold, but I find solace in it. It probably has to do with my Russian genes. Although I was born in the States and have lived here my entire life, my origins will never change.

I wasn't even allowed to adopt the normal American lifestyle. Education? Homeschooled. Fun? Security hazard. Friends? What are those? Clubs and bars? Yeah, they're not an option.

So the fact that I'm in a bar is a miracle that should be engraved in history. It's called Black Moon and is situated at the end of a backstreet in New Jersey.

It took me so much effort to leave home and come here, which is why my trip has got to bring results.

Truth is, I'm absolutely not an expert on these things, but I did my research and also hacked into their system to get an idea of their security measures and the people who come here.

Judging by the trouble I found with their firewalls, I'd say they're good enough.

The place has a classy, comfortable atmosphere that I'm drawn to the moment I walk in. The decor is black and dark brown and the lights are dim, giving the patrons privacy and a sense of anonymity.

Perfect for me.

Still, I feel eyes on me. Lots of them. They're digging into my skull and trying to pull out my true identity—the one that should, under no circumstances, be revealed.

My hand turns clammy and I bring it up, resting it on my chest to calm both its shaking and my heartbeat.

It's all in your head, Ana. It's not real.

With a deep breath, I make my way through the tables and try not to lose the confidence I've been building for days and planned for weeks.

I'm a planner that way. Nothing ever happens without a plan. Not even the small details as to which bar I'll go to.

Since Black Moon is a high-end bar, I came a bit early so that I can get in quickly.

I climb onto one of the chairs and sit at the bar, in direct view of the bartender, whose name tag reads *Simon*. Curly hair falls over his forehead and he's wearing a white shirt with the sleeves rolled up to expose his forearms. When he flashes me a charming grin, I think I have my pick for the night.

A small wave of relief floods me. I don't have to gather more courage and look for someone else.

"What can I get you, miss?"

"Vodka martini. Make it a double, please." I try to sound flirty, but I have no clue if it works. I really suck at this.

But it's not like I've had plenty of opportunities before. This is my first time in a bar. In fact, it's the first time I've been outside of the house alone.

This night is a first for everything.

"Right away." He gets busy and speaks to me over his shoulder, "You like your vodka, I assume?"

"A little."

Okay, that was a white lie. I never thought I would fit the stereotype of how every Russian loves vodka, but when we celebrated my eighteenth birthday two years ago, I was told I needed to drink it and ever since then, I refuse to consume any other type of alcohol.

A smirk lifts Simon's lips as if he's amused by how much I like vodka. "Are you new around here?"

Shit. Shit. He figured me out, didn't he? Everyone does. It doesn't matter if I chose a place out of state or that I faked a driver's license and my age.

One look at me and people know who I am and where I came from. No amount of makeup and red dresses will change what I am.

Who I am.

Maybe I should abort this before it gets too complicated. Maybe I can drive back earlier than planned, and—

I shake my head internally. I worked so hard for this freedom. I'm not going to give it all up now.

So I wear the best smile I can offer as I stare at the bartender for a brief second before I cut off eye contact. "Why are you asking?"

"I just haven't seen you around, is all."

My muscles relax when a shaky breath whooshes out of me.

See? It's nothing. I'm safe here. I made sure no one from my circle comes to this place, after all.

He places the martini in front of me. "Let me know if you need anything else."

"Thanks, Simon."

He grins and I know he's about to strike up a conversation. I can see it in the ease in his eyes and the way his body is leaning toward me.

Learning body language is a given in the world that I've lived in all my life. I might be insignificant in the grand scheme of things, but I recognize these things.

Simon opens his mouth to speak, but he's interrupted when an intruder slides onto the stool right beside me, even though the rest of the chairs are empty.

Oh, please.

It took me a lot of planning to get to a stage where my brain is willing to take things to the next level. I don't do well with people around.

They have eyes. And most of them are judgy and critical and are always out to get me.

Okay, maybe they aren't, but I can't really rationalize that. Because I feel their eyes again. A pair or maybe two.

And they're watching me. Closely. Intently. As if they can rip open my façade and peek inside the shell I've surrounded myself with.

"Macallan, neat."

My fingers tighten around the martini, then I empty half of it in one go. That deep, low voice with the calm undertone is the reason I feel the watchful eyes. I can sense it deep in my heart that's never steered me wrong.

Is it one of the bodyguards I overlooked in my plan? No, that's not possible. They think I'm sick and sleeping in my room so no one will disturb me until the morning.

Using my hair as a curtain, I tilt my head to the side to get a better look. I try not to be obvious about it, try to pretend my legs aren't shaking and my flight mode isn't kicking me to move my butt and bolt out of here.

The man who's sitting beside me has a presence as deep as his voice. There's an unnerving quality to him, even though he's just sitting there.

His physical appearance has something to do with it. He's handsome, shockingly so. Unfairly so. Probably the most beautiful man I've ever seen—and that includes actors and super models. He has the type of physical perfection that makes you stop and stare.

As if that's not enough, he's tall, his legs look long even when sitting, and his shoulders are so broad that the jacket of his Armani suit molds to his developed muscles.

Muscles that could easily overpower me if he chooses to. I shouldn't be thinking about that option. Hell, I should be apprehensive about it, considering all the men in my life, but I can't overlook the fact that this particular man could and would overpower me in a heartbeat.

A sudden flush of heat coats my thighs and I have to clench them together to chase away the sensation. I need to focus on something else, anything but the liquid fire that I shouldn't be feeling.

But I'm slammed with something worse.

His face.

It's a force that hits you out of nowhere. There's a hardness in it, a zing of electricity that's about to electrocute whoever is near.

A volcano that's on the verge of erupting.

I've never found male beauty to be dangerous, and that's saying something considering who I am and whom I encounter on a daily basis.

But his is different. It's not supposed to be dangerous, I realize. His beauty isn't there to teach a lesson or bash someone's head in. He's wearing a designer suit and is drinking Macallan for God's sake, which means he's some sort of a businessman. His thick Swiss watch that's strapped around his wrist must've cost a small fortune. It's luxurious.

He is luxurious. And not in a dangerous way like all the men in my life.

Instead, it's in a powerful, neat way. Like his whiskey. So why is there danger emanating from him?

His hair is light, but not as light as my platinum blonde that's almost white. His is somewhat chestnut, somewhat sandy, and it's styled, which showcases his forehead and killer cheekbones. He has a straight nose and a square jaw that gives him a sharp type of masculinity.

Then I find it.

The reason I associated him with the people from my life.

It's his eyes.

They're greenish with a golden ring, or maybe they're hazel and the lack of light is making me see otherwise. Either way, those eyes are too intense for someone who should be nothing more than a businessman.

There's a fire in them.

A lulling element that appears dormant but could combust at any second. A current that's building in the background. A predator who's watching from the sidelines, waiting for the right moment to strike.

And they're staring right back at me.

Shit.

I quickly drag my gaze back to my martini and finish it off. When I spot Simon close by, I blurt, "Vodka, neat. Make it a double. Actually, a triple."

The last part is whispered, as if I'm ashamed of my drinking habits. And maybe I am a little. I started the night with sophistication and martinis, but now, I just want my vodka, because something alien happened to me just now.

I made extended eye contact with a stranger. A *stranger*. What the fuck?

Maybe I need to run now.

Maybe I need to disappear without carrying out this stupid part of my plan.

What was I thinking anyway? Me, a one-night stand? I must've overestimated my abilities.

Simon flashes me a small smile before he goes to get me the drink. When he hands it to me, I finish half of it, then stare intently at the other half.

Mainly to stop myself from stealing peeks at the stranger next to me who's leisurely sipping from his own drink. His movements are smooth, *too smooth*, like a lion who's lounging on his throne while watching the peasants.

"You can watch. I don't mind."

British. The accent that's spoken near my ear is sinfully British, and now, I'm about to choke on my spit because no one has ever been this close to me aside from my family.

No one.

But instead of bolting, I freeze. Or, more like, I'm *frozen* by the sudden attack. Logically, I realize this isn't in fact an attack and that I'm exaggerating, but my brain doesn't recognize that. It's trapped in a static state and all I can do is slowly lift my head.

I'm not ready for how impossibly close he is, how those eyes are shining, more inwardly than outwardly. And why is he so close, again? Or maybe I'm imagining it because my heartbeat is throbbing in my throat. "Excuse me?"

"I said you can watch, beautiful. I'm better to look at than your drink."

Arrogant. Okay. One point to deduct from the perfect score.

Though he really shouldn't have called me beautiful with that illegal accent of his. It might have added a few more points that even I don't approve of.

"I happen to love my vodka, but thanks for the offer." I sound confident and in my element, when I am, in fact, shaken to the bones by his presence.

His infuriately attractive presence.

The bottom of my belly contracts in short intervals, and I'm going to bet it's not due to the alcohol.

"Does that mean I have to compete with your drink?" There's a unique quality to the way he speaks, a bit amused, a bit flirtatious, and so assertive, I hate him a little for it.

Why do some people get to play the social game so well while others, like me, can barely get words out?

"Why would you?"

"Why do you think? For your attention." His voice drops at the end and so does my stomach. The sensation is so novel that I can't fathom it.

My neck and cheeks heat and the butterfly pendant feels like lava on my skin. "You want my attention?"

"Amongst other things."

"Like?"

He takes a sip of his whiskey, but his intense eyes haven't left mine long after his Adam's apple bobs with the swallow. I can't help gulping the saliva gathered in my mouth as well, then taking a drink. Either the alcohol is loosening my nerves or there's something wrong with me since I can't stop staring at him.

At the way he seems confident in his own skin, unlike me, or the way he takes each action with a simmering control that I feel but can't see.

After he's finished, the British stranger places his elbow on the bar, which allows him to get close. So close that I smell his cologne. A mixture of lime, clean laundry and male musk. It's not strong, but it's as lulling as his presence, trapping me in the confinements of its walls.

The space between us becomes nonexistent when he turns

sideways and his breath skims the shell of my ear. It takes everything in me not to go into flight mode, considering how much of an expert I am at that.

But not tonight.

Tonight is different.

"Like making you squirm." The whisper of his words makes me shudder. It's a full-body one that I can't suppress, despite my attempts.

I don't know where I get the courage to ask, "That's all?"

"Oh, I can do *so* much more." He licks the shell of my ear and I bite my tongue to suppress a moan.

Holy shit. It's like I'm on an aphrodisiac. One touch and I melt. One touch and I'm wiggling and clenching my thighs in search of *something*. What, I have no clue.

Due to being hidden my whole life, everything feels heightened and unreal. As if I left my own body and I'm existing in a different reality.

Just like I planned for this night to be.

"How old are you?" His question is sensual, low-pitched, and makes me shudder again.

"Twenty-three," I lie, because he looks to be in his early thirties and I don't want to appear too young.

"Hmm." There's a vibration in his voice as his tongue lowers to the hollow of my throat. And holy hell, it's like he licked my pussy, because it's wet now. My pussy, not my neck.

Okay, maybe my neck, too, but it's my core that's throbbing for more.

As if knowing exactly what that does to me, he flicks his tongue across the same spot and bites down.

Oh, fuck.

I jam my legs shut, afraid that he'll see how desperate I am for this. How much I need it before I disappear.

It's my "fuck you" to the people who intended to use this part of me to marry me off to the first influential man who comes knocking on our door.

He continues his assault on my throat and his hand skims to my back, my bare back. His skin is similar to fire. A scorching one and he's about to melt me with it, maybe scathe me, maybe drag me to the pits of hell.

"W-what about you?" I ask, assuming that's what's expected in these types of conversations.

Though this can hardly be called a conversation now that his fingers are toying with my butterfly pendant and my flesh at the same time.

"Twenty-eight."

A shudder zips down my spine and it has less to do with his age and more to do with his touch and his voice. Seriously, no voice should be as sinfully attractive as his.

It's like the devil's—whispering and lulling me to my damnation.

"What's your name?" His hot breaths against my throat and his possessive hold on my back send sparks through my whole body.

I'm tingling, throbbing, and aching for something I've never experienced.

Something I never thought was possible in my life.

"No…names," I manage to say in an airy voice I didn't think I was capable of.

"Why?" He bites down on a spot on my neck and it's hard enough that I wince. It's hard enough that I'm clenching my soaked thighs.

"Because anonymity is thrilling."

I expect him to argue, to demand that he know my name, and I have a fake one for that, just in case, but he does something entirely different.

Something that makes my toes curl and my heart hammer.

He laughs, the sound low and sinister and so damn delicious against my neck. When he pulls back, his intense eyes have darkened. They're amused now. Or maybe it's sadism that I'm staring at.

Usually, I can't maintain eye contact for more than a second, but I'm trapped in his.

I can't look away.

I won't.

Because there are words and phrases in that gaze. A book, maybe, and while I'm not able to delve into all of its pages and decrypt its code, I can at least try.

Trying is the first phase of anything.

But I can't figure out the reason behind his reaction, so I ask, "Why are you laughing?"

"Because I just made a decision, beautiful."

"Which is?"

"I'm going to fuck you."

TWO

Anastasia

WHEN I WAS YOUNG, I LIVED IN A HOUSE SURROUNDED BY a forest where no one could enter or leave. It was far from other houses and I had to take trips through that forest with its tall trees and haunting sounds.

With time, I stopped thinking of the trees as ominous and embraced them. I embraced the forest and made it mystical, just like I embraced hiding in narrow places when Mom told me to.

I didn't really like hiding, partially because I knew what would come after, but mostly because it suffocated me. However, I loved the forest. I loved having my white, witchlike hair in braids, wearing my pink dress dusted with glitter, and running throughout the green heaven.

I spoke to the trees and rocks because I thought I was in a fairy tale.

I thought I was like Wendy from *Peter Pan* and no one could find me, catch me, or hurt me.

It was my world and mine alone. I was hidden in Neverland and no one could touch me.

I was invincible.

Until I wasn't.

Until the pirates found me and took me away, and Mom couldn't come along.

That's where I've been living for the past fifteen years, with the pirates, and tonight is the first time I've been able to escape.

Sure, I didn't find my Peter Pan. Hell, he might as well be a devious version of Captain Hook. Sure, he probably won't let me keep my fairy dust and will throw me back to where I came from, but at least I'm free.

I'm *me*.

Even if it's for only one night.

And he said he'd fuck me. He decided it earlier when we were at the Black Moon bar. We're not there now. We're in a hotel, right beside the bar. It's called Black Diamond.

That's the most precious type of diamond and the men I live with deal in it, all around the globe. Not only is it profitable, but it also makes many others bow down in front of them.

I wonder if this British stranger would bow, too. If he'd dirty his Armani suit and mess up his perfect hair and lose his luxurious watch to the men in my life. Or maybe he'll fight them.

The thought of him in a fight makes me shudder with a different type of arousal. I've been in a constant lusty haze since he sucked on my ears and neck and whispered in that hotter-than-sin voice of his.

Oh, and his accent. That's the icing on the cake. It's why I'm sure he's in a different category than the men in my life. Their accent is different to his. Less sophisticated and more dangerous.

Though he might be dangerous, too, since he's managed to do what none of the men I've lived around have even dreamed of.

He's managed to have me.

Or he will soon.

The moment we step into the room, I take a deep breath to

tell him this is a one-time thing, that like the no-names rule, it'll be more thrilling if we never see each other again.

One fuck.

One moment.

And then it's over.

But I don't have the chance to utter any sound except for a gasp. Because the second the door closes, he whirls me around and his body pins me against it. His chest ripples against my spine and there's something hard poking against the small of my back. Not something. It's his erection, massive and ready, and holy shit, did it just twitch?

My breasts heave against the door and my breaths come fast and uncoordinated as I lay my heated cheek on the surface.

As if that's not enough to send me into hyperawareness, he tangles his fingers in my hair and pushes the long strands to the side, baring my back and neck, then wraps his hand around my nape.

He grabs it in a steel-like hold, leaving me no room to move, and the knowledge of that? The fact that I'm completely at his mercy draws a shudder from deep within me. It's long and consuming and leaves me in a daze.

I'm not supposed to surrender to this, right? To the knowledge that I might not be able to escape his clutches, even if I wished to.

It's not in my good-girl genes to want this, but I can't help the subconscious tremors rushing through me.

His teeth find my earlobe and he bites down. I'm drunk on the scent of his cologne, the discreet yet mystic quality to it, just like that forest from my childhood.

Logically, I should've stayed away from it and him, but I can't. I won't.

I'm held hostage by his relentless grip and savage beauty. The type of beauty I didn't know I was attracted to until tonight.

He's still licking my earlobe, nibbling, assaulting it with his tongue, when he whispers, "Now, tell me, beautiful. Do you believe it's a good idea to come with a complete stranger into a hotel room and not ask for his name?"

Shit.

Please don't tell me he actually knows my family? Is this an attempt to lure me into a trap and expose me?

I put a halt to those thoughts before they occupy me. I'm just being paranoid.

That's it. Paranoia and my inability to cope with it.

So I whisper, "I like it."

"What do you like?"

"The no-strings-attached part."

"I like that, too, but do you know what I like about it the most?"

"What?" My voice is too breathy and it has everything to do with his hold on me, with the way his thumb grazes my pulse point and pushes down as if emphasizing it.

"That I can do whatever I want." His voice becomes raspy and it's grabbing me in a chokehold, or maybe it's his words.

Maybe it's a combination of both.

Either way, I'm trapped in a state I've never experienced, and for the life of me, I can't decide whether that's good or bad.

All I know is that not knowing his name and deciding this is a one-time thing makes me lose all my inhibitions.

"You'll let me, won't you, beautiful?"

"Yeah…" I trail off because I wasn't thinking when I agreed. Or maybe I haven't been thinking during this whole night. I want to blame it on the alcohol, but who am I kidding? It's not the vodka that's flowing through my veins right now. It's *him*.

Everything about him.

"Good." He laps his tongue on the shell of my ear. "Now, tell me, are you a virgin?"

The sudden question freezes my limbs and causes my pulse to roar and throb in my veins, right beneath his hold.

"Why are you asking?" I speak so low, I'm surprised he can hear me.

"I don't do virgins."

"Why not?"

"They're a hassle I don't care for. Answer the question. Are you?"

"No," I whisper and hope he takes it as if I'm too overwhelmed with sensations, not something else.

I think it works, because he's pushing his knee between my thighs. "Open your legs."

It's nearly impossible to do so with his presence at my back, possessing me, holding me hostage, but I manage to shuffle my legs a little.

Still holding my nape with one hand, his other one reaches under my dress and I release a gasp when he cups my needy core.

"Fuck. You came ready."

My nerve endings pulse at the arousal in his tone, at how absolutely sinful he sounds when he's taken off guard.

And he's right, I did come ready and he's touching my bare pussy right now. When I made the decision to forgo panties, I thought I would have a quickie and go home. That's still the plan.

But something tells me he won't honor my plan. He'll bulldoze through it, shred it apart, and feed it to me, won't he? It's that intensity of his that I feel with every brush of his skin on mine.

Intensity can't be planned. Which is why I shouldn't have chosen him. But I did, and I couldn't stop this even if I wanted to.

And a deep part of me rejects that option anyway.

"Are you perhaps an escort?" He slides his fingers against my wet folds, making them wetter and more sensitive. "But you would've said that if you were, wouldn't you?"

"Maybe I'm doing pro bono work tonight."

I meant it as a jab, but he chuckles again. It's unnerving, how charming he can get, even though he has sharp edges. It's not supposed to be like this. Charming people don't have the intensity of the men I've known my entire life.

And the combination of both is dangerous, terrifying even.

But my body doesn't seem to care about that fact, because

the moment he thrusts a finger inside me, I go on my tiptoes, stifling a moan.

"You have a mouth on you," he rasps, driving his finger deeper.

"Yeah, and I'm not afraid to use it." Not really, but he doesn't need to know that.

"Does that mean you'll choke on my dick and let me come down that pretty throat?"

I choke, but it's on my barely existent drool. I'm thinking of a comeback when he thrusts an additional finger and tightens his hold on my nape.

I go still, afraid to move or even breathe. Holy fucking shit. It's full, so full that I think I'll burst with the sensation. I've done this to myself before, but it's never felt this...overwhelming.

It's only two fingers.

His fingers that are as hard and sharp as the man himself. But what makes my arousal worse is how he grabs my neck as if he has every right to, how he presses on my pulse point, controlling my shaky, chopped breathing.

"Here's a tip, I don't like talkers," he says casually as he pounds his fingers into me, scissoring and crisscrossing them in rhythm with my shaky inhales and exhales.

"T-too bad; you...g-got one..."

"Looks like I'm not doing it hard enough if you're still able to speak." He drives another finger inside and I shriek, the sound piercing the deafening silence of the hotel room.

If I thought I was full before, I'm bursting right now. And that sensation, the thought that he's so deep inside me that I'm about to explode with him, is enough to make me orgasm.

It's savage and merciless, just like him, like that expression in his eyes that I can't look into, because I'm broken and can't make eye contact.

But I don't have to look to feel the pleasurable wave, to bask in every second of it, in every minuscule detail and every long, deep thrust of his fingers. They're still driving into me, elongating the orgasm, making it ten times wilder.

It's like I've never had an orgasm before. As if my body has been preparing for this type of orgasm, one that shatters my paper-like expectations and blows away my fairy tale dreams.

"You're not talking now, are you, beautiful?" There's a smirk in his voice and it should piss me off, but I'm too drunk on the pleasure to focus on that.

"I…can…"

"Hmm." His fingers slip out of me and before I can make any sound, he grips me by the nape and wrenches me from the door. I gasp when he pushes me to my knees in front of him.

I stare at him for a second. It's only a second, but it's enough to see the dark lust in his hazel eyes. That's their color, I now realize. Instead of being green like the mystic forest from my childhood, they're a mixture of the color of the trees and earth.

I'm distracted from them, though, because he's unzipping his pants and freeing his cock. That's where my wild gaze is focused on right now.

His thick, veiny, and very hard cock. It's so hard that it's changed color, becoming a shade of purple.

A twinge of apprehension zaps through me at the size. He couldn't just have a tiny cock, could he?

I was ready for this not to be satisfying. After all, it's only a mission, and I didn't let my hopes soar high. But just the sight of his dick is enough to make me tingly again. I just had an orgasm, but my body still demands more of him.

Of *that*.

"Do you know what will happen now, beautiful?" There's a tightness in his sharp jaw and his hand flexes around his length as if he's conjuring some form of patience.

I shake my head, still staring at his massive erection. How could it get this hard?

"You're going to make that mouth useful and suck my cock."

My thighs clench together at the image and I lick my lips and then bite my tongue to stop whatever is about to come out.

I'm a good girl and good girls don't make embarrassing sounds.

Good girls don't have one-night stands either, but this is an exception. My last indulgence before everything changes.

The British stranger digs his fingers into the back of my hair and directs his dick at my parted lips. "Open."

Instead of doing as he asks, I wrap my lips around his crown and lick the precum. He groans at that, which means he likes it, so I inch up on my knees and take more of him inside, hollowing my cheeks so I don't graze him with my teeth.

I've never been told how to do this, but I'm good at mixing the little knowledge I've gained through watching porn with the heat of the moment. That's what I do right now, hoping to hell he doesn't realize that I'm figuring this out as I go.

Using his hold on my hair, he pushes me down on his cock and all my doubts vanish. He's deep-throating me, I think, and I can't help my gag reflex when his dick hits the back of my throat.

I splutter, choking on his cock, and even with that, I'm unable to take him all in, unable to fit him into my mouth. I try, though. Instead of letting my gag reflex rule me, I relax my jaw, letting him thrust in a few times before I lick and suck.

Yes, I might not be as experienced as he is, but he's not the only one who gets to wield power over someone else.

I want that, too.

I want to deepen those grunts of pleasure he releases each time he drives his cock deep in my throat, using my tongue for friction. I want to roughen them and turn him into a mess.

So I act on pure instinct and continue loosening my jaw the farthest possible and make that dreaded eye contact. But now, it's not only about the meeting of gazes or exchanging vulnerabilities, it's a challenge.

His lids drop as he slows the rhythm of rocking his hips. "Stop looking at me like that unless you want me to fuck your throat."

I stop moving my mouth altogether and maintain eye contact.

Do it, I say with my eyes. *Fuck my throat.*

"Bloody hell. Who knew I would have a wild one on my hands?"

I like that. Being wild.

But I don't get to think about it further, because now, he's thrusting in—long, hard, and untamed. And my mouth is there for the taking, for his own pleasure, the same way he used his fingers for mine earlier.

And I let him.

Not only that, but I sink into his dominance, swallowing as much of him as possible despite the drool and the tears stinging my eyes.

It's a good type of pain.

The type I didn't think I needed until now. The type that smashes my walls open and leaves me bared and thirsty for more.

And his reaction? I could bask in it for days. I could listen to his low grunts and deep groans forever. The sound turns me on.

That's when it dawns on me.

His pleasure turns me on.

My thoughts are confirmed when I feel that he's close. I want to get him there, I want to make him come undone like he did to me.

And just when I think I'll succeed, he pulls out.

His hard cock is in his hands and it's glistening with precum and saliva. *My* saliva that I'm currently swallowing with his taste.

"Why…?" It's a single word because I've apparently lost the ability to speak properly. Throat-fucking does that, I guess.

"As much as I love your little mouth, I'm going to empty myself inside your cunt, beautiful."

I bite my tongue to stop myself from moaning. His dirty talk is like a lash against my most sensitive part. Seriously, he shouldn't be talking so filthy and ending it with "beautiful." There needs to be a rule against that.

"Bed. Now."

I scramble to my feet, the order twisting something inside me. Something so primal and raw, I can't find a name for it.

Instead of focusing on that, though, I make the short trip to the bed. Before I can reach it, he grabs me by the thin strap of my dress and pulls down the zipper, then yanks the material down my arms, sending my butterfly pendent flying.

It's a full yank, no mercy or softness whatsoever. The way his hand skims over my skin is nothing short of dominant.

He's a man who knows what he wants and won't hesitate to go after it.

Just like the men from my life.

He's probably as dangerous as they are, too.

But that doesn't matter.

No one will be able to find me once I disappear.

I'm standing naked in front of him since I didn't wear a bra either, and it's a vulnerable position, one I never allowed myself to be in before. I don't let self-doubt creep in, though.

Tonight is about my body. Only that.

Without turning me around, he grabs a nipple in his fingers and twists, then squeezes, then twists again.

My toes curl in my heels—the only thing I'm wearing right now aside from my birthday suit.

Then he does something else—while still behind me, he wraps his hand around my neck, but he's not crushing my windpipe. His fingers squeeze on the sides until I'm a bit lightheaded and completely at his command. Then he keeps teasing my nipples. They're so tight, it hurts and sends jolts of pleasure to my pussy. Or maybe it's his hold on my throat that causes it.

Either way, I'm so stimulated, it takes effort to suppress my voice and stop releasing the little noises.

"For a talker, you're so quiet right now," he muses. "Are you biting your tongue?"

I jam my teeth harder until I'm sure I'll break the skin.

"It's useless to hide your voice from me, beautiful." His lips meet my ear again. "You'll scream."

I'm about to say no, that good girls like me don't scream, but then he gives me another order I can't resist. "On your knees."

I fall.

Just like that.

There's something about the way he issues orders, a command that needs to be obeyed, or else it'll wreak havoc.

"I want those tits on the mattress, legs wide apart and your ass in the air."

My cheeks go up in flames at the image, but they nearly explode when I'm in position.

I hear the ripping of something and turn sideways to find him rolling a condom onto his cock. Jeez. I never thought I would find this of all things hot, but on him, it's so much of a turn-on that I gulp.

"Eyes ahead, beautiful." He lowers himself behind me and I stare at the hotel's wallpaper, my ears heating.

I'm the one who's supposed to be against any type of eye contact, but I forgot about my own rule just now.

He grabs both of my wrists and holds them at the small of my back, then something soft wraps around them. That's when I catch a glimpse of his tie from my peripheral vision.

For some reason, it feels as if I'm completely at his mercy now and he proves that when he digs his strong fingers into my hip and thrusts in.

I was ready for it, soaking wet even, but it feels so sudden that my whole body jolts forward.

It doesn't hurt like I thought it would, though. There's a sharp sting, but it quickly vanishes, probably because I'm so aroused that I'm about to burst, or maybe it's because he's so entangled with my body that there's no room for me to feel the extent of the pain.

He pulls out a little, then stops.

Has he figured it out?

Of course he did. The British stranger will know I lied to him and he'll stop and this night will end. My trip to Neverland will finish before it even starts.

But apparently, that's not the case, because the only reason he pulls out is to thrust in again. An electric shock paralyzes my whole body and I wish there was something I could hold on to. My bound wrists forbid me from latching onto anything, and somehow that sends tingles down my spine where my wrists are bound.

He wraps my hair around his fist and my head angles up, even though my chest stays on the mattress which adds friction to my sensitive nipples. The motion is so possessive, drool forms in my mouth.

And it's not only because of the position. It's his mad rhythm. He thrusts deeper, harder, rougher. The pace is so crazy and out of control that only the slaps of flesh against flesh echo in the air. Oh, and the sloppy sounds of my arousal.

I should be ashamed, but I'm not, not even a little.

I'm completely at a stranger's mercy as he fucks me like he hates me. He fucks me like he owns every part of me while still having a vendetta against me, and yet I love it.

I love it more than I should.

It should be demented—handing so much control to a man I just met, but it's a fantasy, right?

And fantasies don't have limits.

Fantasies don't have shame.

Fantasies are just like me when I was a little girl and pretended to be Wendy and had the whole forest as my audience.

My thoughts are scattered when he pulls on my hair harder and then a burning sensation explodes in my neck. He's biting it, I realize. His teeth are so deep in my skin, I can feel it right between my legs.

Drool gathers in my mouth and just when I'm about to shriek, he sucks on the skin with an intensity that leaves me gasping.

What the hell is he doing to me?

I don't get the answer to my question, because he does it again on another mouthful of flesh, then again and again, until I'm in a constant state of bewilderment and arousal.

"Your pussy is tight as fuck, it's strangling me, beautiful."

"Not like my mouth?" I don't know how I speak—it's shaky, like my breasts against the mattress.

"Even better. And that mouth will do another thing for me now."

"What…?"

He slaps my ass and pulls on my hair. "Scream."

My shriek echoes in the air. I can't even bite my tongue, because if I do, I'll just cut it off.

The wild orgasm hits me like a hurricane and I'm helpless in its hold.

In *his* hold.

So I scream, and for the first time tonight, I wish I knew his name because I want to scream it right now, I want him to hear how much he corrupted a good girl.

How much he made a good girl go bad.

A deep grunt echoes in the air as he fucks me even harder and faster, his ferocious pace intensifying by the second. I'm glad he's holding me in place or I would've collapsed to the side a long time ago.

Then he stills inside me and I feel warmth through the condom.

That's the last thing I sense as a smile grazes my lips and my eyes droop.

I'm not supposed to sleep. I should leave, but my mind has another idea and I can't open my eyes.

"Are you okay?" His strong voice barges through my haze.

"Yeah, I just need to sleep a little. Give me five."

There's a pause, a shuffle of his body behind mine before he unties my wrists.

A soft moan leaves me, but it's interrupted when I hear his demanding voice near my ear. "What's your name?"

Jane is my fake name, so I say that, or I try to as I whisper, "Anastasia."

When I wake up, I'm on a bed and I'm not alone.

Oh, God.

Please tell me I didn't stay.

I stare to the side and blink rapidly when I see the man from last night sprawled on the bed, the sheet barely covering his cock.

He's naked. All of him.

I didn't see him naked when we had sex.

No, not sex.

That was definitely fucking. Harsh, raw, and primitive fucking.

My core still tingles in remembrance. It feels tender, too, just like my neck that's bruised from all the marks he left behind, but I don't focus on that. My attention is stolen by something far more important.

Tattoos.

He has a lot of them.

On his upper shoulder and bicep, there's a full, angry-looking samurai as if he's about to go to battle. The details on the warrior's face are striking, haunting even.

And I can't stop staring at him, at the darkened look in his eyes, as if he, too, doesn't like eye contact.

For some reason, I didn't think someone as put-together as this British stranger would have tattoos, but seeing that he does adds even more mystery to him.

Businessmen don't usually have tattoos—not the ones I know, anyway. Unless his background is different from what I've been picturing.

I shake my head.

I really, *really* shouldn't be curious about him. It was a one-time thing and it's now over.

The clock on the wall ticks half past three in the morning. I can drive back before sunrise and sneak back into my room.

Slowly, I shift from under the covers and wince. I'm so sore, it hurts to budge an inch.

He must've cleaned me since there's nothing between my thighs. Not even my own stickiness. He covered me, too, which is a kind gesture I wouldn't have expected from this stranger. He seemed like the "fuck them then leave them" type of man.

Or maybe I'm reading too much into it.

I carefully put on my torn dress, grimacing every few seconds when my core throbs. It takes me some time to work around the ruined dress.

The brute stranger must've ripped it when he was removing it.

It's not only a slight rip. There's a long gash on the side that extends to my hipbone. I can't possibly walk outside like this.

So I grab his jacket and put it on. It swallows me and the dress, but it's better than nothing. His scent fills my nostrils and I try not to think of that or what happened a few hours ago.

It'll just make this complicated.

And I don't need complicated.

"I'm sure you have many of these, so you won't mind if I take it," I whisper. "If you do mind, you shouldn't have ripped my only red dress."

He doesn't even stir and I don't know why I'm disappointed. I shouldn't be.

I'm subconsciously reaching for him—or, my hand is. I just want to touch his hair once, see if it's as soft as it looks.

He shifts and I quickly retract my hand.

What the hell was I thinking?

I can't touch him. I have to completely erase him from my memories.

Not only for my own good, but also for his.

If my family finds out about what we've done, they'll kill him. No questions asked.

It's why I stayed a virgin until twenty.

But I'm not anymore.

And soon, I'll be free.

"Thank you for crossing this off my list," I murmur. "I hope we never meet again."

And with that, I grab my heels and silently step out of the room.

THREE

Knox

GRAY SHADOWS CREEP UP ON ME.

Their ghostly hands reach out to my neck and wrap a noose around it. My trachea jerks and crushes to pieces as the distorted voice whispers.

"Look at me."

My fingers flex, but I don't reach for the hands that are stealing my air. If I touch them, they will force my eyes open, they will make me see.

"Baby boy…" The voice is less distorted now, honeyed, almost in a singsong. "Let me look at those eyes…"

Fuck no.

No.

If I don't look, I'll be safe. If I don't look, I won't know what will happen and it'll all be over faster.

Or that's what I believe as the ghostly harsh fingers jam against my neck and crash the one thing that's giving me air.

"If you don't look, it'll hurt more." The voice is still honeyed, cool, soothing almost, and I would've believed it if I didn't know what hides behind it.

"No…"

"Knox, look at me."

"No."

"I'm going to hit you and make sure to leave marks, you little jerk."

"No!"

That's when my eyes open.

There's a ringing, loud and constant and without any breaks.

At first, I think it's all in my head. The ringing. The pounding against my skull. The fucking shadows.

My head is the place they go to when they decide to visit me occasionally, just to make sure they still have a hold on me. That the little boy inside me that I've been slowly killing over the past twenty years isn't dead.

That he still breathes, still closes his eyes, and has fucking nightmares about the shadows of the past.

He still lives with his demons.

But the ringing isn't in my head. It's from somewhere beside me.

My phone.

I snatch it from the side table, throw an arm over my eyes to darken my vision. Light is blinding in my post-nightmare state. In a way, I become one with my shadows, thirsty for darkness and unable to exist outside of it. So, light and I were never really close friends.

"You better have a good fucking reason for calling me this early in the morning."

"Her Majesty the Queen called and said, "Excuse your bloody French.""

"I'm sure she also told you to go take a wank."

He feigns a gasp. "How dare you put such foul language in her mouth?"

"Is there a reason behind your call, Dan?"

"Blasphemy! What's more important than the Queen?"

"My sleeping time." Though he did wake me up from the nightmare, so I should be thankful, really. "Now, are you dead?"

"Obviously not."

"Are you in a compromised position and need help?"

"Not exactly."

"Then call me back when it's not early morning. If by any chance, you have an emergency before that, call 911."

"First of all, fuck you. Second, I think I told you we're playing golf with the mayor today and you should've been here about… fifteen bloody minutes ago. And finally, it's not early fucking morning."

I slide my arm away from my eyes and peek at the time on my phone. Sure enough, it's past ten.

Considering I'm not the type who sleeps in, this is as weird as a sideways fuck.

"Where the fuck are you anyway?" Daniel asks, sounding more impatient by the minute. He's all fun and games until things don't go according to his plan.

Though most of his plans suck, and they're a bit impulsive sometimes, which might play a role in the sheer number of people he attracts on a daily basis.

He's my only British friend in the States. We studied law together, graduated together, and we now work together.

We've even shagged together. Not he and I. There was always a woman in between.

We don't make a habit out of it, but it's something for when we're bored and need extra endorphins.

"Somewhere…" I squint again due to the light slipping from between my fingers.

Where am I really? A piece is missing from my head, but for the life of me, I can't figure out what it is.

"At least tell me you're back from Jersey?"

"Jersey? Oh, yeah, Jersey. No, I'm still here."

"What the fuck, mate? Weren't you supposed to come back last night after meeting a client?"

"I had a change of plans."

"What about golf?"

"There's been a change of plan for that, too."

"What?"

"Golf is boring and so is the mayor. Now, screw off."

I end the call and stare to my side, expecting to find the woman from last night.

Anastasia, she said her name was.

I don't usually care about their names since they're erased from my head after the night is over, but the fact that she was the one who demanded anonymity was what got my wheels turning.

Usually, they don't.

Usually, I would have to tell them beforehand that this is a one-time thing and then it's over.

I didn't have to with Anastasia since she was the one who practically demanded it.

It's thrilling, she said.

And it was.

Having her completely compliant underneath me as she struggled with holding in her noises got my dick hardening in an instant.

I fuck a lot of women—like, a lot, so many that I've lost count—but none of them have been as memorable as the girl who gave me complete rein.

Not only did she not complain, but she also fell into my rough, fast rhythm as if she enjoyed it as well. As if she couldn't get enough of it.

I knew there was something about her from the time we were at the bar, and I had to explore it, had to get my hands on her and see it until the end. I was supposed to go back to New York last night, but then I decided I would fuck her.

I decided I would have her writhing and screaming beneath me as I held on to her icy blonde hair.

She's easily the best fuck I've had in a long bloody time.

Maybe it's because of that, or curiosity, or another illogical reason, but I didn't leave right after, like I usually do, especially since she gave me an opening by falling asleep.

But for some reason, I couldn't just walk away.

Partly because, despite the powerful release from last night, my dick still demands more. Which is why I was planning to pick up where we left off this morning.

That plan is demolished, however, when I find her side of the bed empty. I run my hand over where she slept, but it's cold, so that means she left some time ago.

Huh.

I sit up, all the sleep vanishing from my eyelids.

She's gone.

Anastasia, the girl who wore red and was mouthy, is no longer here.

Under normal circumstances, I'd let it go. In fact, I should be glad that I don't have one of the clingy ones who demand to have my phone number or tells me to call her.

But the fact that she left without a word sends sparks of fire through my veins.

Women don't disappear on me. *Ever.*

And yet, this Anastasia didn't think twice about it.

That's a fucking first.

I stand up, pushing the sheet away, and don't bother with putting on clothes.

My foot collides with something and I bend down to inspect what it is. It's the butterfly pendant she had dangling against her creamy white back last night.

It's the first thing I saw when I stepped into the bar. The jeweled black butterfly wings against her pale skin grabbed my attention and refused to let go.

Then it was her almost white hair that resembles ice, her soft petite face, and those huge ocean blue eyes that seemed ready to swallow the world while hiding away from it.

She was beautiful, but not in the provocative, seductive way I'm used to. If anything, she seemed naïve at times, not knowing what she was supposed to do and waiting for instructions.

At first, I thought the innocent act was just that—an act. But the more I touched her, the more convinced I was that she had little experience. It was in the little details—how she took time to suck my dick or how she often peeked at me as if waiting for approval of what she was doing.

If I'm wrong and she was in fact an escort, I'll revoke my law license. Or I'll steal an Oscar for her.

Still, no amount of acting could've allowed her to shudder involuntarily or swallow me deep and raw and even like it.

Having had violent tastes all my life makes rough sex a given, but some women don't like it, and I have to slow down so I don't take things too far. I have to keep in mind that not all people are fucked up like me, so I'm forced to handle them a bit more gently.

I didn't have to do that with her, though.

She took everything I dished out and more.

She even orgasmed because of it and screamed in that erotic way that still echoes in my ears like a siren's song.

Then she left.

My hold flexes on the butterfly before I place it on the side table. That's when I notice that my jacket is gone, but my wallet is on the chair with everything inside it.

If she were a thief, it would make more sense to take my cash, but she chose a jacket—worth a few thousand dollars, but still.

She didn't strike me as someone poor. She had the soft, delicate speech and mannerisms of someone well-educated, but maybe all of that was an act as well.

Shaking my head, I go to the bathroom to take a shower.

My gaze falls on the condom in the rubbish bin and I pause. I didn't focus on it last night, probably due to the dim lights and my being sleepy.

But it's there.

Blood.

On the condom and the washcloth I cleaned her with.

When I felt a bit of resistance inside her at first, I thought it was because she was the type who needed to be entered gradually or repeatedly before I found a rhythm.

But that's not the case.

She lied to me.

She was a fucking virgin.

And now, I'm tempted to find her and teach her that no one, no fucking one, lies to me and gets away with it.

FOUR

Anastasia

Two weeks later

TODAY, I'M A NEW PERSON.

I'm no longer Wendy, who's captured by the pirates or who's waiting for Peter Pan to come and get her. I no longer dream about running in that forest with the wind as my only companion.

Now, I can go back to that forest if I want to, but I won't, because it's too small for me now.

At any rate, I'm no longer trapped or nurturing foolish hopes. I snatched my own freedom and no one can find me anymore.

I might have left some of the Lost Boys behind, but they wanted to stay. I can't force someone to see the light when all they're used to is the darkness. Maybe when I have a stronger footing in the new world I've chosen, I'll be able to convince them to leave.

That is, if they don't become pirates themselves.

That's what the pirates do. When they can't control you, they convert you. They've tried that on me for fifteen years, but I escaped before they could succeed.

So now, I'm just a new fairy.

One who wears baggy clothes, has dyed her hair black, put in brown contact lenses, and is wearing black-framed glasses that hide most of my face. They're my crutch, the glasses. Since I had them specifically made with thick lenses, I can't make eye contact and no one can make eye contact with me.

I'm safe.

I hold on to that knowledge as I swipe my card into at entrance of my new workplace.

Weaver & Shaw.

It's one of the most prestigious law firms, not only nationally, but also internationally. The most fascinating part about it is that the two founding partners, Nathaniel Weaver and Kingsley Shaw, have built their reputation in a matter of years.

Where I come from, it takes decades to have any type of reputation—especially one that people talk about.

That doesn't seem to be the case at this law firm.

When I did my research, I found that Weaver & Shaw is one of the most sought-after law firms in their field. Not only due to its two ruthless founding partners, but also due to how efficient the rest of its partners and associate lawyers are.

Weaver & Shaw is a fast-paced firm, from the way they accept cases, to how they process them, and even the way they work paralegals.

Everything around me buzzes with energy. Almost everyone has a phone to their ear and something else in their hands—briefcases, case files, coffee.

I'm only equipped with my laptop bag, the strap glued to my chest. It's the only thing I need in order to navigate in a place full of people, noise, and eye contact.

Logically, I should've chosen a smaller firm or one of W&S's branches in another state—or country, but I had my reasons.

One. I didn't want to leave New York City. The best place to hide from someone? Right under their nose.

Two. A smaller firm doesn't have well-equipped IT departments, and I need that for my disappearance plans.

Those two reasons combined are why I chose to woo W&S. And it did take a lot of wooing to their HR department during the interview process.

My résumé is genius level, and it's not a lie. I did skip grades and attend computer engineering classes when I was young. I may be twenty, but I have valuable skills and have completed an internship at a huge company that shall not be named.

I did mention it in the résumé, though. Because that's where I stole my current name from.

Jane Summers.

She was an intern at that huge company that shall not be named but decided to take a break from college and travel around the world.

I figured that out from a random conversation I heard in the bathroom and built my identity around hers. I had to wait until she left, then I kind of borrowed her name.

Sorry, Jane. I promise to help you with your studies as soon as you get back.

Anyway, W&S's HR board wasn't really convinced, because of my age, so they decided to put me on a month's trial to see how I'll do.

I'm going to prove that age is just a number.

It's one of the few things I believe in from where I came.

After surviving a crowded trip in the elevator, in which I had to fix my glasses a few dozen times and touch my chest a hundred more, I finally arrive at the IT department on the twentieth floor.

I release a long exhale at the sweet sound of silence. There's no fast-paced rhythm and no shuffling of feet.

And definitely no eye contact.

There's just a clean office with marble flooring and blinding natural light coming from the open window at the end of the hall.

My gaze shifts to it and my chaotic brain revs to life like an old engine. My fingers shake on the strap of my bag and my short nails dig into my palms. Why the hell is that window open? Don't they know how risky it is?

"You must be Jane."

I startle from my mini panic attack at the soft voice of the middle-aged woman who's sitting behind the receptionist desk. They did say that I'd have someone from the IT department tell me about the building.

"Yes, that's me." I approach her with slow steps, though I really should stop thinking that one of the people here will bring out a gun and start shooting the whole building down.

This is not the dangerous world I came from.

"My name is Jill and I'm the secretary of the technicians' side of the IT department." She stands, and to my surprise, she's about my height. That's rare as hell since everyone is always taller than me.

Always.

Jill is wearing an orangey lipstick and a scarf that matches it, but it's tucked neatly in her jacket since I'm sure bright colors aren't exactly welcome in a law firm.

"This is where you'll be working." She leads me to an open area with countless screens hanging on the wall. Two men who appear to be in their thirties are already seated in front of their own multi-screens.

One of them wears frameless glasses that seem to be part of his face, and the other is wearing a plaid flannel shirt that's stained—with coffee, I believe.

Both of them type at a rapid speed and monitor the screens, and I instantly feel a sense of belonging. The sound of a keyboard has always made me feel at peace, even in the midst of chaos.

"This is Chad and Ben. Guys, Jane will start working with you today."

They don't acknowledge me. Not even a twitch of fingers or the eye contact that I hate so much.

"Don't worry about them, they're nerds," Jill tells me with a laugh to hide the awkwardness.

I'm a nerd, too, so I don't offer her a reassuring smile, and that instantly makes her uncomfortable.

People are like that. They expect you to comply with what society wants and to avoid confrontation. But I'm done being a doll for show.

I'm done bending myself to fit in settings that don't fit me.

Jill clears her throat. "Anyhow, the cafeteria is on the seventh floor. Your card gives you access to all floors except for the top tier where the managing partners' offices are. You're not allowed there unless they specifically ask for you and grant you security access. You might be called to the partners' floor now and again to take care of computer problems. If you have any questions, let me know."

And with that, she leaves, the clinking of her heels echoing in the silent space like ominous music from a movie.

The two guys are still not acknowledging me, so I sit in the one available seat in front of three switched-off monitors.

Hugging my laptop to my chest, I whirl around to face them. "Do you need my help with anything?"

They pause their tapping for a second to stare at me.

"We don't need a girl," glasses guy, Chad, says.

Ben, the one with the coffee stain, laughs. "Go play with your dolls, Plain Jane."

Okay, so they're the assholish type.

I don't usually let insolence go. Those who do that would pay by my bodyguards' wrath, but I don't have any, and I never will again.

Because I'm free.

And these boys aren't worth my getting all worked up. I no longer follow my family's code of honor.

I follow my own.

So I ignore them and settle on my chair. Then I turn on my computer, enter the login details I was provided, and I start attacking the tasks the head of the IT department left me in an email.

My lips pull in a small smile as I soak in the feeling of having this peaceful, quiet setting with no one barking orders at me. This is what free people do. Work to provide for themselves.

It doesn't take me long to finish the tasks assigned to me. They must be taking it easy on me on my first day, because by the time lunch rolls around, I'm done.

Ben and Chad already left, probably to eat in the cafeteria. From what I gathered, almost all the workers at W&S eat there. Me, however? I never even considered the option of having my lunch there. Lots of people I don't know? No, thanks.

I open my drawer, retrieve my sandwich, unwrap it, and take a bite as I follow a tour on W&S's employee website. I like whoever suggested they add this for newbies like me.

It's sophisticated and there doesn't need to be needless contact with the HR people.

For a moment, I'm focused on the introductory video, but a few minutes later, my mind floats somewhere else.

It's easy to block these thoughts when I'm concentrating on a task, but now that my brain is in a paused state, it's impossible to veer it in another direction.

Because it's already there, at the Black Diamond hotel, where I let a British stranger take my virginity roughly and without holding back. I let a stranger leave angry red marks all over my neck and breasts that I couldn't conceal with foundation, so I had to wear a scarf for some time.

I wish that was all. I wish I'd left that night in Jersey.

But I didn't.

I've been having dreams about it, about his merciless pace and his punishing gaze. About how he grabbed my throat, then fucked it, then grabbed it again. I've been imagining those moments, too, like right now.

And it always gets me squirmy and raises the temperature

a notch. Usually, I'd try to fight these feelings harder, but I don't seem to have the will.

I think I've become sort of obsessed with what happened that night. All I can picture is light chestnut hair, intense hazel eyes, and that angry samurai.

As angry as his thrusts inside me.

As angry as he deep-throated me.

I didn't think I would ever be that type, the one who gets off on violence and being handled roughly, but I should have known better.

I really, *really* should have.

Ever since I was a teen, I've been having nightmares about being held down and ravished. Then I wake up drenched in sweat and with a strange sensation between my legs.

That's when I should've known it wasn't really a nightmare but a fantasy. A dangerous, deadly one.

And the evidence is that I can't stop thinking about it.

It wasn't part of my plan, but it happened, and now, I can't get rid of the memory. Time is supposed to make me forget, isn't it? It's supposed to wipe my memories clean of him, his callous touch, and the scent of his cologne.

But that's the exact opposite of what's happened. Ever since that night, he's magnified to lengths I can't control. He's become the taboo subject that I pictured before I went to sleep and then hoped no one knew what I was thinking.

Or what I've done.

It's over, Ana. You're a new person now.

I keep telling myself that as I dive back into work. I start messing around, creating a mock-up of a security system that could be accessible to everyone.

I'm good at that. Systems. It's not only the perfect way to keep my plans intact, but I can also use them as a façade to appear flawless on the outside despite having broken insides.

My grandmother once told me that imperfect people create perfection and I'm starting to take her words to heart.

At the end of the day, I leave last to avoid the rush of people. Thankfully, when I take the elevator, there's no one in it and I can breathe properly.

The doors open a few floors below and I pray there aren't too many people. My social anxiety and I had a field day today and we just need to go back to our small apartment and hide for an eternity.

Or at least, until tomorrow.

My hold falters on the strap of my laptop bag when my gaze clashes with the same one I've been dreaming about for the past two weeks.

The same stranger I left in that hotel room but can't stop thinking about.

My only one-night stand that I shouldn't have met again.

And he's staring straight through me.

FIVE

Anastasia

THIS ISN'T REAL.

I must be hallucinating.

Or maybe I'm dreaming again, stuck in an imaginary moment and never woke up this morning.

But the more I stare at the man in front of me, the more tangible this becomes. He's not disappearing.

Why isn't he disappearing?

He usually vanishes about now. He becomes one with my dreams and stops bothering me.

Not now, though.

Now he's coming inside the elevator—where I currently am.

Oh, shit.

The need to run hits me out of nowhere and it takes everything in me not to jump out of the elevator like a monkey.

My mission is put to an abrupt halt when the doors slide closed with brutal finality. Now, it's only he and I in the car.

And I can't breathe.

Damn it. Damn it.

Listen, brain, this is about the worst time for your meltdown. Help me out here, please.

I inhale deeply through my nostrils and exhale through my mouth a few times. That's it.

The buzzing in my ears slowly subsides, and it helps that he faces the door, cutting off that intense eye contact. Or maybe I'm the only one who thought of it as intense.

His back is the only thing visible as he focuses on his phone and scrolls through it.

I've forgotten how larger than life he looks, how broad and tall he is. How physically perfect he is that it's impossible to focus on anything but him. He's wearing another Armani suit, dark gray, like the expression on his face when he walked in.

It's been only a few seconds since then, but I could swear that he saw me, that he made eye contact. Did he not recognize me?

It must be the different clothes, hair, and thick glasses. Right. He couldn't possibly relate Anastasia to Jane. We're not the same anymore.

A brick the size of my laptop sinks to the bottom of my stomach, and it's completely illogical. I shouldn't be feeling this way because he didn't recognize me. If anything, I should celebrate it. I should feel lucky.

But that's the last sensation inside me as I dig my nails into the heel of my palm.

Then I peek at him, at the stranger from that night, and I'm once again struck by his majestic presence. He seems different than back then somehow, more serious, hard. Stuck-up.

And I can't help thinking about his dominant orders when he fucked me.

Those dirty, dirty orders that subconsciously make me clench my thighs.

I internally shake my head in an attempt to push those images away.

What's he doing at W&S anyway? Please tell me he's only here on a visit and doesn't actually work in the same building as me.

That would be just…cruel.

Just when I've left everything behind, something has decided to follow me. And not just something. Someone.

The British stranger who should be in New Jersey where I left him after he fucked me senseless.

"Do you work here?"

I jolt at the deep tenor of his voice, and an electric sensation zaps through my entire body. I almost forgot just how commanding his voice is, how it's a bit mellow and cool to the ears.

God, just why does he have an accent?

He's asking me, I realize. Either that or he's speaking to a nonexistent person. I realize I'm praying he sees a ghost lurking in the corner. That would be less catastrophic than the alternative.

Next step of denial: hope that he's merely curious about a random stranger in the elevator.

Though he doesn't strike me as the type.

"Yes," I say as calmly as I can manage. "I…started today."

Please, let it go. Please.

My prayer is obviously not answered when he asks, still not facing me, "Which department?"

"IT."

"What's your name?"

"Jane." My voice is lower now and I hope he doesn't notice it, he doesn't sense the tremor behind it.

But what he does is worse.

He turns around.

As in, he's now facing me and I have a full view of him, of his chiseled face, sharp features, and piercing eyes that are glaring at me now.

He so infuriatingly beautiful, so handsome that there should be a rule against it. And when he glares? It makes him inexplicably hot and scary at the same time. His lips are set in a line, as disapproving as his eyes.

"That's not true, now, is it? If I remember correctly…your name is Anastasia."

Shit.

Fuck.

No.

He recognized me. Even with a completely different appearance, he recognized me. He shouldn't have, but he did. And holy hell, did I tell him my real name? How could I be so careless, just how?

"I don't know what you're talking about." I feign nonchalance even though I'm physically pushing back against the metal railing.

It's a cheap tactic, but it should be effective. People are mistaken for others all the time. This shouldn't be any different. Besides, I did everything in my might to become the opposite of who I am. I wouldn't be recognized by those I've known for years, let alone someone I spent a few hours with.

He steps toward me, or more like, he stalks, moving fluidly and with predatory steps that nearly make me wheeze.

Or maybe it's the way he keeps staring into my eyes as if he's ripping every single one of my façades apart and digging his fingers into the broken parts inside me.

It hits me then, the reason why I'm hyperventilating. I'm being burned alive by his sharp hazel eyes. They're crushing and melting me and I have to stop looking at them.

But I can't.

I feel like if I break eye contact, I'll be in a worse danger than I am right now.

That he'll use the change to confiscate a side of me I've been hiding from the world.

Even from myself.

"You know exactly what I'm talking about." He reaches a hand toward my face and I flinch away, but he wasn't actually going for my face.

His fingers flex around my throat and he digs the pads into

the flesh of my neck as his other hand hits the stop button and something else.

But I don't focus on that.

I can't.

Not when all my blood rushes to where his hand is on the sides of my throat. It's not harsh with the intent of stealing my breath, but it's firm enough to trigger memories of that night.

Memories of him touching me, immobilizing me, and setting me ablaze in a blast of smithereens. And those thoughts are plaguing me right now.

They're tearing me to pieces.

Setting me on fire.

Ripping through my bones.

And I can't stop the images or the full-blown heat that invades my nerve endings, specifically the ones he's touching.

"You don't know me, so this is my first and final piece of advice to you. Don't fuck with me. Not only will you be the one fucked over, but I'll also take pleasure in tearing you apart and feasting on the remains."

I'm used to living under threat. Being offered an ultimatum and never actually having a choice. But his way of doing it, with cold calm, slashes through the fairies in my stomach. They've turned black now, which is a signal to run the fuck away.

But I can't.

Not with his savage hold on my throat. There's a control in it, a simmering firmness, and it's much more ruthless than the dominance I experienced when he fucked me.

This one is laced with a tinge of anger or displeasure. Maybe both.

"Now tell me what your name is. The actual one."

"J-Jane…" I don't mean to stutter, but I did and he must hear it, because his hold tightens on my throat.

"I don't appreciate liars, beautiful. Especially conniving ones."

"I'm not…a…liar…" He has to believe me. Otherwise, the new beginning I painted for myself will be null and void.

He can't know who I actually am.

No one can.

"Your blood that I found on the condom would testify otherwise."

I gasp, wheezing and shaking while he stands there still as a stone, a cold one that could be used as a weapon.

"I thought you weren't a virgin."

I press my lips together, unable to utter a word.

"Turns out, you were a virgin, after all, and since you lied about your name just now, it means you're used to lying. So tell me, what's your purpose, hmm? What are you after, Anastasia?"

"Jane… It's Jane…"

"So it is Anastasia. I suspected it before, but now that you're insisting it's Jane, I'm sure that isn't your true name."

Oh, God.

Just who is he and why is he doing this? Is it just because I lied about my virginity?

But he shouldn't be this intense, angry, and violent about it.

"What's with the name change, Anastasia?"

Every time he says my name, a jolt rips through me. It's fast and sharp and leaves me as breathless as his hold on my throat does.

I tap his arm, choking on my nonexistent inhales, but I don't fight him. If I do, I'll be giving myself away.

Besides, it's not that I need him to release me because he's hurting me. It's more because my reaction to his hold is scaring the shit out of me.

It's scaring me more than the fact that he found me or that he's endangering my new beginning.

He releases me slowly, and I grab the assaulted spot, breathing harshly, the sound ugly in the silence of the elevator.

I should be focused on that, but all I can do is inhale his cologne, basically sucking it into my lungs. The lime and male musk is too familiar. I recognize it because it's been on my mind for two weeks

"You didn't answer my questions, Anastasia."

"Stop calling me that." I adjust my glasses, using them as a shield. "It's Jane. My name is Jane."

He's about to grab me by the throat again. I can tell from the darkening of his eyes, and if he does, I'll find no way out this time.

I won't be able to escape.

So I use a tactic that's common in my family. Distraction.

"I have an idea," I say.

"What's that?"

I duck and before he realizes what I'm doing, I push the elevator button.

The moment it opens, I'm dashing outside, running with all my might.

But I know, I just know this is only a temporary escape.

The war I unintentionally started is far from over.

SIX

Knox

"Hey, Dan. What's the best way to punish liars?"

"Fuck if I know. I don't punish liars, I fuck them."

I stare at Daniel who's sitting on the top of my desk, eating the donuts my assistant brought me. He's a thief that way and couldn't care less what others think about him as long as he gets what he wants.

For him, efficiency comes first and everything else is secondary.

"Why the fuck would you fuck liars?"

"Hello? Because it's fun. Liars are usually the best fuck because you never know what you're in for."

I tighten my fist on the desk to resist agreeing to how true those words are. I hate not knowing what I'm in for. Unlike Dan, I never seek out the thrill. In fact, I prefer it not be part of the equation.

I prefer having everything under my control. I've lost enough of it to the shadows in the past and allowing it to happen again is equal to blowing up everything to pieces.

"Why would you think it's fun when they're using you?"

"You're using them, too." He swings his palm in the air, imitating tapping an arse. "And then it's, 'thank you, have a nice life, love.'"

"That still doesn't give anyone the right to use me."

He raises his brows, studying me, and even pauses eating his donut, which is the equivalent to an event itself. "Since when did you grow morality balls?"

"It's not morality. It's the insult of being taken for a fool."

"Oh, fuck me, this is good." He jumps down from my desk. "Who took you for a fool? I need to buy them a drink. Wait a second, is it someone you fucked without me? I need a redo, one I can participate in."

"No." The word is so firm and final, it surprises me.

I've never said no to sharing before and he knows this, because he's tilting his head with an annoying smirk that creases his cheeks with dimples.

Women love that shit. He's the one they're initially attracted to, due to his wittiness, charm, and conversation skills. I'm usually only along for the ride. It's not that they're not attracted to me, it's that they feel like they should keep their distance from me.

Which is the smart thing to do.

Anastasia was the smartest of the bunch, because she fled the scene while I was sleeping. From the very beginning, she never envisioned anything beyond good old fucking.

And while I might have let that slide under different circumstances, the fact that she's a pathological liar doesn't play in her favor.

She lied not only about the virginity bit, but also about her name and her age. Because I sure as shit got her file from HR after I ran into her in the lift. And fucking surprise, she's only twenty, not twenty-three as she told me that night.

Then there's her weird new appearance. When the lift doors opened, I almost ignored the person inside, almost didn't even look at her, since I was busy checking the group chat with mine and Dan's friends in England.

It was a brief second, barely a lift of my head, but it was enough for me to see her.

And it didn't take me long to recognize her. The blue-eyed, icy-haired girl from Jersey.

Though now, she's nothing like that soft-looking blonde with deep blue eyes. She has black hair that's tied in a twist and wears thick fucking glasses to hide her eyes that have magically turned brown.

Any other person would've been fooled by her appearance, especially with the baggy clothes and the general nerdy aura she gives off. But there's something she couldn't do with her makeover.

She had a habit of touching her chest now and again during that night, as if she was trying to reach for something beneath her flesh and bones. The moment I looked at her, she did that again— brought her hand to her chest and froze.

Those same soft hands with short, elegant bare nails that she couldn't have changed.

If I hadn't thought something was fishy due to the whole new look and the lies, I confirmed it when she ran from the lift as if her life depended on it.

And now, I won't stop until I see the end of it.

Of her and her lies and deceit.

"Am I imagining things or did you just say no to sharing?" Dan licks the chocolate off his fingers slowly, like a cat who just finished eating and is in the mood to play.

"You're not imagining it."

"Why?"

The reasons are blurred in my mind and I couldn't find an explanation even if I tried. One thing's for sure, though. Neither Daniel nor anyone else will put their hands on Anastasia until I deal with this on my own.

"Because."

"No, no." He wraps an arm around my shoulder. "You're not

getting away with "because." I need reasons, reports, and maybe a medical checkup to verify that you're not suffering from mental damage so that I can determine whether or not you should revise your will. Tell me the truth, are you dying? Oh, maybe you fell victim to black magic; that would explain why you're not acting normal."

"I am fucking normal." I push his hand away and go to sit behind my desk.

"No, you're not. Let me think." He makes a dramatic scene of tapping his forefinger against his lip. "Are you acting this way because of the liar?"

"What if I am?"

"You really want to take her on solo?"

"I do."

"But I'm the best wingman. You know that."

"Not this time."

"Why not this time of all times? Did you hit your head somewhere? Bloody hell. Did she give you an STD? First rule of shagging is to always wrap it up. Come on, mate, you're not an amateur."

"It's not that."

"Then what is it? Do I really need to get you that checkup? Maybe I could find a priest and do some exorcism shit. I'm telling you, if there's a demon inside you, I get the rights to sell your story to Hollywood."

"Shut the fuck up, you sorry cunt."

"What? Do you have any idea how many people are suckers for this type of real shit?"

"Either help me brainstorm or get the fuck out, Dan."

He throws his weight on the sofa and flings his arm over the back of it. Then he exaggeratingly flips his chestnut hair back. "I'm all for evil plans. What do you need?"

I knew he wouldn't say no to trouble. Ever since we moved from London to the States ten years ago, we've plotted one disaster after the other.

Or, he has.

For Dan, it's that rush of adrenaline. For me, it's the distraction from the shadows that are often perched on my shoulder.

Either way, we never stop.

Stopping means killing ourselves slowly, and neither of us wants that.

Neither of us has the luxury of surrendering to our demons.

I put my elbows on my desk and steeple my fingers under my chin. "What I need is a background check."

"On who?"

"A tech in the IT department."

"I like where this is going. But aren't two geeky guys the only techs there? Wait a fucking minute, did you change preferences? No judgment here, but I kind of need to know if I'm the reason you flipped the coin. I'm hot and all, but no way in fuck, Knox."

"I could get attracted to the entire world, but not you, fucker. And no, I didn't change preferences. There's a new girl in the IT department."

"Ohhh. Now we're talking. But why would you need the background check? HR must've done their homework."

"Not enough apparently, because she fooled them."

"Blimey." He grins with mischief. "I like her already."

Don't. I want to say that, but I stop myself at the last second. He's already suspicious as it is and I don't want to add fuel to the fire. Considering his bastard tendencies, he'll make a story out of this and sell it out to our friends like a pimp.

"She's a nerd," I say instead, trying to hold on to my calm while sabotaging his image of her.

"What's wrong with nerds? They can be hot as fuck."

"She's a natural blonde."

His playful expression disappears. "Pass."

I can't help the satisfied smile that breaks on my lips. He has a personal thing against them that he's harbored for years. Daniel's type is every woman on the planet aside from blondes—especially natural blondes.

"What are you going to do after you have the background check?" he asks more seriously.

"I don't know. Play with her, punish her. Torment her. The sky is the limit."

During lunchtime, I head to the IT department. Something I don't usually do. Dan and Sebastian, another one of the junior partners who's also Nathaniel Weaver's nephew, gave me a weird look when I ignored our usual lunch gathering.

But I ignored them.

I'm on a mission that will take place on the "nerds' floor," as everyone at W&S calls it.

The receptionist desk is empty and I assume everyone is out for lunch. Everyone except her, because I didn't notice her in the cafeteria yesterday or just now. Which means she takes her lunch here.

And bingo.

She's sitting at her desk, her shoulders and back in a straight line as she eats a sandwich with one hand and types something on her keyboard with the other.

Just like yesterday, her hair is black and tied in a stiff bun, and the thick glasses cover half of her face.

Only her lips remain the same, petite and full, but they're bare, with none of the red from two weeks ago.

Her entire face is free of makeup, but it's still as delicate as I remember. Pale, too. So pale that I make out the thin veins in her throat when I'm within touching distance.

So pale that I left angry red bruises on her hips when I grabbed her by them while I thrust inside her heat.

At the memory, my dick hardens, tenting against my trousers, and I suppress a groan as I adjust it.

Down, boy. It's not time for you…yet.

The distinct scent of orange blossoms and jasmine reaches me and I close my eyes to inhale it. Another thing that's remained the same from that night. Another thing that I can't stop thinking about.

She smells as delicate as she appears. She might be discreet, but something a lot more wild simmers beneath the surface.

Something I've had a taste of and can't erase from my memories.

"If you were changing identities, you should've switched your perfume, too."

She startles, the chair jolting with her sudden movement, and the sandwich remains suspended near her mouth.

Slowly, too slowly, she rotates the chair so that she's facing me. Her throat bobs up and down with a thick swallow and I can't stop watching those fine purple veins moving beneath the transparent skin of her neck.

The neck I held in a chokehold not so long ago, which I itch to repeat. Or maybe that's not the part I'm most thrilled about. Maybe the part that's stuck in my head is how I had her completely at my mercy, where her only way out was me.

"You." It's either a whisper or a pant, I'm not sure which. What I am sure about, however, is that she didn't expect me.

Good.

I like taking people by surprise, both inside and outside the courtroom.

My lips curve in a sardonic smirk. "Me."

"What are you doing here?" She searches around the IT department as if it's her fortress and I broke entry into it. Or maybe she's looking for an ally. Unfortunately for her, there is none.

The best way to crush someone? Leave them with no way out.

"Did you really think you could run away and I'd just forget about it?"

"Well, you should."

"Just because I should, doesn't mean I would."

Her lips twist, and I assume it's because she detected the sarcasm in my tone. "We have…nothing to do with each other."

"I fucked your virgin cunt and made you scream until your

voice turned hoarse, not to mention, the marks I left all over your pale skin. I'd say we have something to do with each other."

She squirms visibly, and it takes her a few gulps to speak. "Even if that were the case—"

"*Even if*? Why are you acting as if it wasn't real?"

"It's in the past. It means nothing." Furious determination laces her sweet, soft voice, and I don't know which pisses me off more: the fact that she's determined it means nothing or that what happened holds no significance to her in the first place.

"I haven't agreed to that."

"I don't think your agreement is of importance."

"I would argue otherwise. After all, I'm the only one at Weaver & Shaw who knows your real name, Anastasia."

She releases a long puff of air. "It's not—"

"Don't utter that lie or you won't get away with it this time."

She blinks slowly, letting the sandwich fall to her lap. "What do you want from me?"

"The truth. All of it. And that includes your real name, true appearance, and your purpose for being here."

"Jane is the only name I have. This is my actual appearance, the other one was fake. As for my purpose, I'm really just trying to work to keep food on the table."

She's still lying. I can tell when someone is, even if they're perfect at it like she is. Usually, people give themselves away with tics or out-of-character body language, but she was completely still and calm when she uttered those lies.

Either she's practiced them for a long time or she's so used to lying that it doesn't faze her anymore.

"That doesn't look like working to me." I motion at the screen behind her, where she has a Google page open with my name at the top.

She throws the sandwich aside and clicks something on the screen that makes it go black.

My smirk widens. "You're not so subtle for a stalker."

"I'm not a stalker."

"Then what was that I just saw? If you want to know more about me, all you have to do is ask."

"I'm only doing my research on all of the firm's employees."

"You should study law. Your impeccable lying skills would come in handy."

"No, thanks. The profession suits shady people like you."

"Hmm. Shady. That's interesting."

She purses her lips and I can tell she's trying to fight with what she should say and shouldn't. Then she levels me with a stare. "Well, aren't you? I'm just trying to work and you're making it impossible."

"That's because you're shady yourself, Jane. Sorry, I mean, *Anastasia.* Did you really think I'd believe that your only purpose is to work here?"

"It is."

"I'll tell Nate about the Anastasia I fucked in Jersey and show him how she transformed into Jane. Then you can take up your case with him. I'm curious to see if he'll believe you're not here for ulterior motives."

She curls her hand into a fist, then lays it on her chest before she whispers, "Don't."

"Why? Because it's true?"

"No… It's… I need this job. Please."

"Fuck that. Try again."

"I really do. I'm…I can't tell you anything, but I want no trouble and I won't put the firm in jeopardy, I promise."

"I don't believe that. In fact, I'm sure trouble is all you know."

"Please."

"Begging doesn't work with me. At least, not under these circumstances."

She pauses and a curious spark ignites in her eyes and her face turns a deep shade of red.

Due to her skin tone, each and every one of her emotions shows on her face. But at this point, I'm not sure if it's bashfulness or anger.

Is she faking that innocence again? Only, she wasn't faking it two weeks ago. It was her first time, after all.

But it feels different now, like a silent rage that's about to decimate everything in its wake.

Dead or alive.

She slowly stands up and fuck, I noticed she was petite when we walked to the hotel together, but I'm once again struck by how small she actually is. How the top of her head barely reaches my shoulder when she steps closer to me, eliminating the distance between us.

Her fingers dig into the lapel of my jacket and she says in a low tone, "If you let it go, I'll give you what you want."

My dick turns rock-fucking-hard, both at her closeness and at the way she looks at me. Even beneath the glasses, there's a fire in her eyes. One I didn't see when I bent her over and took her from behind.

And now, I'm tempted to repeat it. To remove the fucking glasses and sink inside her heat until she's screaming and panting and unable to move.

The images turn more real with each passing second, until I'm two seconds away from bending her over her own desk and taking her from behind like a fucking animal.

"And what do I want, Anastasia?" I ask nonchalantly, despite the fucked up thoughts running rampant in my head.

She lets her hand drop to her side and says coolly, "Me."

SEVEN

Anastasia

I'VE NEVER BEEN THE CONFIDENT TYPE.

It doesn't matter that I believed myself to be a fairy when I was young or that I mingled with pirates all my life. The only truth that remains is I couldn't even make eye contact with people.

But I am right now.

Even though it's through my glasses, I'm staring at him. The stranger whose actual name is Knox Van Doren.

The stranger whom I just so shamelessly told that he could have me—sexually or otherwise, he can just have me.

I sounded confident, too, as if I'm not melting on the inside. As if my skin isn't catching fire and I'm not about to self-combust. That's what happens when things don't go according to plan. I lose it.

Like I lost it when *Babushka* was thrown away and basically given a death sentence. I might not make eye contact, but I can be as lethal as the people who raised me.

If not more.

Knox Van Doren.

That's his full name. I found it after I ran from the elevator and browsed the higher employees in Weaver & Shaw and googled them. Sure enough, his name was there, with the junior partners.

And I might have researched him all night long. He comes from a mega rich family in England. His father owns an empire that's recognized on the international scale and knows tremendous growth.

Not only that, but Knox also gained a reputation in the American press because of his antics and charming side. In the law circuit, he's known to be a cunning devil in disguise who's super picky on which clients to accept.

Those who are lucky to be represented by Van Doren might as well have acquired their "get out of jail free card." Is what one of the magazines wrote about him.

I read countless articles about him and each one painted him in a more sinister light than the previous one.

What? A girl has to look out for herself.

The fact that Knox knows my real name and keeps repeating it and suspecting me is dangerous. Not only that, but it could ruin everything I've worked for. My new beginning.

My freedom.

Babushka's life.

And desperate times call for desperate measures. Which is why I suggested that he have me.

Or that's what I tell myself as I get incinerated by his presence. There's something about it, about being so close to him that our breathing mingles together and I'm trapped by his size and his broad shoulders and those golden, intense eyes that could have been created from the combination of a forest and fire.

Or maybe a forest *on* fire.

There's something about being so far beyond my comfort zone that it feels both foreign and exciting.

Delirious.

Maybe even addicting.

And like any addict, I can't help sniffing in more, breathing in more.

Just taking in more.

"You," he repeats slowly in that deep voice of his, with that eternal calm that still manages to steal shivers from my soul.

"Yeah, me." It's less confident now, betraying all the chipped things inside me.

His index and middle finger sneak beneath my chin and lift. The act is so minimal, but he might as well have doused me with gasoline and set me on fire. A touch. It's a mere touch, so why the hell does it feel like a whole experience?

"What makes you think I want you?"

The sting of his words burns and jostles one of the broken pieces in my chest, but I grab on to my confidence with blood-stained fingers. "You did two weeks ago."

"That was before I knew you were a liar."

"What does that matter when I'm offering myself?"

"You were a good fuck, Anastasia, but not good enough to go against my principles for. I don't do liars. So you'll have to give me something first."

"Forget it then. My offer is off the table."

His lips curve in a cruel smirk. "I'll be the one to decide that, and believe me, when I figure out who you are and what you're after, you'll be well and truly fucked. Hold on to these little lies while you can."

He releases me with a slight shove and I stumble backward, my thigh hitting the chair.

"Oh." He stops at the entrance and turns to face me. "Don't even think about leaving or I'll make this personal."

Then he's out the door.

I slide onto the chair, my nails digging into my palms and my heart nearly hitting the floor.

He'll make this personal? *Personal?* Then what has he been doing ever since he saw me in the elevator? Making it impersonal?

Just what type of man did I get involved with?

Even my desperate attempt of offering myself has failed. How the hell am I supposed to keep myself and *Babushka* alive now?

"How are you, my little bunny?"

I clench the phone in my hands and resist the urge to bawl my eyes out, to tell her everything is not fine, that it won't be anymore.

That I could be in danger and so will she.

Instead, I force a smile, straighten my spine, and stare out the window at the gigantic buildings of NYC. Then I speak in Russian since her English is rusty, "I'm fine, *Babushka*. How are you? Are they treating you well in the clinic?"

"Of course. The nurses are so nice and the food is exquisite. Not as good as your momma's, but it's close enough. How is she? Did she leave that lowlife yet?"

This time, I can't help the tears that gather in my lids. *Babushka* isn't my blood-related grandmother, but she practically raised me when I was young. She hid me in her house whenever Mom told me to run. The reason I traveled through the forest was to reach her place.

She protected me when she didn't have to and made me my favorite orange cake and gave me treats.

Then she sang to me in Russian so I would fall asleep and not think about what Mom was going through.

In the morning, she'd braid my hair, heat me some milk, and give me cookies. She kept me safe until Mom could come to fetch me.

Even though she was old, she never once complained about taking care of me and always laughed when I told her stories about my fairy adventures.

She's much older now, though, in her late seventies, and suffers from dementia that requires intensive care. It's one of the main reasons I left, to get her the medical help she needs.

All the money I stole from my family is slowly being paid to the Swiss clinic where she's staying right now. As soon as I disappeared, that's where I went—moving her to Switzerland from a small town in West Russia. The small town she was expelled to soon after my mother died.

I cried and begged and even asked for help, but no one heard me. In fact, I was reprimanded for it because we can't show weakness and we certainly don't beg for those beneath us.

That's when I decided to take things into my own hands.

It took me years to find her, and I'm still not officially reunited with her. Actually, she barely remembers me now, but that's okay.

She protected me when I was young and I'll do the same now that she's old.

"Yeah," I say in a cheerful tone. "She left."

"Good. Good. I was always telling her he was no good for her or you, but Sofia was too scared and always flinched the moment he walked in. She should've asked your father for help, but she was so stubborn, saying that your papa could be even worse."

"He's not." I'm breathing heavily into the phone, forming a sheen of perspiration on the screen.

"Right? Just because he leads that type of life doesn't mean he won't take care of you both. I'll talk some sense into her again when I see her."

"She's…gone, *Babushka*."

"Gone?"

"Yeah. She's no longer with us. She died fifteen years ago."

"No…that's not true… I was talking to her just yesterday when I did your hair…"

There's a shuffle from the other side before the nurse's voice reaches me. She speaks in English. "She's a bit tired."

"Is she okay?"

"Don't worry. These episodes happen often in cases like hers, but she'll be fine in a bit. She does ask about you all the time."

A tinge of guilt wraps a noose around my neck. I should be with her, but I can't. If they find me with her, they'll blame her for the whole rebellion I singlehandedly plotted.

This time, they'll make sure to end her life. In front of me, too, so I'll learn to never mess with the system.

I hang up after I tell the nurse to call me if anything happens. It takes me a few seconds to gather myself, wipe my eyes, and stop being caught in the memories of the past.

Then, as I do during every lunch break, I take the elevator to the floor where the partners' offices are.

It's been a week since I joined W&S and was caught by Knox. Anyone else would do their best to keep their distance. Not me.

My family was a lot of things, but careless wasn't one of them. I learned early on that the best way to beat an enemy is to learn as much as possible about them.

Their daily habits, their morning routines, and even their night ones. That's where their weaknesses lie.

In the habits. In the routines.

That's why I hacked into his computer, his phone, and his car's GPS. What? I needed to know what he was up to at all times. And yes, that might sound a little bit stalkerish, but he messed with me first. He threatened me *first*.

No one threatens me and gets away with it. No one.

I shake my head at that. I really sound like them right now, even though I've done everything possible to be separated from them.

In my digging about, I discovered that his father isn't his biological one, but he's still the foster son of a powerhouse English businessman, Ethan Steel, and has a twin and a foster sister. Said foster sister married into the King family, which is another influential name in the UK.

He comes from money and power, something I should've expected, but it still makes me antsy. I hate those two words. Money and power. They belong to the world I escaped from.

And I need to escape his orbit, too. Because even though he didn't pay me a visit, I can feel him biding his time, waiting, pining for the right moment to attack.

If anyone is going to do that first, it'll be me.

So I head to the open office area that situates the interns, junior associates, and some paralegals. The junior partners' offices are on the opposite side, where they can overlook the interns if they open their blinds.

Knox's are always open, giving everyone a 3D view through the glass wall of his office. It's like he has nothing to hide.

And he doesn't. From what I've learned, he's a ruthless criminal defense attorney and is always in demand, probably because of his offensive style in court.

He's known to be provocative, even toward the victims, which has earned him a notorious reputation. Naturally, he gets a lot of case requests, but I also found out that he refuses about eighty percent of them. Another thing that's bizarre for lawyers, but apparently, the founding partners of W&S give him free rein on that. Which I assume is why he refused every other firm's offer to join them.

When I come here, I pretend to be getting a coffee from the break area that's dedicated to the staff and try to gauge if anything is different.

Usually, there's nothing, and I'd have to sneak out before he notices me.

Today, however, is different.

The moment I step out of the elevator, the sound of hushed murmurs reaches me in waves. I slowly inch forward to find a small crowd watching a scene.

And the location is Knox's office.

A girl stands in the middle, wearing a pale violet dress and matching heels. Her face is red and even from a distance, I can see the tears and anguish in her eyes.

She's a myriad of motions; her hands flailing around as she talks, then she hugs herself and more tears follow.

My spine snaps in a line at the scene. It's so similar to Mom's when she was married to my abusive stepfather.

The self-comfort. The involuntary jerking. Even the tears that don't seem to be planned.

In the midst of her small breakdown, Knox sits behind his desk, fingers forming a steeple at his chin, listening.

There's not an ounce of emotion on his hard face. Not even the fake empathy some people wear as a façade.

He's in his true element. Unfeeling. Completely detached from her anguish as if she and her grief don't exist.

My nails dig into the heels of my palms as I clench my fists. Is that how my mom felt with Papa?

That he was too emotionless to feel for her?

That no matter how much she cried, he'd never see those tears or her pain? Is that why she refused to ask him for help?

"Twenty bucks says that he'll reject her," one of the interns, a brunette with darker skin, says.

"Call," her colleague, a tall ginger male replies. "I say that he'll accept her case."

"No way." The brunette shakes her head. "He hasn't moved during her entire speech."

"He's just listening to the facts like he always does." The ginger waves two bills. "Who's with me?"

Not many are. A debate breaks out among them about how Knox doesn't accept many cases and that he's been on a rejection spree lately.

I'm half-listening to them, half-focused on the girl who keeps touching her hands, her elbow, anywhere she can reach.

"Who are we betting on?" a friendly voice asks, having just arrived to the party.

I immediately recognize him by the accent and slowly step back. It's Daniel Sterling, another junior partner and Knox's closest friend. If they're not working or in court, they're together.

Unlike Knox, Daniel specializes in international law and has a generally charming presence. Probably because the dimples make him appear friendly, but the jury is still out on whether or not he is.

Despite my spy skills, I haven't figured him or Knox out. On the outside, they appear to be two hotshot Englishmen who came to study and work here. Their reputations are stellar—or mostly good, aside from their manwhorish ways—and they built their careers tremendously in so little time. They're often in the limelight at social events and are the talk of magazines and the press—the press I only became aware of after I became Jane, since I didn't have hardly any focus on it as Anastasia.

However, something tells me that's not the end of it. I lived in a dangerous world long enough to know that what lurks beneath the surface is often much more nefarious than what's visible.

"We're betting twenty bucks on whether or not Knox will reject her," the brunette replies without looking at him.

"I'll raise you a hundred on that. He'll reject her. See that slight twitch of his fingers? It means he's bored and will kick her out in about twenty seconds."

Everyone turns around to Daniel and he grins at them, showing his dimples.

They're flustered for a second, only a second, but then he hops to a sitting position on one of the desks and beckons them over. "Anyone here have popcorn?"

Low laughter breaks out and then they're all surrounding him, watching the show and chatting among themselves.

I stay on the outskirts, feeling like I need to be there for some reason.

"Three, two…" Daniel counts with his fingers. "And go."

At that exact moment, Knox stands up, opens the door to his office, and directs the girl out.

She doesn't move, sniffling and jerking in place, then she goes to him. "Please…I have no one to ask for help."

"Yes, you do. A thousand other attorneys, in fact. I'll have my secretary send you a list of recommendations." He's speaking calmly albeit emotionlessly, like when he promised to find what I'm hiding the other day. "Besides, I'm a criminal defense attorney. Come back when you need to stay out of prison."

"I don't care. I've done my research and I know you aren't afraid of a challenge and could take on a civil case if you wanted to."

"I just said I don't want to. Best of luck finding another attorney."

"No one is like you. Please. They're scared to go against him."

"Not my problem. Have a nice day."

And with that, he goes back to his office and closes the door and pulls down the blinds. The girl nearly collapses and has to grip the wall for balance.

"Told you." Daniel grins. "You'll pay me later. Now, back to work."

They buzz to their desks and he strides to his office humming a tune.

The scene from a moment ago vanishes as if it never existed.

Everyone seems to have forgotten about the girl who's slowly walking to the elevators, still using the wall to hold her up.

I follow her and click the call button when her hand shakes, unable to push it.

"Thank you." She sniffles, wiping her eyes with the back of her hand. Then she's touching her elbow again, and there's a spot there, a hint of something violet that seems to have been hidden with foundation.

My chest squeezes and all I can see is how Mom used to do the same to hide the bruises, especially from me.

"Don't take it personally," I whisper. "He doesn't accept many cases."

"I know, but he was my last hope. I heard he doesn't care who he goes up against, but maybe he does. Maybe everyone is right. Maybe I shouldn't have started this."

"No," I tell her without thinking. "Don't say that, please. You're doing the right thing."

She looks up at me then, her dark eyes filled with moisture, but she's not crying anymore, because there's a little smile there. "Thank you for saying that. You don't know how much it means to me."

The elevator dings open and she smiles again before she steps in.

But I don't like the way it disappears the moment she's inside, how her shoulders hunch and the tears come back.

Maybe there's something I can do.

A crazy idea forms in my mind.

Knox told me he's coming after me, but he won't know what hit him when the tables are turned.

EIGHT

Knox

CLENCH AND UNCLENCH MY FINGERS, BUT IT'S IMPOSSIBLE TO keep typing.

The hurricane that's brewing inside me is unable to be squashed or derailed. It's not only eating everything in its path, but it's also destroying any semblance of calm I've held on to for decades.

The shadows crowd over my shoulders, whispering, murmuring, getting sickeningly close to my ears.

They started when I was five and haven't stopped.

They never will.

"Fuck, fuck, fuck!"

I push away from my desk and inhale a few sharp intakes of air, but it's like I'm breathing smoke, thick and foggy and fucking asphyxiating.

It's not Sandra Bell's words that play in my head like a distorted record anymore, it's not her voice that I'm hearing.

It's mine and my twin sister's.

And they're more haunting than hers, more fucking deranged and raw. I can still smell the rotten stench of our hellhole. The pungent smell of alcohol, cigarettes, and disgusting male musk.

It was twenty years ago, but it feels like only twenty minutes.

The twenty minutes Sandra spent telling me her story.

I can listen to tales of murder all day long and not blink an eye. I should've been desensitized to child abuse by now, too.

I've come a long way from when it all happened. I didn't stand there, waiting for the hit.

I fucking punched back and rose above the shadows and their bloody rotten smell. I grabbed my sister's hand and ran away without a look back, so why the fuck are those shadows dragging me under again?

My phone vibrates and I'm about to hit Ignore. The last thing I should do in my state is talk to people. They wouldn't recognize me when I'm like this. I'm not the charming, fun-loving Knox they know, I'm the Knox from that hellhole.

A kid in an adult's body.

A man who still sees his demons.

The picture that flashes on the screen makes me pause.

Teal. My twin sister.

In it, she's in the middle while both her husband and son kiss each of her cheeks. But that's not all, she's smiling.

No, laughing.

When we were growing up, she never had any of these joyful expressions. She also barely spoke for years and only when it was absolutely necessary.

But look at her now. A wife, a mother, and a successful businesswoman.

My finger hovers over the Ignore button, but I don't press it. If it were anyone else, I wouldn't reply, but Teal is different. Teal is my other half.

Falling back onto my seat, I accept the video call, plastering a smile on my face. "Hey, T."

My sister and I obviously aren't identical twins, so she doesn't look much like me. Her eyes are darker, bigger, and used to be sadder. Not now, though. There's a light in them, a spark.

Life.

That's what she lacked until she met her husband during our senior year in secondary school.

She's not smiling back, though, a deep frown etching between her brows.

"Where's my nephew?" I search behind her. "How dare you video call and not show me Remi?"

"He's having a bath with his father." She inches forward to the screen and her black hair follows the motion, framing her face. "Are you okay?"

"Why wouldn't I be?"

"I just got a weird feeling. You know, twin hunch."

"There's no such thing as twin hunch, T. Especially for fraternal twins, so you're just making that up to get information."

"Stop the lawyer talk, Knox, and yes, there's such a thing as a twin hunch. That's how we found each other when I was lost in the market while we were kids, remember?"

I grunt.

"So?" she insists, squaring her shoulders and crossing her arms over her chest. "What's going on?"

"Work."

"And?"

"And shagging." I grin. "You want to hear details about that?"

"Ew, no, and you're not changing the subject."

"You're a pain in the arse, T."

"And glad of it. Now, are you going to tell me what's going on or should I smash your Metallica collection?"

"You wouldn't fucking dare."

"Yes, I will if you don't spill."

"I'm bribing Dad to watch them for me, so screw you, T."

"I'll just bribe Dad more and have him film me while I do it, then I'll take the next plane to New York so I can find out what's going on myself."

"I'll call Ronan and tell him his wife is on the loose."

"Joke's on you because I'll just bring him with me so he'll annoy the shit out of you."

I groan.

"That's what I thought. Now, spill, Knox."

I release a sigh. I can win a million battles in court but not one against Teal's sense of infuriating perseverance. Especially when she senses that something is wrong.

"It's really just a case, T."

"What type of case?"

"Nothing you need to worry about."

"Apparently, I do." She softens her tone. "Please, Knox, tell me. I won't be able to sleep if I'm worried about you. Isn't it enough that I can't see you as much as I want? I feel like you're slipping away."

"I'm here, T. I'll always be here." I inhale deeply, thinking about how to deliver this.

The best option is to lie, but she'll see straight through that. No matter how much I've perfected my façade, she's the only one who detects my bullshit and calls me out on it.

She's waiting for me, her face blank, but she doesn't say anything.

Words never were and never will be her strength. She's also really a pain in the arse, because she knows she can get to me with a look alone. That's how she used to communicate her discomfort to me when we were kids and she didn't speak.

After a moment of fruitless deliberation, I say, "A woman wanted me to represent her because she's suing her father for sexual abuse and is demanding monetary compensation."

That look returns, the dimmed one that kills all the light in her eyes. Eyes that were dead for so long and finally started being alive ten years ago. That's gone now as if, like me, she's back to that hellhole in Birmingham. The hole filled with the stench of alcohol, drugs, and men.

And I want to fucking shoot myself. This is why I don't want to tell her, why I keep it all buried inside.

I'm a fucking bastard, but I had one purpose—protecting my baby sister.

And I just screwed it up with flying colors.

"Listen, T, it's not…"

"I knew it," she says in a calm tone.

"Knew what?"

"You're hiding things from me."

"I'm not hiding anything. It's just work. There's really nothing you should worry about."

"But it's affecting you. I can see the hardness forming on your face, Knox."

"I'm fine."

"I said that, too, and we both know how that ended up."

"I'm a criminal defense attorney, T. I've handled worse than this."

"Worse, yes, but not that exact subject."

"Didn't you tell me to defend those who are as defenseless as we were?"

"Not if it triggers you, not if it takes away your humanity and steals you from me."

"Who's stealing who?" a male voice calls from her end before Ronan, her husband, appears by her side. He's shirtless and carrying a half-naked Remington in his arms. They're both wearing towels and their hair is wet. Is that shampoo on Remi's head?

"Daddy…" My nephew claps, then points at me. "Uncle Nokth…"

That's what I am to my three-year-old nephew—a gibberish of consonants and vowels.

"Hey, there, buddy." I smile at him, thankful for their interruption. If they hadn't shown up, the conversation with Teal would've veered into disastrous territory.

"Hey, Uncle Nokth!" He claps again. "Daddy made me a bath."

"That's right. Who's your favorite?" Ronan gives him a fist and he bumps it, giggling uncontrollably.

"Daddy!"

"Okay, go change now and let me talk to your uncle Knox." Teal kisses her son's cheek.

"Not until we clear this whole thing up." Ronan leans forward. He passed almost all of his genes to Remi, from the brown eye color to the straight aristocratic nose that he himself inherited from his earl father. "Are you going to steal my wife, Knox? Because Remi and I won't allow it."

"Won't allow it," Remi repeats, mimicking his father's frown.

"No way. In fact, I have work to do, so you can take her back."

"Knox, don't you dare!" Teal objects.

"Bye, Remi."

"Bye, Uncle Nokth!!"

My smile drops as soon as I disconnect.

I attempt to get my head occupied with work, but after an hour or so of reading a case file, it's impossible to ward off the tension that's building in my shoulders.

So I opt to get out and change the scenery.

Preferably by fucking someone.

It's the best way to get rid of accumulating tension, but there's one tiny problem about that.

Ever since I fucked Anastasia three weeks ago, I haven't had the appetite for anyone else.

It's not that I don't want to fuck. It's that I want to fuck *her*. No one else but the lying, conniving thief that I should've outed by now.

The background check Daniel did on her is squeaky clean, which is suspicious as hell. Just like her.

And I'll handle it.

I just haven't figured out how. Because every time I see her, I picture my dick in her mouth or her tight pussy.

And that's not very productive. Or maybe it is, depending on which angle one looks at it from.

I leave my briefcase in my office and take the lift to the car park. Someone stops it a floor below, one of the assistants. She smiles and I fake one right back.

It's easy now, to pretend that I'm normal, that I can automatically smile upon seeing another human instead of having nefarious thoughts about throwing them from the highest floor.

I might act friendly, but I don't trust people. Not after the kindest-looking ones made mine and my sister's lives hell.

The rotten people looked posh, elegant, and had all the right connections and money to hide their nefarious tendencies. They used their power to prey on the vulnerable and feed their fucked up animalistic urges.

Which is why I made it my mission to make them pay any chance I got. The press and everyone in the law circuit says I'm picky, but they don't know the actual reason behind that.

I refuse to represent a person if I doubt they're rotten.

They have a stench—the rotten ones—and I can smell it from a mile apart. It's a sixth sense that I've had ever since I was a child.

Don't get me wrong. That doesn't mean I give a fuck a fuck about justice. At least not in the traditional sense.

If a woman comes to me because she murdered her abusive husband, good for her. I'll get her out of prison in a heartbeat.

If a man killed his gold digging, emotionally abusive wife, good for him, too. I'll give him a new page so he can start over.

Yes, I get murderers out of prison, but not any murderers.

Not any abusers.

Just the ones I don't smell that rotten stench on them.

When the lift is about to close, I spot a very petite and very familiar woman walking at a brisk pace in the opposite direction.

I don't even think about it as I hit the button that opens the doors before it closes. This is not the IT department, so what's she doing here?

That girl is shady as fuck, and today, I won't let it go.

I follow after her, keeping a safe distance. She doesn't notice me, though, since she has that nerdy way of being so focused either on her computer, or on her feet, like right now.

She's carrying her laptop case and lowering her head as she cuts the distance in record time. She's fast, but not forceful, almost like a breeze passing through.

Her destination is, apparently, a staff supply room that's rarely used. She stops in front of it and checks her surroundings like a thief before breaking and entering. I hide around the corner until she goes inside.

I wonder what the little daredevil is doing on a floor that shouldn't concern her and in a supply room. I doubt it's because a tech was needed here.

Instead of following right after, I wait five minutes. I need her to be engrossed in whatever her task is so she doesn't get the chance to hide.

I'm patient like that. Hunting doesn't happen with only speed. Stalking before the attack is the best way to leave the prey with no way out.

Once the five minutes are up, I stride to the door and slowly open it. Sure enough, she's sitting cross-legged on the floor in the midst of stacks of papers and typing away at her computer.

The blue light reflects in her glasses as her fingers move at lightning speed. She's facing me, so I can't see what she's working on, but she doesn't notice me, even when I close the door, trapping us both inside.

Click.

The sound echoes in the air and she lifts her head, her lips forming an O.

With the door closed, the only light in the pitch-black supply room comes from beneath the door and her laptop. There's light, but I don't use it.

For me, darkness is familiar. Light is not.

Due to the blue glow, I can make out the parting of her full lips. Lips that should've never left my dick since that first time.

"W-what are you doing here?"

"That should be my question." I stalk toward her. "What are you plotting now? Another identity? Another name?"

She tracks my movements as if I'm indeed the predator that's coming after her. I lean forward to peek at the computer. "What do you have there, Anastasia? Why do you need to come here to do it?"

As if just realizing what I'm after, she slams the laptop shut, filling our surroundings with dark shadows.

"Do you think that will stop me?" I reach for it and she tries to curl up around it.

I slip my hand onto her stomach and she's forced to get on her back, keeping the laptop overhead so I can't reach it.

So I climb on top of her, my chest glued to hers, and that stops her from wiggling about. She strains, her fingers clutching the laptop in a death-grip.

"What are you doing?" She pants, half-mortified, half-strained.

"I told you, I'll uncover you, and now is as good a time as any."

"There's nothing to uncover, let me go."

"Hmm. I would've believed that if you weren't going through so much trouble to protect your crime weapon."

"Laptops are personal, asshole."

"Not if they're at the crime scene."

"Ugh…you're crushing me."

"Then give it up."

In one last-ditch attempt, she tries to knee me in the balls. I grip her knee with one hand and stroke her thigh. A smile stretches my lips, a real one, though it probably looks like an evil smirk in the dark. "You really shouldn't have played dirty. Now, I'm tempted to do something."

"D-do what?"

"Make you squirm." My fingers inch closer to her hips, and even though I'm touching her through her clothes, I feel her warmth and the shudder going through her body.

"Y-you said you wouldn't touch me."

"I changed my mind."

"Why?"

"Because your body gets so pliant underneath me and I might like that."

"It does not."

"Hmm. Should I prove it?"

"D-don't."

"Challenge accepted, my little butterfly."

After all, she's the reason I lost my sexual appetite and it's only fair that I get it back through her.

Yes, she's a liar, but she might be the best form of distraction I've ever had.

NINE

Anastasia

MY LITTLE BUTTERFLY.

That's what he just called me, right?

My chest tightens and my eyes grow in size, desperate to make him out. In the darkness, I can't see him, but the sharp lines of his face are visible and so is the glint in his intense eyes.

I'm trapped beneath the hardness of his body and the sheer size of him. I'm crushed and can't breathe. And that cologne I searched for at the department stores? It's suffocating me now, robbing my thought process and stopping me from thinking beyond this moment.

"You…you have my butterfly?"

"Why would you think that?"

"You just called me a little butterfly."

"Could have done that for any reason."

"But it was specific enough."

"Hmm. What are you going to do to find out whether I have

it or not?" His voice is deep, dark velvet that's wrapping itself around my neck.

"I..."

My words trail off when his hand that's been on my thigh glides to the inner side of it.

I clench my legs together tightly, even though it tingles, even though every illogical thought in my head is urging me to let go.

I can't.

Not when I can sense ripples of darkness emanating from him. The same darkness I fought tooth and nail to leave behind.

I think I've always sensed it on him, even during that night in Jersey, but back then, it was fine because it was a one-time thing and I foolishly thought I wouldn't see him again.

I foolishly thought I would just keep him in my memories and that's it.

But he's right here, and he's coming after me and that's not good.

It's downright frightening for *Babushka*'s and my destiny.

His fingers hover at the apex of my thighs and even though he's not forcing entry, he's lingering there, biding his time.

"What's going on?" There's slight amusement in his tone, bordering on sadism. "Feeling shy all of a sudden?"

"That's not...oh..." My words end in a moan because he's pressing a finger against my clit now, and although it's through my pants and underwear, I can feel the throbbing of my veins in my core.

"You shouldn't be." He's speaking against my ear, his voice hotter and sexier in the low range.

For a second, I'm so focused on that, on his voice and range, that I momentarily forget what's at stake here. My brain has tuned out all environmental elements so all I can feel is his cut body that has a warrior tattoo hidden beneath the prim and proper suit.

A lot of muscles, too, that I saw that day and currently feel against the softness of my belly and breasts.

Everything about me is so soft while he's so hard and big that he makes me feel small. So small and breakable, but instead of becoming apprehensive, my skin catches fire and a strange type of arousal spreads inside me.

That's wrong, though, isn't it? I'm not supposed to be turned on by our size difference. If anything, I should be wary of it, should think of what's at stake.

Like my laptop.

Knox must've gotten this close to aim for my laptop that I'm holding with both hands and keeping it out of reach above my head.

But he doesn't.

Instead, he flicks his tongue on the shell of my ear and I can't help the zaps of pleasure that burst in waves across my sensitive flesh. When his deep whisper follows, I'm on the verge of something so harsh, it steals my breath.

"You shouldn't be shy. After all…" He digs his fingers in my pussy and I bite my tongue to suppress a moan. "I made this cunt bleed for the first time."

Shit.

Why does he make the act of taking my virginity sound so hot? It shouldn't, not when I always considered it a burden that could be used to marry me off to the first suitable man my family found for me. Not when all I cared about was getting rid of it. But hearing him say those words makes everything sound more twisted, perverted, and completely deviant.

"Open." The firm, non-negotiable order sends a blast of sparks inside me.

He doesn't need to use his fingers to force my legs apart, because they fall open on their own. My mind is conditioned to all the delicious authoritativeness that I felt that night, to the surrender I experienced for the first time in my life.

And it's not the forced type where I had no choice, because I did, I had the option to walk away, but I chose not to.

I chose to stay.

Because for the first time, I wasn't the daughter of a dangerous family or the fake Jane. It was just me.

As if he's thinking the same, Knox reaches for my glasses. I want to stop him, but I can't let go of the laptop, and just like that, he removes them. I don't think he's able to see my eyes in the darkness, and if he does, he'll only look into the contacts. However, when he does look at me, it feels different, like we're back at that moment.

Where we were anonymous.

"Open wider," he commands, and this time, I don't have to part my legs much since his hand is already on the zipper of my pants. He easily pulls them down, then slides his fingers into my panties.

It's a jolt, a shock reaction that causes my back to arch off the floor and my hands to become sweaty on the laptop.

This isn't the first time he's touched me this intimately, but it feels like it is.

"Hmm. Someone got turned on by the wrestling." It's that sadism again, but it's mixed with a foggy type of lust.

Or maybe that's me.

He rubs the length of his massive erection on my stomach and I go still, my breathing shattering. "Your little wiggling got me rock-fucking-hard, beautiful. You will take care of that, won't you?"

I don't understand what he's talking about, partly because his fingers continue rubbing my soaking folds, and partly because his erection is growing by the second.

The sound of his zipper echoes in the air and I hold my breath, even though I'm overwhelmed by all types of sensations. Even though my heart is about to jump out to where his fingers are on my pussy.

The way he touches me is slow and firm, as if he knows exactly what he's doing and where he's taking this. And I'm helpless in front of that, completely and utterly caught in a trap I can't escape.

Then something happens.

His erection that I was feeling on my stomach only a

few seconds ago replaces his fingers, rubbing against my panties-covered pussy.

The sparks of pleasure turn into full-blown bursts, but that's not all, because he's thrusting against my opening while it's still covered and for some reason, that feels perverted and causes more arousal to coat both of us.

"I want to fuck you," he grunts as he thrusts, rubs, and slides his cock up and down my panties. "I want to yank down your fake identity's clothes and pound into your tight cunt until you're screaming."

Do it, I want to say.

Just do it already. I've been having withdrawals I didn't think I would suffer from ever since the first time he touched me.

Ever since I found out what sex is all about.

And not sex with just anyone. Sex with him and his deliciously intense dominance. Ordinarily, I'd run away from it, but with Knox, I'm slamming straight into it.

Consciously and subconsciously.

"See how your cunt is swallowing me, my liar? You want my cock inside you, don't you? You want me to fuck you hard and fast and with no restraint."

I'm on the edge and I can't look away from it. I'm right there and it's not only because of the pace of his cock. It's a combination of everything.

It's due to his dirty talk and the deep tenor of his voice.

It's due to his firm touch as he takes what he wants without an ounce of apology.

It's due to the air that's rippling and crowding with tension, oozing with sex and his intoxicating cologne.

But the most important element of all is him. The man who should've been a one-time thing but is turning into more.

And that's strangely a turn-on. A button that I didn't think I even had inside me.

"Do you want me to fuck you, Anastasia?"

The sound of my name should've quenched my desire, but it heightens it to a wildfire.

He knows me—well, not really—but he at least doesn't think I'm the fake I worked so hard to build. And while usually that would be alarming, it isn't right now.

Because it's me.

"Do you?" he insists, and I'm so close to shouting it, to telling him to fuck me.

It's only a one-time thing anyway.

That's what I said the other time and I was obviously wrong.

But I nod anyway, it's barely-there, but he notices it and picks up his pace. If it weren't for his chest on mine, I would be jumping up from the heat of the sensations.

"I won't, though, not until you tell me a truth about yourself."

"Ugh…" The frustration that spills out of my throat is spontaneous and it makes him chuckle. But the sound is nowhere near light. It's dark and somewhat disturbed.

"You thought I would let you play me, my little liar?"

"That's not…I'm not…"

"You're not what?"

"Playing you." If anything, he's the one doing that, toying with me until I'm about to burst.

"Then say something."

"Anastasia is…my real name."

It's a little information, something that he was suspecting all along, but saying it aloud knocks a weight from my chest.

"I already knew that."

"You…didn't know for sure."

"Hmm. I still can't fuck you, though."

"Why not?"

"I don't have a condom on me. Usually, I don't come to work with plans to fuck an employee."

My nails dig into the laptop and I nearly scream from frustration. I bite my tongue instead, not wanting him to feel how much of an effect he has on me.

How much his words just filled me with inexplicable disappointment.

"But I'll change that going forward." He thrusts his dick against my opening a few times with increasing force. The tiny jerks are so pleasurable that I subconsciously release my tongue.

The orgasm hits me with a blinding force and then I'm falling, shattering, but there's no landing in sight. Not even when I blink rapidly, trying to rein in my reaction. The force of the pleasure is stronger than my attempts at self-control, and I just scream.

He wraps a hand around my mouth. "Shh, people will hear."

Shit.

I completely forgot about that, about the fact that we're at the firm and that I'm protecting my plans in the laptop from him, even though my hands are still over my head.

As the wave slowly subsides, I lie there, catching my breath and my thoughts. I'm a bit sleepy, too.

It's a problem if I constantly want to collapse after a powerful orgasm. Doesn't that defy the whole purpose behind it?

In my haze, I make out Knox climbing up my body until his knees are on either side of my head. His dark shadow falls over me like doom, a thrilling one at that. One that I can't stop staring at.

And then I taste something salty—his precum. In my daze, I didn't notice that he was placing the tip of his dick on my mouth. "I need these lips on my cock."

I open slowly, taking him inside. It's different from the other time because now, I don't even attempt to have any control. It's all his for the taking.

He snakes a hand beneath my head, gripping me by the hair, and thrusts into my mouth with brute force. He hits the back of my throat and I choke on him, spluttering and gasping for air.

"Relax your throat," he coaxes, almost half ordering, and then thrusts again. "That's it, beautiful."

My heartbeat thunders and my pussy clenches with a renewed need at his words. The fact that he's still calling me beautiful, that he's enjoying it.

I really do get off on his pleasure. On the fact that I'm the reason behind it, the reason he's groaning deep in his throat.

And I want more of that.

So I relax my throat more, letting him fuck it hard and fast and without restraint. I moan around him, too, because I like this feeling of power.

I like how his hips jerk as if he's unable to control the pleasure.

"Fuck, beautiful. I'm going to release my cum down that pretty throat." And with one last grunt, he does as promised, shooting his release so deep that I barely get to taste him as I swallow.

When he pulls out, a trail of cum forms between my mouth and his dick, and I'm utterly fascinated by the view that I can't look away from it.

From *him*.

He wipes the side of my mouth with his thumb and I can almost hear the smirk in his voice as he says, "I'm going to have fun playing with you, my little liar."

TEN

Knox

THE MOMENT I GET OFF HER, ANASTASIA CRAWLS BACKWARD until her back hits the side of a shelf, but she holds the laptop protectively to her chest.

She didn't let it go, even while she was shattering against my cock and I had to muffle her screams.

I tuck myself in and grunt at the twitch in my dick. Apparently, coming down her pretty throat isn't enough. I'm resisting the urge to grab her by the throat and fuck her against the wall. Condoms be damned.

Though, not really. I'm not my sister and I'm not interested in kids now. Or ever. Why bring a child to this cruel world, then force them to fend for themselves?

Remi is the only kid allowed in my life, and only from afar.

Nevertheless, I'm seriously contemplating bending her over the nearest table and fucking her tight little cunt. I can pull out before I'm finished or—

Fuck, what am I even thinking about? I shouldn't be

entertaining this idea in the first place, let alone finding loopholes around it.

I don't fuck without a condom and that's that. I'm pissed off that I even considered the option.

This is only because I haven't shagged in a while. That's it.

That's *all*.

Anastasia grabs the laptop with one hand and zips her pants with the other. That's her name, Anastasia, her *real* name.

In admitting that, she also indirectly insinuated that the whole Jane persona is just that—a persona. None of it is real; not her appearance and definitely not those fake brown eyes that are currently tracking my every movement.

Sometimes, she looks like prey, a smart one who does the watching instead of waiting to be eaten.

Now that I think about it, this is what she's been doing ever since that first time I saw her in that bar. She was watching from behind those icy blonde strands and determining what to do next.

Is it curiosity or perhaps caution?

Just who the fuck is she? The mere question in my head boils my blood with annoyance. I'm not a good man. I'm not even decent. Needless to say, I'm not the type who asks women their names, let alone about their life story.

So why the fuck do I want to jam my fingers inside her and pull out whatever the fuck she's hiding?

Why her?

Because she's a little fucking liar, that's why.

While I'm used to criminals lying to me all the time, it's different when it's on a personal scale.

Once I'm all tucked in, I open the door with more force than needed. The light from outside slips inside, bathing the room and her in a soft hue.

Her cheeks are still red, her expression like a deer caught in the headlights, but she takes the motion of me opening the door as meaning I'm done with her and bends over to grab her laptop case.

The moment she does, I snatch it from between her fingers.

At first, she freezes as if not understanding what just happened, then a blush covers her cheeks. The light coming through the door turns her brown eyes lighter, almost streaked with blue. Which I'm sure is her actual eye color.

"Give it back!"

"Tell me something about the real you first."

She jumps, but I'm holding the laptop up. Considering our size difference, she won't be able to reach it no matter how much she tries.

But she does just that—try. She grabs my arm and uses it as leverage to jump higher. Her face turns a deeper shade of red with each passing second and her breathing comes out harsh and guttural.

Finally, she pushes back, her brow furrowing before she raises her nose. "You won't be able to open it anyway. It's password protected."

"I'll figure out a way." I shake the laptop in the air. "I wonder what skeletons I'll find here."

She purses her lips. "Why do you want to know about me?"

"Because I'm not a big fan of liars. Besides, you know so much about me from all that googling, it's only fair that I'm in the know, too."

She stares at my hand for a second and I can tell the exact moment she decides to have one last-ditch attempt.

But even as she jumps, she doesn't manage to reach half the distance.

"Nice try." I smirk.

She glares, but it's only a fraction of a second before she breaks eye contact. I noticed that she doesn't do that a lot, looking into other people's or my eyes, as if she's escaping something by avoiding them.

Crouching down, she grabs her glasses that I threw away earlier and puts them on, using them as some sort of armor, a weapon against the world.

Or maybe just against me.

"I have a condition."

"A condition? What makes you think you're in a position to have those? I have your laptop, remember?"

"I won't tell you anything unless you agree to my condition."

"And what is that?"

She inhales a deep breath, places her hand on her chest, then says, "Can't you accept that woman's case?"

I narrow my eyes. "Were you spying on me?"

"I just…happened to be passing by."

"For such an excellent liar, you're doing a rubbish job with your speech pattern right now. But it doesn't matter, because the answer is no."

A frown appears between her delicate brows and she drops her hand from her chest. "Why not? She was obviously abused."

"How do you know that?"

"She had purple marks on her wrist that she was hiding with makeup. It's typical behavior shown by abused women."

"And you're an expert because…"

"Mom was in an abusive relationship and I witnessed it all. From the beatings to the lying to the flinching. *All* of it. I was there when she used foundation to hide the bruises but I wasn't there when she sent me to the neighbor in order to protect me. It takes a lot of courage to go against one's abuser. I know, because Mom couldn't, and when she did, it was already too late. So please, help that woman if you can."

I pause, lowering my hand with the laptop to my side. The emotions in her voice are so raw and real. More real than anything I've heard from her before. I always suspected that she was hiding something, that she was cunning and conniving for a reason, but I never thought it would be this.

She's not even focused on her laptop anymore, only me. There's desperation in her stiff posture, in the way she continuously adjusts her glasses and touches her chest as if that keeps her rooted in the moment.

I flex my fingers on the laptop. "Why was it too late?"

"What?"

"You said your mum couldn't ask for help and when she did, it was too late. Why?"

"Because…" She strokes the edge of her glasses, clutches her shirt in her fist, then swallows thickly. "Because…the person she asked for help wasn't exactly a knight in shining armor."

"And you think I am?"

"You're a lawyer."

"Doesn't make me a hero."

"A hero is the last thing women like my mom and that girl need."

"Why is that?"

"Because heroes follow rules and think about the world's wellbeing. They're shackled by outdated codes of honor and self-imposed morals, and that might work in a black and white platonic idealism, but that's not reality, that's not how it works. In life, sometimes, the hero has to turn into a villain."

"Is that what I am? A villain?"

"I heard you could be if the situation requires it."

"So I'm a part-time villain?"

"I prefer the term, dark warrior of justice."

"And do you believe in that? Justice?"

"I have to, because if I don't, I'll have nothing to believe in, nothing to hope for, and that's just…too bleak to think about." She stares at me for that fraction of a second, then lowers her head. "Do you?"

"Do I what?"

"Believe in justice?"

"Not really."

"Then…why did you become a lawyer?"

"Because justice fucked me over once upon a time and I'm fucking it right back. It's a grudge of sorts. Justice and I have what people call a love-hate relationship." No clue why the fuck I'm telling her all of this when I don't talk about it with anyone, not even T.

My perception about justice has been warped ever since I was a kid, and it only got more complicated as I grew up. I hate justice most of the time, but using it has been giving my life meaning.

However, I don't like others finding out about my relationship with it, so the fact that I just told her all that is a first.

It could be because she opened up about her mother. Could be because of the way she steals glances at me, even though her head is usually lowered, worshipping the ground.

Or maybe it's due to the fact that I discovered another depth to her, one that's toying with my fucking shadows, and I want those gone.

The depth and the shadows.

Or maybe I want them to clash together, to hit rock bottom so that I can watch the type of mayhem it'll create.

"Justice fucked them over, too," she whispers. "People like that woman and Mom, I mean. No one heard them scream or saw their hidden bruises. No one stopped to offer them a helping hand or even listened to them. But you can."

"I'm not exactly a benevolent person."

"You don't have to be. Just do what you do best."

"And what is that?"

She smiles and it's soft yet raw, just like her words from earlier. As if she's not only baring her teeth but also a piece of her hidden soul in the process. "Fuck justice over on their behalf."

I can't help the tinge of amusement in my voice. "I thought you believed in justice. Now, you want me to fuck it over?"

"When it's being an asshole, yeah." She peeks at me through her lashes. "So?"

"I'm still not convinced. You'll have to try harder."

A determined fire takes refuge in her eyes. "I will."

"Are you sure? I'm not the type who easily changes their mind."

She snatches the laptop from my fingers, and even though I saw it coming, I don't stop her.

A gleeful, victorious expression covers her features. "And I'm not the type who easily gives up."

⚖️

"I'm in." I slide to the seat across from Aspen and focus on the man sitting behind the desk.

Nate, the *Weaver* of Weaver & Shaw and the managing partner of the firm stares at me as if I've grown two heads.

He's in his late thirties, has a strong bone structure, and is strict as fuck when it comes to running W&S. While he doesn't interfere with how we pick our clients, he doesn't let us completely loose either.

One way or another, he's involved in every single case that comes knocking on our doors, which is why I'm sure he already knows about Sandra's.

Either his spying elves told him or Daniel's big mouth took care of the job. Either way, he doesn't seem very surprised, just skeptical, really.

That makes two of us.

It took me a few hours of mental processing to come to this decision. After I parted ways with Anastasia earlier today, I went back to my office and thought about the pros and cons.

Naturally, for me, the cons are greater. Not only is this a civil case, but it also hits too close to home, and that's usually a deal-breaker.

But something Anastasia said kept nagging at me.

No one heard them scream or saw their hidden bruises. No one stopped to offer them a helping hand or even listened to them. But you can.

It reminded me of Dad. If he hadn't found me and Teal, if he'd rejected us, we would've headed down a destructive path. We wouldn't have become the people we are today.

As if it's a sign, he called me earlier and asked if I needed anything. I'm a successful twenty-eight-year-old man with a fortune that I'm investing around the globe, but my dad still calls and asks me if I need anything.

He's never once made me feel as if I'm not his biological son.

When I fucked up as a teen, he got mad at me like a normal father would and taught me what the world is all about. When I did something right, he rewarded me and made me feel appreciated and loved.

The combination of his and Teal's call, as well as Anastasia's words, sealed the deal for me.

Despite the cons glaring at me from a distance, I'm getting out of my comfort zone.

It was getting boring in there anyway.

Nate continues watching me and so does Aspen. She's a redhead and one of the most attractive women I've ever seen—aside from the icy-haired, blue-eyed little liar.

I take a calming breath to shoo her away from my thoughts.

Back to the topic at hand, Aspen is the only female senior partner at W&S and Nate's right-hand woman. She's also Kingsley's archenemy, so the whole dynamic between the three of them is amusing at best.

She takes a sip from her coffee. "Didn't you turn her away?"

"I changed my mind."

"You rarely change your mind, if ever, Van Doren." Nate leans forward in his chair. "Why now?"

"I didn't know that her father was being represented by Pearce & Powers, our biggest rivals last I checked." I lean back in my chair and cross my legs at the ankles. "We can't let this chance to crush them slide."

"How about you let me and King worry about Pearce & Powers and tell me the real reason?"

"I smell something fishy, too." Aspen places her coffee on the table and two pairs of critical, judgmental eyes zero in on me.

"I'm merely interested in the case. What more reason do you need? Just take my word for it and let me do my magic. Needless to say, you guys are invited to have front-row seats."

"Are you sure?" Nate raises a brow. "You'll handle the civil side of this case, considering that Sandra Bell is demanding compensation."

"Yes, but the criminal case might happen right after this and I can assist Sandra."

"You're well aware that this case will be media-heavy, not only because of the nature of the lawsuit but also due to who she's going against. Matt Bell is a known producer and that makes him a public figure."

"Which will bring more awareness to these types of cases—and the firm, of course. It doesn't matter who Matt Bell is, I'm going to crush him and his lawyer."

Aspen gives me a little smile. Despite her behind-the-scenes role, she doesn't miss a chance to give scums what they deserve. "My little elves tell me the prosecutor will be charging him with a Class B violent felony for the sexual abuse."

"Since she's related to him by blood, the opposing counsel will argue for a Class E felony. Then they'll easily get him put on probation and it'll be as if it never happened." Nate is stating facts in his cool tone that's slightly provocative, as he does in court. "That's if the prosecutor finds proof of the sexual assault. If it turns into a his-word-versus-hers scenario, who do you think will come out of it unscathed?"

"Not that lowlife, for sure."

"He already got bail for the criminal case, so it's not looking good," he says.

"Then I will change things to my favor. I'll even find evidence to force the prosecutor's hand."

"I wouldn't be so cocky if I were you." Aspen crosses her legs. "Reginald Pearce himself is representing Matt Bell. Not to mention that the DA appointed Gerard as the prosecutor and he's besties with Pearce & Powers."

"Thanks for all the depressing news, Aspen, but as I said, I don't give a fuck who I go up against. It might as well be the Supreme Court and I will still fuck them over." I smile at that.

And no, Anastasia didn't play a part in my decision. Fine, maybe a little, but it's more for me.

She gave me a genius idea earlier.

This is another chance to fuck up the system that left gigantic loopholes for predators like Matt Bell to take advantage of.

"Even the mafia?" It's Nate who asks.

"The mafia?"

"Russian mafia. Matt uses his position in showbiz to launder their dirty money and bring them profitable ventures, among other things."

I grow silent.

Aspen fixates me with a smug look. "Want me to take over?"

"Fuck no. The mafia's involvement will make this even more fun."

"You mean, dangerous. This is a bad idea for your first large-scale case."

"You forgot something, Nate. I love bad ideas."

Like Anastasia.

She's the worst idea of all, but all I'm thinking about is keeping her coming for more.

ELEVEN

Anastasia

I KNOW I SAID I'M NOT THE TYPE WHO GIVES UP, BUT convincing Knox to change his mind is harder than I thought.

I wish his brain was a computer I could hack into and alter its wires, maybe leave a malware there to pay him back for being an asshole.

Unfortunately, I'm out of my depth and definitely not dealing with a computer. He's a man, a beautiful jerk at that. A jerk who knows which buttons of mine to push and which will set me on fire.

I've never dealt with men before. Yes, I've been surrounded by them all my life, but they only ever treated me like a princess. One with no crown and no say in anything.

My interactions with them were few and far between, so I'm absolutely clueless about how to persuade a man—or a woman, to be completely honest.

Sometimes, I feel so helpless that I consider running again, disappearing again to where no one can find me. Especially Knox.

But that would mean I'd have to abandon Sandra and that's just too similar to abandoning my mother.

I can't even consider that option, so I have to stay, despite my struggles, despite the constant irritation and strange arousal I feel every time Knox and I speak to each other.

As of now, all I'm able to do is hold on to the perseverance I thought I had tons of.

It was implemented in my upbringing, in the life that was chosen for me.

Turns out, there are limits to that, too, because Knox is a fucking manipulator.

There's this thing he invented that's called "convincing sessions." They all happen in that supply room he caught me in three days ago. They all start with his hand around my throat and end with me on the floor or against the wall as he wrenches violent pleasure out of me.

Then he uses my mouth and marks me with his cum.

"I'm still not convinced. Try harder tomorrow." Are his words after we finish.

Or more like, *he* finishes, because I'm a marionette in his hands. A doll he can do whatever he pleases with. I probably should fight harder, push him away, and stop this endless loop.

But what's the point when I can't remove him from my head? Not only that, but I've also started looking forward to coming to work, to being cornered by him. I've even grown fond of that small nook that I was going to use as my hideout for when I do research on the life I left behind. Or when I used the firm's servers to learn more about what's going on between its walls.

And maybe, just maybe, that first taste I had a few weeks ago has turned me into an addict. Maybe I'm craving more of it and stupidly telling myself "one more time."

But he's keeping me on the edge. He hasn't fucked me, and I'm sure it's not because there isn't a condom.

It's a game of his, something that he enjoys doing to make me frustrated.

But if he thinks I'll give him the satisfaction of asking for it, he'll have to wait a long time. We'll see who will give in first in this game.

God. This is so different from who I am. *What* I am. I don't usually let anyone play with me—not that they ever got close enough to do so. But now, the promise itself makes my skin tingle with something I've never been allowed to feel before.

Excitement.

And maybe that's dangerous. Maybe I should say no. But for the life of me, I can't.

It's harmless fun. Just sex.

Nothing more. Nothing less.

I plug in my earbuds and hit Play on my "Oldies" playlist. The sound of the eighties and nineties rock music puts me in a serene mood. I've always been a lover of vintage music, even though new technology is my jam. I'm a paradox that way.

I rarely listen to my music when I'm working, but ever since I encountered the hostile situation Chad and Ben have been creating, I've become religious about it. Not only do I get to enjoy good music, but I also get to tune them out.

Win-win.

I think they're mostly jealous and while I don't pay them much attention, I also don't stay quiet when they start throwing jabs my way. I might not make eye contact with them, but I won't allow anyone to treat me as if I'm a pushover.

A finger taps my shoulder while I'm typing away and I pause, thinking it's one of them coming to start shit.

It's not.

The girl who's looking down at me smiles widely and holds out a small basket of baked goods. Her name is Gwyneth—or Gwen, as she asked me to call her.

She's a pre-law student who's interning at W&S during the summer and we're the same age. We met two days ago and I had her help me with a new system I was creating. Ever since then, she's started coming to the IT department frequently because the other interns are avoiding her.

I didn't know why at the time, but she told me yesterday that she's actually Kingsley Shaw's daughter. As in, the *Shaw* of Weaver & Shaw, and apparently, that makes everyone wary of her. She's even interning for Nathaniel himself. I know he doesn't really take interns, but it makes sense since she's the daughter of his partner, who can't monitor his daughter due to being in a coma.

I remove my earbuds and offer her a small smile back.

"I brought you cupcakes." She pushes the basket at my chest. "I had to save some from Daniel. He's a cupcake monster."

"Then maybe you shouldn't make them all the time. I heard everyone wants some now."

"It's okay. I like it when I make people happy through cupcakes." She looks at Chad and Ben. "Not those nerds, though."

They glare at her and she places a hand on her hip and glares right back. She developed an animosity toward them on my behalf after she heard them call me Plain Jane. She has a weirdly cute sense of justice, which is different from Knox's warped one.

When I learned her identity and that she's actually known Knox, Daniel, and the other partners for years, I contemplated asking her to convince Knox about taking the girl's case. However, that would mean sharing too much information with someone I just met. Besides, I don't want anyone to know about what Knox and I have.

It's our dirty little secret.

"Go ahead, try them." She pulls up a chair and watches me expectantly with eyes so colorful, they look a little freaky. She has rare heterochromia that creates a mash-up of green, blue, and gray in her irises, as if she's a mythical creature from the folklore tales *Babushka* used to read to me.

I take a bite from the dainty-looking cupcake. "Vanilla again?"

"Hey! Vanilla is the best flavor."

"It's pretty standard."

"Uh, excuse you. It's versatile."

I smile at that as I continue eating.

"What are you smiling at? It really is the best."

"You're one of the minority who think that." She's also one of the few people who's willingly gotten close to me, not caring about my appearance or how asocial I actually am.

Gwen snatches one of the cupcakes she brought and starts eating. A strand of her auburn hair falls to her forehead and she unsuccessfully tries to blow it back.

"Shouldn't you be working?" I ask.

"Nah, I finished reading through the docs Nate gave me. Besides, he has a meeting with the other partners about an important case Knox is taking on, so he can't give me any new tasks or make my life hell for being half a minute late."

I lean forward in my seat. "Wait. Did you say an important case?"

"Yeah." She licks her fingers, then nearly butts her head with mine when she slides her chair closer. "The offender is Matt Bell. You know, that famous producer? His daughter is suing him for sexual assault and demanding compensation, and Knox has accepted the case. Which is weird, because I'm pretty sure I heard Dan say he rejected it. But maybe he saw the case from a different perspective and changed his mind."

My fingers tighten around the cupcake, and I'd smash it if I weren't aware that Gwen would kill me for it.

Did she just say Knox accepted the case? The same case he said I needed to convince him to take on?

"This case is getting so much media attention," Gwen continues. "It's going to be wild."

"Really?" I don't have to ask her what I actually want to know, which is if Knox is up for this. Gwen is talkative by nature and tells me anything with simple nudges.

"Absolutely! But if anyone can do it, it's Knox. Though everyone is skeptical that he's taking a civil law case, but it's probably going to happen at the same time as the criminal one and he's done that before. Dad watched that one personally and was especially proud of how Knox drove both the prosecutor and the opposing counsel insane. So, I'm totally sure he can nail this as well."

"How can you be so sure?"

"He's a strategist, you know."

"A strategist?"

"Yeah, like at first, it looks as if he's going to lose, but he's really plotting several deadly blows. And when he actually delivers them? It's game over."

I believe her. I do. As a matter of fact, I think he used that tactic on me.

A fire burns inside me and it takes everything in me to continue listening to Gwen talking about a horror movie she watched last night. It takes everything in me not to unleash that fire on him.

On the man who's been manipulating me all along.

The asshole.

By the time Gwen leaves, I'm fuming. No, I'm about to let all the destructive energy consume me.

I can't even concentrate on the system I've been carefully building for days. The codes keep blurring in front of my vision no matter how much I take deep breaths and clean my glasses.

My phone vibrates and I retrieve it with a jerk. I know who it is before I even check. The only two people who know this number are the clinic where *Babushka* stays and the asshole who unapologetically exchanged numbers with me after that first time in the supply room.

Knox: In five minutes, I'm going to fuck you.

I'm so tempted to send him a middle finger emoji, but I think better of it.

I'm going to do it in person.

TWELVE

Knox

THERE'S BEEN TENSION IN MY BLOODSTREAM FOR DAYS. Maybe even weeks.

Since the day I fucked Anastasia and she disappeared on me, leaving only her virgin blood and a black butterfly behind.

Back then, I resisted the urge to find her, because fuck that. I don't chase girls. They always fall into my lap and bombard my phone with calls.

But during those weeks, I couldn't touch any of those girls and Dan started sending stupid messages in the group chat we have with our friends in England. Two of whom are Ronan and Aiden, my brothers-in-law.

Daniel: Breaking news from the Empire State. Knox's dick is broken.

Aiden: Now, this is interesting. Tell us more.

Daniel: He hasn't shagged for weeks.

Aiden: Bit weird that you even know of his shagging schedule, Sterling, but okay.

Daniel: That's not the point here, fucker. It's that he. Hasn't. Shagged.

Cole: Agreed. Kind of a record for Van Doren.

Ronan: Did someone mention my dear brother-in-law?

Daniel: The one whose dick is broken, yes.

Ronan: I take back the dear part and also the brother-in-law part. I know no one whose dick is broken.

Aiden: Should we start to pretend he doesn't exist in public, Astor?

Ronan: Eventually.

Cole: What's the exact story, Dan?

Daniel: Nothing specific, just the fact that he refuses to shag. Real question, should I take him to the doctor? Trick him into it maybe? Because he needs his dick checked.

Aiden: Or you need to be less obsessed with his dick, maybe.

Daniel: You shut up. Any suggestions?

Ronan: Hookers, a solution as old as time and just as efficient. No doctors are needed, Danny boy.

Cole: Does Teal know you're talking about hookers?

Ronan: For her brother, not me, and fuck you, Cole.

Ronan: Un-fuck you. Don't bring it up to Teal.

Cole: Screenshot shared as we speak.

Ronan: You fucking bastard…

Daniel: Hey, motherfuckers. This is about Knox and his broken dick.

Aiden: He's probably fucking someone behind your back.

Daniel: What? Why would he do that?

Aiden: Let me take a wild guess. Your unhealthy obsession with his dick, maybe?

Ronan: Or maybe Knox just lost his balls.

Cole: RIP.

Knox: I'm right fucking here in case you forgot, arseholes.

Aiden: Even fucking better.

Needless to say, it's become a running joke in that fucking group chat that I'm contemplating muting until someone else becomes the joke. The most likely candidate—Ron.

Point is, this whole mess is because of Anastasia.

Deep in the back of my mind, I recognize that this is headed to the unhealthy obsession level, that I shouldn't allow myself to be sucked into such a bottomless pit.

Which is why I have to fuck her out of my system, once and for all. That's the plan, anyway, when I walk into the supply room.

But I'm greeted with light.

There's never light when I take her against the wall and wrench one orgasm after the other from her. Anastasia hates it, I realize—the light. She's more comfortable in the darkness, like me, where we can be ourselves without thinking about our identities, where we are, or the consequences.

It's on now, the supply room's white neon light, and it highlights the dullness of the space. The unorganized piles of papers lying around that should be in the archives.

It also puts focus on the tiny woman standing in the middle of it all, arms crossed and foot tapping on the floor. A red flush covers her cheeks and her lips are pursed in a stiff line.

I know I should probably focus on her obvious displeasure, but my gaze is stolen by the undone third button of her blouse and the hint of her lace bra and creamy breast. I would've never pegged her as the lacy type, but she is and it's a fucking turn-on.

"Do you have anything to tell me?" she asks in a tone as rigid as her posture.

"I love the view."

She follows my gaze and bunches her hand in her shirt, then jerkily buttons it. "You're such a pervert."

"Let me turn off the lights and I'll show you how much of a pervert I actually am."

"Like hell you will." She stomps toward me, the force in her steps rattling her small body. "Didn't you say you hate liars?"

"I did."

"Then why are you one yourself?"

"Me?"

"Oh, don't give me that tone. Gwen told me you accepted Sandra's case."

Gwen. Of course. I should've known that she'd tell her the news, given that they've grown close ever since King's daughter started interning for Nate. Not that I'm watching Anastasia all the time.

Fine, so I do watch whenever I have the chance, but it's only to find out what she's up to.

Nothing more.

"I thought I needed to convince you," she continues.

"You do."

"No, I don't. You already accepted the case."

"You need to keep convincing me so I don't drop it."

"You can't do that to her."

"Believe me, I can." I won't, but Anastasia doesn't need to know that.

"You're an asshole."

"Glad we agree. Now, are you done?"

"I'm not done." She's glaring, and I can feel the heat of it through her thick glasses. "I don't like liars either."

"Even when you're one yourself?"

"I have my reasons."

"And what makes you think I don't?"

"What are they then?"

I reach a hand out and grab her by the throat. I don't do it suddenly, but she startles, her body going still in my hold, and the anger slowly dissipates from her features. "Continuing to touch you, to make you squirm and have that fuck-me look. Or maybe I just want to play with you, maybe it's to debauch and fuck you up until I get my fill. Maybe it's all of the above. Do you have a problem with that?"

She's silent, her lips parting, and I can't resist the urge to run my thumb over their fullness, feeling her shudder.

"W-what if I do?"

"What if you what? Have a problem with it or don't like me touching you?"

"Both?"

"Then I'll stop."

Her breath stutters and I smile, tightening my hold on her throat. "For *now*. But I'll still come back for more. I'll still find you in every corner and every fucking nook. I will haunt the fuck out of you, Anastasia, until you have no way out but back to me."

I feel her melting as she leans closer, her lips pulsing against my fingers. The heat of them alone makes my cock rock-fucking-hard.

An inexplicable need I've never felt before thunders and roars inside me with a wrecking force.

The need to slam her against the wall and fuck her.

The need to drive so deep inside her, I won't know where she ends and I begin.

The need to have her so full of me that she'll struggle to breathe like that first time.

I don't have such thoughts about the women I fuck. Not even close. They're always a means to an end, a way to release the pressure and get it over with. It's been a chore at times, a fucking instinct like breathing and eating.

It's different with Anastasia.

Because I know, I just know that if I fuck her again, everything will be blown out of proportion. And not only because I rarely fuck the same woman twice or because she's turning into an unhealthy obsession.

It's all of that and more.

It's the way she easily submits to my dominance, how she trembles in my hold, even when she's bent on defying me.

The way her small body feels so close to mine and how her breathing hitches the moment my fingers dig into the sensitive, easily reddening skin of her throat.

"What if I keep running?" Her voice is low, so low that I barely hear it.

"I'll keep chasing you."

"What if I run fast and disappear? What if you can't find me? Will you give up then?"

"I'm not who you're running from, beautiful. I won't slow down and I sure as fuck won't give up. So if you feel like running, do it. Believe me, I will enjoy every second of hunting you down."

She licks her lips and her tongue grazes my thumb. "And then what?"

"Then?"

"When you find me, when you catch me and forbid me from running anymore, what are you going to do?"

"Bend you over the nearest object and fuck that tight cunt of yours until you can no longer hold in those screams. Until I have to grab you by the throat and jam my fingers into this mouth to mute you, but guess what?"

"W-what?"

"You'll probably never shut up, will you? You'll just keep screaming until everyone can hear you. Until everyone knows you're being fucked deep and raw by me."

She's flat out shaking now, a different type of red that's nothing like the anger that was covering her cheeks. And my cock becomes painfully hard, so hard that I can barely contain it without adjusting my trousers.

"Wouldn't everyone think you're harassing me since you're a partner and I'm just a lowly employee?"

"Am I harassing you, my little liar?"

"Maybe you are."

"Maybe you're too scared to admit how much you like it."

"Maybe you're too arrogant and think everyone will fall for your charms."

"I don't just think it, I believe it."

"That's what all arrogant jerks say."

"I think I have enough reasons to be arrogant."

"Like what?"

"My looks, for starters. Even you fell for it that first time in the bar."

"That wasn't a very studied decision. Besides, I would've slept with the first man who appeared. I wasn't being picky."

My jaw clenches so hard, I'm surprised a tendon doesn't snap. "You would've slept with anyone. Interesting."

"Yeah, so it's not about your looks or your accent or the scent of your cologne."

I smile. "Good to know what you liked about me."

"I'm saying that so you have no misconceptions."

"I don't have those, beautiful. Do you know why?"

"Why?"

"Because you would've slept with anyone, but you didn't. You let me fuck you any way I wanted. You didn't even comment on being tied up or thrown down, you took it all like the good little submissive you are."

"I…am not."

"If you repeat that a hundred times before you fall asleep, you might start to believe it."

"Don't flatter yourself." She grabs the forearm of my hand that's on her throat. "You're not the only fish in the sea, Knox."

"What?"

"You're not the only one with a useful dick out there. So if I want more fun or to let go, I'll just go to a bar and pick someone else to spend the night with."

A muscle tics in my jaw again. My body tightens and so does my hold on her throat. She wheezes, her face reddening with the lack of air and I release her because I'm two seconds away from suffocating the fuck out of her.

"You don't want to play that game with me, Anastasia." My voice is eerily calm considering the fire that's eating me from the inside out.

"Why? Because you're the only one allowed to play games?" She tilts her head to the side. "You don't know who you're up against, Knox. You really, *really* should've pretended you didn't know me, but you made it hard for both of us and started a needless game. One that I decided to play."

"Hmm. We're playing, then?"

"We are. And guess what the first rule is?"

"Enlighten me."

"No fucking."

"Today?"

"Ever."

I chuckle, the sound dark and ominous to my own ears. I approach her and she must see the menacing look in my eyes, because her feet falter. But she does manage to stop herself before she steps back, I'll give her that.

I tower over her tiny frame so that I'm looking down on her. She's so small, I want to throw her over my fucking shoulder. "Let's see how long you'll last, because I promise that I'll fuck those words out of you, beautiful."

THIRTEEN

Anastasia

I F THERE'S ANYTHING I CAN COUNT ON FROM GWEN, IT'S THAT she'll try to take me out for lunch every single day.

At first, I fought it and tried to come up with different excuses about how I couldn't be outside, but she's persistent and definitely doesn't take no for an answer. I think that part of her determined personality is due to her father's and Nathaniel's influence. Growing up surrounded by powerful people can have one of two effects on you.

Either you become as powerful as they are, like my cousin, or you retreat into yourself trying to survive each day on its own, like me.

Gwen is in the middle. She's not too out there, but she's definitely not a recluse either.

And because of her, we're having lunch in a huge restaurant downtown with one of her friends from college—an intern who joined the firm at the same time that she did. His name is Chris and he has long hair that reaches his nape and obviously hates suit jackets, because his is lying on the chair beside him. Along with his tie.

The clinking of utensils and a low hum of chatter echo in the air like a distorted symphony with a horrible orchestra. Not only that, but the smell of food and a mixture of perfumes make the atmosphere as suffocating as trying to breathe underwater.

Gwen is laughing at something Chris said while eating a slice of her pepperoni pizza. I, on the other hand? I keep watching the windows, the door, the servers. Even the lady sitting at the corner opposite us who's eating on her own and observing everyone. Is she searching for me? Did they send an old lady now?

"Jane!" Gwen snaps her fingers in front of my face.

"Uh…yeah?"

She observes me with those colorful eyes that seem to be in a world all of their own. "You're not eating or listening. Are you feeling unwell?"

If being on the verge of hyperventilating is unwell, then sure, I think I'm one stage beyond that. Maybe I'm close to having a panic attack. Otherwise, why is Gwen blurring and why the hell is that lady still looking at me?

Maybe it's one of the men in disguise so I won't suspect them. Maybe they'll jump in front of me, like in my scariest nightmares, and tell me the fun is over.

"Jane?" It's Chris who calls my name this time.

"I…I'm fine."

"Are you sure?" He runs a hand in front of my face. "You look pale."

"And you're trembling." Gwen motions at my fingers that are clutching the fork and knife, and yup, they're flat out shaking.

Is this how I'm going to be in public for the rest of my life? A pale, trembling mess who can't get a hold of her life?

No. I already have control of my life. I'm my own person now.

"Yeah," I say in a more assertive voice, slowly trying to erase the woman and the rest of the restaurant from my peripheral vision.

Gwen and Chris's presence helps, because I can use them as crutches.

I feel bad for calling them that, even in my head, but I really wouldn't have anyone to hold on to if they weren't here.

"Did you even hear a word we said?" Gwen asks.

"Of course. Chris was taunting you about Nathaniel."

Gwen's face turns red and she plays with her spoon on her plate. She's really not subtle at all about anything Nathaniel. He's eighteen years older than her and is her father's best friend and partner. Oh, and her boss, whom she always complains about being too stern, but all of that seems null and void to her. Like none of those obstacles exist and her feelings for him make complete sense.

It's been about two weeks since she started her internship and those feelings seem to be getting stronger every day.

And the worst part is, Nathaniel is the most stoic, aloof person I know. He's cold to a fault and seems to be a working machine, so I'm worried that her feelings won't be returned.

I never thought I'd worry about anyone else besides *Babushka* and my cousin, but Gwen is the type who jumps in front of you and gives you no choice but to become friends with her.

And the best part? She didn't choose to be friends with just anyone, even though she could have. This cheerful, albeit a little weird, girl chose me.

Not anyone else. *Me.*

The knowledge of that makes me feel special in a warm, fuzzy way.

"First of all, it's Nate. You're the only one who calls him Nathaniel, Jane. Second of all, Chris is jealous that I'm interning with the managing partner of W&S."

"I have nothing to be jealous about since I'm interning with the rising star of W&S, Knox. The same Knox you wanted to intern with but couldn't."

Gwen slams her cup on the table. "It's not that I couldn't. It's that Nate was being difficult."

"Whatever. I'm with Knox and we're having so much fun with the Bell case while you rot in corporate law."

She pokes him with the spoon. "No need to rub it in."

Chris pokes her back. "I totally will. This will look so good on my law school application."

"And so will all the large corporate cases I'm doing with Nate."

"*Boring* corporate cases."

"They're NOT boring. Don't you dare call anything Nate does boring or I will kill you in your sleep."

"But they are! None of them compare to the fun I'm having with Knox. You should've seen the way he prepares the case, it's so strategic and ruthless."

"Nate is strategic and to the point. There's no one like him, not even my dad."

"Knox is better."

"No, Nate is, and as proof he's the managing partner."

"Just because he's older."

"Hey!"

"I'm just saying. Knox is better."

"No, it's Nate."

"Knox."

"Nate."

They're both crossing their arms and glaring at each other so hard, sparks fly between them.

Both of them have a tendency to start an argument or debate that goes on for several minutes. Usually, I'd sit there, watching while sipping water.

But the subject of choice is making me all hot today. I want to jump in with Chris and take his side, but then what? Defend Knox?

Why the hell would I do that?

It's not like he took Sandra's case out of the goodness of his heart. It's probably his way to reach for the glory, to be a public figure in front of the flashing cameras.

It's been eleven days since I told him he can't fuck me. That I'll find a replacement.

It was a challenge, mostly empty and out of spite because he was being impossibly arrogant. But maybe he took it as real, because he hasn't texted me to meet in the supply room since then.

He doesn't text me, period.

Or talk to me, really.

At first, I ignored him as much as he did me. At the time, I believed it was all part of a game, a push and pull of sorts.

But there's only been a push.

If I don't go up to his floor for a spying session, I go a whole day without seeing him.

At some point, I became angry, I became so angry that I considered doing exactly what I threatened. To go to a bar and fuck someone. A stranger. A random person.

Maybe that would ease all the tension gathered in my chest.

But then again, I wouldn't do something like that out of spite. It's just wrong.

Like everything lately.

Even my "Oldies" playlist doesn't sound the same anymore. The songs are too sad, too colorless.

And they shouldn't be. They're the most colorful thing in my life. The things that give me the power to push through the day, to create more systems, and just survive.

That's what has always been my goal, right? To survive.

"Jane, you choose." Gwen's voice brings me back to the present and that's when I notice that they're both looking at me after their glaring session.

"Yeah, you choose, Jane. Isn't Knox better?"

"Nope, it's totally Nate. Don't you dare choose anyone but Nate."

I take a sip of my water to soothe the dryness in my throat and say the exact opposite of what I'm thinking, "I'll go with Nathaniel. He's more experienced and level-headed."

Gwen slaps both her palms on the table. "Thank you!"

"You have terrible taste in lawyers, Jane." Chris side-eyes me. "Both of you will eat your words when he wins Bell versus Bell."

Gwen flips her hair back. "That's *if* he wins. I heard Mathew Bell is backed by the mafia."

I choke on my water and it snorts through my nose and splatters all over my lap.

"Jesus, Jane. Are you okay?" Chris offers me a napkin, but I'm unable to focus on it, because all I can hear are Gwen's words.

"T-the…the what?" I stare at her with what must look like an expression from a scene in a horror movie.

"The mafia."

"Which mafia, Gwen?" My voice is all choked up like my insides.

"Russian, I think? I don't know for sure. I overheard Nate talking about it with Aspen the other day, not that I'm spying on them or anything. I swear I was just passing by, and fine, maybe I stayed on purpose to hear what they talk about when they're together, but it's not like I had any ill intention or anything. I swear on my sacred vanilla."

Gwen's hyper speech dims to the background and something much more nefarious pops to the surface. I think I'm going to throw up.

Or maybe choke.

Or faint.

And I can't do that in front of Gwen and Chris or they'll find out I'm broken. So I stand up as slowly as possible, because if I do it faster, I'm definitely going to end up on the floor.

"I'll be back," I whisper and turn around, heading to the bathroom.

That lady is watching me again. She has her eyes on me and it's more intense now, more focused.

She knows me.

She knows exactly who I am, despite the glasses and the disguise and everything, and she'll tell them. She'll say she saw me here, that she found me, and they'll come for me—

Stop.

You need to stop.

I suck in deep inhales of oxygen and head to the bathroom. Removing the glasses, I place them in my pocket and splash a copious amount of water on my face.

"You're going to be fine," I whisper at my disheveled reflection in the mirror. "They can't find you."

It takes me a few seconds to be able to control my breathing before I go out, slipping my glasses back on.

I slam into someone and wince.

"Watch where you're going."

I freeze.

Was that an accent I just heard with *that* voice? The same voice I'm familiar with?

Slowly, too slowly, I peek at the person I slammed into. He's tall, broad, and wears glasses. They're not as thick as mine and they make him look smart, camouflaging his true dangerous nature.

Kirill.

A pirate.

One of them, anyway. And he's so powerful and cunning that no one dares to cross his path.

He's judging me now with his light eyes that are covered by the glasses, and for a moment, I think it's over.

For a moment, I think he'll reach out, pluck off my fake glasses, poke out my contact lenses, and drag me back by my hair.

A man steps in front of him. He's scrawnier, shorter, and has feminine looks, but he never fooled me. Behind that appearance hides one of the most lethal human weapons. Aleksander. Another pirate whose purpose is to guard Kirill.

He's the one who told me to watch where I'm going, and he's also the one who's glaring down at me.

I'm under both their scrutiny now and I wish the earth would open up and swallow me.

I wish I'd stayed in the bathroom.

I wish I'd never come here.

Hell, at this moment, I wish I was never born.

"What are you looking at?" Aleksander asks in his not-so-deep yet threatening voice.

I can't stop staring at them, can't stop the shaking, the heart pounding. All of it.

This is a meltdown, isn't it? I'm going to have it in front of them and destroy everything.

"This little insolent piece of shit…" Aleksander reaches out for me and I can see it, his hand, the violence it promises, but I can't move. I'm unable to.

And then he's grabbing me by the collar and lifting me up. My feet leave the ground and my throat closes with his savage grip, blocking my air.

My nails find his arm in a desperate attempt to peel him off me, but that only manages to make him tighten his choke-hold on me, bringing tears to my eyes.

Shit.

Shit.

I stare at Kirill, who's right beside him, watching the scene without moving a muscle. As if he's bored and his guard is providing him his daily dose of entertainment.

Aleksander shakes me so that my attention slides back to him. "You don't look at him, you don't cross his path. You apologize for disturbing him, or I will bury you where no one can find you."

I'm about to call their names, to beg, but I don't. If I do, for what purpose did I come this far? Why am I here?

Something moves in my peripheral vision and then Aleksander is forced to let me go.

I'm on the ground again, a strong hand holding me by the shoulder, and warmth I haven't been able to forget surrounds me.

My eyes sting and my lungs burn with the unhealthy amount of air I've inhaled in such a short time. But none of that matters, because all I can focus on is the man standing beside me.

The man who's turned my life upside down so many times but still holds it in balance.

"I have the entire scene recorded, so prepare to pay a hefty settlement when she sues for assault."

I stare up at him, at Knox, the man who's not even supposed to be here, but he's holding me by the shoulders and speaking on my behalf.

And just like that, the tears I held in for so long gather in my lids.

"Knox?" I whisper.

"Don't worry, beautiful." He winks down at me. "I'll protect you."

FOURTEEN

Knox

'VE HAD PEOPLE LOOK AT ME IN DIFFERENT WAYS.

Some have pitied me, others have had expectations of me, and even those closest to me, such as my family, have had questions in their eyes about me. Sometimes it's worry. Other times, curiosity.

But no one has ever looked at me the way Anastasia is right now. As if she were falling down a bottomless well and I pulled her out.

As if she were choking and I gave her back her air.

She's wheezing, a full-body shudder gripping her. Her shoulders tremble beneath my hand and her lips are twitching. I don't have to see the look in her eyes beneath the glasses to know she's falling into a loop.

That she's out of her element and way out of her comfort zone.

When Christoph mentioned that he'd be having lunch at this restaurant, I guessed that he'd be accompanied by Gwen and

Anastasia—or Jane, as they know her. The three of them have become close over the last couple of weeks, almost inseparable.

So whenever I want information about her, all I have to do is drop ambiguous questions to Christoph and he happily answers them all. Though I'm a bit annoyed that she spends more time with him than me.

Fine, not annoyed. It's way more than that.

The game Anastasia and I started to play was supposed to make me get over her, remove her from my system and allow me to finally move on, but it's only made the fire burn hotter, stronger.

Instead of purging her, I've been engraving her in, searching for every moment I can catch a glimpse of her. Even if she's only passing by.

It's that unhealthy obsession again, the lack of control I've been fighting all my life.

And I did plan to continue fighting it, to reject it and keep this fucked-up fixation under wraps.

But that was before.

Before I stepped into the restaurant and saw her heading to the bathroom, only for her to take a long time to come out.

And that's when I followed her and witnessed a fucking arsehole grabbing her by the throat and suffocating her. I lied about filming the whole thing, because the moment I saw someone hurting her, my first thought was to release her and punch the two fuckers who are currently glaring at me.

One of them is taller and broader and wears a tailored suit and black-framed glasses. He's the silent one who didn't talk or take action during the whole ordeal.

The other one is much smaller, leaner, but still strong, because he effortlessly lifted Anastasia by the collar of her shirt.

He's also the bloody wanker who has me thinking about the best way to murder. No one touches Anastasia and gets away with it.

No one.

"Who are you?" the leaner one asks with a tinge of an accent. Russian? Eastern European?

"Her attorney." I tighten my hold on Anastasia, who's shaking even worse than a few seconds ago. "You just committed physical assault, and not only will I have you arrested for it…"

"This little…" He storms toward me, his face tight with the intention of violence. I swiftly push Anastasia behind me, ready for the impact of his clenched fist.

One more assault to drag this bastard down with.

But before he can reach me, the other man grabs him by the arm and the leaner one immediately comes to a halt. He's breathing heavily, his fists still clenched, and his glare alone is about to cut me open.

The groomed man with glasses shakes his head at the other one. No words are spoken as he stares at me, then at the hint of Anastasia behind me. I don't know why I feel the need to hide her from their watchful gaze.

It's an instinctive feeling that I have no control over, but it turns my whole body rigid. If they want a fight, that's exactly what they'll will get.

But the man adjusts his glasses, turns, and leaves.

"Consider yourself lucky." The leaner man tells me before he follows the other one. His jacket flies behind him and I catch a glimpse of something metallic tucked in his pants.

A gun.

I narrow my eyes on their backs as they disappear down the hall. There's something about them. What, I don't know.

Anastasia must've felt it, too, when she was cornered by them, because even now that they're gone, her fingers are digging into my jacket and she's still behind me, trembling uncontrollably.

I turn around and the scene that greets me makes me pause.

Tears stream down her cheeks, fogging her glasses, and she appears so helpless, so scared and small that I want to find those two men and shoot them with their own guns.

"They're gone," I say in a cool voice, trying to make her feel at ease.

She doesn't say anything, doesn't move. Only moisture cascades silently down her cheeks as she stands there like a statue.

"Anastasia…"

"Don't…don't…please…please don't call me that, please, I'm begging you…I'll do anything…just…just…"

"Hey, relax. It's fine."

She stares up at me then, her tears sliding to her chin and neck with the motion. "It's not…it will not be. Nothing is fine. They're watching me…that lady from the restaurant was watching me and now, they're here and it's never going to be fine."

A few passers-by watch us questioningly and though I'm not sure if she's focused on them, I can tell that she's well and truly on the path of having a breakdown. Otherwise, she wouldn't let people see her in this state.

So I grab her by the arm and drag her behind me. She doesn't protest as I guide her out through the restaurant's back exit and release her against the wall.

We're in a small alleyway that's hidden from sight. It's not so bright and there aren't people watching her every move.

But she's still crying silently, her body stiff.

I reach out for her glasses and remove them. She tries to fight me, to keep them in place, because they're her camouflage from the world. Something she can hide behind and hope no one will see her.

"Give them back," she whispers.

"So you can return to your bubble?"

She glares at me. "What's wrong with bubbles? They're safe and no one hurts you when you're in them."

"They're a delusion that will disappear sooner or later. All you'll be left with is more suffering."

"I'll deal with that when it happens."

"Or you can deal with it now instead of hiding."

"I'm not hiding. I'm fine."

I retrieve my phone, open the camera, then place it in front of her face. "Does that look like someone who's fine?"

Her lips part and tremble and a fresh wave of tears gather in her fake eyes. I hate that she changed the color, that I can barely see a glimpse of the ethereal blue I stared into that first time I met her.

The blue that tells a mystic story without her having to say a word.

She pushes the phone away and stares to the side. When she speaks, her voice is so low, it's almost unintelligible. "Sometimes, hiding is the only option people like me have. So let me be."

I drop her glasses in my pocket and place one hand on the wall by her head, then grab her by the throat with the other one and lean into her. "See, that's the problem. I can't."

Her breath hitches as my chest is glued to hers until we're both feeling the booming of heartbeats and the skyrocketing pulse.

Until we're both trapped in the present moment.

"What are you doing—"

Her words are cut off when I lower my head and lick her tears. I drink the salty taste and her anguish, fear, and anxiety. I take it all, my tongue sucking at her scorching hot cheeks, then her nose and her chin, and I finish with her mouth.

My lips brush against hers and I lick them, nibble on them, reveling in each of her shudders, tremors, and small moans, and then I'm thrusting my tongue into her mouth.

The same tongue that tasted her tears is now making her drink them, too, feed on them from me.

My hold tightens on her throat as I kiss her slow at first, then hard and fast and so out of control that she's gasping in my mouth.

She's wheezing for air, her fingers holding on to my jacket with everything in her might, and when I open my eyes to stare into hers, they're closed.

Her head is tilted back and she's letting me ravish her, my tongue feasting on hers and my teeth biting and nibbling and sending tiny sparks of pain through her.

That's what I do, after all. I'm a master of pain. Pleasure can't happen without it; there needs to be a balance between the good and the bad.

The pretty and the ugly.

And Anastasia doesn't seem to mind it, the bites between the licks, the nibbles between the sucks. If anything, she's getting lost in it as deeply as I am.

The need that explodes in my groin is unmistakable. I'm so hard that it's painful, so painful that my trousers can't contain it. She must feel my erection against her soft belly, because her eyes open wide, even though my tongue is playing with hers, even though she's still shuddering like when I licked away her tears.

And the way she looks at me?

Fuck.

It's like she wants me to repeat it all over again. She wants me to be the only one who makes her tears stop and lick them away.

She wants to cry for me so I'll confiscate those tears and have them for my own.

And that's not something I should wish for or want. It's not even something I should be thinking about.

Yet, deep down, in the dark corners that I spent decades trying to squash, there's a part of me that wants exactly that.

Worse, that part might want something even more nefarious. Something that I'll probably regret once this whole thing is over.

But that time isn't today. So I don't allow myself to think as I pull away from her mouth. Her lips release mine slowly, leaving a trail of saliva between us and sticking to her lower lip.

So I lick it, darting my tongue out to get all of it.

"Knox…" she whispers, her breath hitching as my tongue leaves her lips.

"Shhh." I turn her around so she's facing the wall and keep my hold on her throat. "I'm going to need you to be real quiet for me when I fuck you, beautiful."

FIFTEEN

Anastasia

I THINK THERE'S SOMETHING WRONG WITH ME.

With him.

With us.

Otherwise, why the hell am I so hot and bothered like never before?

And it didn't start just now, no. This overstimulation started when he pinned me against the wall, grabbed me by the throat, and licked away my tears. He darted his tongue out and licked them all away. I should've been repulsed, should've flinched away or attempted to stop him.

But something much worse happened.

I liked it.

Every lash of his tongue was as if he was lapping at my pussy, parting my legs to get more access.

And when he thrust his tongue inside my mouth, I could almost feel his cock driving deep into my channel.

I still feel it now, the uncontrollable need, and I'm not sure if it's his or mine.

Or maybe it's a combination of both.

His larger body pins me against the wall and I can't breathe, not because he's crushing me, but because of everything else.

Like his breath on the side of my face and the sharp tingles it provokes.

Or the scent of his cologne that envelops me whole as he did in front of Kirill and Aleksander.

But most of all, it's his warmth, the sense of safety I've never allowed myself to feel, not even with my father.

Because he didn't say that, my father, he never said he'd protect me. That's why I left, that's why I wore contact lenses and glasses and changed my hair color.

That's why I stole from him.

But Knox said it in front of those two dangerous men. He didn't care that they were dangerous or that they could snap his neck with a motion from Kirill's hand.

That's exactly what would've happened if there weren't people around. Kirill would've given Aleksander a sign and his guard would've stabbed Knox to death, then buried him on some construction site.

But Knox didn't give a fuck about any of that.

He said he'd protect me.

And maybe that's why I'm melting against the wall. I'm breathing so harshly, so gutturally, I think I'm hyperventilating.

However, Knox's hold on my neck keeps me anchored in the moment and to him. And even though I have no clue where he's taking this, a part of me, the rebellious spiky part that decided to steal and leave, doesn't care.

Knox doesn't care either, because his cock is nuzzling against my ass cheeks, hard and thick and hot. So hot that I catch fire.

All the tension I've been feeling since that day he walked out of the supply room returns with a vengeance. The onslaught of emotions wrap around my throat, matching his grip. He has his index finger against my jaw, forbidding me from attempting to move.

But that's not the only thing wrapped around me. His other hand loops around my waist and reaches for the zipper of my pants, undoing it, then pulling the cloth down to beneath my ass.

A gust of air hits my skin and my eyes widen. "Knox…?"

"Shh. I told you to stay quiet."

"Oh my God, you can't be serious?"

"I perfectly am. What did you think "I'll fuck you" means, my little liar?"

That's the thing, I didn't think. Or maybe I thought he was joking, but that's obviously not the case.

"Here?" I murmur, my voice shaking, but it's not out of trepidation.

"Here." It's one word, one single word, but he whispers it in that deep, sensual voice of his and it feels like a thrust into my starving core.

"But…but we're in public."

"So?"

"Anyone can see."

"And?"

"That's not right."

"All the best things aren't, beautiful."

I can't think of a reply, because he's cupping me through my panties and their soaked with so much arousal, it's strange and exciting at the same time.

"Hmm. You're wet at the thought of being fucked in public."

"No…"

"No? Your cunt that's dripping due to the promise alone would argue otherwise. Do you like the thought of someone showing up and watching?"

"I don't…"

"Good. Do you know why?" He pulls down my panties, so that they join my pants, and exposes my pussy; however, I still think he'll back down and end the madness.

But I should've known better.

Knox and madness go hand in hand.

Sometimes, *he* is the madness.

He's that piece of insanity that makes the most sense.

The foolishness in the midst of logic.

That's how it feels now. So right and wrong at the same time.

The only right thing in the wrong.

The sound of his own zipper echoes in the air in the small nook behind the restaurant where anyone could pass by. Where any staff member could step out the door to throw something away or take a smoke break.

And I think he's right. The possibility alone makes me wetter, stickier, messier.

He's the reason why I'm this way. I was always a goody two shoes. A wallflower. Boring and mild.

Hell, I thought I would only like sex with the lights off and on scheduled days.

And no, those fantasies I had about being held down and fucked don't count.

But he proved that they do. Very much so.

Ever since that first time, he's provoked that part of me I reserved for nightmares. He's taught me that I want more than mild and boring. That sex without lights and on Saturdays isn't enough.

That sex isn't enough.

I prefer fucking. Primal, rough, and out of control.

I prefer relinquishing all control and not thinking, even though we're in public.

Even though this isn't how my second time is supposed to be.

His lips meet my ear as he whispers, "I won't let them see. They can wish, they can imagine, but they'll never have you like I do, beautiful. They won't even dream about seeing this pussy, let alone fucking it."

And with that, he thrusts inside me from behind. The motion is so deep and raw that I get on my tiptoes.

Holy shit.

Is it possible to come from penetration alone? Because I think I'm there. The orgasm isn't as hard as the other time, but it's shaking me, it's gripping and dragging and filling me to the brim.

"You like this, don't you, my little liar?" He's still whispering in my ear, one hand on my hip and the other holding me by the throat. "You like the threat of being found out, of being seen while surrendering to the most carnal part of you."

"Oh…" I trail off because he's pounding into me now, hard and fast and unrestrained. I'm bumping against the wall, my legs shaking and my heart about to spill to the ground.

My nails scratch on the wall for balance, but it's impossible with his pace. His mad, harsh, and savage pace that's building a hurricane inside me.

"Say you like it, Anastasia." He slows to low, deep thrusts that make my toes curl.

"Like w-what?"

"The depravity of it all, the promise of the unknown. The fact that someone can walk up now." *Thrust.* "Or now."

He drives in again, deeper this time, and I moan, the vibration bouncing from my throat and against his fingers.

"I do…" I whimper.

"You do, don't you? You like being fucked rough and fast in a place where people can find us…where they can see who you belong to…"

"Oh, God…" I'm coming again and it's stronger this time, more consuming, and without restraint.

I can feel myself strangling his cock, clenching around him, and pulling him deeper with the force of my orgasm.

"So fucking tight, my Anastasia," he grunts near my ear.

As if possible, my release gains more power, stretching and pulling at a place inside me I didn't think existed.

But that doesn't make Knox stop.

If anything, he's pounding into me more ruthlessly, so much that I'm bouncing off the wall. My nipples peak and pucker against my bra and the friction on the solid surface makes them ache so much, it's almost unbearable.

Everything is so sensitive, sore, and so utterly pleased. Like that first time, but multiplied by ten.

"Fuck," I hear him groan at my ear. "Fuck how tight and beautiful and bloody addictive you are. Fuck!"

And then his chest turns rigid at my back, and then he's spilling inside me. Hot spurts of his cum warming my pussy.

Holy shit.

"You…you…" I pant. "You didn't use a condom?"

The question is stupid because I can feel him bare inside me, I can feel the hot spurt of his cum in me.

There's a long pause. One so silent that I fidget and slowly stare back at him, making that eye contact that I hate so much.

Knox is standing there, covering my back, his cock still inside me and his hands on my hip and throat, and he looks so savage.

So raw.

So dark, even.

It's not like that first time, though I don't really remember it since I passed out right afterward.

I would've done the same just now if it weren't for being faced with the reality that he didn't use a condom.

That he just came inside me.

I think I'm at the point of hyperventilating, because my breathing is harsh and uneven and I think I'm going to faint.

"I'm clean," he says in a low voice.

"I am, too, but that's not the problem."

"Then what is?" He pauses, probably noticing how I'm breathing so heavily and reaching the point of collapsing. "You're on birth control, right?"

I gulp. Once, twice.

His hold tightens on my throat. "Bloody hell. You are, right?"

"No." The word is so quiet, so damn inaudible that I'm surprised he even hears it.

"Fuck." He pulls out of my aching pussy and releases me.

I stand there, lamely getting my clothes together and trying to resist the remnants of a panic attack that's trying to grab hold of me.

Knox's movements are jerkier than mine—violent, even—as he zips his pants and runs a hand through his glorious hair. "Why aren't you on birth control? Who the fuck is not on birth control these days?"

"Me." I get in his face and snatch my glasses that he placed in his pocket, then put them on. "And why are you angry at *me*? You're the one who didn't use a condom."

"I don't exactly walk around with them in the street."

"Well, you shouldn't have fucked me in the street then."

He stares down at me, his golden eyes catching a glimpse of the sun and shining just as bright.

"Bloody hell," he mutters under his breath. "Just take the morning-after pill."

"I don't need you to tell me. I was going to do it anyway."

"Fantastic."

"Great."

"Perfect."

"Awesome." I tip my chin at him, then we both stare away at the same time, and I mutter, "Hmph, as if I would ever want something else with you."

He's in my face in a second. "What is that supposed to mean?"

"Nothing."

"Next time, either say what you're thinking or don't say it at all."

"There won't be a next time."

He smiles, and it's beautiful and a little sadistic, and I can't help feeling like I'm caught right in the middle of it.

"Oh, there fucking will be. Especially now that you're joining my team."

SIXTEEN

Knox

"**H**AVE YOU EVER FORGOTTEN TO WRAP IT?"

I realize the mistake in asking the question the moment it leaves my lips. The fucker Dan stares at me funny, tilting his head to the side and nearly dropping the cup of coffee from his hand.

He swallows the contents of his mouth slowly, then places the cup on the table. "Did you just say forget to wrap it? As in, *you* forgot to wrap it?"

I stand, facing the window that overlooks New York City, and think of a million ways to somehow go back a minute in time.

Or maybe a day, because ever since I fucked Anastasia in public, *bare* and against a fucking wall, I haven't been able to stop thinking about it.

About the way she felt, how she moaned and clenched and came undone around me.

She was a masterpiece, one I didn't know I needed until she was there, at that moment, all mine for the taking.

And fuck me if I remembered to put on a condom.

Yes, I lied. I did in fact have a condom on me. Ever since that first time in the supply room, I always walk around with one.

But at that moment when she was completely at my mercy, her wetness soaking my fingers and her body glued to mine, I completely forgot about the bloody condom.

I never fuck without a condom. Fucking *ever*.

All that information was background noise with Anastasia. Completely and utterly unimportant.

"I'm just asking you. It's a hypothetical situation, Dan."

"Don't give me that bollocks. It's you, isn't it?" He stands up and circles me like a curious cat. "You did! Who was it? Just tell me it's not a blonde."

"It is." Originally, at least.

"Blimey, that's a game-changer, but it's fine." He holds an imaginary microphone. "What's her name? Her number? Why didn't you invite me to fuck her?"

"That won't be happening."

"What? Why? Wait a minute. You found your girl from Jersey! She's also blonde and you're all secretive about her."

"She's not…" I trail off, because the thought of her being my girl turns my blood hot. If it were any other time, it would've been freezing cold at the thought of commitment.

I've never liked that, commitment, never seen the point behind it. Which is why I've never had a relationship or brought a girl home, never introduced them to Dad or my sisters.

The possibility of Anastasia meeting them makes me pause. I wonder how they'd feel about her and if—

I internally shake my head, forbidding those thoughts from going any further.

"She's not what?"

"From Jersey."

"Uh-huh. Give me her number and I'll check myself. Something tells me you're lying and she's not a blonde. Which is uncool, mate. I don't mind sharing with you, do I? So you should give me the same privileges."

A red-hot fire grabs hold of me at the image of Daniel calling her or getting close to her.

If he touches her…I'll fucking throw him out the window.

I'm not the type who has violent thoughts, *usually*, but because of her, I'm having constant pulses of strange emotions.

"You won't be getting it, Dan," I say with a calm I don't feel.

"Why?" he asks with a wide smile that's openly provocative. "Because you didn't wrap it up and she's probably pregnant with your child?"

"Jesus."

"He'll be visiting, too, when your baby mama gives birth."

I flip him the finger. "Sod off, Dan."

"Nope, this is getting fun." He retrieves his phone and holds it in front of him.

At first, I think he's taking a selfie since he loves flaunting himself all over social media, but then a ringing sound follows and a very familiar voice answers, "I don't know about you, but I'm working."

"Shut up, Ron. This is serious." Dan grins. "I've got the scoop for you, right from the center of New York."

My brother-in-law, and one of Dan's closest friends, pauses. "Oh? Do tell, Danny boy."

"Guess who forgot to wrap it?" Daniel's smile widens and I wish I could punch him from this distance.

So I settle with a whispered, "Don't you dare."

"Let's give it up for our one and only, the man, the legend. Knox Van Doren!" Daniel turns the phone so Ronan is facing me.

He's in his office since he's now leading his father's company. My brother-in-law stares at the camera blankly. At first, anyway, before a slow grin stretches his lips.

"I need to tell Teal the news. She's always thinking that you'd never settle down."

"Don't, Ron." I breathe harshly. "And please hold while I kill a pest called Daniel."

My friend jumps away from me. "Yes, do tell Teal, Ron. We should be planning global baby showers."

"It's that serious?" Ronan asks.

"Serious? Try monumental. He refuses to give me her number and I'm pretty sure he lied about her being blonde. I don't know about you, but in my dictionary, that's pronounced dead serious."

"So Aiden was right and he's shagging someone behind your back?"

"I know. I'm wounded, gutted, disappointed, but not as much as I'm ecstatic about the turn of events for our chap here."

"Teal will be thrilled."

"Don't tell her, Ron." I snatch the phone from Daniel. "You'll give her empty hope."

"It can't be empty when there was no condom, Van Doren."

"Damn straight." Dan jams his face in. "Prepare for a weekend of celebration in London."

"You got it, Danny boy. Leave all the parties to me and just take care of Van Doren's baby mama."

"Roger that."

"Fuck you both." I try to kick Daniel, but he darts away at the last second like a damn lizard.

As soon as he disconnects the call with Ronan, I grab him in a choke-hold. "Do you have a fucking death wish?"

"Don't kill me yet, Knox. I still have to tell the rest of the guys about this hidden gem."

The guys—as in, our friends from secondary school that we're still close with. We played football together and the five of them, Ronan included, are married and have kids.

"Like fuck you will. Say a word about it and I'll send a blonde hooker to your door every day."

"Oh, you shouldn't have done that. Now that you've provoked me, I'm sure as hell telling everyone. Can't wait for what they'll say when they learn you're expecting a baby."

"I'm not."

He tries to push me away and I use the chance to mess his hair the fuck up. The same hair that he spends half an hour to put every strand in order.

A knock on the door interrupts us and I release him with a shove. Thank fuck I kept the blinds down. Two lawyers fighting is probably frowned upon by the general public.

"Come in," I say, and whisper to Dan, "Expect blonde hookers starting tonight."

"Fuck you." He flips me both his middle fingers, then heads to the door.

He leaves and Sandra Bell flinches back, giving him room. "Am I early?"

"No, you're right on time." I smooth my voice to a professional tone. "Come in, please."

She does so hesitantly and I hit the intercom for my assistant. "I need Lauren and Chris here. Oh, and Jane from IT."

"Right away, sir."

I sit across from Sandra, and she tugs her skirt and then the sleeves of her jacket down. "Are you uncomfortable being with me alone?"

Her head jerks up. "It's not—"

"Don't lie."

"A…little."

"Good. You'll be ten times more uncomfortable when you're faced with him in front of people who don't believe your story. Get used to this feeling."

She gulps, her fingers linking and unlinking at a steady pace. But instead of sparing her the discomfort, I lean back in my chair and stare at her, mostly unblinking.

She instantly shifts focus to her lap.

Hmm. I called her therapist and asked her whether or not Sandra could mentally and emotionally handle the courtroom, and the doctor assured me she could.

Doesn't seem like it.

If anything, Sandra appears more and more perturbed. Is the therapist even doing her job?

There's a knock on the door followed by the shuffling of feet. My associate lawyer, Lauren, comes in first. She's about my age but passed the bar a few years after me.

She usually works with Aspen, but she lent her to me since she has a knack for dealing with sexual assault cases.

Chris and Anastasia come in next. The latter remains near the door as if she's looking for an escape route. Ever since I told her that Sandra wants her on the team because she feels comfortable in her presence, she's had that weird expression on her face.

As if she's about to faint.

Or maybe that's because of what happened yesterday and the no-condom event in public.

Fuck.

Focus. This is work.

"You already met Lauren and Christoph," I tell Sandra. "As you requested, Jane will also be sitting in. This is the only friendly face you'll be allowed."

Sandra smiles at her a little and Anastasia smiles back.

I stand and that gets everyone's attention. "Have you read the questions I'll be asking you?"

Sandra nods.

"No nodding in court. If it's a yes or no question, that's what you'll say."

"Yes, I read them."

"Are you confident in how you'll reply?"

"I think so."

"Again, a yes or no question, Ms. Bell."

"Yes…I can do it."

"How about the prosecutor's possible questions?"

"I learned them."

"Good. Now, we'll move on to the possible questions the opposing counsel could ask you."

Lauren gives her documentation. "These are the points we

believe they'll focus on. Reginald Pearce is known to play offense at the first chance he gets so you need to be extra ready."

"We'll help you out." Chris smiles at her and she stares at her lap again.

"From this point on, I'm Reginald." I stand in front of her, pacing slowly like he does in court. "Ms. Bell, you said that your father has been touching you against your volition. Is that correct?"

She swallows. "Yes."

"Since when?"

"Since I was young."

"How young exactly? Nine? Eight?"

"I...I don't remember."

"You claimed it was since around eight, right?"

"Objection." Lauren stands. "Counsel is leading the witness."

"That would be overruled, Lauren. Counsel has the right to lead the witness in a cross-examination," I say, still pacing without breaking eye contact with Sandra. "Now tell me, do you remember when the first time he touched you was?"

"Not really, I..."

"So, you don't remember. You're only placing these allegations on faulty memories that even you don't have a recollection of in order to slander a man of your father's standing..."

"Objection..."

"The truth is, you've been in a consensual relationship with him all this time. There are pictures of you wearing provocative clothes that you sent him from your phone."

"That's not true!" Sandra's bawling. "I didn't...he made me wear those and took the pictures...I didn't..."

"Ms. Bell, there's hard evidence that points to it being consensual, whereas the evidence of the claimed sexual assault is nonexistent."

"Objection. Counsel is stating his own conclusions..."

"He did it...he..." Sandra stands abruptly, her whole body shaking. "He did it!"

"You can't say that when there's no evidence. Isn't it true

that you're just doing this to slander my client's reputation? That you came up with these allegations so that you could take his hard-earned money? Are you—"

"Stop." The low voice catches me off guard.

It's Anastasia. She's grabbing Sandra by the arm, tears shining in her eyes. "Stop it, please."

"If she can't take this, she won't be able to be a witness in court."

"I just need a moment." Sandra sniffles before she bolts out of the office.

Anastasia stares at me funny, like she wants to punch me. "You don't have to be a monster to drive a point home."

I step closer until I'm toe to toe with her. "Didn't you say you needed a dark warrior of justice? This is what we look like."

Her lips purse before she releases them. "I'm going to see how she's doing."

And then she's out the door, too, her orange blossom scent lingering behind her.

Or maybe I'm the only one who smells it.

I grab a file the prosecutor sent us and fall back into my seat.

Lauren rolls her chair so that she's facing me. "Ms. Bell needs a lot of prepping and we don't have much time before the trial."

We don't.

Sandra reported the charges against her father a few months back after she ran away from home and lived off the trust fund her mother left her. Since they're paid off by Matt and his defense, the police and the DA office attempted to sweep everything under the rug, but Sandra was smart and sent the report to the media. Considering her father's public status, the press latched onto the case like hungry sharks after smelling blood. As a result, the prosecutor was obliged to file the criminal case against Matt Bell, but he's been carefully backpedaling and hoping this whole thing will be old news so he can drop the charges.

But the press wouldn't leave this alone. There are support

groups and women organizations involved now and they all have their eyes on how the prosecutor will handle this case.

Sandra had a restraining order against Matt, but she got her recent bruises when she went back home to get something and he suddenly showed up and beat her again for daring to go against him.

Which is why she decided to sue him civilly as well.

Point is, the prosecutor could take the criminal case to trial any time now. Especially since Matt's defense attorney used every trick under the sun and underhanded methods to push the civil case forward. I assume they're counting on Sandra to freak out and handle the civil case poorly, which will give the prosecutor all the reasons to dismiss the criminal case.

I don't trust the prosecutor. I don't trust the whole fucking system, which means in order for Sandra to get her justice in both cases, I need to twist his arm with evidence I will present in the civil trial.

"Let's brainstorm, Lauren. We have to get more media attention and for that, we need to play harder on their emotions."

Even though I'm sure Anastasia won't like it. But this is what she asked for and this is what I'm going to give her.

And the world.

SEVENTEEN

Anastasia

I STEP OUT OF KNOX'S OFFICE, BUT I COULDN'T FOLLOW SANDRA even if I wanted to. My legs shake so badly that they're hardly holding me up.

So I lean against the wall in the corner to catch my breath. I really don't think I'm fit for comforting people.

I've never been good at it.

Being raised to remain in the background put shackles on me—like never standing out. Never offering a hand or a shoulder to cry on.

My cousin, Rai, is the only woman who's been by my side since Mom died, and while she loves me, she didn't need any comforting from me. She's strong, stronger than some men, and I've never seen her weak.

She also treated me with kid gloves as if one wrong touch would break me.

A twinge spreads in my chest when I think of her reaction to my disappearance. She must be so disappointed in me, so angry.

But I can't afford to think about the family I left. Not now.

My fingers tremble as I retrieve my phone and scroll to one of the few pictures I have with Mom and *Babushka*. I was so young at the time, probably four, and I'm sitting on Mom's lap, giggling uncontrollably.

I'm a carbon copy of her, whether it's the white-blonde hair, the deep blue eyes, or the tiny features. But she always looked broken, tired, almost as if she was exhausted of existing.

Mom wasn't the type to smile, but she has a small smile in the picture as she stares at me. *Babushka* is grinning, too, her entire attention also on me.

These two women loved me unconditionally and if fate had worked in different patterns, I would've been able to recreate this image.

The more I continue staring at the picture, the more it anchors me, giving me a sense of safety.

"I'll always be with you, even when I'm far away, Ana." That's what my mother used to say and as a child, I could feel her close, near me.

Now, too.

And I have to do the right thing. I have to be there for Sandra, even while knowing who stands with her father.

Even while knowing that I could be compromised.

But I can't just abandon someone who's asking for help. How is that any different from abandoning my own mom?

After hiding the phone, I walk to the bathroom, where I expect Sandra to be. However, I find her near the window, grabbing her chest and leaning forward.

I hurry toward her, then stop a safe distance away so I don't startle her. "Are you okay?"

She slowly lifts her head, the tears still streaming down her cheeks. "Uh...yeah...I think so."

"I know he was harsh, but he's really good at what he does, so trust the process, okay?"

"Maybe he's right. If I...can't handle this with people who are on my side, how am I going to do in court? In front of *him*? I'm going to make a fool out of myself, aren't I?"

"No, don't say that." I approach her slowly. "You are a brave girl, Sandra. Not many are as brave as you and that deserves to be worn as a badge of honor."

A small smile peeks through the tears. "Thank you for saying that."

"It's not just words. I believe them."

"Why?"

"Because...my mother was abused when I was younger and I didn't have the power to protect her. There hasn't been a day in my life where I didn't blame myself for being useless, but there's one thing I don't regret."

Her lips part. "What?"

"Asking for help when I could, even if it was from someone who's cold."

"Cold like Knox?"

"Worse. But you know, people like them bring in results. They're well aware of how jerks think and can counter them efficiently, so you're in good hands."

"Really? Should I trust him?"

I don't miss the hesitation in her voice, the way she hugs herself and touches her elbows. So I don't think twice when I say, "You should."

"Do *you* trust him?"

"With anything legal? I do."

She sniffles, so I reach into my pocket, then give her a tissue. Sandra wipes her tears and peeks at me through her long lashes. "You'll be there during the whole trial, right?"

I gulp. Being in court means the possibility of running into someone from my previous life, and that sure as hell isn't going to happen. "I'm from the IT department so I really shouldn't be around."

"Please." She clutches my hands. "You're the only friendly face I know. I already asked Knox and he agreed to have you on the team."

"I'll do whatever I can. So even if I'm not there in person, I'll call you prior to the trial. You can also call me whenever you like."

"Thank you." Her eyes shine with fresh tears.

"We…should probably go back."

Her smile falls, but she tightens her hold on my hand while we walk back to Knox's office.

We find Lauren, Chris, and him deep in conversation about the case. They're throwing around legal terms that I don't recognize and at such a fast pace that I can't keep up.

When they finally notice us, they halt their conversation.

Lauren smiles and Chris releases a long breath, but Knox doesn't act the least bit relieved. If anything, he appears calm, way too calm, as if the episode didn't happen in the first place.

His eyes meet mine for a brief second. They're sharp and dark, as if I'm staring into the haunted soul of a completely different person.

The moment barely lasts before he slides his attention to Sandra. "We'll resume where we left off. If you run away again, you can find yourself another attorney."

I glare at him when she goes stiff, but he ignores me the whole time he continues to prep Sandra. His questions are still harsh, but he does pause when he sees her having a hard time.

I don't think anyone notices, but it's like he's also taking a break. At first, I think I'm making things up and he's only doing it for Sandra's sake, but then I focus on him—like, really focus.

He's flipping through a document, and although his movements are calm and measured, they're longer than usual—as if he's enduring something.

As if he's in the midst of a crisis and he needs to remain calm for it.

His shoulders crowd with tension and his eyes are still dark, less gold, less bright. Almost as if the color has been sucked out of them.

There's something else, too. His breathing, it's short and clipped, and his chest rises and falls in a slightly irregular rhythm.

But when he speaks next, his voice is still in that calm range, as if it's disconnected from the rest of him.

By the time he announces we're done for the day, everyone appears drained.

Not him.

He looks furious. Almost like he has otherworldly energy accumulating inside him and he can't get rid of it.

Or *won't*.

I want to stay behind and…do what exactly? It's not like I can ask him what's wrong and actually get an answer.

But I can try…right?

For some reason, it feels like he shouldn't be alone right now; if he is, some sort of a disaster will follow.

I'm probably reading too much into it. In what world is Knox not okay? He always appears to be put-together and so perfect, I'm kind of envious.

And okay, maybe I've often wondered what I'd see if I reached into his armor and took a peek.

Maybe he's not so perfect on the inside, maybe there's a haunted, troubled part I could see for myself.

"Jane?" Sandra's voice pulls me away from my hyperfocus on him.

"Yeah?"

"Can you walk me out?"

"Sure." I steal one last glance at Knox, but he's concentrating on some paperwork, so I leave without even a glimpse of his golden gaze.

Isn't it weird that I have an unhealthy phobia of eye contact, but I crave it with him?

That should be strange.

Abnormal.

And yet, it's all I keep thinking about for the rest of the day.

His eyes, his perturbed state.

Him.

I contemplate texting him, so I type.

Are you okay?

Then I delete the text before I send it. We're not really on good terms, especially after yesterday's public unprotected sex incident.

But even after I get home, I'm not looking forward to my lonely night where I'll eat leftovers and spend the rest of my evening searching the internet for what the men in my old life are up to. I'll be focusing over every detail and be a paranoia freak.

I sit in my dimly lit studio apartment. It's shabby and old, but it's not in a bad neighborhood, so I don't have to worry about unwanted attention.

My typing slows and I stare blankly at the hundreds of pages open on my laptop.

Is this how I'm going to be for the rest of my life? On the run, obsessed, and always scared?

The thought of *Babushka* being hurt forces my hands to carry on the spying mission. If any of them find out what I'm doing—

I shake my head, refusing to think about the consequences. It's not that I'm doing something wrong; I'm only trying to protect myself and my grandma.

The doorbell rings and I freeze, then immediately close my laptop.

Holy shit.

They found me.

"Deep breaths," I whisper to myself in a shaky tone. "They can't find me. I used a firewall, I blocked my IP address. There's no way in hell they can find me."

Unless Kirill and Aleksander suspected something and followed me?

No, no. They would've been here yesterday if that were the case. Hell, they would've grabbed me by the hair in the restaurant and dragged me back instead of letting me go.

But what if Kirill told Adrian?

Shit. He's the mastermind of hacking. He could've broken through my firewall and intercepted my IP and found me. He's here now and will—

"Anastasia, open up, I know you're in there."

My breakdown pauses at that voice. The beautifully accented voice that I would recognize not only from behind closed doors but even if it were coming from underwater.

A weight slowly lifts off my chest and vanishes into thin air as I head to the entrance.

I stare through the peephole to make sure it's him.

Sure enough, Knox stands there, impatiently waiting for me to open the door, judging by that hard look in his eyes.

And it dawns on me then.

Knox is here. In front of my shabby apartment, and he wants me to let him in.

I have to take a moment to breathe.

To not let all the gloomy feelings from earlier manifest in front of him.

When I feel marginally better, I open the door.

No amount of moments or deep breaths could've prepared me for how sinfully attractive he looks.

For the way his hair is styled and how his clothes are impeccably in place, even after a whole day at work.

It's unfair.

So, so unfair that he's physical perfection no one else can match.

It's also unfair that he was my first, and now, I can't see any other man but him. The bar is just too high for anyone else to reach, not that I would allow them.

He ruined me.

Corrupted me.

And I keep wanting more.

"How did you find out where I live?" I whisper.

"Your résumé."

"Why are you here—"

My words end with a moan because he's grabbing me by the throat and slamming his lips against mine.

EIGHTEEN

Knox

THERE ARE TIMES WHEN I CAN CONTROL THE SHADOWS AND times when they control me.

This is the second instance.

I haven't been able to get rid of them since this morning. They've been looming and spreading over me until their gray clouds are the only thing I breathe, see, or touch.

That's how I found myself at Anastasia's flat.

I resisted not seeing her, especially when I'm in this state. I don't let anyone see me with my shadows, not even my twin sister.

But I desperately needed the distraction. I needed to feel the heat of her body and hear the tiny gasps she makes when I take her by surprise.

Like now.

She lets out small noises in my mouth as her fingers latch to my side. I kick the door to her flat shut and back her up with my hold on her neck. Her pulse throbs beneath my fingers as if she's caught by the same adrenaline wave that's holding me hostage, and I grab her throat tighter until I'm her only anchor.

And she's mine.

Because even now, I'm still surrounded by those shadows, and they're vicious and harsh, needing a pound of flesh.

Hers.

She makes them feel bare, and they don't like that. They don't like being exposed or weakened or even seen.

And she did see them. Today. Back in the office. When no one even thought twice about my state of being, she was staring at me funny, as if she could make eye contact with them.

Sense them.

Drag them the fuck out.

So this is vengeance. This is their way to taint her, tarnish her, and ruin her so badly that she'll no longer dare to make eye contact.

That she'll run the other fucking way when she notices them.

My tongue thrusts to the roof of her mouth and I kiss her with a savageness that hardens my dick and twists my fucking spine.

But I don't stop.

Not when she gasps.

Not when she trembles.

And definitely not when her feet fail her with my relentless movements.

I hold her upright by the throat, squeezing until she opens her mouth wider, probably to breathe. But I claim that mouth, I suck on her tongue, then nibble down so hard, I'm surprised I don't taste blood.

Her moans and whimpers are music to my ears, an aphrodisiac to my fucked-up shadows.

And they want more.

So much bloody more.

When she loses her footing again, I let her fall to the wooden flooring, but I hold her tighter to lessen the impact.

Her eyes widen when her back meets the ground and I release her lips with one last bite.

As much as I'd like to keep feasting on her, she needs air. But even as I allow her that, I don't let go of her throat. She's the only armor I have against the shadows and there's no way in fuck I'm releasing her.

Yes, that's selfish. Yes, they should probably find me a deeper pit in hell than the one previously designated for me, but that's all on her.

She shouldn't have stopped and stared this morning, shouldn't have put her nose where it doesn't belong.

Shouldn't have seen the side of me I keep under wraps.

But she did and now, she needs to pay for it.

Anastasia swallows thickly and darts her tongue out to lick her lips that I've turned swollen and red. "What…what are you doing?"

"I'm going to fuck you like it's your first and last time, my little liar." Still tightening my hold on her throat, I kneel between her legs and unbuckle my trousers. "You'll take it, won't you?"

For a second, she just stares, her mouth agape. Her legs are still splayed in an awkward angle from the fall. Her baggy hoodie rides up her pale thighs, revealing her white lace panties.

White and lace.

Fuck me. The way she dresses beneath the hoodie is nothing like what her new persona is supposed to be. She looks like that icy-haired, blue-eyed stranger from the bar right now. The same stranger who should've been a one-time fuck yet turned into so much more.

But she's not. She has the glasses on, and she's still wearing the brown contacts that hide her true eyes from me.

I begrudgingly release her throat and yank the hoodie over her head. Her tits gently bounce, the rosy peaks taunting me, so I grab both of them and pull her up using them.

She gasps, then moans when my lips find hers again while

I continue pinching her nipples, twisting them as hard as I suck on her tongue.

She's trembling, I realize, with anticipation or something else, I don't know, and at the moment, I don't have the state of mind to focus on it.

All I give a fuck about is the feel of her shaking in my arms, her tongue tentatively taking licks of mine, even when she can't keep up with my pace and her whimpers grow in volume.

"Ugh…" She tries to pull back, her glasses fogging up. "Knox…d-do something."

"Something?"

"Anything…" Her voice is breathy, low, and so aroused that I feel it through her chest where I'm pinching her taut, throbbing nipples.

"It's not going to be anything, it's going to be filthy and raw. I'll take your cunt on the floor, and I'm going to fuck it rough, fuck it right, until all you can do is scream."

"O-okay…" Her voice is barely a whisper, or maybe it's a whimper, but it's all the confirmation I need.

Releasing one of her nipples, I pluck off the glasses and throw them away. Her eyes, her fake brown eyes are drooped and barely open. But she's looking at me. Like in the office earlier, she's only looking at me. As if I'm the only one who exists in the world.

As if I'm the only one she can look at.

Part of me wants to reach out and bring out her actual eyes, the real ones that I have memorized deep in my soul. But the most logical part wins, the part that shouldn't care which eyes are genuine. I don't like them in the first place.

Eyes.

They're the part of the face that hold the most contempt. They're what T and I tried to escape and still couldn't, not even after we ran away.

So I grab Anastasia by the hip and flip her onto her stomach. She gasps, the sound echoing in the small flat as her head lifts, probably to look at me, but I grab her by the nape and pin her to the ground. "Stay like that."

Her harsh breathing is audible and I feel her stiffening beneath me, but soon after, she relaxes, her cheek resting on the floor.

As if my callous, violent treatment is normal and she accepts it.

As if…she trusts me.

Bloody hell.

Why the fuck would she trust me when I promised to hurt her? I sensed that she was a masochist that first night, but is this even still under that category?

Despite myself, though, a small nook inside me rejoices at that fact, at how she trusts me enough to let go when she's not the type to.

When she's clearly hiding so much shit and being a little liar.

My fingers latch onto her underwear, pulling them down, and she opens her legs, letting me settle between them as if I always belonged here. Between her fucking legs.

I throw the underwear away and my hand finds her soaking folds. "Hmm. So fucking wet. Did the promise of rough sex turn you on, beautiful?"

She doesn't say anything, but I get my answer when her juices coat my fingers and drip between her thighs.

"Tell me you got on some sort of birth control today."

"I'm on the shot."

"Thank fuck."

"You're not…going to use a condom?" She tries to twist her head back, but I hold it forward.

"Now that I've felt your cunt bare, I'm not going back to using a barrier."

I grab her wrists and lock them at the small of her back, then use them and my hold on her nape as leverage as I thrust into her tight heat in one ruthless go.

Fuck.

I came here with the promise of violence, revenge even, but

the moment her walls clench around me, it's like I've reached a different level of existence.

One where only the two of us exist.

She moans, the sound shattered when I pull out to the crown, then drive in harder this time, as violently as my shadows.

My fingers tighten on her neck and I thrust in and out of her cunt with a speed even I didn't know I was capable of. The sloppy sounds of her arousal keep me going on and on as the slaps of flesh against flesh reverberate around us.

I fuck her like a madman with no cure, like this is the last fuck of my life, like she's my prize and I have to have her one final time.

Sex never felt this raw to me, this…fucking primal. Yes, I've always loved it rough, but never to the point where I didn't want to stop.

Where I wanted to be inside a woman forever.

The thought gives me pause, but only for a second before I'm pounding in her again.

Faster, wilder, until she's sliding on the floor and my hold is the only thing keeping her in place.

"You're so fucking tight, my little liar. This hole is made for me, isn't it?"

She releases an unintelligible sound, so I repeat, "This hole is mine, isn't it?"

"N-no…"

The pads of my fingers dig into her nape. "Did you just say no?"

"You…don't…own me…"

"Is that fucking right?" I up my pace, ramming into her the fastest I ever have until her whimpers and moans break. Until her small body is completely at my mercy—or lack thereof.

"Here's the thing, my little liar. I do own you, I own this hole and every other hole you have to offer. The longer you deny it, the harder I'll fuck it in you."

"Oh, fuck…" she curses, her walls tightening around me. "Knox…Knox…oh, shit…I…can't take it…"

"Then admit it. Admit that your cunt is mine to own and fuck."

"Oooh…"

"That's not the word."

"Just…just let me come…"

"Not until you say that your cunt is mine."

"It's…it's yours…" Her voice is barely above a murmur, but I hear it.

I hear it so loud and clear that the inexplicable possessiveness veering on madness takes hold of me.

"Good girl." I rotate my hips until I hit deeper, and that makes her moans louder and sharper. "Do you like that?"

"Yes…yes…there…please…"

I roll my hips again, driving deeper instead of harder, then repeat it a few more times until I feel her shattering around me. "Here?"

"Yes!!" she screams, spluttering and murmuring my name like a chant as she comes undone.

I feel her clamping around me, swallowing me inside and milking my dick as if she can't come alone and is inviting me along for the ride.

My pace turns frantic, fueled by her pleasure. It's something only she is capable of, making me so attuned to her orgasms and the tremors in her body that I can't help the need to follow her.

To be with her.

To fucking own her.

At that thought, the one about owning her, my cum spurts inside her with a wrecking force I've never felt before.

As if with a vengeance.

As if I want her every pore to be stuffed with my seed.

I slowly pull out of her, my gaze following the trickling of my cum out of her pussy, smearing her thighs and pooling on the floor.

The shadows slowly dissipate to the background when a raging sense of possessiveness bulldozes to the forefront, tearing through my flesh and smashing straight into my bones.

I've always hidden my tendencies of obsession—the need to be number one, to be Dad's favorite, and even to be T's only support. And I've been trying to get rid of those bad habits since after secondary school.

This is the first time I've felt a blinding possessiveness for someone I fucked. It's close to being a dark obsession.

A dangerous one, where my shadows will come out and play.

And yet, I can't stop staring at the evidence of my ownership dripping out of her.

I can't let her go, even though we're both panting and perspiration covers our skin.

It's a primal thing that I have no control over. A raw feeling that holds me hostage and refuses to let go.

A soft whimper rips from her and the sound shakes me out of my trance. I slowly release her, then stagger to my feet, tucking in my semi-hard dick.

Yes, I just emptied inside her, but the view of my cum pouring out of her cunt is taunting my dick for another round.

But it's not about that.

I didn't come here for multiple rounds or even to fuck at all. I'm here so Anastasia will stop looking at me, so she'll stop being attuned to me when she has no business to.

She turns around and slowly gets into a kneeling position, then stares up at me. My cock twitches at the view of her completely naked. There are a few red marks on her pale skin from when I gripped her—around her neck, on her wrists, and on the creamy flesh of her breasts. Her nipples have become red and puffy from my assault. Her lips, too. They're swollen, plump, and tempting me to shove my dick between them.

But what really gets me is the look in her eyes, the satisfaction in them, the fucking pleasure that she's not ashamed to show.

Because we're compatible, she and I. Other women wouldn't appreciate the roughness and dirty sex, but my Anastasia gets off on it.

Wait. *My?*

Since fucking when did I start thinking of her that way in my mind?

I need to go home and erase these cancerous thoughts from my head.

This is fucking.

Only fucking.

I haven't taken even one step when she asks, "Do you want to grab something to eat?"

I should turn and leave. Should ignore that fuck-me look in her eyes or the hope in them. If it were any other situation, I would personally crush that hope.

But I don't.

I go against my principles one more time and stay.

And the shadows have no say in it this time.

NINETEEN

Anastasia

I THINK I DID SOMETHING WRONG.

Because the tension that's been floating in the air for the past half hour is suffocating.

Even more than when he fucked me on the floor, face down, and made me come the strongest I ever have.

Without a condom.

Again.

But for some reason, that doesn't make me mad. Deep down, I liked the sensation of his hot cum inside me and the friction of his skin against mine.

In fact, I liked it so much, I might be a little bit obsessed with it. And his rough dominance.

And devious fucking.

And everything about him, really.

But that's wrong. I shouldn't be so tangled up with him that I can't escape his trap.

Even now, I can't stop staring at him, at his broad shoulders that are stretching his shirt. But that's not the only thing straining against his shirt; there's also his bulging biceps, his pectoral muscles, and even his abdomen.

A wave of heat slaughters the fairies in my stomach and I clench my thighs together to trap whatever sensation is trying to escape.

I pulled on my hoodie earlier, but I couldn't locate my panties, so I'm bare and that feels so revealing. Vulnerable, even.

My breathing is harsh and I'm glad I put on my "Oldies" playlist when we sat down so he can't hear the loud inhales and exhales or how much I'm crossing and uncrossing my legs.

Besides, even on a low volume, my playlist gives me peace and a sense of courage. It's even stronger than liquor in that department.

We're sitting across from each other at the coffee table, eating the pizza I ordered. Or, I'm nibbling; he's studying my small place with a critical eye. From his point of view, this must look so subpar. There are smoke lines on the cracked ceiling that is decorated by some star drawings the previous tenant left behind.

My furniture is sparse to none. Since this is a studio apartment, I only have a sofa that can be turned into a bed and a table—the one we're sitting around. On the floor.

But he's not looking at those, his attention is on the clothes scattered everywhere and the dishes piled up in the sink.

"I was going to clean them," I blurt.

He focuses back on me with a small smirk. "Did I say anything?"

"I can tell you were going to."

"You can tell how?"

"Well, people like you don't appreciate the chaos."

"People like me?"

"Prim and proper."

"Liking things organized doesn't have anything to do with being prim and proper."

"Yes, it does."

"No. You're living proof of that."

"How is that?"

"You're prim and proper yourself, but you're not organized."

"I'm...not prim and proper."

"Wearing lace panties, drinking water with a straw, and always keeping your nails clean and trimmed says otherwise. Besides, your manner of speech is calm and measured, as if you were taught by private tutors to speak a certain way."

My mouth falls open and the slice of pizza remains suspended mid-air. How and when the hell did he even notice those things?

Hell, even I don't pay attention to half of them.

I should've known he'd be a danger to me. I should've pushed him away harder when I could've.

But that's not possible now, is it?

Not when I've become inexplicably addicted to him, to his ethereal face and that delicious accent in his deep voice.

Not when seeing him brings a sense of peace I've never experienced before.

He leans back on his hand, the gleam in his eyes so similar to a predator who's enjoying toying with his prey. "Tell me, what made you prim and proper, Anastasia?"

"I don't know what you're talking about." I take a bite of my pizza.

"Let me guess. It has something to do with your real identity, which is why you changed it. Was it suffocating where you came from? Is that why you left?"

My ears heat, but instead of playing into his hands, I strike back. "How about you?"

"What about me?"

"How did you become prim and proper?"

"Again, I'm not prim and proper, but I did have a cool foster father who saved me and my twin sister from the slums. It's because of him that I changed from an ugly duckling to a beautiful swan." He winks, but there's no playfulness behind it. If anything, it seems like a camouflage for something dark and sinister trying to peek through.

"How about your parents?" Usually, I wouldn't ask. I don't really get curious about people in general, because I'd rather not get involved, but I am curious about him.

About the reason behind the darkening in his golden eyes.

He takes a bite of the pizza, chews slowly, as if he has all the time in the world. "Never knew my father, and my mother was a whore, who was as clueless as us about the identity of the man who impregnated her. When she got mad at us when we were six, she said we were the product of a gang bang from which she received her stash of drugs for the month, and the only reason she kept us was because many of her clients had pregnancy and lactation kinks."

I gulp the mouthful of food, but that has less to do with the information and more to do with his tone when he talked about his mother.

In all my life among monsters, I've never heard someone speak with so much venom and pure hatred about their parent. It's as if he wishes she were on the edge of a cliff so that he could push her off and watch as she meets her demise.

Knox leans back on his palm again and tilts his head to the side. "Now that the boring information is out of the way, why don't you tell me about *your* parents?"

"What about them?"

"You mentioned your mum was abused and since you spoke about her in the past tense, I assume she's no longer alive?"

The food gets stuck in my throat and it takes me a few swallows before I can push past the clog that's built up there. "She's not."

"How about your father?"

"He's around…"

"And?"

"What?"

"Are you close?"

"Maybe. Maybe not."

"Do you not want to be around him?"

"No."

"And why is that?"

I tighten my hold on the slice of pizza until it's almost crushed. "Because."

"I see. Is he the reason behind the identity change?"

My head jerks and I realize my mistake when he smiles in that predatory way.

"So he is."

"I don't want to talk about him."

"Then what do you want to talk about? How about how suspicious you are or…" he trails off when the opening of "Nothing Else Matters" by Metallica echoes from my phone. "You get a small pass for having good taste in music."

My eyes bug out. "You like Metallica, too?"

"Like? Their music has been running in my veins since I knew what music is all about. Attending their concerts is always the highlight of my year."

"Do you by any chance have a collection of their merch?" I always wished to own music-themed merchandise, but that was forbidden in my house.

"I collected a lot of T-shirts, jackets, hoodies, and other Metallica-themed merch in my teenage years. I even had a pair of headphones with the name of the band engraved on it. I kind of dropped endless hints about wanting it so Dad could get it for my birthday. They're back in England and my sister always threatens to destroy them when I don't do things her way."

I can't help the smile that curves my lips at how carefree he speaks about Metallica and his sister. It's the first time I've witnessed this easygoing part of him.

He's always been intense in some way or another, but now, it's dulled down.

"Your sister seems fun."

"No, she's usually a pain in the arse. Headstrong and has a no-nonsense personality."

"I get along with that type. My cousin is that way and we're close…" I trail off as a tendril of sadness splashes inside me. "*Were* close."

"I assume you left her behind, too?"

"I didn't leave her behind. We're just…on different sides of the battle."

"Battle. Interesting terminology."

I clear my throat, needing to derail his attention. He's like a cat with a mouse, once he sees a chance to strike, he won't hesitate to use it. "Do you listen to anything aside from Metallica?"

"I used to listen to Slipknot, Megadeth, and Iron Maiden when I was a teenager. Dad used to be fussy because I went to sleep and woke up with loud metal music in my ears."

"You don't do that anymore?"

"Not really."

"Why not?"

"In law school, I didn't really listen to much music and it just extended to after I passed the bar and started working."

"I don't understand how someone can move on from music. It's what helps me concentrate better."

"I know that."

"You do?"

"You usually have earbuds in when you're working. I also know you listen to vintage music."

"Are you a stalker?"

"I prefer professional watcher, just like you."

"M-me?"

"Yeah, beautiful. I know you come to watch me sometimes."

My cheeks are burning hot. "I do not."

"We have glass walls, in case you haven't noticed, and that means I can see you through them."

I stare down at my lap. "I…wasn't there for you."

"Uh-huh. Your denial is adorable."

I glare at him. "Don't call me adorable."

"Well, you are. Deal with it." He motions at my phone. "Why do you like vintage music?"

"I'm an old soul that way. I like historical novels, music from decades ago, and everything vintage."

"But you're in IT."

"An old soul with a futuristic mindset."

The corners of his lips curve in a smile before it spreads all over his face. "I like that."

My breath catches and it takes me a few tries to swallow it down. Hearing him say he likes that while smiling makes me think that maybe he likes me.

And that's just stupid.

If there's anything Knox has proved thus far, it's that whatever is between us is only sexual, so I better kill that small voice whispering inside me.

"What's your favorite band?" he asks.

"I don't really have one."

"Come on, everyone does."

"Guns N' Roses, I guess. They make me feel powerful."

"You mean their music does."

"What's the difference?"

He's poker-faced as he says, "There's one. It's their music, not the men in the band."

"No clue about the logic in that, but whatever."

We continue eating in silence, listening to the music and stealing peeks at each other. Or I am, anyway. Knox watches me openly, periodically narrowing his eyes on me and pursing his lips as if he disapproves of something.

"What?" I ask when he continues doing it.

"I want to see your real eyes."

"W-what?"

"The blue ones. And don't even dare say these are real. Without the glasses, they look fake as fuck."

"I...can't."

"Why not? I already know your real name and what you look like."

"Just...no."

"Why?"

"Because...I don't like it. Just like you don't like looking into my eyes during sex. Do you see me asking about that?"

"Who told you I don't like looking at your eyes?"

"Well, you've always fucked me or touched me from behind. Isn't that indication enough?"

"I prefer that position."

"And I prefer having these eyes."

A muscle tics in his jaw and I expect him to insist, but he does something entirely different.

His voice lowers when he speaks. "I don't like fucking from the front. It makes me feel less in control and brings back dark shadows from a past I like to keep buried."

I'm suddenly hyperaware of the tension floating between us, as if he summoned it and its sole purpose is to suffocate us both.

"What type of past?" I ask in a murmur.

He shakes his head slowly. "You don't get to ask that when you're hiding yours."

"I told you about my mom."

"She's not what you're hiding from, so that doesn't count."

I purse my lips and attack another slice of pizza.

He just leans back on his palms, watching me with a grin. The asshole. "That's what I thought."

"I want my butterfly back," I blurt out of nowhere.

He's still grinning and I'm considering the best way to wipe it off his face, aside from the obvious option—murder.

"What makes you think I have it?"

"You mentioned it the other day, so that means you do."

"Maybe if you show me your real eyes."

"I will not."

"Then I don't have it."

"Knox! That butterfly is important to me."

"Apparently not enough, because you refuse to compromise."

But it's not a compromise. He's demanding to see a part of me that will make me vulnerable and I refuse to play that game. "Are you always an asshole or only with me?"

"A little bit of both." His grin widens.

"I hate you right now."

"We have all the time in the world, so I'll convince you otherwise."

"No, we don't."

"Of course we do." His voice drops when he says the words that make me shiver, "I'm not even close to being done with you, beautiful."

TWENTY

Knox

"ARE YOU SURE YOU'RE ONLY CHOPPING THE POTATOES AND not murdering them?"

Anastasia stares up at me from behind the kitchen counter, a delicate frown appearing between her brows.

She's wearing a hoodie that barely reaches mid-thigh and keeps flashing me her lace panties every time she bends over or reaches up.

Needless to say, my dick has been twitching non-stop at the view. It's one of the reasons I agreed to let her help me make dinner, despite the fact that she's absolutely helpless when it comes to cooking.

However, she's taking it seriously. Way too seriously, considering the concentration that's written all over her delicate face, accentuated by the light hanging from the ceiling.

"I am chopping," she says matter-of-factly, motioning at the potatoes with the knife.

"They look murdered to me."

"But I did it slowly like you told me."

"It's still not right."

Her shoulders hunch as if she's failed something monumental. "Whatever. You do it."

"Let's do it together."

"How—"

I wrap my arms around her from behind and she goes still, the word she was about to say remaining stuck in the air between us.

A full-body shudder goes through her and I can't help inhaling deeply, breathing in her orange blossom perfume mixed with her delicate natural scent.

Everything about her is delicate. Whether it's her tiny features, her small frame, or her pale skin that can be bruised with a single press of my thumb against it.

For some reason, her softness always drags out the primal part of me, the part that needs to claim her every second of the day, then repeat it all over again.

The part that can't get enough, no matter how many times I've fucked her, touched her, and made her scream my name.

Despite loving the feel of her writhing body beneath me and how she demands the roughness I give, I'm starting to think it's not only due to the need to fuck her. Or else I wouldn't have shown up here every single day for the past week.

I knew I shouldn't have stayed when she asked me to. I shouldn't have given in to the temptation of her gentle voice and her inviting warmth, but I did.

And now, I can't force myself to leave.

I can't bring myself to spend a single night without her wrapped around me as if I'm a lifeline. In a way, I'm thankful for her small sofa that only allows us to sleep when we're glued together or she's lying partially on top of me.

Now, I feel it again. The way she relaxes against me as if her little body belongs in the crook of mine. My jaw clenches as my dick begins tenting against my trousers, but I refuse to let him take rein this time. I refuse to bend her over the kitchen counter and take her rough and hard.

At least, not at this moment.

For some reason, I want to keep feeling her like this, in the silence, with her body so attuned to mine that we breathe in sync.

"Aren't you supposed to be helping me chop potatoes?" she whispers when I grab each of her hands in mine but don't do anything.

"One moment," I murmur against her hair, rubbing my nose in it. "I haven't gotten my fill of your smell."

She squirms, a tremor going through her hand. "I can feel it, you know."

"It?" I ask with a note of amusement.

"Your…thing."

"It's called a cock, not a thing, Anastasia."

"Yeah, well, it's poking my ass."

"That's because my cock is demanding access."

Her face turns a deep shade of red. "Pervert."

"Me or my cock?"

"Both!"

"Then you're stuck with two perverts, beautiful. Aren't you the lucky one?"

She wiggles again and that only serves to aggravate the state of my unsatisfied erection.

"You might want to stop that unless you're planning on being my dinner."

I feel the hitching of her breath against my chest as she goes still, then murmurs, "What about me? I don't get dinner?"

"You can choke on my cock if you want."

"Stop it." She laughs, elbowing me. "I want real food."

Her hit isn't strong, but I stagger back due to the force of something entirely different—her laughter.

It's such a rare occurrence to hear the musical sound of her laughter. Her eyes close slightly and her head tips back a little as if she can't contain it.

I'm trapped in it, in how fucking carefree she looks. Ever since I first met her, she's been a bit reserved, careful, and always counting her steps. But over the past week, she's been slowly but surely getting more comfortable around me.

The fact that I'm the only one who brings out this side of her fills me with a raw sense of possessiveness and a deep feeling of pride.

I'm the only one she laughs around.

Only *me*.

"Come on. We need to make something before the movie starts." She nudges me when I remain frozen, completely and utterly fucking smitten with a view that meant shit to me in the past.

"You mean, I need to make something since you're hopeless at it," I joke to camouflage my inexplicable reaction to her. "And I'm not watching another *Harry Potter* film tonight."

"Why not? They're fun!"

"They're unrealistic."

"It's fantasy, so that's the whole point."

"Still not my thing."

"You're weird." She rolls her eyes. "Next, you'll tell me you didn't read the books."

"I didn't."

"Oh my God, who are you and where have you been living?"

"In England, where those books were set and I'm still not interested."

"How about *Lord of the Rings*? *The Hobbit*?"

"No and no."

She gasps inaudibly, her mouth closing, then opening a few times. "How is that even possible? Wait. Are you from another planet?"

"Nope, earthling through and through."

"This won't do." She shakes her head with pity written all over her face. "I'm going to have to fill in the gaps you're missing. We'll start with the books and then the movies."

"Why in that order?"

"The books are always better, duh."

I smile at the way she says "duh." It's a new word for her, something that she most likely learned from Gwen.

"What if I don't like any of them?" I ask with a poker face, egging her on.

She takes the bait, a frown appearing between her brows. "Then we'll reread them until you do."

"We?"

"Yeah, I'll read them for you."

"Hmm. Depends."

"On what?"

"On whether or not I get to touch you during the process."

Her face goes red again and it's fucking adorable. "Does everything have to include touching?"

"If I can help it."

"Fine. But you need to focus on the story."

"I'm good at multitasking." I grab her by the waist and lift her up on the counter. She squeals, her fingers latching onto my gray T-shirt. "Which book are we starting with?"

"Which one do you want?" she asks breathlessly.

"What's your favorite fantasy book?"

"*Peter Pan.*"

"Why?"

"Because I used to think I was Wendy when I was a kid. She was a free fairy and could fly away any time she wanted."

"Is that what you want?"

Her lashes flutter against her cheeks as she lets out a low, "Maybe."

"Even now?"

She lifts her head and her fake eyes meet mine, but the emotions in them are guttural and so fucking real, they stab me in the chest.

The moment she opens her mouth to speak, her phone vibrates on the counter beside her and she startles. I'm about to throw the fucking thing away, but the moment she sees "Sandra" flashing on the screen, Anastasia grabs the phone and wiggles away from me.

She hops down from the counter and escapes to the living area. "Hey, Sandra. Is everything okay…? No, yes, I mean, of course I can talk…"

I tilt my head to the side, watching as she flops onto the sofa, her complete attention on what Sandra is telling her.

Ever since that time in my office, they often talk on the phone and it's had a positive impact on Sandra's mental state. I'm a bit annoyed at my client for interrupting me, but at the same time, I admire how selfless Anastasia is when it comes to Sandra. She went out of her way and waited outside during the pretrial hearings of the civil case, despite having a form of social anxiety that makes her antsy in public places.

When I told her she didn't need to come anymore, she vehemently shook her head and said, "What I feel is nothing compared to what Sandra is going through. She needs as many friendly faces as possible in there."

Still, Sandra has the worst timing.

She cut Anastasia off when she was about to say something monumental. I release a breath and go to salvage the mess she made of the potatoes.

All I keep thinking about is why the hell I don't want to ask her what her reply would have been.

Why the hell am I fucking frustrated that she might've said yes?

That if given the chance, Anastasia would become her favorite fucking Wendy again and fly away from this world.

Me included.

TWENTY-ONE

Anastasia

A RUSTLING STARTLES ME AWAKE.

For a moment, I think I'm back in my house and there's an emergency and everyone needs to evacuate the property.

But before I can stumble from the bed, the ceiling with stars that glow in the dark comes into view.

A breath whooshes out of me, but it gets stuck in my throat when I make out the reason behind the rustling.

Knox.

I'm lying partially on top of him like we've done every night for the two weeks since he started living here. Because I'm usually a deep sleeper, I only wake up when the alarms go off. *Plural.* This is the first time I've been hauled out of sleep in the middle of the night; it's because of the Red Bull I had with Gwen and Chris yesterday afternoon. I told them caffeine messes with my system, but they called me weird for never trying an energy drink in my twenty-year-old life, and my pride was kind of wounded, so I drank it.

I'm glad I did. Otherwise, I wouldn't have seen the scene beneath me.

Knox's eyes are slammed shut and sweat covers his naked chest and glistens against his tattoos. The samurai looks gruesome in the darkness, haunted even. I click on the flashlight of my phone, bathing the room in soft white light, then slowly shake his shoulder.

He seems to be having a nightmare, a really bad one, judging by how his lips are pursed and the way his beautiful face appears to be in agony.

It hurts. Seeing him so deep in torment is similar to being slashed open and bleeding out.

"Knox…" I whisper. "Wake up."

My free hand strokes his cheek and I try to smooth the lines between his brows, but they get deeper with each passing second.

"Knox…please wake up—"

My words turn into a yelp when he grabs me by the shoulder and hauls me off him. I think I'm about to fly off the sofa and land on the floor headfirst, but my back hits the cushion and a large body hovers over me.

Knox.

He stares down at me with a glassy look, the hazel in his eyes muted and his shoulder and chest muscles flexing. One hand grabs my shoulder and the other shoots to my throat. But he doesn't grab the sides of it, where I get a bit lightheaded but absolutely delirious with pleasure, like he usually does.

This time, he chokes my windpipe.

As if his sole purpose is to suffocate the hell out of me.

My lungs burn from the lack of oxygen and I try to thrash beneath him, my nails digging into his arm, but it's like an ant is wrestling a buffalo. I'm unable to move him even an inch.

And the worst part is, he doesn't seem to be seeing me.

"K-Knox…" I choke out.

He blinks a few times and he freezes. He doesn't release me, but he's not actively trying to suffocate me to death either.

Slowly, too slowly, the golden gleam seeps into his eyes and he pushes off of me with a sudden shove, then scrambles to his feet and runs a hand through his hair. "Fuck!"

I drag in copious amounts of air through my nose and wince at the burn of every inhale and exhale.

Before I'm able to get my bearings, strong hands grab me by the shoulders, pulling me into a sitting position. I stare into Knox's eyes and a wild sense of comfort slams through me.

The thought that I'd lost him even for a moment filled me with damning trepidation.

"Are you okay?" He inspects me, then his face scrunches with pain when he focuses on my neck. "Bloody hell."

"I'm fine."

"The red marks on your neck indicate otherwise."

"It's nothing."

"It's not fucking nothing. I almost choked you to death just now."

"But you didn't."

"Why the fuck did you even touch me? You're usually out of it until the morning."

"Wait…does that mean this happens a lot?"

He's silent, his sharp jaw flexing as if he's suppressing something.

Inching closer, I place my unsteady fingers on his cheeks, cupping them. "What's plaguing you so much that you have constant nightmares about it?"

"Why would you care?" There's no accusation in his tone. In fact, it sounds a bit vulnerable, as if he wants me to care but is scared that I don't.

"Why wouldn't I? I don't want you in pain." I stroke my fingers over his cheeks and he leans into it.

He often does when I touch him lately, whether I'm reading fantasy books to him or we're watching movies or bingeing on some crime show. As per his rules, he always gets to touch me until even I can't concentrate on what I'm reading, but it feels more intimate now.

We've fallen into a peaceful rhythm that scares the shit out of me sometimes. It feels too real and too different from the no-strings-attached arrangement we started with.

There are so many strings attached now that I can't count them.

"I'm fine," he says coolly, seeming to be more in control of himself.

"You're obviously not. Tell me, Knox. What is it?"

"If I do, if I bare myself to you, will you do the same?"

I gulp, my fingers freezing on his face. "I can't talk about my past. It's dangerous."

"Maybe mine is, too. So I guess we'll both leave it at that."

He starts to release me, but I wrap my legs around his waist to stop him from getting up. "It doesn't matter."

Knox gives me a questioning glance but remains in his position.

"It's okay if our pasts remain in the past. We can just focus on the present for now."

"For now?"

"My mom once told me we can't escape our pasts forever. There will be a day when we'll have to face it." I brush my lips against his briefly, letting myself taste him on my tongue. "But that day isn't today."

He remains silent for a long second, staring, unblinking.

Shit. Did I say something wrong?

I'm about to backpedal or pull away, but he captures my mouth in a long, passionate kiss that steals my breath away.

Then we fall back asleep with his heartbeat against mine.

TWENTY-TWO

Anastasia

WHEN KNOX SAID HE'S NOT CLOSE TO BEING DONE WITH me, he absolutely meant it.

It's been three weeks since he ambushed me in my apartment and there hasn't been a day that he hasn't shown up at my door.

He basically lives here now, brings groceries, and helps me cook. Oh, and he's totally in control of cleaning my place, keeping it spotless. The other day, he bought wallpaper and furniture, then remodeled the whole thing, hiding the smoke marks and asymmetrical stars.

But no matter how much he cleans my place, he makes it dirty again with all the sex. He doesn't get enough, ever. Whether it's in the kitchen, the shower, or even when I'm sitting peacefully trying to create systems, he just swoops in and fucks me like he hasn't touched me in decades.

His presence in my living space feels weirdly domesticated, and I've been trying not to get used to the company, to keep reminding myself that I'm on my own.

That at the end of whatever fucked-up fixation he has on me, I'll be alone again.

But it gets harder every day, especially since the little bonding moment we had after his nightmare. We feel closer now, more in tune with each other than ever before.

His presence is like a potent chemical reaction—impossible to ignore and leaves me craving more.

And it's not only about sex.

It's about how I've converted him to being a fantasy novel fan and how he dedicates time to watching movies with me. Not only that, but Knox is also a fun conversationalist with a dark sense of humor that I relate to. With him, I get to be nerdy and talk about the latest technology without him judging me. If anything, he listens to me talk as if my words are the most sacred things to ever exist.

However, since he's here most of the time, I have to call *Babushka* during work or before he gets here. I also check on the people from my previous life when he's sleeping so that he doesn't get a glimpse of them.

If it were up to me, I'd keep them and Knox worlds apart, but that's wishful thinking, especially since they're affiliated with Matt Bell—the man Knox is trying to defeat.

Sandra had a panic attack at the civil case pretrial hearing. I was on the verge of one as well from being in the midst of all those people, even though I hid outside.

The media's attention to the case is insane, like absolutely atrocious, and all their questions to Sandra were vicious. Not only do they hunt her down every chance they get, but they also asked if she faked the panic attack to play on the judge's sympathy.

Although I remained in the background most of the time, it was almost as if eyes were on me, as if my worst nightmare was coming true and everything would end.

I was more paranoid than usual and I nearly gave into the irrational fear, but I didn't, because Sandra needed me. So I had to be there for her, even if my skin was crawling.

Even if I contemplated running away again and never coming back.

However, I don't think that's possible anymore, not when I've established roots I don't like to admit having.

And most of those have to do with the man who sets my body and soul on fire and doesn't shy away from being caught in the flames.

I wish I had his confidence or straightforwardness. I wish I was as assertive or as otherworldly as he is. Although I admit to being attached to him, I can't admit that it could be more than mere attachment or simply a way to drive away the loneliness.

It's becoming so much more, and it's eating me up from the inside out to consider the hidden meaning.

As a direct impact of that thought, I can't help the tinge of emptiness that grabs hold of me whenever he's done fucking me.

Like now.

We're in the supply room. He takes his time putting my clothes back on—and feeling me up in the process—after he fucked me fast and raw against the door. I'm barely standing, my limbs shaking and my pussy still throbbing. Knox does that to me all the time. The power of his thrusts often makes me delirious for a long while after.

And I'm glad he's the one who puts my clothes in order, because I can hardly move, let alone function.

Finally, he places the glasses on my nose. He never fucks me with them on or allows me to wear them in my apartment, but he does respect my need to remain hidden in public. He doesn't push me to answer his questions about my real identity either, even though he continues to ask them.

His lips brush against mine and I shudder, my heart lurching in my chest.

It's such a light contact, a brush of lips and not even a kiss, definitely not as raw and passionate as before he fucks me.

But as much as I love his primal kisses, I'm addicted to his soft after-sex kisses, completely attuned to them and unable to get enough.

Because he doesn't have to give me them, not when we're well aware of the status of our relationship, but he still claims my lips.

He still kisses me as if he can't get enough.

As if, like me, he could be feeling so much more than sex.

I internally shake my head, trying to push back that thought. If I get caught up in it and trick my brain into believing it, things will decline for the worst.

"I'll see you tonight," he whispers in that sensually sinful accent of his and pushes a stray strand of hair behind my ear.

"Are you going to cook?"

"If you'd like."

"Of course I do." I don't really enjoy cooking. Before he came along, most of my meals were takeout or some burned dish I tried to follow the recipe for online.

I'm not ashamed to admit he's much better at it than me, and he seems to enjoy it, too.

He pinches my cheek playfully, "You're such a princess."

"I'm not a princess."

"You hate cooking, cleaning, and any house chores, basically."

"It's not that I hate them. I'm just not good at them."

"Because you're a princess." He smiles. "But don't worry, I've got you."

And with that, he steps out of the supply room, leaving me absolutely helpless and confused and maybe a little bit lightheaded, too, because I keep licking my lips for the remnants of his taste.

I'm really hopeless.

It takes me a few seconds to get my bearings. Though there aren't usually people on this part of the floor, I'll have to explain to Chris and Gwen why I disappeared during the lunch we were supposed to have together.

Knox texted me to meet him in the supply room earlier, and when I ignored it, he barged into the IT department, kicked Gwen and Chris out, then said, "Now, you have nothing stopping you."

I asked him not to do that again, but I don't have much hope in him following through with it. He's too headstrong for that.

But even he should know that my friends will be suspicious at some point.

I smile at that as I leave the supply room.

Friends.

I never thought I would ever use that word or actually have the opportunity to make friends.

When I was little, I was lonely, which is why I became the fairy of the forest and had trees and stones for friends. And after I moved in with Papa, the idea of friends became impossible.

People like me aren't allowed such a luxury.

"So, it's you."

I freeze, my stomach dropping at the sound of the accented voice coming from my right. It's British, too, and while it's calm and collected, it's not Knox's.

If anything, it's even more sinister.

I whirl around to find Daniel leaning against the wall, arms and ankles crossed and a look of pure contempt darkening his cobalt blue eyes.

Holy shit.

Was he there all along? Wait, no. Knox would've seen him if he was and he would've told me and—

"I was becoming suspicious with his frequent visits to the fourth floor so I decided to start my own private investigation and followed him. I had to wait until he was out to find out who he was coming here for." He stares at his watch. "Twenty minutes is a record for him. He usually gets bored and finishes quicker than that."

My skin heats and crawls, and I wish I could somehow vanish into thin air as if I never existed.

Daniel watches me intently, as if he can comb through my thoughts and my deepest, darkest desires.

"I...I don't know what you're talking about." I attempt to play dumb, but my unsteady voice doesn't cooperate.

"Really now? Do you mind telling me what you did in that supply room all this time?"

"Work."

"Is that a new word for sex?" His expression and tone don't change. They're actually more composed, as if he's completely in his element.

I've heard a lot of things about Daniel, mostly that he's a player and easygoing, but no one mentioned his threatening, sinister side, because that's what it feels like right now.

Being threatened.

Watched.

Desiccated.

He pushes off the wall, and it takes everything in me not to turn around and run. Because I know, I just know that it would encourage him to come after me even stronger.

Daniel circles me and the hairs on my nape stand on end as he stops in front of me. "You're not his usual type, so now, I'm wondering what made him interested in you. Do you care to shed some light on the mystery?"

"How will I do that?"

"Simple. Let's fuck."

"W-what?"

"Tonight?"

"No!"

"Why not? Oh, not a good time?"

"Not a good pairing. Why would you think I would ever want to have sex with you?"

He appears genuinely baffled. "Why not? Knox and I go three-way with no problem."

"Huh?"

"We fuck the same women, often at the same time."

My stomach lurches and I think I'm going to throw up the cupcakes Gwen gave me earlier.

Did Daniel say he and Knox fuck the same women at the same time?

Yes, I think he did.

But that's not what's bothering me. What's bothering me is the fact that Knox could and would share me with his friend.

The thought causes my stomach to cramp and my heart to shrink in its ribcage.

If he's so used to that, why wouldn't he do it now? After all, our relationship is all about sex.

"So?" Daniel asks. "What do you think?"

"About?"

"Fucking me. For the record, everyone prefers me since I'm obviously more charming." He accentuates his words with a grin that showcases his dimples.

And I can see it, his charm, the reason why many women would prefer him. Daniel is the type that oozes sex appeal and can effortlessly grab anyone's attention. He has a striking kind of beauty that glows from afar and blinds once you get close.

But he doesn't have Knox's intensity and he certainly doesn't make me feel like I'll jump out of my skin due to his presence alone.

"No," I say simply, easily, and with so much assertiveness, it makes him pause.

"You don't have to answer now. Think about it."

"I don't need to."

"This is interesting." He circles me again before stopping in front of me. "Is it because of Knox? He wouldn't care."

Well, I would. But I don't say that, because I don't have the voice to. So I just shrug, even though my heart is bleeding.

It's not supposed to, but it's metaphorically dripping all over the ground.

It's funny that I left my family to avoid being hurt and used, but it feels as if I've landed in something much deeper and more painful.

And I need to distance myself from it.

From him.

The source of the shattering pain in my chest.

TWENTY-THREE

Knox

SOMETHING'S CHANGED.

I can't quite pinpoint it, but it's there in Anastasia's stiff movements and silence.

Last night, when I fucked her against the kitchen counter, she was oddly quiet, then she curled up on the sofa and fell asleep

Usually, we have dinner together and talk about the case, or anything, actually. She talks nerdy to me about some new software or coding, her eyes brightening the more I listen. I'm not really interested in all that stuff, but the fact that she talks to me with that hyper tone of hers is an accomplishment. It's the only time she leaves the prim and proper side of herself in the background.

In return, I find myself telling her about the friends and family I left in London or my antics with Dad, Ronan, and everyone else.

It's so easy to talk to her, so easy to spend hours in her company without having to do anything.

It's even better when she's the one who talks about herself. Sometimes, she slips and mentions her cousin, her father, and her family. It's in passing, though, and whenever she mentions them, her shoulders hunch and she changes the subject.

She talks more about Gwen, Chris, and Sandra than her actual past, and sometimes, it feels like she's stuck in the middle.

Not fully Jane and not fully Anastasia either.

I'm along for the ride, enjoying every bit of her contradictions and letting it seep beneath my skin.

Not last night or this morning, though.

It's like a barrier has materialized between us. The fact that I have no clue where it came from has been driving me bloody insane.

She's also been *busy* today and can't go to the supply room. I call bullshit on that, because she's the most efficient member of the IT department and often finishes her tasks in the first half of the workday.

Stepping out of my car, I stare at the text message she sent me a few hours ago when I asked her what she wanted for dinner.

Anastasia: I'm going out with Gwen and Chris, so I won't be home for dinner.

If there's anything I've learned about her, it's that she dislikes being in public, so going out is not the norm for her.

Either Gwen is corrupting her—and I wouldn't be surprised if that were to be the case—or more logically, she's avoiding me.

Which I will not have.

So I called Chris and made him tell me where they are.

"We're at a club!" he shouted over the music, then texted me the address.

That's where I am right now. At the fucking club.

Loud music nearly punctures my eardrums as I make my way through the crowd of writhing bodies. Blue light flashes in sync with trendy music and people go crazy when the beat drops.

Usually, this is my scene.

I live for the rush of adrenaline, alcohol, and sex. It's what distracts me from my head and keeps my shadows at bay.

But that stopped being the norm ever since I met her. Ever

since I owned her and inserted myself in her life as deeply as she invaded mine.

It's been several weeks since the last time I was in a place like this, despite Dan's constant bitching and the group chat's eternal teasing.

The club feels a bit foreign now.

Maybe because my idea of fun has strangely switched from a loud nightclub to a small, quiet flat.

At first, I spot Gwen and Chris because they're loud as fuck. Both of them are chugging drinks while dancing sporadically. Another guy, about their age, moves with them, and the three laugh in unison.

Gwen is barely staying on her feet, but that's not my job to worry about.

I scan their surroundings, knowing Anastasia can't be far if she came with them. Sure enough, I find her sitting alone at a secluded booth.

In my head, I'm forging ahead and grabbing her by the throat, but my feet don't move. I'm stunned and rooted in place by her appearance.

Anastasia owns three types of clothes—baggy trousers, oversized shirts, and hoodies. Oh, and sexy-as-fuck lace panties.

Those are the only things in her closet.

So where the fuck did she get that dress from?

A tight black one that reveals her curves in silhouette form. Its straps might as well be nonexistent; not only are they thin and barely cover anything, but one of them also falls down her shoulder constantly. Although the dress isn't too short, it reveals her pale legs and fuck-me heels. She's also released her black hair, letting it fall in waves to her shoulders.

She seems to be wearing some makeup, too, even though she still has those thick glasses on.

My dick instantly twitches to life and I have to adjust the sorry fuck with teenage fantasies.

Or maybe they're not teenage-level, after all, because the only thought running through my head is to rip that dress off her and fuck her on its shreds. With those heels on.

I don't really care what she looks like, but this appearance is eerily similar to the first time I saw her in that bar.

Though she's not a blonde and she doesn't have those enchanting blue eyes, the aura is similar.

And for some reason, that Anastasia seems more real than the Jane persona she's hiding behind.

A straw hangs in her mouth as she drinks from a sparkly blue glass and frantically checks her surroundings.

She looks a little bit lost, unfocused, almost like all the external stimuli are about to crush her in their clutches. I can taste her anxiety in the air with every step I take toward her.

Not only is she gripping her drink tight, but she also adjusts her glasses every second and lowers her head whenever she makes random eye contact with someone.

Inexplicably, that makes me want to reach out to people's eyeballs and blind them for causing her to feel such distress.

For being the cause of her discomfort.

And that's wrong, isn't it?

I'm not supposed to be on the verge of losing it only because she's staring at people and hates it. I'm not supposed to be this worked up about a girl who's so secretive about who she is that it drives me bloody insane sometimes.

Upon seeing me approaching, her posture stiffens and she's about to stand up, but before she does, I sit beside her and grab her by the thigh. "Where do you think you're going, beautiful?"

"To find Gwen and the others."

"Why? To parade this new look of yours? I thought Jane doesn't like dressing up."

"I…don't. Gwen made me do it."

"Hmm. But you went along with it anyway. Maybe you do like it." My voice is too calm, despite the unhinged emotions going on inside me at the same time.

She lifts her chin. "Maybe I do."

"What did you just say?"

"I said, maybe I do like it."

"What exactly? Dressing up in a low-cut dress or coming to clubs to show it off? Or maybe it's dancing with boys and having them look at what that dress hides. Maybe you want them to imagine what's underneath it." My fingers latch onto the fallen strap and I lift it up her shoulder, enjoying her shudder. "Maybe you like being a little fucking tease."

"Maybe...I do."

"Is that so?" I snap the strap back in place, my voice battling to keep its cool, but my touch is sure and firm as I sneak my other hand that's on her thigh underneath her dress. "Do you want them to feel what it's like between your thighs, beautiful?"

She places her drink on the table, hands trembling when my fingers meet the edge of her underwear. "No..."

"No...what? You don't want them to feel how soaking wet you are, my little liar?" I glide my fingers against her folds, then twirl her clit, and she slouches forward, her shoulder brushing against my arm.

"Oh, God..."

"You still didn't answer my question, Anastasia. Do you like it when they see you like this, all done up and beautiful?"

"I...I do."

I pinch her clit and she whimpers, the sound so erotic that my dick responds immediately, tenting in my trousers.

"Do you fantasize about them touching you here? Playing with your clit and thrusting their fingers in your soaking little cunt?"

She stares at me then, and even though the club is dimly lit, I can see the mixture of emotions in her eyes. The hurt and the determination. The pain and the promise for retribution.

It's something about her. Even when she's down and overwhelmed, she never acts like a weakling or a pushover.

She definitely feels more and more like a princess, since her dignity always comes first.

"Maybe you do," she whispers.

"What?"

"Maybe you like imagining them touching me, thrusting their fingers and dicks inside me while you watch."

I grab her by the cunt harshly and she hisses in a breath. "*Me?*"

"Yes, you."

I pull her panties aside and thrust two fingers inside her in one go. She moans, snuggling into my side and gripping my hand over her dress.

But it's pointless because I'm pounding inside her now and adding a third finger until she whimpers. Until she's holding on to me and staring at me with frantic eyes as I touch her savagely.

As I touch her with the intent to make her come as hard as possible.

I want her to detonate here and now, for the world to see who the fuck she belongs to.

My fingers drive deep into her pussy, needing to purge those fucking thoughts out of her, needing her to only see and think about me.

To only be with me.

Her short nails dig into my arm as she trembles violently and then she hides her face in my neck, biting down on the flesh of my pulse as she shakes violently.

The shattering force of her orgasm swallows my fingers, but I don't release her, keeping them deep inside her.

She's breathing harshly against my neck, panting as she releases my flesh.

"You think I want anyone to feel you like this? Or that I would let them fucking touch you?"

"I don't know," she whispers. "Daniel said you share with him."

"You talked to Daniel?"

"Yeah."

I'm going to fucking kill him.

"Was he lying?" she asks slowly, painfully even.

"He wasn't. We did share, but that doesn't apply to you. I won't share you with Daniel or anyone else."

She pulls back, moisture shining in her eyes. "Why?"

"Because you're fucking mine, beautiful. No one gets to look at you or touch you. And if they make that mistake, I will end their miserable lives."

"Even Daniel?"

"Especially Daniel. His name is at the top of my shit list."

She smiles a little and it's bright and fucking innocent. "I told him no, anyway."

"You did?"

"Yeah. He's not really my type."

My chest expands with a strange warmth that I hadn't felt in…forever. This is the first time anyone ever said Daniel isn't their type—he's *everyone's* type—and the fact that she, from all people, is saying it does shit to me.

It takes all myself control to ask, "And I am?"

"Maybe."

"Hmm. I have to make that a "certainly." I pull my fingers out of her and she releases a small erotic sound that makes me rock-hard.

I stand up and pull her by the hand. She stumbles before landing against me.

"Where are we going?" Her voice is so breathy, I want to fuck her right here and now.

But that means an audience and I'm not a fan of that.

"Home."

"But…I came with Gwen and Chris and their friend…I have to tell them."

"Forget them."

"I can't leave Gwen alone. She's drunk."

I grunt as I keep dragging her behind me. I should've known Gwen's drunken state would cause a problem.

Luckily, I know the right person for this situation.

Tightening my hold on Anastasia, I dial Nate.

Let him take care of his best friend's drunk daughter so that I can focus on Anastasia.

My Anastasia.

TWENTY-FOUR

Anastasia

"**Y**OU'RE MARRIED?" I STARE DUMBFOUNDED AT GWEN AND she takes a long slurp of her milkshake.

I was ready to be told off about the way I disappeared on them last night. As a gesture of apology, I invited them over to the IT department for a coffee break and I bought her favorite vanilla milkshake and Chris an iced coffee.

But he pushed his drink aside and said in an overly hyperactive voice, "Where the hell were you last night, Jane? You missed the epic moment when Nate announced that Gwen is his wife."

My friend groans, then stares down before meeting our expectant gazes. "Let me explain."

"Hell yeah, you'll explain." Chris nudges her. "I've been in suspense all night long, waiting for morning, despite being drunk as fuck."

"You couldn't have been as drunk as I was. I have the worst hangover in human history today." Gwen massages her temples.

"That doesn't give you the right to escape answering to what the hell is going on." Chris lowers his voice. "You're really married to the managing partner of W&S, who happens to be your dad's closest friend, WHILE your father is in a coma?"

She grimaces. "Sort of."

"What does "sort of" mean? No?"

"We are married, but it's not what you think. I just…it's just for convenience."

"But isn't he twice your age?"

"He's not twice my age, he's only eighteen years older than me."

"Which is two years away from being twice your age, Gwen."

She shifts, her gaze getting somber, and the colors in her eyes clash into an undecipherable mix.

"Are you happy?" I ask.

"That's not what you should be asking her, Jane. You should make her explain."

"Why would she? They're both adults and Nathaniel doesn't seem like the type who'd make impulsive decisions, so it must've been for a good reason."

"It was." Gwen's voice trembles. "Do you think this is all okay? Me married to Nate, I mean. His mother dropped by yesterday and she made me feel shitty by bringing up the outside world. Why can't it be just me and him? And yeah, I know he's Dad's best friend-slash-partner and almost twice my age, and when I was eighteen and kissed him, he was twice my age, but—"

"Wait," Chris interrupts. "You kissed him when you were eighteen?"

"I did and I don't regret it, okay?" She focuses back on me as if I'm her safe haven. "Do you think my feelings for him are weird?"

"I don't really have the right to judge and neither does Chris." I glare at him, then smile at her. "It's your life so live it as you wish."

"Thanks." She abandons her tight hold on the milkshake and takes my hand in hers. "I'm so glad you at least understand."

"But I don't." Chris rolls his eyes. "You have to admit the whole thing is off. I can't imagine you married to Nate."

"Why not?" She purses her lips.

"Because he's so strict and no-nonsense and you're…well… talkative and active and many other things that he isn't."

"I also think it's a very unlikely pairing."

"Jane." She releases my hand and hits my shoulder. "I thought you were on my side."

"Even Jane can't ignore the facts," Chris teases. "Do you drive him insane with all the talking?"

"Screw you, okay? He's never complained about that."

"He probably will soon."

I laugh as they go at each other's throats and bicker. It feels light, nice, normal.

And I have no clue why that makes my stomach drop with each passing second.

In the back of my mind, I know people like me aren't allowed to have this kind of ordinary life, or happiness, or anything that doesn't include a conflict.

Yes, I ran away, but that doesn't mean they won't chase me. Hurt me—or *Babushka*.

Or the people I've started to care about despite vowing to stay alone. Despite my efforts and the walls I've built around me.

And because I've been having these small bursts of anxiety since this morning, I've been manically checking on *Babushka* and making sure she's okay.

It's probably a play of my imagination, a trick of my brain, which is rejecting how alive I've been lately.

So absolutely alive.

My phone vibrates and I hide it from Gwen and Chris as I check the text.

Knox: My office. Now.

I type discreetly, even though they're both still bickering.

Me: Not the supply room?

Knox: I know your pussy misses me, but this is about work.

Despite the tinge of disappointment, I stand, clearing my throat. "They need me on the partners' floor."

A frown appears between Gwen's brows. "Now?"

"Yeah, I'll catch up with you later."

I grab my laptop case and leave before either of them can say anything. I know it's about work, but if I can see his face, that's fine.

No clue when seeing Knox became this vital, and I think I have an unhealthy fixation, but it's there and it's impossible to get rid of it.

And maybe, just maybe, I don't want to.

When he came to find me at the club yesterday, my chest squeezed the hardest it ever has, and everything that followed made it even tighter and narrower until I couldn't breathe.

Or maybe I breathed way past my capacity until I had no air left besides what his mouth fed me when he kissed me senseless in the car.

I'm practically jogging to his office and when I reach it, I stop to catch my breath and fix my hair. Before, I never felt the need to be beautiful for anyone, but now, I keep thinking about being in my best shape, just so I can deepen that gleam in his eyes.

But that means becoming Anastasia again. That means being a wallflower whose life is dictated for her, and I refuse to do that.

Inhaling deeply, I tap on Knox's office door and his gruff "Come in" makes me clench my thighs.

Get a grip, Ana.

I slip inside and find him sitting majestically behind his desk, reading from a file. He's so beautiful, it's a little painful, especially when he's concentrating on his task, his thick brows knit together and his strong hands flipping through the pages.

Why am I not those measly pieces of paper?

As if reading my thoughts, he lifts his head and a sly smirk tilts his lips. "You're here."

"You said you needed me."

"Needed you?"

"For work."

"If you keep staring at me with those come-and-fuck-me eyes, that plan will change."

I gulp, looking at the floor.

"No, Anastasia. You never break eye contact with me, not for any reason."

I slowly lift my head and take in a few steadying breaths. "What do you want me to work on?"

"I'm forming an offensive strategy for Sandra's case. I emailed you a list of leads that I want you to go through."

"So it's about gathering intel?"

"In a not-so-legal way. Are you up for it?"

"I'll be happy to help."

"If Nate or anyone else finds out about this, they'll fire you."

"And they'll probably call a disciplinary board meeting for you."

He smiles. "You're worried about me, beautiful?"

"No, I'm...not."

"As you shouldn't be. They can't hurt me for this."

"But what if the opposing lawyers find out? You could lose your license, right?"

"This is between you and me, so unless you betray me, no one will find out."

"Only...the two of us know?"

"Yeah."

"Why?"

"Because of all the complications that could arise from it."

My nails dig into the strap of the laptop case and I try not to be disappointed that he didn't say the words I didn't know I wanted to hear, but now, I do.

I wanted him to say he trusted me.

But that's stupid. Why would he trust me when my background is a mystery and he's well aware that I've adopted a different identity than my own?

It's the reason I haven't shown him my eyes; I needed to keep a piece of myself hidden.

And maybe he wants to hide a piece of himself, too, because he's never fucked me while looking at me.

Like me, he has high walls and prefers to keep them that way.

I should be fine with that. After all, this arrangement suits me the best, but that's not the case.

So instead of focusing on those somber thoughts, I sit on the sofa and get lost in work, typing away at my computer.

I'm at it for some time, not sure how long, since I kind of forget about my surroundings when I'm creating systems or breaking through firewalls.

"You're fucking hot when you're in your nerdy zone, beautiful."

I stare up at that, my breath catching in my throat, and my cheeks burn bright. "Stop it."

"Stop what?" His voice drops as he glides his finger on the edge of the paper. "Telling you how hot you are?"

"Distracting me."

"You're distracting me, too, so it's only fair that you suffer with me."

"But I'm not doing anything."

"Still distracting as fuck."

"Maybe I should work from the IT department."

"Fuck no. I finally found an excuse to get you here."

"I thought this was for the case."

"That, too." He tilts his head in my direction. "But why do you think I have the blinds down?"

"I…don't know."

"So you can flash me those gorgeous tits anytime you please."

"I won't do that."

"But you can. Anytime, beautiful."

"Pervert."

"I won't deny the charge."

"The harassment charge, you mean?"

"I beg to differ."

"Well, isn't that how harassment in the workplace happens? A higher-up bullies an employee to do their sexual bidding."

"But does said employee wait for their boss in a dark room while only wearing lace panties and dripping in them with the anticipation of being fucked?"

My cheeks go up in flames at the retelling of one of the times I waited for him in only my panties. I don't know what came over me then. I just wanted to see that lusty look in his eyes and feel the way he couldn't seem to get enough of me.

I ended up bent over on the floor and fucked so thoroughly that I couldn't move.

"I suppose not," I murmur.

"Does that mean you're going to show me your tits now? Or your cunt? Maybe both?"

My fingers itch and burn, and I do want it. I want to get naked for him and watch the darkening of his golden eyes.

But before I can get on board with that crazy idea, the door to his office busts open and Daniel strides in.

"Stop sending me blonde fucking hookers, you bloody wanker. There were two of them last night."

I freeze, but Knox simply smirks. "There will be three today."

"What the fuck?"

"Four tomorrow. By the weekend, you'll have an army of them."

"Do you have a fucking death wish?"

"Apparently, you do. So I'll kill you slowly with blonde hookers."

I try to suppress my laughter and that alerts Daniel to my presence, because his head whips in my direction. His eyes narrow on me, then back on Knox. "Wait a minute. Is it because of her?"

Knox purses his lips but says nothing.

Daniel throws his weight on the chair in front of Knox, seemingly a bit calmer. "I see. If you don't like me making a move on your girl, all you have to do is say so. There's no need to be a dick."

My cheeks heat at that. Or, more specifically, the part where he called me Knox's girl.

I'm not, right?

"I did tell you, but you didn't listen, so the hookers are your punishment until further notice."

"Oh, fuck you." He tilts his head to the side toward me. "Are you sure you won't change your mind? I'm a way better fuck than he is."

Knox stands abruptly, so abruptly that I push back against the sofa, startled.

"Repeat that one more time and I'll beat you the fuck up, then I'll pay a dozen blonde hookers to wank you in your sleep. Don't test my fucking patience."

Instead of being mad, Daniel's lips pull in a wide grin. "My, my, Van Doren. Isn't this fucking interesting?"

"Get out."

"Not when it's getting juicy. Should I order my best man suit?"

I swallow, my heart hammering at what he's insinuating. I stand up so fast, the room starts spinning for a bit, but I plant my feet firmly on the ground. "I...I'm going back to the IT department."

Knox is about to say something, but I can't listen to him in my disheveled state or with the way my heart threatens to jump out of my ribcage.

And the feeling doesn't go away for the rest of the day, not when I'm working or having lunch with Gwen and Chris, and definitely not when I go home alone.

Knox sends me a text that he's having a late work meeting and will go to his apartment tonight before coming over.

So that gives me a long time on my own. Hours, to be specific. I should probably sleep them off until he comes along.

Jeez.

Since when did he become the highlight of my day? As I slip the key into the door of my apartment, I can feel the gloominess of being alone in this place.

Is this even healthy anymore?

Mom used to tell me that love is a game one will always lose and I'm starting to realize exactly what those words mean.

Though, this isn't love.

No, nope. We're merely fuck buddies.

Yeah, keep telling yourself that.

The moment I open the door and step inside, the hairs on my nape stand on end. And it's not because Knox isn't here.

It's something darker, sharper, and much more nefarious.

My blood roars with the need to run, to disappear and never come back.

My feet shift in place and I turn around to do just that, but a hand shoots out from the darkness and slams the door shut.

The faintly accented voice makes my stomach drop. "Long time no see, Anastasia."

TWENTY-FIVE

Anastasia

EVERYTHING I'VE WORKED FOR CRUMBLES AND SPLINTERS into a million pieces right before my eyes.

And all I can do is watch.

For a few seconds, anyway, as the reality of being found strikes me to my bones, crushes them, and leaves me with no air.

But the moment I can breathe again, the second oxygen burns my lungs, I lunge toward the door. I just need to run, to hide. If I disappear properly, they won't be able to find me this time.

They won't—

A hand wraps around my wrist with brute force and I'm helpless, absolutely powerless when that same force yanks me back.

I stumble and nearly fall on my face, but the same hold keeps me upright with effortless ease. As if this is a normal occurrence for them. Who am I kidding? It is normal.

The likes of him kidnap, torture, and kill for the mere fun of it.

My insides crumble to my feet and my heart beats out of rhythm.

This is just a nightmare, right? The worst nightmare possible.

If I blink, I'll wake up and put this whole thing behind me.

But when I slam my eyes shut and open them again, reality crashes into me with no introductions or preparation.

My gaze meets the one who's grabbing me savagely. Aleksander. The same Aleksander who I should've known wouldn't just forget that incident in the restaurant from a few weeks ago.

He stares at me blankly, his light eyes resembling an icy storm, not to be budged or survived. They're the same as his hold on me—merciless, savage, and with a coldness that will soon freeze me to death.

And that's not the worst part.

No matter how violent and efficient Aleksander is, he's only the right-hand man of a much more dangerous opponent.

And sure enough, when I look ahead, I find his boss. One of the four kings, the most secretive, the most cunning, and the one who might as well be the deadliest.

Kirill sits on my sofa, flipping through one of the takeout menus. But seeing him isn't what nearly makes me go into a full on panic mode.

It's the fact that he's not alone.

Beside him is the strongest man in the *Bratva*. Some even say he's more powerful than my father. He's not only the strategist and the brains, but he's also the most ruthless man I've ever known.

Adrian Volkov.

And he's going through my spare laptop, his fingers typing at supersonic speed.

Shit. Shit.

"Come join us, princess," Kirill says with absolute nonchalance, still flipping through the menus. "Let her go, Sasha."

Aleksander—whose nickname in Russian is Sasha—shoves me forward and I wince as I massage my wrist.

"Now, Sasha," Kirill reprimands in a tone that suggests he's used to his senior guard's brute ways. "No hurting the *Pakhan*'s only daughter…yet."

My lips tremble, but it's not just because of Kirill's unveiled threat or the fact that he and Aleksander found me, it's Adrian.

I can't stop looking at him, even though he hasn't acknowledged my existence yet. He's tall, dark, and has an imposing presence that sparks fear without him having to do anything.

His reputation precedes him. Of all people, I'm well aware of how he erases his enemies when they show the slightest bit of disrespect. Anyone in the world I came from avoids his wrath with any means necessary. The moment he puts someone in his sights, they might as well be considered dead.

One thing's for certain: his loyalty only lies with the *Bratva* and his family.

And as a runaway, I don't belong to the *Bratva* anymore. So if he chooses to, he could shoot me in the head and cover up the whole incident as if it didn't happen.

Kirill will sure as hell take his side, not mine. Especially since he's been not-so-subtly eyeing my father's position for a while now.

Everyone in the *Bratva* has.

The king's throne is the most coveted spot. The princess's only role is to nod her head and be used by whomever the king sees fit.

That's why I left.

That's why I risked Adrian's wrath, Kirill's violence, and everyone else's death sentence.

"Did you recognize me a few weeks ago?" I ask Kirill, my attention bouncing between him and Adrian.

I don't even attempt to run again. It's useless since not only is Aleksander standing at my back like a demon ready to strike, but I'm sure that Adrian's senior guards are also surrounding the place or hiding somewhere I can't see.

He never goes anywhere unprepared, and he sure as hell wouldn't give me a chance to escape or leave until he's through with what he's here for.

"I suspected it, yes." Kirill smirks, throwing the menu on the table. "I must admit you did a great job, but it wasn't perfect enough to fool me. Besides, your mannerisms will always give you away, Anastasia."

I never wanted to hear my name pronounced the Russian way again. It feels like I'm back in the confinements of that prison, unable to use my fairy wings that I always dreamed would let me fly.

"The *Pakhan*, Rai, and dear Vladimir said you were continuing your studies in Russia. So it didn't make sense for you to be roaming the streets of New York as an unflattering version of yourself." Kirill tilts his head to the side. "Am I right?"

My lips part, my mind stuck on the bit of information he just revealed.

The fact that Papa, my cousin, Rai, who's the head of the *Bratva*'s legal front, V Corp, and Vladimir, who's always been like a big brother to me, said I was in Russia.

I obviously wasn't. They had no idea where I was, except for the note I left saying, "I'm sorry."

But they…covered up for me?

My eyes fill with unwanted tears at that thought, the fact that they protected me from everyone else. That they didn't let me take the fall, even though I was prepared for that.

Even though I should've taken it.

I've been part of the brotherhood for fifteen years, and I know better than anyone that any betrayal's punishment is death.

No matter who or what you are.

Papa, Rai, and Vladimir didn't allow that. Despite being the strictest people when it comes to the *Bratva*'s code, they bent it for me.

"Am I right?" Kirill repeats, raising a brow.

Since I have no clue what Papa, Rai, and Vladimir said, I choose to stay quiet. I'd rather pay with my life than betray my family.

A hand nudges me forward, rattling my whole body. Aleksander. "He asked you a question. Answer it."

Kirill tsks. "No violence, Sasha."

I hear what resembles a scoff from Aleksander, but he doesn't touch me again.

"It's fine if she doesn't answer, because I am right. The whole situation reeks of lies and manipulation, and I'm not a fan of those." Kirill smirks, sliding his glasses up his nose. "Unless I'm the one inflicting them, of course. So, to rectify things, I had a little chat with my number one source of intel, Adrian. Color me surprised when he revealed that you weren't in Russia. In fact, no one—your father, Rai, and Vladimir included—knew where you were. So I teamed up with this one here to find you, even though I'm still wounded he kept information from me."

Adrian doesn't acknowledge Kirill or anyone in the room and continues to type away.

And for a moment, I can't look away from him. Just what is he searching for? I never keep incriminating information on my laptops, ever.

I always delete everything before I go to bed and make sure to clean any traces. But this is Adrian.

What if he's able to restore some data?

I'm distracted from him because Kirill keeps watching me with that slight tilt of his head. As if he's waiting for a bomb to drop.

Just what else has he told Adrian?

Hell, how did he find out that Papa and the others covered for me?

Kirill taps his mouth in a contemplative move. "Now, the real question is, why were you running, Anastasia?"

My gaze strays to Adrian and for the first time, he raises his head. I always thought he was beautiful in a dangerous type of way. He has a rugged type of beauty with his dark hair, sharp cheekbones, and massive build. I swallow when his harsh yet seemingly calm gray eyes fixate on me.

Kirill doesn't know the reason.

Adrian doesn't have to say it for me to catch the memo. I'm sure he has his reasons behind not revealing it and he'll probably use it against me at some point, but that doesn't matter.

If I can at least have Kirill off my back, it's worth it.

"I just wanted to get away from it all," I whisper.

"You don't get away from the *Bratva*, little princess. You're cute to think there's a way out other than death."

My muscles lock together and my first thought is *Babushka*. If I'm gone, no one will be able to take care of her. Hell, if they found me, they might be able to track her down and make her join me and Mom.

"You'll come back with us," Kirill announces.

"No!"

"You don't have a say in it. The *Pakhan*'s daughter won't be roaming the streets as a nerdy tech at a law firm."

"I don't want to."

"What you want doesn't matter. Either you come willingly or Sasha will be given free rein to use force."

"I'm not going back. I don't care what you'll do."

Kirill stands, sliding his glasses up his nose with his middle finger. It's crazy how he can make that single motion appear threatening. When I adjust my glasses, it looks anxious at best. "You don't want me to act on my threats. I could, and would, put your father's position in jeopardy. The choice of going back is the only courtesy I'll offer you."

My fist clenches and I can feel the bulging of the tendons in my neck. When I made this decision, I thought Papa wouldn't care, as usual. I thought he'd definitely choose the brotherhood over me.

He always has.

He's so loyal to the *Bratva*, and so is Vladimir and Rai.

At one point, I thought my great-cousin could probably help me. She always took care of me after Papa killed my stepfather and brought me to live with him. All after Mom was beaten to death by said stepfather.

But I didn't want to put her in jeopardy after everything she'd worked for. She's a leader in the brotherhood and an executive manager at V Corp, and it took her so much struggle to be the only powerful woman in the midst of wolves.

And now, if I say or do something wrong, I'll hurt the only people who ever cared for me.

The only family I've ever had.

"Let her stay at Weaver & Shaw."

Kirill's and my attention snaps to Adrian, who finally looks up from the laptop, then slowly closes it and places it on the table.

"What the fuck are you talking about, Adrian? Let her stay? The *Pakhan*'s only daughter can't be left alone at some law firm."

"We need to win Matt's lawsuits since we use his production company to launder money. Weaver & Shaw is representing his daughter and are digging their noses where they shouldn't. As a member of the brotherhood, the *Pakhan*'s daughter will play her role and become our eyes and ears there. It shouldn't be hard with the tech department access and your *interesting* set of skills. Right, Anastasia?"

A full-body shudder takes hold of me. *Interesting set of skills.* He knows. Even though my spare laptop doesn't have anything incriminating on it, Adrian somehow figured out about the hacking.

Does that mean he knows about the stolen funds?

Kirill narrows his eyes at me, then at Adrian as if he's figured out that something is amiss. He always does. He's like a dog who can smell anything fishy from a mile away.

But instead of being obvious about it, he lets the subject go. "Though I don't like it, we do need to win the whole Matt thing. Do as you're told and I'll pretend I didn't see you."

I'm about to say no, but Adrian meets my gaze again and I clamp my lips shut.

He stands up in one swift motion. He and Kirill are so large that they dwarf my small apartment, stealing all the air.

"Sasha will keep an eye on you to make sure nothing goes awry." Kirill smiles, but there's no warmth behind it. "And when the case is over, I'll personally take you back, little princess."

And with that, he leaves, his guard following after.

I expect Adrian to join them, but he leans close and speaks in a low tone, "We'll play this my way, Anastasia. You don't contact Sergei, Vladimir, or Rai. You continue the charade and live as Jane until I allow you to come back. If you don't, the brotherhood will know you stole hundreds of thousands of dollars and everyone will be out not only for your head, but also for Sergei's, Vladimir's, and Rai's because they helped cover up the theft for you."

A lone tear slides down my cheek and hangs on to my chin. "They…didn't do anything."

"They lied and that, too, is considered a betrayal."

"Why…why don't you reveal it now?"

"Because I can use you."

"Against my father?"

"You allowed yourself to be used, so don't act victimized. I also need to know where that money went since you're obviously not using it."

So he doesn't know about *Babushka*.

Yet.

Because I have no doubt that if he puts his mind to it, he'll eventually figure it out.

"What if I don't help you? What if I don't want to interfere in the Matt Bell case?"

"Whether you help or not doesn't really matter. We'll win either way. Whether or not we'll use violence is what you should worry about." He pauses. "You don't want your boyfriend to accidentally lose his head, do you?"

I'm flat out shaking, cold sweat covering my temples because I know, I just know that Adrian doesn't make idle threats.

That he doesn't target anyone just because.

That he didn't haphazardly pick Knox without a reason.

"What…did he do?"

"Put his nose where it doesn't belong. If you want him safe, make him lose or drop the case. Either would work."

"He won't listen to me. We're just casual, so neither of us is important to the other." I lie through my teeth.

"I'll be the one who decides that. Play your part and be smart about it, Anastasia. If you do, I might let you come back without shedding any blood."

TWENTY-SIX

Knox

An ominous feeling has been metaphorically crushing my windpipe for the past hour.

So I called my family. Teal, Dad, my foster sister, Elsa, and even that grumpy fucker Agnus, Dad's husband, who raised me and my twin sister.

Everyone seemed safe.

Unless they lied to me?

I have a weird sense of intuition. I always have, ever since I realized that it's possibly the only thing that's able to save me.

That aside from myself, no one will stand up for me, no one will give me what was taken. So I had to rely on my sixth sense more often than not, and it's that intuition that saved my arse more times than I can count. It's what made me escape with my skin unscathed.

So I don't ignore it.

Ever.

I think about calling Dan to make sure he's all right, but fuck that wanker. I'm still contemplating the best way to get back at him for what he insinuated today.

My blood boils just thinking about him near Anastasia. If he so much as touches a hair on her head, I might as well quit being a lawyer and become a criminal.

So, no, I won't complain if he meets his maker sooner rather than later.

Besides, he's definitely not the reason behind the clenching and unclenching of my chest or the fucking twist in my heart.

I refuse to think about why I'm here, in front of Anastasia's flat, when I'm supposed to be in a meeting, but I am.

Here.

And the feelings are escalating to dangerous heights.

There's no way in fuck I could concentrate in that meeting when my ribcage was about to burst open. Aside from my family, there's only one other person who could be the cause of this reaction.

I use the spare key she gave me a while back and open the door slowly. For some reason, it feels as if I shouldn't make any sudden movements.

The lock is a bit crooked and I pause at that, but only for a second, before I step inside.

The flat is dark, silent, which is different from usual, or at least, ever since I started coming here on a regular basis. On normal nights, Anastasia would either be singing along to her favorite old songs in a low voice, or she'd be silently listening to them while typing away on her laptop. Either way, the music would be blasting.

None of those scenarios are present. There's no music or typing sounds that I'm starting to only associate with her.

The defective silence slowly gives way to something more frantic and ominous. As if someone is rummaging through things.

Sure enough, when I stride to the closet, I find her shoving clothes into a bag, her face flushed and her movements sporadic.

I hit the light switch. "What are you doing?"

Anastasia jumps, her wild eyes meeting mine. She's not

wearing the glasses tonight and she appears so young and fragile, like a rose that can be broken with a single touch.

Her chest rises and falls with heavy breaths that she doesn't seem to be able to control.

"Knox."

My name is a haunted whisper on her lips, a sound that she doesn't seem to be able to control.

She clears her throat. "Shouldn't you be in a meeting?"

"It's over." *Lie.* I left early, feigning an emergency, and from what I'm seeing, I'm glad I did. "Where are you going?"

She swallows a few consecutive times, her blunt nails digging into the strap of the bag. "Away."

"Away where?"

"Just away. I'm leaving."

The dooming feeling from earlier crashes against my ribcage and a blind sense of anger spreads throughout my bloodstream. "Like fuck you are."

"You can't tell me what to do."

"Well, I am. And you're not going anywhere, Anastasia."

"This whole thing was only meant to be temporary."

"This whole thing?"

She throws her hands in the air. "The sex, the arrangement, me being here. All of it. I was never meant to stay."

"Well, I'm telling you that you *will* stay, whether you like it or not."

Moisture gathers in her lower lids. "You…don't understand."

"I do, perfectly. You're running away again, just like you ran from your previous life, because that's what you do best, right? Leaving. Running. All the fucking time."

She releases the bag, letting it fall to the ground, and barges in front of me. "You don't have the right to stand there and judge me when you have no clue about my life."

"And whose fault is that? You're the one who's hiding on top of running."

"That's none of your business."

"I'm making it my business, my little liar. Did you really think I'd stand by and let you run as if I never happened?"

"You should."

"Think again, beautiful. Do you know me to be the type who gives up? Ever?"

Her shoulders hunch as she comes to the same conclusion herself. We might have been together for only a few weeks, but she knows me better than anyone else.

She knows I wouldn't let it go.

"Why don't you tell me what's going on instead of choosing the running route?"

"I can't." She sounds so pained, so defeated, as if the weight of the world has settled on her slender shoulders.

So I soften my voice, "Does it have something to do with your family?"

"You don't need to know."

"So it does." I pause. "Is that why the lock was messed up. Was someone here?"

She stiffens. "N-no."

"You're such a bad fucking liar. Who was here?"

"No one."

My hand shoots out and wraps around her throat. It's so I can attach myself to her, to keep myself from letting my anger loose, because that motherfucker is on the verge of burning everything in its path as we speak.

Her eyes snap to mine and even though they're brown and fake, the emotions behind them aren't. There's a multitude of them, rising and falling in the favor of others. I don't recognize them all, but I recognize the most prominent one—fear.

Not of me—or at least, I hope not.

But it's there and it's eating at something inside her.

And inside me.

I never thought I would ever be attuned to another human being other than my twin sister. Never thought I'd feel her emotions before she's even aware of them herself.

But at this moment, right here, I know, I just know that I would do anything to make these emotions go away.

"Anastasia, I'm on your side here, so don't make me force you to speak. Who was here?"

"No…one…" It's a whisper now, a haunted one at that.

My hold tightens on her, the pads of my fingers digging into the sensitive flesh of her pale throat. When I speak, it's in a low warning tone. "Anastasia…"

"Just leave me alone, Knox." A tear slides down her cheek. "Let me go."

"No."

"Why? Just why the hell do you keep holding on to me?"

"Because I'm not done with you." And I probably never will be. But I don't voice that thought aloud in case it would freak the hell out of her as fast as it's growing roots inside me.

"What if I'm done with you?"

"You'll have to mean that first, and even if you are, I'll win you over again."

"Even if I hurt you?"

"Even if you hurt me."

"You're not supposed to say that." Her tears soak her cheeks unchecked.

"Then what am I supposed to say?"

"That you won't let me or anyone hurt you."

"I won't."

She swallows. "Promise."

"I promise. I also promise that no one will hurt you under my watch."

Her lips part, then she swallows thickly. "I never asked for your protection."

"You'll get it anyway." I release her throat. "Now, continue packing, because you're coming with me."

"W-what?"

"I'm not leaving you in a place someone broke into, Anastasia. You'll be safer with me."

"But…"

"No buts. This is not up for negotiation."

"You…don't have to do this for me."

"Who said it's only for you? I get to fuck you anytime I like, so I have advantages as well."

She smiles a little through the tears, even though it's sad, even though the fear isn't completely gone. But I'll make sure to make it go away if it's the last thing I do.

Because Anastasia is mine and I protect what's mine.

TWENTY-SEVEN

Anastasia

W HEN KNOX SAID I WAS COMING WITH HIM, I KNEW HE'D
take me to his apartment. He's often suggested that I pay
him a visit, but I always change the subject.

Why?

Because it's too close, too intimate, and I won't be able to keep
the distance I've been fruitlessly trying to maintain between us.

And now, it's worse.

It's dangerous.

Fatal.

For his life, not mine. Despite everything, I'm still the *Pakhan*'s
daughter, I'm still of value one way or another.

I'm one of them. The mafia men I often called pirates because
once they came into my life, my childhood fantasy of being the
forest fairy ended.

Knox is an outsider, an antagonizing one at that, and Adrian
wouldn't hesitate to eliminate him from his path. He'd erase him

from the world as if he never existed. He wouldn't be fast and swift about it either; he'd torture him first, until he wishes for death.

The images that play in my mind make me sick to my stomach and I have to place a hand on it to stop myself from vomiting.

But no matter how much I begged Knox to let me stay in my apartment, it didn't make a difference. He merely threw me over his shoulder, took my bag and laptop case, then carried me to his car.

The drive to his apartment was mostly me arguing that I'm fine, and him ignoring me. I'm starting to learn that the moment he makes a decision, no one will be able to convince him otherwise.

Then, the second we stepped into his apartment, he grabbed me by the throat and fucked me against the door from behind. It was fast and dirty and I still haven't been able to catch my breath.

Even now, as I lie on the sofa, I'm still dizzy, a bit disoriented. Which happens all the time after sex with Knox.

He has a mysterious ability to wipe my mind clean. It's like we're transported to an alternate reality where only he and I exist.

But I shouldn't let that happen.

Not when Aleksander is probably watching me and could interfere any second and smash every ounce of happiness I'm feeling or trying to soak up.

But I'll leave soon. One day, I'll have to.

However, that day isn't today.

Since I didn't have the chance to check out his place earlier due to obvious reasons, I do that now.

My gaze flits around the glamorous apartment—sorry, *penthouse*. Of course someone like Knox would live in a penthouse. Not only is it on the highest floor of a building in the heart of the city, but it also has a dreamy view of New York.

The furniture and decor are classy and elegant, but they scream impersonal. As if he just paid someone to put things in place to get it over with.

It must be lonely to live such a glamorous life with no personal touches. I'm one to talk, considering my whole life has been dictated.

At least Knox has complete hold of his.

"Are you cold?" he asks from his position on the chair, looking up at me as his fingers pause on his laptop.

He still has work to do, but he told me not to move or put on anything—after he stripped me bare at the entrance while he remained fully clothed, as usual.

I can actually count the number of times I've seen him fully naked on one hand, and that was mostly in the shower. He has a lean but very muscled body, and it's a shame to hide it and those gorgeous tattoos.

He told me to lie naked on the sofa opposite him and not make a sound while he works.

"I'll be done with this in ten minutes, then I'm coming for round two," is what he said.

I shift and bite my lower lip when I feel his cum pouring out of me and messing up my thighs. "Not too cold."

He unbuttons his shirt and my eyes take in the perfection of his muscled chest and cut abdomen, then I focus on the samurai tattoo, the dark warrior that's fascinated me since that first time I woke up beside him.

It's like I'm staring at another facet of Knox, a part that he doesn't like to show often.

Or ever.

The intricate design swirls around his shoulder and over his chest, and it's like there are wires wrapped around him and the warrior.

I wonder if that has a meaning or if he just did it for the aesthetics. For some reason, I don't believe he'd get that tattoo just because it looks good.

"When did you get your tattoos?" I ask, laying my head on my propped hand.

He continues unbuttoning his shirt. "Some in secondary school, but the bigger ones were after I left London or I would've risked being murdered by my dad."

I smile a little at his tone. He always sounds so different and carefree whenever he speaks about his family—which can't be said about me. "Is there a reason you chose a samurai?"

"I wanted something that represents strength, and from the sketches the artist made, I liked this the most. Probably because of the black eyes, though. They hinted at hidden darkness."

"How about the wires?"

"No matter how strong one is, there's always something that holds them back." A distant look covers his eyes—pain, or memories sprinkled with pain.

I want to ask more, to learn about what possibly could hold someone like him back, but I don't have the chance before he throws the shirt my way.

"Does this mean I can go to sleep?" I tease.

"Fuck no. I'll be with you in a minute."

"I thought I had to be naked for that."

"You do, but I don't want you cold either, so you can wear that."

I smile, putting on the shirt that swallows me and falls to the middle of my thighs. I have to roll the sleeves up to reveal my hands.

When I look up again, Knox's eyes have darkened as they watch me with intense focus. His fingers still hover over the keyboard without typing and his jaw is clenched tight.

I sit up in case I've done something wrong, and that makes more cum coat my thighs because he totally didn't let me wash up. "W-what?"

"From now on, you'll either be naked or wear my shirt. No in-between." There's a raw possessiveness in his tone, a non-negotiable quality that robs me of breath.

"I can't just wear your shirt all day."

"No, but you can be naked."

"Indoors."

"For now."

"For now?"

"I'll find an outdoor place where you can be naked for me and only me."

"Pervert."

He stands up, and even though it's not too abrupt, my heart lunges to my throat and I can't help rubbing my thighs together.

It's so rare to see him in his half-naked glory. His tattoos aren't for show like they are for many people. Even the leaders of the *Bratva* consider it an honor to showcase their tattoos and explain what each one means, especially if it's related to the brotherhood.

That's not the case for Knox.

They seem to exist only for him.

He hovers over me, looking larger than life, but that doesn't last too long when his body slowly lowers to mine.

My palms flatten on his shoulders and I suck in a sharp breath at how good he feels, shirtless, just for me.

Showing his tattoos only to me.

I never thought such a trivial thing would make me so elated, so ethereal.

"Aren't you supposed to be working?" I ask in a low voice, stroking my fingers on his skin like a junkie who's toying with a drug before inhaling it.

"Not when you're distracting as bloody hell." He reaches a hand between my legs and a deep grunt leaves him when his fingers are coated with both our arousal. "Fuck, beautiful. Mmm. This might be my new favorite thing."

Before I can ask what that is, he gathers his cum with two fingers and thrusts inside me. A moan rips out of me, though it shouldn't.

I shouldn't be feeling this turned on by the act of him smearing his seed inside me, but I am and the guttural sounds that leave me are foreign to my ears.

He does it leisurely, fucking his fingers inside me with purpose.

"You look fucking beautiful with my cum in this tight cunt."

"Please…"

"You want more?"

My nod is barely intelligible, but he catches it and he's about to flip me to my stomach. This is what he does when he fucks me, always from behind.

I'm used to it after all this time, but I don't want that now. I don't want the distance.

I want him to show me the rest of him as he did with his tattoos.

I want him. Period.

So I dig my short nails into his skin, holding on to a hope I shouldn't be having.

I'm hoping and buzzing with wishes that have no place in whatever relationship we have.

His hand finds my hip, which is his cue to turn me onto my stomach. My nails dig into his skin and I slowly shake my head.

The thrusting of his fingers slows until it's an agonizing ache that's torturous. But his features darken, his eyes turning a molten hazel that's the weirdest I've seen.

His hold on my hip is as tight as his face, urging me to release him, but I don't.

I can't.

I don't want to.

"Let go." It's two words. Two single words, but they sound non-negotiable and harsh.

When I don't, he effortlessly removes my fingers from his shoulder, then easily flips me over. My breasts flatten against the sofa and my body heats so fast that it feels like I've been set on fire while being doused in gasoline.

Strange energy rushes through me, demanding I kick and fight, that I hit and claw.

Something. *Anything.* As long as I'm not in this position, beneath him, where he doesn't want to look at me.

I think I must've moved, because when he gets behind me, he feels stiff, hard almost, as if he's seeing my inner turmoil.

"What the fuck is wrong with you?" His tone is clipped, which is the tone he only uses when he's mad.

And he shouldn't be right now.

Like I shouldn't be having these weird feelings.

"I don't like it," I whisper, burying my face in the pillow.

"You don't like what?"

"This." There's a brokenness in my voice, and I wish it was because of Kirill and Adrian finding me. I wish it had something to do with them or my double life, but it doesn't.

Because ever since I stepped into Knox's apartment, I haven't thought about that or them.

I've only ever thought about him.

The man who's now pushing off of me. The absence of his weight and his touch make me feel empty, desolate even.

Slowly, too slowly, I turn my head to the side and catch a glimpse of him standing there like a god. His hands are crossed over his muscled chest and he's narrowing his eyes at me.

"What's the problem?" His question is calm, but the tone isn't.

There's so much tension there, so much punch behind his words that it tightens my throat.

"I just..."

"What? You're just what?"

"I want to have sex while I look at you."

"And I want to see your eyes, your *real* eyes, but neither of us is getting what we want."

"Why are you so obsessed with seeing my real eyes?"

"Because I'd see the real you behind them. Not the Anastasia from that night or the Jane you became. Just you."

My lips part and a flash of emotions attack my belly in need of a release.

So I stand up, bent on going to him, on kissing him, on telling him that if he wants to see my eyes, he can.

He's the only one who can.

Because unlike everyone else who knows me, he wouldn't see me as Anastasia Sokolov, the only daughter of Sergei Sokolov, the *Pakhan* of the New York *Bratva*.

He wouldn't see me as a sheltered princess to be protected

or used. He would just see me. The Anastasia who escaped her jail to be free, to live.

To be alive.

But my impulsive moment is put to a halt when the doorbell rings.

It sounds like an alarm in the stilled silence and I flinch.

Knox, however, seems more annoyed than surprised. "I'll go get rid of whoever is there and then I'm coming back to see this to the end. Don't fucking move."

I wouldn't even if he hadn't ordered me, because I'm watching his strong back as he marches to the door.

My toes curl and I'm not sure if it's because of him or what he said. I like how he never lets misunderstandings stand between us, that he's always looking forward.

Never backward.

Never sideways.

Always ahead.

And I think it's rubbing off on me, because I want to be that way, too—a forward-looking person who doesn't let the past shackle them down.

But I have to talk about it first with him, no?

I have to strip myself bare and actually let him see a part of me that even I'm scared about showing to anyone.

"Good evening, punk." An older male voice says from the door in a very distinctive, proper British accent.

Before I can wonder who it is, Knox's next word answers my unasked question. "Dad?"

TWENTY-EIGHT

Anastasia

DID HE JUST SAY "DAD"?

My heart thumps against my ribcage and my throat is drying with each passing second. I quickly button my shirt—Knox's shirt—and I'm grateful it's big enough to cover my nakedness.

Before I can run to hide into the bedroom or even the kitchen, Knox reappears in the living room accompanied by a much older man who's probably in his early fifties. He's wearing a sharp three-piece suit and has light blond stubble covering his jaw.

Two women are on either side of him, both are shorter than him and look nothing alike. One is slim, blonde, and tall like my cousin, Rai, and the other is petite, wears her black hair short, and has tiny features.

Knox's twin sister.

I don't even have to guess. Although her eyes are a darker brown and she's way shorter than him, the look in her eyes is similar to his.

A little bit haunted.

A little bit odd.

And just…deep.

It's as if they've both seen the world and didn't like it, but they won't give it the satisfaction of leaving. They both have this determination of "I'm here to stay."

And as much as that fascinates me, I don't have the luxury of feeling it right now, because I'm half-naked. In front of who I assume are Knox's dad and sisters.

Assume, as in, I stalked them on social media when I first came to W&S and met Knox again.

What? I had to look out for myself.

Is it too late to actually disappear? Because I feel like I'm about to catch fire from the way three pairs of eyes are watching me intently.

"Did we come at a bad time?" his father asks with a slight smirk.

"Who are you?" the blonde asks with more amusement than judgment.

I rub my foot against the back of my calf. "I…uh…"

"No one you should worry about." Knox strides to my side and even though he's not touching me, his presence brings much-needed comfort.

"Nonsense," his father says with the same tilt of his mouth. "My name is Ethan Steel. I'm Knox's father. This is Teal, his twin sister, and this one is Elsa, his other sister. What's your name?"

"J-Jane."

I bite my lip after the stutter. Why the hell did I want to say "Anastasia" just now? It doesn't make sense when I should be keeping my other identity completely under wraps.

"Nice to meet you, Jane." Elsa leaves her father's side and takes my hand in a handshake. "I can't wait to hear all about you."

"Or…" Knox stands between us and tactfully pushes her back. "You can take the next plane back to London. Take Dad and T with you while you're at it."

"Not going to happen. We didn't come all this way just to leave. Right, Teal?"

Knox's twin sister nods. "Yes. After all, I'm here because I was wondering what's making you so different lately."

"T!"

"What? You wouldn't tell me."

"There's nothing to tell."

"Obviously, there is." Elsa smiles with clear mischief. "I'm so glad we decided to tag along on Dad's business trip."

"Well, I'm not. So the three of you can leave."

"No," Teal announces point-blank.

Elsa hugs her by the shoulder. "What she said."

"I'm calling your husbands." He reaches into his pocket and retrieves his phone and then he puts it on speakerphone as it rings.

I fidget when I read the caller ID—Aiden.

He picks up with a deep, bored, "Hey, fucker."

"Hello to you, too, arsehole. In case you didn't know, Elsa is here, in New York. I don't see you anywhere near her, which, if I remember correctly, hasn't happened in the past thousand years."

"So?"

Knox pauses, then shakes the phone as if he can physically shake the person on the other end. "Hello? Is this Aiden King's phone? Who are you and what the bloody hell did you do to the crazy fucker?"

"Shut the fuck up and take care of Elsa for these couple of days." There's a tinge of annoyance in Aiden's deep voice. He sounds a bit murderous, too.

I only heard him on the phone, but that's enough to send a shiver down my spine. I can't imagine what it's like to meet him in real life.

My gaze flits to Elsa, who seems nonchalant. She's gorgeous and appears laid back—which can't be said about her husband. And I find myself wondering how they're even together.

Knox's grip tightens on the phone and that brings my

attention back to him. "Or you can come here yourself and pick her up or something? Send your plane over."

"Not until the forty-eight hours are over."

"Are you sure you didn't hit your head? Because there's no way in fuck you'd let her be away from you for this long."

Aiden pauses before he says, "I was promised things."

Elsa smiles, then whispers, "Plural."

Aiden, who seemingly didn't know he was on speakerphone, releases a breath, then lowers his voice until it takes an edge. "Fucking plural, sweetheart."

"I can't believe you let her manipulate you, King," Knox taunts. "You've lost your touch."

"Fuck you. If she comes back with one hair on her head hurt, consider yourself dead, Van Doren."

And with that, he hangs up.

Knox curses, then narrows his eyes on Elsa. "What did you promise that crazy fuck so that he'd let you out of his sight."

"It's our secret." She winks.

"Eww. Disgusting. But this isn't over." He directs his phone at them as if it's a weapon, then dials another number. This time, I see the name "Ronan" on his screen.

As soon as he answers, Knox says, "Come pick up your wife, Ron. She's an unwanted guest in my flat."

"On my way," he says with cheerfulness.

"Don't you dare, Ronan," Teal says.

"But he said you're an unwanted guest, *ma belle*. I have to come there and beat him the fuck up for calling you that."

"You promised," she enunciates.

"Fine, whatever." He sounds dejected. "Remi and I miss you."

"Miss you, Mummy." A tiny voice comes through the phone.

"Miss you, too, hon." She smiles for the first time since she got here. "Mummy is going to stay with Uncle Knox for a few days, then I'll come back, okay?"

"Okay! Me and Daddy will wait."

"That's a good boy."

"Ron." Knox grits his teeth, his words sounding clipped. "Say or do something."

"My hands are tied, Van Doren. I lost a fucking bet, so I don't have a say in this."

"Why do I have to suffer the downfall?"

"Don't call my Teal and Ellie downfall or I'll fuck up your face, mkay?"

By the end of the call, Knox is breathing heavily, Teal and Elsa are smiling, and Ethan is obviously amused.

I'm about to dig my own grave for feeling so out of place.

They're a family, and I'm just an outsider. Someone who shouldn't even exist in the midst of what seems to be their usual form of interaction.

But when I try to think of an excuse to disappear from their immediate vicinity, Elsa grabs me by the shoulder. "Teal and I need to talk to Jane. Dad, can you and Knox cook us something?"

"Why the hell would I cook?" Knox narrows his eyes on where Elsa is holding me. "And what are you going to talk to her about?"

"You don't need to know." She pulls me with her to the bedroom and Teal closes the door, despite protests from the other side.

When Elsa sits me on the bed, my skin tingles and I clasp my hands together so tightly, it hurts. But not as much as the unknown or the situation I'm in.

I was never a people person, *ever*. Being sheltered my whole life and witnessing countless assassination attempts on my father and the leaders of the *Bratva* made me careful about each step I took. Each breath I inhaled and every word I uttered.

It's not merely a personality trait, it's how I learned to survive. It's how the *Pakhan*'s daughter is supposed to be. Silent, demure, and follows orders.

A beautiful bird in a gilded cage.

Even though I thought I escaped it, maybe I was only upgraded to a bigger one where I supposedly have freedom, but it could be snatched away at any second.

However, this situation, being in the company of two women

I've never met, who also happen to be Knox's sisters, isn't something I thought I would find myself experiencing.

I grew up surrounded by men, lots of them, and they were harsh and unyielding. The only prominent female presence I had with me was my cousin, Rai, who's as hard as they are.

So I really, really, have no clue how to act, aside from letting a panic attack take hold of me and make a fool out of myself.

And that's just absurd. They're not scary…I don't think. Because while Elsa is sitting beside me wearing a soft smile and still watching me with a gleam of curiosity, Teal is standing right across from me, slowly tapping her foot on the floor.

"Why are you with my brother? Do you like him?" she asks out of the blue, no introductions whatsoever.

"I…I'm…" How the hell am I supposed to answer that question when my brain hasn't even accepted their presence?

Elsa touches my shoulder as if to bring my attention to her. "What she meant to say is, we haven't seen Knox with the same girl for more than a couple of days since…well, ever. So imagine our surprise when she overheard Daniel's phone call with Ronan, in which he said that Knox wouldn't even let him touch you."

"You know Daniel?" I ask, almost whispering.

"Of course. We've belonged to the same group of friends since secondary school. Which is more important now since we can bribe him for information about Knox. That brother of ours tends to be a tad bit too secretive and we always worry about him."

"You don't have to. He's doing really well for someone his age."

"Work-wise, you mean," Teal says.

"Uh…yeah."

"Come on, Teal. It's not only related to work. He has Jane, too, now, right?"

"I don't think…that's the case…" I try to argue. How do I explain that our arrangement is purely sexual when I don't want to believe that anymore?

"She's hiding something," Teal cuts me off in her no-nonsense tone. I think she normally sounds like Knox when he doesn't bother to wear a mask. "I don't like it."

"We all hide secrets, Teal," Elsa says in a smooth voice.

"Not like her." Her dark eyes fixate on me. "You're dangerous."

I gulp. Did she figure all that out by just looking at me?

"Stop being paranoid. Besides, weren't you the one who was wishing Knox would settle down so you wouldn't have to worry about him all the time?"

Teal clears her throat. "I didn't say that."

"Not those exact words, but you definitely did." Elsa smiles at me. "I like Jane."

You shouldn't, I want to say.

You really, really, really shouldn't.

Because Teal is right. I am dangerous. So freaking dangerous, I might end up hurting Knox myself.

And when I do, I'm going to hurt these women, too.

The sisters who worry about their brother, who want to see him do well, who come on an impromptu visit because they suspect something is wrong.

I don't deserve Elsa's trust.

I don't even deserve Knox's care.

Because I know, I just know that I'll shatter both to pieces.

I'll hurt them.

That's what happens to people in my vicinity. They get hurt. Badly.

Most of the time, they die.

Like my mom.

TWENTY-NINE

Knox

"**I**'M NOT DOING THIS."

I throw away the vegetables I'm supposed to be preparing, but Dad catches them before they reach the sink, then pushes them against my chest. "Keep cutting if you want to eat tonight."

"We can just order something." I'm in in no mood to cook, because not only was I ambushed by my family out of nowhere, but Elsa and Teal have been with Anastasia for exactly twenty-three minutes and fifty-four seconds, talking about fuck knows what.

Maybe my twin sister is bringing up the psycho side of both of us and telling her what an absolute arse I am.

Maybe they're hurting her.

A strong hand clutches me by the shoulder, swinging my attention to the present. "Relax, it's going fine."

He's smiling and has the audacity to be all relaxed. Though this is in fact his usual mood.

Ethan Steel might own a large corporation, but he doesn't show his business beast side in front of us.

I don't remember the last time I saw him mad, and when he is, it's usually because of his children—us.

"You don't have the right to say that when you brought them here without telling me. This is a low blow and I'm officially not giving you a present on Dad's day."

"First of all, I can't take sides with you. That's a sure way to start a war. Second of all, if I don't get my present, I'll just bring them both back here again."

I narrow my eyes and he narrows his back. "Now, chop-chop. No takeaways."

Sighing, I grab the potato and start chopping. I can't help glaring at him now and again. Despite being in his mid-fifties, Dad looks way younger than that. His hair is still a dark blond with barely any white strands and his eyes are a deep blue, which is the only thing he passed down to Elsa—his biological daughter.

The look in his gaze is wise and collected, as if he's seen the whole world and nothing could perturb him anymore.

He comes from money—old, powerful, and influential. However, he didn't only use what he inherited to get where he is today. He invested it and started countless business ventures that made him tenfold richer and more untouchable than his father ever was.

But when we were growing up, he didn't allow us to be spoiled by that money, never let us use it as a blanket excuse for our actions or a crutch we could fall back on when things didn't work out.

We have one motto in our family—everyone is responsible for their own actions.

Even Dad himself.

Sometimes, it feels as if he brought together people who could never fit in the same puzzle, and yet, we somehow do.

We're somehow the most cohesive family I know.

Despite our dark and bloody past.

"Since you've brought the whole of London, why didn't you finish the job and invite Agnus so he could cook?"

"He came with us, but he chose to finish some pending work at the hotel." He smiles at the mention of his childhood friend/right-hand man-turned-husband. "And he's Dad to you."

"No way in fuck will I call him Dad after I've known him as Agnus all my life."

"Teal does that just fine. Or you could call him Papa, like Elsa does."

"Eww, no way in fuck. And Elsa does that just to egg him on. She still doesn't like him, in case you didn't notice."

"She'll get there."

"Those are empty dreams and you know it, Dad."

A dark look covers his features and I realize I fucked up by reminding him of facts he doesn't like to think about. My father's personal life has always been a mess of epic proportions. His first wife, Elsa's mother, was a psycho who captured me and Teal after we ran away from our mother, because she wanted us to look like her lost son.

As if that wasn't enough, he was shot by her and spent nine years in a coma, during which time, Agnus took care of us. And when he woke up, it was like he'd become a different person. When we were young, he used to be more outgoing, but after sleeping for almost a decade, he changed.

The only person who stood with him through it all was Agnus. That man can be mistaken for a mute and Elsa calls him a psycho to his face, and honestly, he does have antisocial tendencies, but I knew early on how much he cared for Dad.

In fact, he only took care of us in his absence for Dad's sake.

What surprised me, however, was when Dad invited the three of us to a family dinner and announced that he and Agnus were in a relationship.

While I always assumed Agnus was fluid orientation-wise, Dad is the straightest person I know. And he still is, I guess.

He once told me that Agnus is the only man he's attracted to. It's not about his gender, it's about *him*.

So for the first time in his life, he has stability with the one person who understands him the most. The fact that there's bad blood between his only biological daughter and his husband has always sat wrong with him.

And in hindsight, I shouldn't have brought their animosity up, so I redirect the convo to a topic Dad likes—praising his husband.

"By the way, I got the annual report of the portfolio Agnus handled for me, and the profit tripled."

A rare smirk tugs his lips. "He knows what he's doing."

"Obviously. I have more money than I can ever spend."

"You could start your own firm."

"Not yet. I need to get a few more years of experience first."

He fixes me with a glare.

I search my surroundings, then focus back on him. "What?"

"Did you send Agnus a thank-you gift for tripling your profit?"

"He doesn't like those." I resist the urge to mention that Agnus is a bit antisocial.

Okay, a lot. I'm a million percent sure that he would've become a serial killer if he hadn't met Dad early on in their childhood.

"Send it."

"Fine. Is he coming over here later?"

"No, he'll spend the night at the hotel."

"Why?"

"I told you, for work."

I squint. "Since when does Agnus choose work over being your shadow?"

"It's a special type of work. Drop it."

"Hmm."

Dad pauses mixing the soup and stares at me. "What?"

"I'm curious, is all."

"And I'm curious about your girl and the reasons why you didn't introduce her to us. Is it not serious with her?"

My spine snaps in a line at his swift way of changing the

subject and putting me in the limelight. I take a moment to think, then say in a low tone, "It's not that. It's…different."

"Different as in, you don't wrap it when you're with her?" A smile tilts his lips, amusement shining in his eyes.

"How did you…? I'm going to fucking kill Daniel."

"It was Ronan, actually. He animatedly told the story to approximately thirty people at a party. It was entertaining."

I close my eyes and take a deep breath. "Please tell me Teal and Elsa weren't there."

"They were the first in line."

"Fuck."

"It's due to that piece of information they decided to tag along." He continues mixing the ingredients slowly, taking his time with the task.

Dad has always been the type of person who doesn't rush into anything. Whether it's business or his personal life. He's steady, almost never provoked, to the point that it's creepy sometimes.

"Are you going to define "different," Knox?"

"I don't know how to explain it. I guess I feel more at peace when I'm with her, a little less perturbed, maybe. Just…not stuck in my head or with my shadows or in the past."

"Interesting."

"Do you think that's normal?"

"Depends on your reasons for feeling that way."

"What if I don't know those reasons?"

"You do. You just don't recognize them yet, which is to be expected considering you closed yourself off for decades."

"I…didn't close myself off."

"Yes, you did." His voice takes on a more soothing tone. "The first day I met you, you were this scrawny kid with protruding bones and marks all over your body. You were obviously hurt, hungry, thirsty, and scared. You were so scared, you shook with it, but even then, at eight years old, you pushed Teal behind you and came out first. Even though it seemed like your brain told you to run, you didn't. You stood there, head held high and eyes never looking sideways. It was as if you were giving the world the middle finger and telling it that you wouldn't run anymore, you wouldn't hide. You wouldn't be told what to do. From that point on, you'd fight. For yourself and your sister. You had a fire in your eyes, one that rose from the ashes of sealing your past. That fire is the reason I decided to raise you, Knox, but I always knew it hid a deeper layer, a layer you refuse to face, even as an adult."

My grip tightens on the knife and I take a deep breath to slow down the fucking pounding in my chest. "What do you want me to face, Dad? My whore mother who sold us out for some drugs or the father whose identity she didn't even know? They're both gone, and it's pointless to think about them."

He faces me, a dip appearing between his brows. "That's where you're wrong. They're may be gone, but the damage they left behind isn't."

"I'm fine, Dad. I'm a lawyer, the youngest partner in the firm, in fact, and bloody brilliant at what I do. I'm not a criminal or a lowlife or a manipulator. I. Am. Fine."

"That's what Teal said before she broke down."

I pause, letting the knife fall to the chopping board because I'm tempted to jam it against my own veins just to see blood.

That was one of the reoccurring thoughts I had as a teen, but I resisted, knowing it would make Dad and T sad. There was no way in fuck I would be the cause of misery for the people I cared about the most.

He meets my gaze, his voice lowering even further, as if he doesn't want to disturb my shadows. "Teal only got better when she faced it, Knox."

"I'm not her."

"No, you're not. You're worse. At least she recognizes something is wrong and doesn't go pretending everything is perfect. You need to start doing the same if you wish to keep that girl. No woman likes a man trapped with demons from his childhood."

Before I can say anything, the door to my bedroom opens and

my focus immediately shifts in that direction. Teal comes out first, alone, wearing her poker face, which is a typical expression of hers.

She really only laughs and smiles easily around her husband and son. Gone are the days when I was the only one she smiled at.

I might have hated Ronan a bit at first for taking her away, but I couldn't hold a grudge for long, considering how much he means to her.

How alive she is when he's around.

Elsa is arm in arm with Anastasia, who's now wearing a pair of my sweatpants, and although she's rolled them up her stomach, they're still skimming the ground.

Fuck. Seeing her in my clothes is a fucking turn-on.

Would I be yelled at and blacklisted from the next Christmas family gathering if I kicked everyone out so I could fuck her against the door?

I'd probably take that risk.

However, my master plan is put to a halt when I realize Anastasia's attention isn't on me.

She's focused on something Elsa is showing her on her phone and smiling. It's soft, demure, and appears genuinely happy.

"So that's your son?" she asks in that delicate voice of hers.

"Yeah, his name is Eli."

"He…doesn't look anything like you."

"I know." Elsa furrows her brow, appearing dejected. "He's taking after his father and grandfather, but I'm holding on to a slight bit of hope that his personality will at least resemble mine."

"Don't hold out too much hope, princess." Dad interferes with his usual warmth, as if we weren't having a heavy as fuck conversation just now. "He's becoming a King more and more."

"Dad! You're supposed to be on my side. Don't you want your grandkid to take after you?"

"Well, I still have Remi and the dozen children Knox said he's planning to have."

Anastasia's eyes widen and her cheeks flush a deep shade of red while Elsa grins.

"I never said that." I try to be calm but fail.

"Really, now? I'm pretty sure I heard you say before how comfortable you feel around—" I place a hand to his mouth, cutting him off mid-sentence, and shake my head.

His eyes shine and Teal steps between us, staring us down, which is comical at best because we're tall and she's so small that it takes effort on her part. "What are you two hiding? Let me in."

"Nothing you need to worry about, T. And you might need to stop craning your neck before you sprain it. I don't want Ron on my case."

"Screw you." She elbows my side.

"Oh, you're fucked, T." I release Dad to grab her ticklish spot. She starts snorting and begging me to stop, but I don't.

It's how I used to cheer her up when she was down, which was most of the time, before she met her husband.

I catch Elsa telling Anastasia, "I'm the grown-up in all of this. Excuse the children's behavior."

"You're on, Ellie," I say, then Teal and I bring her into the midst of us. Even though she tries to fight it, she's helpless when we both attack her ticklish side.

"I'm sorry, Jane," Dad tells her with a smile. "My children aren't usually this immature."

She shakes her head, grinning, though her mannerisms are still reserved. "You have a beautiful family, Mr. Steel."

"Ethan is fine. After all, you're part of us now."

I expect Anastasia to be shy, maybe shocked, but her smile drops and she looks absolutely horrified.

As if a ghost from her past has appeared in front of her.

THIRTY

Anastasia

WHEN KIRILL SAID ALEKSANDER WOULD KEEP AN EYE ON me, I didn't think it would be close.

As in, across from the firm close. As in, he's in his car, watching me like a hawk while I walk through the front entrance with coffee.

Usually, Gwen gets the coffee, or Chris. Anyone but me basically, since I try to keep human contact as minimum as possible.

But today, both of them were busy and I had to go. I had to cross the distance to the coffee shop and pretend that I wasn't being shadowed by a scary man in a black suit.

It's been like this for a week. Ever since I was ambushed in my apartment by Kirill and Adrian and told that I had a role to play.

That no matter what I do, I'll never stop being the *Bratva*'s princess.

As promised, Adrian must've not told my father, or he would've sent his guards to fetch me.

Kirill kept his word about not leaving me unsupervised, which is why his right-hand man, Aleksander, has been following me around discretely. To people on the outside, it wouldn't be noticeable since he changes car models, plates, and even the color of his clothes.

He's a professional, after all.

Though this is a rare occasion where he's not acting like Kirill's shadow.

And because I'm attuned to him and to the danger he represents, I spotted him the first time Knox and I left his penthouse together.

I had to distract him from looking at the rearview mirror so he wouldn't realize we were being followed. The last thing I want is for him to clash with the other men from my life.

Especially after I met his family, a welcoming one with their distinctive sense of humor and mannerisms.

That night, they stayed over. We had dinner together and played board games. Ethan and Elsa told me all sorts of stories about Knox's teenage years and how competitive he was—still is. I listened with keen interest to every detail, every piece of information about a version of Knox I've never met.

No clue why I held on to every word, but it felt vital in a way. Like a memento I needed to keep close.

Or maybe I just care about Knox more than I want to admit.

Teal wasn't much of a willing participant in telling stories, but I loved the seamless relationship she has with her brother.

The way they understand each other without having to say a word.

Before they left the following morning, she stood there with her hands crossed over her chest and told me point-blank, "You better not hurt my brother."

That sentence stayed with me the most after their visit.

It's as if she knew that's exactly what would happen.

I don't blame her for disliking me. I actually respect her for looking out for her brother. That's what family does.

Unlike mine.

My gaze flits to Aleksander's car. Even though it has tinted windows, I can almost picture him staring back with that cold gaze of his that only ever softens around Kirill.

He must've figured out my relationship with Knox, and if Adrian's threat is any indication, they wouldn't hesitate to use him against me.

To hurt him because of me.

Because that's what they do in the brotherhood. They use people, break hearts, and crunch bones.

And I'm no exception.

If anything, I'm placed on a high pedestal for being the *Pakhan*'s daughter. It's a cruel twist of fate that my mom got pregnant after a short fling with my father—the number one man in the *Bratva*.

She married my stepfather afterward and I should've been a normal citizen. But that jerk was abusing her, both physically and emotionally, and although she tried to protect me, she knew she couldn't.

That's why she took me to the park that day. I won't forget it, ever. Not only because Mom was shaking, but also because she seemed relieved when a tall man with harsh features came.

And I remember how his shadow blocked the sun as he stood there, watching us. Or more like, watching me.

She told me he was my father and I grabbed onto her, thinking she'd leave me with him, but she didn't.

They just talked while I played hide-and-seek with one of the other tall men who came with him.

Before Mom and I left, Papa patted my hair. I remember having eyes so big, they nearly reached my hairline. My stepfather never did that, never treated me like more than a pest in his path.

One he kicked around whenever he saw fit.

Papa also gave me a piece of paper with his number on it and told me to call him if I needed anything.

In hindsight, I should never have done that.

It's why I got trapped in his world in the first place.

But it's not like I had any other option that night.

Now that I think about it, the moment I called him, crying on the phone, was when I sealed my fate.

That was when I became part of the *Bratva*.

My phone vibrates in my pocket, bringing me out of my reverie.

It's a text from an unknown number.

I don't see the lawyer losing any cases. On the contrary, he's coming on even stronger. Here's a little incentive for you.

My thumb shakes as I click on the attached video. It's taken from a parking garage's surveillance camera. The building in which Knox's apartment is. I recognize it from the yellow lines on the ground and the strong light.

It's dimmer in the video, though, as if someone cut off the power on purpose.

My heart hammers in my throat when Knox steps out of his car, carrying his briefcase and talking on the phone. He's wearing the black suit that I helped him put on yesterday. I clearly remember it because he decided to fuck me at the last second before we went to work and ordered me not to mess up our clothes.

This footage was taken when he got home last night, later than usual, since he had a long meeting with Lauren about Sandra's case.

At exactly that moment when he was getting home, I was trying to fix something for dinner. Elsa called me and I burned the pasta anyway, so I kept talking to her and ordered something.

It all seems normal until the angle shifts to following Knox from behind as he walks to the elevator.

I gasp, nearly spilling the coffee when I make out what's at the back of his head.

A red dot.

A sniper rifle's red dot.

And it's following him all the way to the elevator until the video ends.

I'm about to have an epic meltdown when another text comes through.

If you don't do as you're told, the next footage will show a bullet in his head.

My legs tremble, refusing to hold me upright, and it takes everything in me not to collapse in the middle of the street.

It's Adrian.

I knew his threats wouldn't be empty ones and I just got first-hand proof that he already has someone following Knox, and not just anyone. A sniper.

Moisture stings my eyes at the thought that he could've died in that instant while I was completely clueless.

It doesn't matter who I am or who my father is. When push comes to shove, I'm unable to do anything except for playing by the rules.

My focus falls on Aleksander's car across the street and I hide my phone, then quicken my pace to inside the building, my mind nearly exploding with a thousand thoughts.

If I suspected it before, then I'm sure about it now.

I'm a danger to Knox.

If I don't stay away from him, he'll sure as hell get killed.

My heart squeezes, then thumps loudly in a sporadic rhythm. The possibility of something happening to him churns the contents of my stomach until I feel like I'm going to throw up on the sidewalk.

I place a hand on my chest, trying to quench the nausea rising to my throat.

But it only gets worse.

I shouldn't have slept with him that day.

I shouldn't have been selfish and wished for something I'm not allowed to have.

What's more, I should've run as fast as I could the day I met him again. Just why the hell did I let it go so far?

Why did I allow him to become such a vital part of my life that I feel physically sick at the thought of parting from him?

"What is it?"

I jolt near the reception area and nearly spill the coffee. I realize I'm grasping the holder in a death-grip and my whole body is tight as I look over my shoulder.

To where I left Aleksander across the street.

I didn't even notice Knox approaching me. He's standing in front of me now, wearing a sharp gray suit and holding his leather briefcase.

Lauren and Chris are a few steps behind him. They're going to a hearing, I recall. Sandra's. I said I wouldn't be able to attend today, because I'm sure Adrian or Kirill will be there. Or worse, someone else.

And if I were to see any of them, I'd have a meltdown of epic proportions.

"Jane." There's a warning in his tone, a demand for me to answer his question.

On one hand, I'm thankful he respects my choice about my public persona and didn't call me Anastasia. But on the other hand, I'm starting to hate this name.

The fake one.

The *wrong* one.

"It's…nothing."

He grabs me by the elbow and pushes me to the hall, away from eavesdroppers.

Then he's towering over me, his height and presence blocking any outside interference and causing my stomach to tighten. I've always loved having him so close that I can't see anyone past him.

When did this position become my favorite?

He observes me for a second, his lethal eyes narrowing for a beat. "Are you going to tell me what's wrong?"

"There's really n—"

"Don't finish that lie." His features harden and a muscle works in his jaw. That's when I know that I won't like what he'll say next. "You think I haven't noticed your jumpy, shifty attitude since I caught you packing and ready to run? I've given you enough time to mull it over and I need an answer now."

My focus shifts sideways when someone passes us by. "This isn't the time or place. Don't you have a hearing?"

"I'm not moving from here until you give me something. Is it about the car that's been following you for the past week?"

I flinch, my back hitting the wall behind me. "W-what?"

"No amount of distraction on your part will scatter my focus from my surroundings, Anastasia. So tell me, is it about that? Are they people from your past?"

"Why are you so sure they were following me? Maybe they were following you."

"They didn't when I left the firm, but they just did when you went out to get coffee."

Shit.

It was wishful thinking to believe he wouldn't notice.

This is Knox, after all. He's so attuned to details, it's disturbing sometimes. But even he didn't notice Adrian's sniper. Instead of being in-your-face like Aleksander, Adrian and Kirill more discreet yet highly efficient.

If Adrian chooses to, he can kill him in a heartbeat.

My lips tremble at that and I force them shut because Knox is still looking at me, waiting for an answer.

I swallow, resisting the urge to put a hand on my chest, since he knows it's a nervous habit. "It's really nothing. I swear."

He jams his fist at the wall beside my head and I startle, even though the move isn't strong or surprising. I think it's the expression on his face that shoots tendrils of fear to the bottom of my stomach.

Knox isn't the type to get angry often or without a reason, but his jaw is clenching now and a muscle jumps in the veins of his neck.

His anger is raw, furious yet still calm. And I'm in the middle of it now. Worse, I think I'll be swept away by it.

"If you repeat the word "nothing" one more time, I swear to fuck..." he trails off, his nostrils flaring.

"Can't you just leave it alone?"

"No."

"Knox…"

"Why are you building a wall between us, Anastasia? Hmm?"

"I am?"

"I feel it, and it keeps getting taller with every passing second."

"Maybe that wall was supposed to be there from the beginning. It's safer. For both of us."

"You mean, for you."

All the anxiety and fear of the unknown rush to the surface, exploding in a myriad of red-hot temper. "Yes, for me! You have no idea who I am or what you've gotten yourself into. The day you do, you'll curse the moment you met me. I'm defective, okay? Do you know what I do to people? I destroy them."

"You can't destroy me, beautiful. That was done way before you came along, so how about you tell me what's haunting you?"

"How do you know something's haunting me?"

"I saw it that night. In your ocean blue eyes. They were a little bit haunted, a little bit broken. Just like me. Usually, I don't get close to people who give off vibes that resemble mine, but you were the exception, my little liar. You still are."

"You shouldn't have made me an exception." I sniffle. "I'm bad for you."

"And I'm bad for you, too. You don't see me asking you to leave because of that. In fact, I never will since I happen to be fucking selfish. When I covet something, I keep it. I don't throw it away and I certainly don't let it slip from my hands. So you're fucking stuck with me, Anastasia."

"What if I want to leave?"

"No, you don't. You're just running away because that's what you're good at, but you'll quit that fucking habit with me. Do you know why?"

"Why?"

"Because I'm keeping you. Whether you like it or not."

I see it then. The determination.

The stubborn determination and the raw possessiveness.

And something tells me it'll just get worse from here on. That he'll not only demand to know more, but he'll also keep me. Whether I like it or not, as he said.

If anything, the more I fight, the harder he'll chain me to him.

Because he's decided that he covets me. Wants me.

He won't allow me to run or escape or search for an alternative solution.

And I can't stay. Not if I want to keep Adrian and Kirill away from him.

The painful decision thuds against my ribcage with crushing reality, leaving me hollow.

My words are barely audible when I whisper, "I want to break up."

A muscle works in his jaw and his fist flexes on the wall. I think he'll move his hand, whether to choke or grab me, I don't know, but he doesn't. Instead, it remains there, as stonelike as his presence, as if he's pining for patience. "What the fuck did you just say?"

"I…want to end this. Whatever this is."

There's a manic light in his eyes that I've never seen before. "Hmm. I don't think you were listening, Anastasia, because I just told you that won't be happening."

"You can't tell me what to do. I'm breaking up with you." My heart bleeds with every word out of my mouth, but I'm so thankful for my calm tone and the false composure in it.

My brain realizes this is the only way to protect him. The only way I'll keep him out of the sniper's range.

If he's out of the picture, Adrian won't have anything to threaten me with.

This time, Knox's hand finds my throat, the hold is tight and unyielding, as if he's driving his words home. "You can break up with me all you want, but you're still fucking mine."

THIRTY-ONE

Knox

MY MOOD HAS BEEN SHIT SINCE YESTERDAY.

Since Anastasia said we were breaking up.

I haven't seen her—properly, at least—since that encounter in the firm's hallway. Not only did she leave work after dropping that bomb, but she's also ignored my calls.

I was a few seconds away from turning into a raging arsehole. Even though, per Dan's words, I already was one.

He invited me and Sebastian for dinner at one of the few restaurants he approves of. He's posh like that, a picky eater to a fault, and never eats out unless it's absolutely necessary.

I might have glared and glowered during that whole dinner until they'd finally had enough and kicked me out for ruining their meal.

When I went to her flat, Anastasia was already sleeping in a curled-up position on the sofa. I wanted to wake her and continue where we left off, but I couldn't when I saw that delicate frown on her face.

This morning, she got up earlier than me and went to work.

With all the prep I've had to do with Sandra, I haven't been able to go find her. And when I finally got the chance during a small break, she wasn't in the IT department. Chris mentioned she was out with Gwen.

So I shot her a text.

Me: Meet me after work or I swear to fucking God, this will get real ugly, real fast. You don't want to get on my nerves any more than you already have, my little liar.

She didn't answer.

Not that I expected her to.

Which means she's taking the difficult road. A stupid mistake that she'll pay for once I'm finished with court today.

That's where I am right now, in court, barely holding on to my patience, because although I prepped Sandra, she's on the verge of breaking down again.

Pearce didn't even bring out the big guns yet, but a simple look at her father and she starts shaking all over.

"If you keep giving that reaction, it'll only play in his favor," I whisper to her. "You're not here to win his case for him, you're here to make him pay. Are we clear?"

She nods, sniffles, then slowly regains her composure after exchanging looks with Lauren. My associate lawyer is definitely better at the sentimental stuff than I am.

Anastasia is, too, but she chose not to be present today, and it's fucking with my head more than I'd like to admit. Maybe, like me, Sandra is used to her silent support and gentle touches and fucking natural softness. Maybe like me, she feels like she's losing her footing and will be stumbling into nowhere.

I internally shake my head to focus on Pearce, who was questioning Matt's wife, and Sandra's stepmother, who's been basically calling her stepdaughter a whore for the past ten minutes.

"Your witness." Pearce gives me a lopsided smile that makes his face appear maniacal.

He's so sure he'll win both the criminal and the civil case, and he has all the right circumstances to fall back on. Not only is the prosecutor in charge of the criminal case not aggressive enough, but the amount of bribing happening in the background is astounding, to say the least.

That fucker Matt, who's sitting in a relaxed position with a permanent smirk on his face, seems to be waiting for the whole charade to end. And once it does, I'm sure that big-bellied bastard with the slowly balding head will make Sandra's life a living hell for merely going up against him.

That's what bastards like him do; when you stand up to them, you either have to kill them or they'll chop your head off.

The first time I tried to run away with Teal and Mum had found us, we were in for brutal floggings that broke our skin. Then she locked us in a closet for a whole day with no food or access to the bathroom.

She only let us out when a "client" specifically asked for us. She bathed us then, made us look pretty for her fucking pedophiles and told us that if we ran again, she'd kill us and sell our corpses.

After that incident, Teal withdrew further into her shell and barely talked. Me, however? I knew that if we didn't escape, that bitch would kill us anyway or she'd get us hooked on drugs so we'd never get the chance to leave.

So I planned our next attempt well. I waited until the fucking bitch was half passed out on drugs, then gave her a bottle of water that I'd put sleeping powder in. The same powder she'd put in my drink when she had pedophiles over, because when I turned eight, I started to fight, and the fuckers didn't like that.

"Did you ever love us?" I asked her when she was half-dazed, close to collapsing.

I'll never forget the lunatic snarl on her face when she grabbed me by the hair so harshly, she ripped some out. "Are you fucking daft? How can someone love their golden goose?"

She laughed then and I pushed her away so hard, she passed out. It was the first time I'd done it, and it filled me with waves of adrenaline.

So much so that I grabbed Teal's hand and we left.

Once and for fucking all.

So no, Sandra's case is not a mere case. It's her chance to finally break free.

Ignoring Pearce's obvious attempts to rile me up, I stand, buttoning my jacket. "Mrs. Bell, you said you knew Sandra way before you married Mr. Bell. Is that right?"

Karen Bell, a woman in her forties with a bony body structure and bleached hair, twists her lips, but answers, "Yes."

"For how long before the marriage?"

"Three years, I think."

"You married Mr. Bell when Sandra was thirteen years old, so that means you've known her since she was ten, is that correct?"

"Yes."

"That means you've been around the family for a considerable amount of time."

"Objection." Pearce stands. "Counsel isn't asking a question."

"I will."

"Then do so, Mr. Van Doren," the judge, a middle-aged black man, says.

I focus back on Karen. "Did Ms. Bell ever show signs of abuse at that time?"

Karen twists her lips again. "No."

"Not even when she asked you to take her to the clinic because she was bleeding before her period came along?"

"Objection! Hearsay."

I carry on, pushing into Karen's space until she's trembling slightly. "Not when she begged you and cried on her knees in front of your office and asked you to help her because she couldn't walk on her own? Because she had blood on her skirt and down her legs and suffered from a ripped hymen? What did you do then, Mrs. Bell? When a ten-year-old was bleeding because she was raped by her father, what did you do?"

"Objection, Your Honor. Counsel is reciting unfounded information without evidence."

"Sustained." The judge glares at me. "Unless you have evidence to back your claim, I'm going to strike everything you said from the record."

"I have evidence." I step back, then take the file Lauren has ready for me and try to ignore the tears in Sandra's eyes as she locks them with Karen's. "I would like to submit into evidence, the testimony of Dr. Norman Schmidt, Mrs. Karen Bell's ex-partner, who's now residing in Switzerland."

The judge summons both me and Pearce to the bench and I give him the file while speaking in a low tone, so the jury can't listen. "This is the medical record Dr. Schmidt created when Mrs. Bell, then Miss Rens, called him to Mr. Bell's house to look at an unconscious child with bleeding from her vagina. She told him not to report it and that taking the girl to the hospital was not an option. When Dr. Schmidt insisted on taking her with him to the ER, Mrs. Bell kicked him out. I've also included a copy of the testimony he gave at the police station, which the police chief reportedly "lost" the same day. A day later, Immigration and Customs Enforcement agents barged into Dr. Schmidt's office and informed him that he was being deported for accumulated charges of malpractice—which he had no idea existed until ICE gave him a one-way ticket back to Switzerland."

Pearce makes a face as the judge reads the files. "Mr. Norman Schmidt is a doctor who was deported and had malpractice claims filed against him for raping two women, Your Honor."

"Dr. Schmidt was never convicted."

"He can't be cross-examined since he's in Switzerland, Your Honor," Pearce says.

"The *certified* medical records he sent can still be used in court." I smile and Pearce's face instantly darkens.

The judge stares between the two of us, then tells everyone present, "We'll take a recess to review the newly submitted evidence."

As the attendees slowly rise to leave, Matt shares a patronizing look with his wife and she immediately lowers her head, her fingers still shaking.

Hmm. Interesting.

Instead of tucking his tail between his legs and crying to his beloved mafia for help, he walks to Sandra, whose eyes widen as her shoulders hunch. "You're making a grave mistake, you ungrateful little—"

"One more word and I'm reporting this," I cut him off as I stand by her side, then glare at Pearce. "Control your client better, would you? Or does that also need to be done for you like every single case you've taken?"

His lips curl in a snarl. "This isn't over, Van Doren."

"It sure as hell isn't. Because your client just breached the restraining order." And with that, Lauren and I escort Sandra out of the courtroom.

"Thank you," she whispers shyly.

"Don't thank me yet. We're not done." I make eye contact with the prosecutor in charge, Gerard. He's been present during the trial since it's strongly tied to the criminal case.

His brows are knit together and he doesn't seem amused by the new evidence I brought forward. I could've given it to him or discussed it with him beforehand, but he's on Pearce's side, not mine.

Which is why I metaphorically twisted his arm so he'd look further into it and, for once, go aggressively against Matt.

He narrows his eyes at me and I wink.

That's right, motherfucker. Either you do the right thing or the media will riot against you. Many humanitarian and women's associations are backing Sandra on this. Even the public switched to her side once Lauren and I tactfully leaked pictures Sandra secretly took of her bruised skin over the past year.

She didn't want to do it at first, but after a chat with Lauren, Sandra agreed.

It's been submitted into evidence, too, but there's still no medical report to back it up. Some fuckers on social media even suggested that she could've paid someone to beat her. Anastasia used to methodically hack into various platforms and delete those comments so Sandra didn't see them.

She didn't tell anyone this, but I caught her once while she thought I was sleeping.

We spend all day in the courtroom and it's bloody annoying and fucking exhausting, or maybe it's because I'm irritated and all I want to do is go home.

No, that's not the part I'm more interested in.

It's the person I'll find at home. The woman who's been watching her back every step of the way and decided to push me out of her life.

It's not going to happen.

Ever.

Not when she's not telling me the real reason behind it.

Hell, even if she does, we'll work around it. There's no way in fuck I'm ending what I've finally found.

The light to my shadows.

Sure, it's not bright or constant. Fuck, it could be mistaken for darkness, too. It's dim, but it's there, the light that I've probably been coveting since the first time I saw her.

Since the first time I laid eyes on her.

I just didn't fucking realize it then.

Lauren, Chris, and I go back to the firm for a short meeting, but I need to see her first, so I tell them to start without me.

After every day spent in court for Sandra's case, I get into this funky dark mood that makes my blood boil.

And Anastasia is the only one who drives it away.

I don't care how often she tells me we have to break up, I'll just refuse until she comes to her senses.

When I reach the IT department, though, she's not there. I find Gwen lounging at her post, drinking a milkshake and reading from a stack of files Nate probably gave her.

When she notices me, she releases the straw in her mouth. "Oh, Knox. What are you doing here?"

"Have you seen Jane?" Usually, I try to be around here as little as possible, mainly because Anastasia likes to keep everything a secret.

But fuck that, she was never my dirty little secret.

Gwen narrows her eyes. "Why?"

"You don't need to know."

"Of course, I do. Don't think I haven't noticed you roaming around her, trying to intimidate her and stuff." She stands up and places a hand on her hip, her drink clutched tightly in the other hand. "I protect my friends, you know."

"And you'll do that with a milkshake? I suppose this is the time I should act scared?"

"Not with a milkshake. I'll tell Nate and he'll fire you."

"He can't fire me, Gwen. I'm a junior partner, so he'll have to make the board agree first."

"Then he'll just do that."

"Uh-huh."

"Can you just not bully the only female friend I've ever had?"

There's desperation in her tone that makes me pause my arseholish remarks. Gwen might as well be Anastasia's only friend, too.

She's that lonely and used to acting solo.

"I'm not bullying her, Gwen." My voice softens a little.

"How can I be sure?"

"Because I like her."

We both freeze at that, me more than her, because what the fuck am I saying?

"Ohhhh." She grins. "That sneak Jane never told me. You must be the friend she's staying with these days."

So I've become a fucking friend now?

"I am. Now, can you tell me where she is?"

"She took her laptop and went to the fourth floor. Apparently, there's a place she can focus there. I haven't been to it, but Jane says…"

I'm striding out before she can finish her sentence.

"You're welcome!" Gwen shouts behind me.

I don't focus on her, because I'm on a mission to get to Anastasia. She must be in the supply room.

Our room at the firm.

No idea why that fills me with a strange type of energy.

The moment I arrive, I barge inside and pause in the doorway. Soft light bathes the room, which is different from when we're usually here.

And the reason for the change punches me right across the face when I find Anastasia sitting between someone's legs, unbuttoning his shirt.

Someone.

Not me.

Someone else.

As in, another fucking man who has his hand on her arm.

The man is Daniel and he's touching what's fucking mine.

My vision turns pure bloody red.

Red like I've never experienced.

Red like I've never seen before.

Something inside me crashes, splinters, and blasts into a million fucking pieces.

And in the midst of the blinding, searing pain, only one thought remains.

The need to fucking hurt.

THIRTY-TWO

Anastasia

"**W**HAT THE FUCK IS GOING ON?"

There's a clipped quality to his voice. The voice that I would recognize anywhere. The voice that's been haunting my reality and my nightmares.

I raise my head slowly, my throat drying, and my skin suddenly turns freezing cold. The air thickens with suffocating tension and my breaths become deeper but shorter, like none of it is reaching my lungs.

And I don't think it's only due to the lack of air or his rough, savage voice. It's his entire presence. The tightness in his shoulders, the clenching of his jaw, the bulging veins in his neck.

Mostly, it's the light slowly but surely leaving his golden eyes. The light I always found refuge in. The light that anchored me when I needed something to lean on.

It's gone now.

What's left behind is worse than rage or even anger.

It's nothingness. A bottomless black hole that has no end in sight.

Daniel pushes me away and I scramble to my feet as he stands up, the first buttons of his shirt still undone.

He carefully walks up to Knox. "Mate—"

Whatever he was going to say is cut off when Knox drives his fist into his face with a force that makes me gasp.

Daniel reels backward, cradling his nose with both hands. When he checks his palms, I lean over and startle when I see droplets of blood. "The fuck, Knox? Not the face, you bloody wanker!"

As if not hearing a word he said, Knox lunges forward, probably about to finish what he started. I don't know how I do it, how I get the courage to jump forward.

Usually, I don't get involved. I'm neither a pacifier nor a shit-stirrer. I just stay in the background, watching with my mouth shut.

But I think that part was purged out of me when I started becoming Jane. When my life took a sharp dive in a direction I don't recognize.

The old Anastasia would've never gotten involved in fights, but the new me doesn't think twice as I slide in front of Daniel, flinging my arms wide.

Knox stops mid-punch, his fist still raised in the air, and he's breathing harshly through his nostrils, uncontrollably even. "Step away."

"No," I whisper.

"Step the fuck away."

"No! Daniel has nothing to do with this. I was the one who asked him to join me here. I was the one who came on to him, so if you want to punch someone, punch me."

"No one came on to anyone…" Daniel starts.

"I did. I wanted him," I say firmly to Knox's face, despite feeling something splinter to a million pieces inside me.

I feel bad for using Daniel and putting him in this position without asking him about it first, but this is the only chance I have.

Knox's fist clenches until the veins on the back of his hand pop, and just when I think he'll punch or strangle me, he lets his hand drop to his side.

Even though it's still balled in a tight grip.

We're both breathing heavily, his skyrocketing adrenaline rubbing off mine, his anger scratching on my fragile emotions.

He grabs me by the arm, his fingers leaving bruising marks on my skin as he hauls me closer to him. "I don't want to deal with you right now, so fucking disappear."

"Why? So you can beat Daniel up?"

"That's none of your fucking business, and stop taking his side in front of me before I drive my fist into his windpipe and end his motherfucking life."

"Ouch," Daniel says from behind me. "And I'm still over here, bleeding, thanks so much for asking, everyone."

"You shut the fuck up. I'll be with you in a second," Knox enunciates from between gritted teeth before narrowing his eyes on me. "And, you. Go."

"No. You have no right to do this. I already broke up with you."

He grinds his back teeth together, then drags in a long inhale. "I never fucking agreed to that."

"That doesn't mean it isn't true."

"That's exactly what it fucking means." He shakes me by my arm, his voice becoming guttural and asphyxiating. "You're mine, and no one touches what's mine. You don't let anyone put their hands on you or it'll be the last time they touch anything."

My breath hitches and it's not only due to the raw possessiveness in his tone, or that his heat nearly melts me. It's that I feel his words instead of merely hearing them.

They sneak beneath my skin and flow into my bloodstream faster and thicker than blood. I'm speechless in the wake of their intensity.

Completely and utterly helpless.

His fingers dig further into my skin as if driving the point home. "I mean it, so don't make me act on it."

"I also mean it. We're over." I sound calm and composed, even though a war is bursting through my limbs, destroying me from the inside out.

"Anastasia…" The thickness in his voice nearly makes me crumble.

I'm so weak for him, I realize. So damn helpless in front of these golden eyes that hold the world in their depths. A world I recognize myself in. A world I never wanted to leave.

Every part of me is urging me to explain, to throw myself in his arms and cry.

But that will only hurt him.

And me.

"Let me go," I murmur.

"Not in this fucking lifetime."

"Let me go, Knox. Just let me go!" I'm two seconds away from crying, from ruining the fragile façade I've been wearing since he came in.

"Not going to happen."

Daniel steps to my side, still wiping the blood from his nose. "She said to let her go."

"You keep your mouth shut and send any goodbye messages before I fucking murder you."

"Knox…" Daniel grabs his arm and shakes his head, speaking slowly though with a firm edge that I've never heard from him before, "Let her go. You're hurting her."

I don't know how he noticed it when I've been hiding my reaction, but his words prompt Knox out of his haze. He focuses on where his fingers are digging into my arm and releases me with a jerk.

I wince, not because of the pain, but because he's no longer touching me. I prefer the pain over completely losing his touch.

The pain means he's there, but its absence is no different than being abandoned.

Daniel sniffs, the blood still coating his nose. "You need to calm the heck down, mate."

Knox raises his fist and punches him in the face and he jerks back, cursing.

"Fucking fuck, Knox. What the bloody hell is wrong with you? This face is real estate!"

He completely ignores him, his attention solely on me. His hazel eyes are dark and unreadable, a bit scary, even. "This isn't over."

The staring contest continues for a few more seconds, or maybe minutes, before he turns and leaves.

As soon as he's out the door, my feet falter and I nearly drop to the floor.

Oh, God.

Is it supposed to feel this miserable? As if something is tearing up my insides and leaving them out in the open?

The door I've been staring at since Knox left is blocked when Daniel stands in front of me. "Are you okay?"

I internally shake my head and focus on him. On the blood that's trailing down his chin and dripping onto his white shirt and the lapel of his jacket. "I should be the one asking you that. I'm so sorry."

"He'll be the one who's sorry when I sue him for assault."

"Please don't do that."

"You're still defending him after he fucked up my face? The same face that's worth millions of dollars and on the cover of countless magazines?"

"I'm really sorry. I'm sure he didn't mean to."

"You must really love him if you're apologizing on his behalf after you clearly broke his heart."

A ball the size of my fist thickens in my throat. "It's... complicated."

"I can see that. He called you Anastasia and I assume it's not because of some role-play kink I didn't know he had. Is that why you asked me to come in here? And what's with the coming on to me bullshit when we both know it's not true?"

I bite my lower lip. I really didn't mean for Knox to catch us, not that there was anything going on. I only spilled my water on Daniel and I was trying to wipe it off when Knox walked in.

Daniel dabs the back of his hand against his nose before his scrutinizing attention falls on me. "I might not look like it, but I don't allow anyone to use me, especially when it comes to hurting my best friend."

"I'm not using you...I just wanted to ask for your help."

"Concerning what?"

"Knox's safety. If you care about him, don't explain this situation to him. Let him believe that I came on to you."

"So he'll hate you?"

My lips tremble. "Yeah."

"That means he'll hate me, too, and I'm not game for that. So you'll have to give me something more to go on with this plan."

I take a deep breath. "I'm leaving."

He lets his hand fall to the side and tilts his head as if I finally have his undivided attention. "Why?"

"Because I'm a danger to his life, and if I stay, he'll be dead in no time."

Daniel doesn't react strongly. In fact, he doesn't react at all, which is to be expected of a lawyer, I guess. He leans against the wall, crossing his arms over his chest. "Explain in more detail."

"And you'll help me?"

"If your goal is to protect him, I will."

Okay.

I can do this.

If there's anyone who can help me keep Knox away, it's Daniel. Even if it means hurting him in the process.

However, no amount of emotional pain compares to what would happen to him if he insists on staying with me.

Surprisingly, the words don't feel heavy when I confess to Daniel, "Because my father is the leader of the New York Russian mafia and Knox is under threat because of that."

THIRTY-THREE

Knox

THE NEED FOR VIOLENCE HASN'T LEFT MY SYSTEM.

If anything, it's growing and intensifying, despite being in the process of murdering the punching bag in my building's gym.

I keep pummeling on and on, imagining Daniel's face as its substitute. Or any other man's face who ever put their hands on her.

Any.

All.

This isn't normal, is it? Being on the verge of destruction and feeling like I'll burst any second. It isn't normal to have urges I thought I got rid of long ago.

Like standing at the top of something high, spreading my arms, and plummeting down, just so I can kill the shadows swirling around me from every side.

Or maybe cutting open my veins so they'll fucking bleed out

so I can stop them from whispering, murmuring, and hissing in my ears.

I haven't had these thoughts for…years. Or maybe I've done a fantastic job pretending they weren't there anymore.

That I was fine.

Perfect.

Completely over my past

Dad is right, after all. It's impossible to pretend all is well when it isn't.

One incident, one moment in time is able to make me back-pedal into the worse version of myself.

The version that resisted the urge to jump or cut open my veins because I couldn't leave Teal. Because I was responsible for my sister and abandoning her was a betrayal of the vow I made to protect her.

But she doesn't need my protection now. Not only does she have her husband and son, but I can finally admit that she's in a better place than I am.

I always thought I was her rock and anchor, that I had to be strong for her, but I didn't stop to think about how much that fake strength would eat away at the edges and seep inside.

That's how it feels right now—like I'm dissolving from the outside in.

The scene of Anastasia clinging to Daniel keeps replaying at the back of my mind in a loop, in spite of my attempts to stop it. It's whirling, repeating, and fucking up my breathing.

The way her lips parted when she looked at him and knelt between his legs. Lips that were only mine to kiss. Lips that only smiled at me.

Not anymore, though.

We're over.

That's what she said and when I didn't agree, she proceeded to fucking prove it.

I hit the bag harder until my knuckles and muscles scream

with pain and exertion. Until my vision is hazy with sweat and a red mist.

"Are you done murdering the punching bag or should I come back in a bit?"

My head whips to the side to find the fucker Daniel casually leaning against the wall, his legs crossed at the ankles.

I abandon the bag and stride toward him. Thank God the gym is empty, because it's about to turn into a crime scene.

Sweat drips from my lashes and temples, and the exhaustion from punching the bag slowly recedes as adrenaline moves to the forefront.

Daniel raises his hands and backs away. "Whoa, calm down, mate. You're making a grave mistake."

"I'll worry about that after it happens."

He keeps backing away and I'm on him, my strides longer and with intent.

"I notarized a new will just now that says if I die under mysterious circumstances, Knox killed me."

"Might as well make it happen then."

"You're being an unreasonable bloody idiot right now."

"I'm the unreasonable bloody idiot? Are you sure that's not you? Since…I don't know. *You* are the one who put their fucking hands on her. On the one person that I've ever called mine. Let's break down the fucking reason, shall we? What was it, exactly? Jealousy? Or maybe it's your constant need to feel something after your secondary school crush broke your heart and stomped all over it as if it were mere rubbish? Is it because the only person you wanted never wanted you back, and that made you develop a phobia of blondes you still struggle with even as an adult?"

He stops backing away, his shoulders turning tense and his features gradually shutting down. The agreeable mask he wears for everyone slowly disappears, allowing his true image to show.

The raging, bitter fucker who also hates himself. That's the one thing we had in common when we got close, and no matter how much he's hid that fact, it's still a huge part of who he is.

"Shut the fuck up, Knox." There's a warning in his clipped tone.

Bloody fantastic. Now, we're getting down to business.

"It hurts, doesn't it? Being hit upside the head by the truth. Being reminded that you can have any woman except the one you really want, because she only ever used you, right? You were *nothing* to her and always will be."

His fists clench at his sides and I expect him to punch me. I'm waiting for him to make the first move so I can pummel him to the ground. However, his lips curve, and the holes in his cheeks appear grotesque as he smirks. "Just like you're nothing to Anastasia, you mean? She threw you away the first chance she got. And guess who she chose? *Moi.*"

I lunge at him and he's waiting with a raised fist. I punch him first and he punches back just as hard. I might've been the one who was working out on the bag, but his hits are fueled with as much adrenaline as mine.

It's like he's waited for this moment to release all the pent-up energy that's been growing inside him as well.

I tackle him to the ground, but before I can pin him down, he rolls us around and kicks me in the balls.

"Motherfucker!" I curse, grabbing the throbbing area and stare up at him, because he's standing, panting, his eyes shadowed. "That's a fucking low blow."

"Just like bringing *her* up. Do that again and your dick will be next."

"Not if I kill you first."

"You can try. Doesn't mean you'll succeed."

I crawl to a sitting position, wincing at the pain in my balls. The fucking bastard got me good.

As much as I want to rearrange his features and sell them for parts, I know he meant it about my dick. He can be a raging arsehole when provoked and I definitely did that by mentioning his Achilles' heel.

So unless I break his dick first, he'll come after mine.

Besides, it's like all the destructive energy I stored inside is slowly deflating. All I'm left with is a bitter taste at the back of my fucking throat.

I stare up at him—or, more accurately, glare. "Just tell me why, Daniel. Why her?"

"No reason."

"Either you tell me or I swear to fuck I'm going to find the blonde from your past and fuck her, then send you the pictures." I wouldn't, because that would mean touching another woman besides Anastasia, and as much as I want to strangle the fuck out of her, I don't want any other woman but her.

However, my words get me the intended reaction. He grabs me by the shirt and hauls me off the ground. "Don't you fucking dare."

"Why? I thought you were over her, or is that another lie?"

"I'm going to fuck up your life, Knox."

"You do that while I'm busy fucking her into oblivion."

"Shut the fuck up or I'll fuck Anastasia for real."

I'm about to punch him to death when his words register. He said *for real*, as in, it didn't happen.

"You didn't do anything with her, did you?" I ask slowly, the haze dissipating from my vision.

"I will in about half an hour if you don't stop being a dick."

"Like fuck you will." I stand to my full height and push him away. "Why did you make me believe something happened?"

"I didn't make you believe something happened. You painted that whole scenario yourself. I specifically told you I didn't come on to her, but you weren't listening."

"Why did she say she came on to you?"

"Hello? She obviously realized I'm a catch."

"Daniel," I warn.

"Why don't you ask her?"

"Well, I'm asking you."

"Even if I knew something, why would I spill the beans? You get fewer brownie points for being a bloody fucking wanker. Not only did you believe I would do such a thing to you, but you also brought *her* up. We agreed to never fucking do that."

"What did you expect me to do? You were lying to me."

"I was cooperating for your bloody sake, but fuck you."

"*My* sake? What is that supposed to mean?"

"She said she's doing this for you."

"For me?"

"That's all I'm telling you. You'll have to find out everything else from her."

It still feels wrong that she even went to him instead of coming to me and I want to punch him to death for that reason alone, but I suck in deep breaths to conjure some much-needed calm.

Anastasia has a lot to answer to, and a lot to learn, like the fact that she can't take any other man's side but mine. Or tell me it's over.

She can do whatever the fuck she wants, but only while she's with me.

"Where did you see her last?" I ask Daniel.

"At the firm, but I wouldn't look there or at her flat."

"Why the fuck not?"

He sighs, long and deep. "Because she said she's going back to where she came from."

THIRTY-FOUR

Anastasia

WHEN I LEFT MY FATHER'S HOUSE TWO MONTHS AGO, I never thought I'd ever come back.

At least, not alive.

But here I am. In front of the black metal gate, waiting for the guards to open it. I don't have to wonder whether or not they spotted me since countless cameras and drones survey the mansion.

If someone is stupid enough to consider intruding on the *Pakhan*'s house, they'll have machine guns at their temples before they can blink.

The guards recruited to specifically protect the *Pakhan* don't only rely on technology, though. They own countless weapons, some smuggled from Russia, and others from the merchandise they've acquired from arms dealers.

I've just seen the weapons vault once, and only because I was passing by when they were loading new guns in it. That thing resembled an army's arsenal waiting to wage war.

Needless to say, I never went near it again.

Like Little Miss Ostrich, I pretended none of it mattered and I had nothing to do with it. Until I couldn't keep up the façade anymore and I had to leave.

But now, I'm back.

Now, I'm sitting in front of the huge gate, staring at the blinking cameras. The guards must've seen me by now and told my father that the daughter who stole from the *Bratva* and he covered up for is back.

No clue what's taking them so long. It couldn't be because they don't recognize me.

I stripped my hair and bleached it back to its original platinum blonde and I also removed the glasses and the contacts. I even wore a soft pink flowery dress and elegant high heels—the style everyone knows me by.

Just like that, Jane vanished. I snuffed her out as if she never existed.

I left my resignation letter with HR and two different letters to Gwen and Chris, apologizing for not being truthful about who I truly am and telling them that it's better if they forget they ever met me.

Neither of them were supposed to happen in my new life, but they did, and for the first time, I realize that I'm capable of having friends.

It hurt to leave them, but it's for their sake.

It's for the best.

I'm back where I always belonged and foolishly thought I could leave.

And the worst part is, this isn't the only thing I was so foolish about.

There's also the belief that I could have a normal relationship.

My chest aches at the reminder of him, Knox, the man who showed me the world, but I left him with a bitter betrayal.

It's been a day since he caught me with Daniel and left with that angry frown I wish I could erase. Only one day, but it feels like an eternity, like I haven't seen him in forever.

The fact that he thinks so little of me adds insult to injury, but hopefully, with time, when he realizes why I'm doing this, he'll understand.

The key word being *hopefully*.

Two guards appear behind the gate as it slowly creaks opens. They're dressed in black suits and have assault rifles slung over their shoulders.

Then someone else walks through them, but it isn't a guard. He's a tall, bearded man who's always protected me since I was a child.

It's only been a short time since I saw him last, but he looks different, a little bit monstrous, even. Not that he's ever been an angel, but I guess I only ever considered him a big brother. One who wouldn't hesitate to break someone's arm and smash another person's face just because they touched me—even accidentally.

But that was before I turned my back on him and the brotherhood.

"Hi, Vladimir," I whisper, unsure.

"Don't hi me." He has a thick Russian accent and a glare that can serve as a weapon. "Where have you been?"

That means Kirill and Adrian didn't tell anyone about my whereabouts. That gives me less to worry about.

"Around."

"Around isn't a place."

"It was nowhere important. Now, can I come in or are you going to keep interrogating me here?"

His lips press together, and I'm sure he has a million other questions he still wants to ask, but even he must realize this isn't the place to do it.

"Follow me," he grunts, then turns around without waiting to see if I'll do as he says.

My feet carry me inside and my heart shrinks as the echo of the metal gate reverberates behind me.

It sounds final, as if I've signed some sort of a deal with the devil and will never be able to escape.

The guards fall in behind us as we step into the main building. The shrinking in my chest gets worse when my gaze falls on the giant painting in the entry hall.

A painting that Papa and my dead uncle—the previous *Pakhan*—put here for every visitor to see.

The clashing of angels and demons in a ferocious battle is depicted in raw detail. If you look closely, you can feel the blood coating your fingers and hear the howls of pain deep in your soul.

It's an indirect message that lets everyone know what's waiting for them.

It's meant to bring assurance to every ally of the *Bratva* yet terrorize them in case they think of betrayal.

And I see myself in the dark side of the picture, the one that's shadowed by the lighter color and unable to win.

I'm the slaughtered demon lying on the ground, clutching his chest and choking on blood.

My ominous thoughts are brought to a halt when Vladimir stops in front of the double golden doors of the dining room, where Papa conducts his meetings with the leaders of the brotherhood.

Meetings I were never allowed to attend.

My pulse skyrockets and any semblance of calm shreds into a million pieces. Does this mean Papa will confront me in front of everyone? Adrian and Kirill included?

Shit. I'd hoped to talk to Adrian first, because if he finds out I didn't abide by his orders, he won't hesitate to make his threat about Knox a reality.

Before I get the chance to hyperventilate, Vladimir opens the door and I freeze.

Because I'm attacked by a hug out of nowhere.

A warm, soft hug that I've known since I was five, when she promised to protect me.

My great-cousin, Uncle's granddaughter, Rai, pulls back to check me out as if I'm a soldier home from war.

She's wearing a beige pantsuit and her hair is pulled up in an elegant twist. It's blonde, too, but it's a bit darker than mine.

Everything about Rai is darker than me. Whether it's her childhood or how involved she is in this world.

"Are you okay? Did anyone hurt you? Just give me a name and I will personally make sure they know their place."

I resist a smile at her overprotectiveness. She's always acted like my shield against this world, but unfortunately, that was never enough.

"No one hurt me, Rai."

She focuses on my face for the first time, a frown deepening between her brows. "Then where were you?"

"She willingly left, as she mentioned in that measly note she wrote before disappearing." The apathy in the older male voice turns my blood to ice.

I stare over Rai's shoulder and my eyes meet those that are identical to mine.

The same eyes that I considered safe when I first met him.

Sergei Sokolov.

Even though I found his eyes safe that first time we met him at the park, I didn't want to leave with him, because that meant abandoning my mom.

That same day, however, someone told my stepfather that they saw Mom with a man and he beat her up so badly, I couldn't remain hiding under the bed anymore.

I rummaged through my pocket for his number and called him. Papa. I begged him for help and he came within half an hour.

It was too late, though.

Because my stepfather had finally managed to beat Mom to death. I'll never forget the scene I walked in on that night.

Mom's head was lolled to the side, blood splattered on the table, and her teary eyes stared at nothing.

My stepdad was on his back next to her, a bloody hole lodged between his eyes.

In the midst of the gruesome scene stood Papa, a gun in hand.

When he saw me, he hid the weapon and reached his hand out to me. That time, I didn't hesitate to take it.

Because I had no one but him. The man who ended the nightmare my stepdad represented, even though it was too late.

That same man is now staring at me with ice-cold eyes that rip through my soul. He's so much older than back then. His hair has whitened and wrinkles have appeared around his eyes.

But no amount of aging can take the killer out of him. No amount of changes can deny how powerful he is.

The Sokolovs were born to do great things, he told me when I was young, but I don't think he meant using my skills to steal from the brotherhood.

I slowly walk to him and reach for his hand to kiss the back of it the way everyone is expected to greet the *Pakhan*, but he turns his face away from me in clear rejection.

My trembling hand falls to my side and I swallow thickly.

"You have some explaining to do," he says without masking the coldness in his voice.

"Granduncle…" Rai starts in a placating tone. "She just came back."

"When she shouldn't have left in the first place."

Vladimir closes the door and locks it, trapping the four of us inside, then starts inspecting the room, for bugs, I presume.

We all remain silent until he finishes his thorough checkup and nods at us to proceed.

It's Papa who says, "You have one minute to explain why you stole funds from V Corp and disappeared."

"I'm sorry," I whisper, hanging my head. "I didn't think the three of you would cover up for me."

"Then what did you think? That I would paint my own daughter as a criminal and risk losing the leader position? Did I or did I not tell you that you needed to think about who you are before making a single move? It's not only about you anymore. It's about the Sokolov name. So why don't you tell us what made you betray it."

"I didn't betray you…"

"You left with funds and without telling any of us." Vladimir crosses his arms. "That's the definition of betrayal."

"That's not what I intended."

"Then what did you intend?" It's Rai who speaks, her voice softer but no less firm than Vladimir's. "Tell us, Ana."

I let out a breath. "I wanted to protect *Babushka*."

Rai frowns. "You don't have a grandmother."

"I do. She's not my real grandmother, but she raised me and protected me. But Papa expelled her back to Russia, where no one can help her, because he said she's a bad influence. She has dementia and is suffering, but he forbade me to see her, so I had to come up with this plan." I don't miss the way I'm talking about my father in third person in his presence.

I can't even look at him, because I know his wrath won't be easy to handle.

"Why didn't you tell me?" Rai asks.

"I wanted to, but you were so busy with your marriage and the *Bratva*, and I couldn't add more to it. Besides, I wanted to do something myself for once instead of always relying on you."

"That was foolish, Anastasia." Vladimir steps from the door, his bulk eating up half the space. "Even though we covered for you and returned the funds out of our own pockets, Adrian found out about what you've done and that nearly cost your father his position and life. Ours, too. He pulled a huge favor from the *Pakhan* in exchange for not harming you or exposing what you did."

My head whips up. "I…didn't think it'd come to this. I'm so sorry."

"Apologies don't fix what's already broken." Papa is still not looking at me, his face closed off and his expression dark. "You'll not leave the house until you receive further instructions."

"But…"

"That is final."

"Please don't hurt *Babushka*. Please."

"That depends on how you act from now on." Papa looks at me and I wish he hadn't. He appears so much older, so much sadder. "You've disappointed me, Anastasia."

He stands up and leaves, and I finally let the tears loose.

Home sweet home.

THIRTY-FIVE

Anastasia

I't's been three days since I came back to Papa's house and it feels like two months.

Maybe two years.

Being in the unknown about *Babushka*'s and my fate is slowly killing me. Rai promised that she won't let anyone hurt her, but even she has no say whatsoever when Papa decides how things will go.

I have no access to my phone, which I predicted, and I threw away the one I used as Jane, so no one can retrieve it. Also, since Papa found out that the way I got all those funds was through hacking, he had Vladimir confiscate my laptop as well.

So I'm sort of cut off from the world, but I've figured out a way to follow Sandra's case, and it's through the most traditional way possible. TV.

I don't want to watch it in the main hall since anyone can walk in, so I sneak into the staff's quarters.

Distinct chatter in Russian reaches me from the kitchen, where many guards sit down for snacks or meals.

I slip into the adjoining room and leave the door ajar so I can continue listening to the rumble of their voices. The moment they stop talking, I'll know I have to leave. The last thing I want is for them to report my sneaking around to Vladimir. Or worse, Papa.

He'd really lock me up in my room this time.

I turn on the TV and scroll to the local news channel, keeping the sound as low as possible.

My heart pounds when images of the Bell case fill the screen. Sandra is mobbed by reporters, but Knox singlehandedly pushes them off her and tells them his client has no statements to make.

This was during yesterday's hearing. The reporter says that they're being backed into a corner and the testimony of an important witness from Switzerland is very likely to be rejected. That leaves Sandra's side with fewer options and their mission is starting to look impossible.

My feet tremble and it takes all my strength to remain standing. I know, I just know that the *Bratva* has something to do with it.

It doesn't matter that I left, Kirill and especially Adrian won't stop until they get what they want.

I press Pause on the picture frame that shows Knox grabbing Sandra's elbow while he and Lauren guide her away from the crowd.

It's a bit blurry, but I can see every line of his face and the cut of his jaw. I can even see the frown in his forehead and that perturbed look in his eyes. My shaky fingers reach out to the screen and I run them over his face, lingering on his cheek and mouth.

God, I miss him.

I miss him like I've never missed anyone before, and the knowledge that this ache will never disappear splinters the bones in my ribcage and digs them into my heart.

As I look closer at him, I notice something is wrong. I don't know if it's how dark his eyes are or how stiff he appears, but it's there and I can't look away from it.

The need to find out what's wrong and make it better overwhelms me. But what can I do when I'm under house arrest?

"So this is the reason you returned."

My body goes rigid at that familiar voice. The chatter of the guards from the next room is still ongoing, so I thought I was safe.

But I can never be safe from Adrian. I slowly turn to face him and he's leaning against the wall, watching me and the TV screen as if he's been here for a while. Maybe ever since I first got here.

I didn't sense him. I couldn't have even if I'd tried, because he moves quietly and takes action just as secretly.

But apparently, I've lost all semblance of fear, because I stride toward him. "Are you the one behind this?"

"Behind what?"

"Making him lose."

"So what if I am? In fact, last time I checked, you should've been our spy at Weaver & Shaw. Instead, you decided to come back without informing me. Isn't that very bold of you?"

"I will not let you use me against him. Never."

"Does that mean you wouldn't care if the rest of the brotherhood found out what you did?"

"I don't care. Papa is already punishing me, so if there's another one I have to take, I will. Yes, I stole from V Corp, but only so I could protect my *babushka*. She raised me and gave me the affection no one else did, so I wasn't going to abandon her at her old age."

Something flickers in his eyes—a brightness, a recognition, or maybe it's an understanding. Now that I think about it, Vladimir once told me that Adrian had a better relationship with his stepmother than his birth mother when he was young.

So he must know what it feels like to have that sort of a bond with someone not related to you by blood. Instead of taking the aggressive route, I force my body to relax. "Adrian...please don't do this."

"Do what?"

"Let a sexual predator get away with his crimes. Even if Matt is of business value, he still committed a crime that he needs to be punished for."

"It's not proven yet."

"It can and will be. All I'm asking is for you to stop interfering and you'll see justice take its course."

"You still believe in that empty concept?"

"It's not empty."

"Yes, it is. You're a hopeless dreamer, Anastasia, and I have a piece of advice for you. Crush those vain dreams or they'll eventually crush you. There's no room for them in this world."

"You don't believe that, or you wouldn't have married Lia."

A muscle works in his jaw at the mention of his wife, but I don't stop. "She is a dreamer, too, right? And you liked that about her, or you wouldn't have gone against everyone and chosen her."

"Stop," he grinds out. "Bringing my wife into the conversation won't give you any extra points. If anything, it'll deduct them."

"Fine. Take it as if I'm begging you and stop meddling, Adrian. Please."

"Let's say I agree to that. Do you think your father will let this slide? He doesn't believe in justice any more than I do."

"Yes, he does. He killed my stepfather because he killed my mother."

"That was not justice. It was cold-blooded revenge." He pauses. "But here's the thing, if you convince Sergei to cut off Matt, I'll back off."

"Really?"

"Yes. I can also forget about the whole mess you made by stealing from V Corp if you do another thing for me."

My throat is suddenly dry, but I ask anyway, "What type of thing?"

"I don't have anything in mind right now, but if I need your hacking services in the future, you'll provide them. No questions asked."

That can range from a mild operation to something absolutely dangerous, but I don't care. At least Adrian would be by my side, and he's one of the best allies I could ever have. He might as well be the deadliest around here and I have to be smart about siding with him.

"Deal." I offer my hand.

He shakes it with a slight twitch to his lips. "Good luck convincing Sergei."

"I thought you don't believe in luck."

"I don't, but if there's such a thing, you'll need lots of it."

He's right, I will.

But instead of only feeling intimidation, a sense of determination washes over me.

I might not be Jane anymore, but I'm not the weak Anastasia who bowed her head and went with the flow either.

This time, I'll make a change.

Deciding something and actually doing it are completely different.

I spend the whole day pacing and avoiding confrontation with Papa.

So I'm basically hiding in order to come up with a plan. Rai is working, so I can't even ask her for backup.

Vladimir is a little mad at me for disappearing, not that I blame him. But even if he weren't, he's too loyal to Papa to take anyone else's or my side over his.

While I'm thinking about the best way to broach the subject, a knock sounds on my door, startling me. I'm surprised to find Papa's senior guard standing there like an impenetrable wall.

"Do you need something?" I ask in Russian since that's the only language allowed in this house.

"The *Pakhan* is asking for you."

The nerves I thought I had under control bulldoze to the surface. I wipe my clammy hands on my floral dress and follow the guard down the hall.

Why is he asking for me when he treated me as if I were invisible over the last three days? He even refused to have meals with me, and I pretended that it didn't split me open.

Rai told me he'd eventually come around, but I didn't think he'd do it this fast.

The guard opens the door to Dad's office and steps aside to let me in.

It's vast and has tall bookshelves that extend from the floor to the ceiling. I've always been apprehensive about this place. It's only ever been meant for business, and for ruining people's lives.

My movements are careful as I walk in, my hands sweatier than they were earlier. Before I can wipe them on my dress, however, I'm caught off guard by the man sitting across from Papa.

His dark hair is mussed, as if he couldn't have cared less about brushing it when he rolled out of bed this morning. Not only that, but the first few buttons of his white shirt are also undone. I don't remember the last time he's ever worn a complete suit or a jacket.

He's rugged that way, an absolute rebel, and extremely volatile.

Damien Orlov.

One of the four kings who reign over the *Bratva*, the youngest of them all, and the most violent.

No kidding. I've heard horror stories about him dislodging a man's head from his shoulders with his bare hands. I also witnessed him going on a killing spree at Rai's wedding as if he were on a "who kills more" competition.

Those with violent tendencies and a potent bloodlust like him are a wild card. It's why Vladimir and Rai monitor him so he doesn't spiral out of control.

Papa has always been wary of his potential, despite what he does for the *Bratva*. Everyone in and outside of the organization calls him a dark horse and it's not empty words.

Finding him alone with Papa is a surprise, to say the least. He's usually either bickering with Kirill or flirting with Rai—attempting to, anyway, because she only has eyes for her husband.

Stopping near the entrance, I say, "You asked for me, Papa?"

At my words, Damien faces me with a frown. "Why did no one tell me you were back? I thought you preferred Russia and the fucking cold over New York. Is that not the case anymore, Nastyusha?"

I swallow, clearing my throat. Only those close to me call me by the Russian endearment version of my name. Namely *Babushka*, Rai, and Papa—when he wasn't mad at me. Even Vladimir has never used it.

But Damien informed me once that he'll call me what Rai does and I'll have to deal with it.

"She returned to where she belongs." It's my father who answers him before he tips his head to the chair that's across from Damien.

I approach them carefully, then sit down, wondering why he has both of us here when that's never happened before.

"That's good and all, but why did you ask for me first thing in the morning, *Pakhan*? I kind of need my beauty sleep after killing five motherfuckers last night...or were there ten? I lost count with all the screams and begging."

"It's almost afternoon, not morning," Papa says.

"So what? It's been a while since you've been in the field, but let me tell you, it takes some time to recharge before the next killing spree, *Pakhan*. So do me a tiny favor and make it quick."

I stare at Papa, but he doesn't appear angry. Damien is probably the only one who gets away with being insolent to everyone, his own *Pakhan* included.

Okay, everyone but Kirill. They're always at each other's throats.

"I just need you to agree to something and then you can go back to sleep, Orlov."

"Consider it done," Damien says with finality.

"Good. Then you'll marry my daughter in a month's time."

A shudder goes through me and my heart shrinks in my ribcage.

I've always known that Papa wanted to marry me off within

the *Bratva*. Rai took the fall for me once and got married to her ex-nemesis, but she couldn't do that every time. Sooner or later, Papa would married me off to the one he found most suitable, which is part of the reason why I left.

I just didn't want to be in this life forever, caught in the middle of violence and shootouts and betrayals.

But as I stare at Papa, I know my fate is sealed, because he's already made a decision about this marriage and I have no say in it.

Unlike me, however, Damien isn't fazed. If anything, he appears bored. "What's with everyone matchmaking me? I'm not husband material last I checked... Or am I?"

"Just do it."

"I can't."

"Why not?" Papa asks.

"Because Rai matchmade me with some *Yakuza* princess and I might have given her father my word to go along with it. Now, I'd drank too much vodka at the time, so I don't really remember the details, but Abe's already acting as if I'm his son-in-law."

"I never agreed to that marriage, so consider the agreement null and void. You'll marry a Russian."

"Fine, but you'll get Abe off my back. He's a bit clingy, so good luck with that."

"Leave it to me. I'll take care of it."

"Wait a minute." Damien faces me, his expression turning serious. "I have a very important question to ask first. Do you drink vodka?"

"A little."

"Better than nothing. Now, if you don't need me, I'm out of here. And, *Pakhan*, do us both a favor and only call for me in the evenings from now on." He starts to leave, then leans in to whisper so only I can hear, "I'll give you a chance to ruin this marriage before I ruin you, Nastyusha."

Then he stands to his full height and gives me a sadistic smile before he stalks out the door as lazily as a giant black cat.

"Start preparing for the wedding," Papa says as soon as the door closes behind Damien.

"Papa, please. I know you're mad at me and that I did something unforgivable, but you don't have to do this."

"On the contrary, I should've done this a long time ago. If I had, you wouldn't have had the chance to be a thief and a backstabber."

"I didn't backstab you, Papa. I was only looking out for the woman who took care of me when you weren't there, when you didn't even know I existed and I had to hide from my stepdad so he wouldn't hit me with a belt."

"So you're blaming me now? Am I at fault for taking you away from that life? For offering you a better one?"

"It's not better, Papa. I can't…I can't live in the midst of danger all the time. I can't stay on my toes and avoid the outside world because I could be attacked at any second. I might survive the first time or the second, but what about the rest of my life? What about when you're gone and I become an even bigger target?"

"You'll be no target if you marry Damien. Everyone is too scared of him to even think about attacking him."

"I don't want to, Papa. Please."

"Then what do you want? A certain lawyer who's currently going against us in court?"

My lips part. "How…how do you know about him?"

"Adrian told me everything."

Of course, Adrian would be playing both sides. I was foolish to believe he wouldn't.

"I also heard you want him to win." His expression becomes closed off. "Against us."

"He's defending a physical and sexual abuse victim, Papa, just like my mother was. If she ever meant anything to you, if I mean anything to you, please stop interfering. You killed an abuser once. Don't let this one walk free."

"So you want me to think you're doing this for the girl, not a certain…" he trails off, staring at a file in front of him. "Knox Van Doren."

Something slashes my insides at the thought that Papa already has a file on him. Was it Adrian again? Or maybe Kirill?

"He has nothing to do with this," I murmur.

"He better not or he'll be collateral damage."

"Papa, don't…please."

"He's not what you think, Nastyusha."

"What do you mean?"

"This case is personal to him."

"How could it be personal? He doesn't know either Sandra or Matt."

"No, but he's well-acquainted with Sandra's circumstances since he went through something similar himself. My people went to a lot of trouble to get me this information since his foster father practically buried it, but he couldn't have hidden it from me."

"What are you talking about, Papa?" I realize I'm shaking, my fingers clasped together and sweat gathering between my brows. "What information are you talking about?"

"His mother was a prostitute and a drug addict."

"He already told me that."

"Did he also tell you that when her body no longer had any value, she prostituted her two children to pedophiles?"

I gasp, my hands going to cover my mouth. The information Papa just revealed ever so casually crashes against my ribcage and splits it open.

Despite my attempts to reject it, to tell him it's not true, many pieces of the puzzle fall into place. Like how Knox doesn't like to have sex from the front, Teal's overprotectiveness, and especially his stiffness ever since he met Sandra.

I thought it was him being an asshole, but it must've been because she triggered him somehow. Because her story brought back awful memories from his own past.

Oh, God. I was clueless.

So damn clueless.

"He's not for you, Anastasia."

My mouth falls open as I stare my father square in the eye. "And the man who kills a village for dinner is? What type of logic is that, Papa?"

"Damien will protect you."

"He won't care about me enough to protect me. Down the line, he might become no different than my stepdad. The man whose file you have in front of you, however, does. Even when I lied to him and hid my identity, all he did was take care of me."

"An outsider is out of the question."

"Rai married Kyle and he's British."

"Kyle might have been raised in England, but he's not an outsider. His father is one of our leaders."

"But…"

"My decision is final. Don't make me get rid of him."

"Papa!"

"Do as you're told, Anastasia. Marry Damien and cut any relations with this lawyer and I'll spare him. I'll even stop backing Matt."

A tear slides down my cheek because the decision I'll have to make will burn me alive.

THIRTY-SIX

Knox

ROUND OF APPLAUSE GREETS ME AS SOON AS I'M INSIDE THE office. Even Lauren and Chris step aside and join the others in the celebratory greeting.

Every senior and junior partner is present, in addition to all the assistant lawyers and even the interns.

Nate and Aspen are at the front of them all, wearing what seems to be proud expressions. The managing partner of W&S strides toward me and grabs me by the shoulder with a little squeeze. "Great job."

"You're saying that as if I had a chance to lose."

"You did." It's Aspen who speaks with a slight lift in her brows. "In fact, you might have gotten lucky at the end."

"Turning the defense's witness against him isn't lucky, Aspen. It's hard work." Though luck might have played a little part in it.

Our evidence wasn't rejected as we thought it would be. Not only that, but Karen, Sandra's stepmother, visited me late at night to tell me she wanted to make up for her mistake.

The look on Matt's face was priceless when she took the stand as a witness in Sandra's favor for all the shit she'd witnessed over the years.

Pearce wasn't even trying to save face at the end and kind of let Matt fall on his own. I demanded his entire fortune for compensation but only got sixty percent, and Sandra just announced to the press that she'd donate most of it to the women's and children's organizations in hopes of helping people like her.

Now, the prosecutor is pushing harder for the criminal case. He gave Matt a plea deal to take twenty-five years in prison or he won't only charge him with a Class B felony, but will also file each case of physical assault separately.

I demanded that of the prosecutor after I met with him or I would've dragged him in front of the media. They're fans of me, Sandra, and Lauren, and started a movement called #SaveSandra, so if I called for a press conference and accused him of slacking, he would've received huge backlash.

So he decided to do the right thing. For once in his bloody rotten existence.

I still think twenty-five years in prison is too little for all that Sandra suffered, but it's better than the alternative.

Even though she still has a long road ahead of her, this is a good start.

Despite my relief about the outcome, the sense of joy I thought I would feel is nonexistent. It's muddied by a gloomy shadow that keeps hovering over my head.

A shadow so large and thick that I can't see through it.

I don't let anything show on my face, though. I smile and take the others' congratulations with my usual arrogance while all I want is to vanish into thin air.

When I finally get to my office, I throw my weight on the sofa and close my eyes. My hand fists then flexes on my thigh in sync with my loud heartbeats.

I might have won today, but something is off. Or more like, a few things.

First, Pearce's apathy. Second, the general atmosphere in the courtroom. And last but not least, the way everything fell into place without any interference.

It's almost as if Matt was dropped by the mob, which explains his pale face even before he lost. It's like he had a premonition about what would happen and only waited for the other shoe to drop.

There's a knock on my office door and I open my eyes as Daniel walks in.

It's been a week since the day I nearly beat him to death, but instead of giving us the space we both need, he's been there like a thorn in my side, one I'm tempted to punch every time I see him.

"I see congratulations are in order." He smiles, flopping on the chair across from me.

"You fuck off."

"You sure? I thought you'd want to hear what Anastasia told me that day."

I sit up straighter, every bone in my body coming to attention at the mention of her name. It's only her name, but it's gained a presence, a sharp one at that, and it's slashing through my chest and fucking up my organs.

For a whole week, I haven't been able to live properly. Each inhale is filled with the suffocating lack of her presence. And each exhale is choked with the emptiness she left behind.

Whenever I look, there's no sign of her soft smile and peaceful presence. It's as if she was never there in the first place.

But she was.

Every inch of me remembers her sweet scent, her delicate skin, and how right she felt in my arms. Every inch of me remembers her, whether as Anastasia or Jane doesn't matter. She was only ever one person to me.

And I got used to her more than I'd like to admit. I got so used to her that my life has felt dysfunctional since she's been gone.

It's become so bad that I smelled the orange-scented shampoo she left behind in a fruitless attempt to recreate her presence.

Needless to say, it was useless, and after that, I damn near lost my mind trying to find her.

I searched for her everywhere. I stalked her flat and even hired a PI to look for her.

Not only that, but I was on Chris's and Gwen's case since they were close to her, but even they had no idea where she went. However, she left them notes, ones where she apologized and wished them well.

I got no such note.

And I might have been extra hard on Chris for no apparent reason that day.

So after her complete desertion, this is the first time I might have a lead, even if it's coming from the little bastard, Daniel.

"Spill it," I say.

"Repeat that again and add a please."

"Fuck you, Dan. Now, talk."

"You're a bloody idiot and a sorry cunt. I just want to put that out there."

"Any day now."

He raises a brow. "You also realize that there was something wrong with your win, don't you?"

"How do you know that?"

"Anyone who watched the case closely would know that Matt is no longer the *Bratva*'s favorite boy and if you think that happened by coincidence, you're way off the mark. In fact, the last person you'd expect helped you."

"Who do you mean?"

"Anastasia."

"What does she have to do with it?"

"She asked me not to tell you since you were in danger, but I don't see why I should keep it from you now."

"Keep what? And stop the suspense bollocks."

"She's a mafia princess. The daughter of the Russian mafia's leader in New York, to be more specific."

The information should reel me off my axis, but it doesn't. If anything, the pieces of the puzzle slowly come together.

Whether it's the way she ran away from her past and avoided it or how she didn't want to talk about her family. There's also the makeover and the way she seemed innocent yet dangerous that first day.

All of it.

She was a woman with baggage from the beginning and I knew it. I think I actually fell for it at some point.

So finding out that she has ties to the mafia makes complete sense. The guard who followed her makes sense, too. The fact that Daniel couldn't find anything on her when he did a background check is plausible, too. He must've done a paperwork, superficial one, but even if he dug deeper, she had the skills to hide her skeletons.

That woman had a double life, after all.

"What do you mean, I was in danger?" I ask Daniel.

"You were snooping around in *Bratva* business and hurting their associate, so the higher-ups threatened her with your life. They even told her to betray you, but she chose the third option."

"To go back to them." I don't phrase it as a question, because I know that's what she did.

She hurt me on purpose with the whole Daniel thing so I would forget her and not search for her.

Well, the fucking joke's on her because I'm never letting her go. Not even if I have to barge headfirst into her world.

Daniel lifts his shoulder. "She didn't tell me that, but I assume so."

"What else did she tell you? Don't leave anything out."

"That I should keep an eye on you, that I shouldn't get mad when you become an arsehole, and that you mean well." He snorts. "She believed in you more than you believe in yourself, and didn't seem to care about her own wellbeing as long as you were alright. I have to say, you're a lucky son of a bitch to have found someone like her."

I am.

I fucking am.

And now, I have to get her back to where she belongs.

By my fucking side.

THIRTY-SEVEN

Anastasia

Papa is telling me to prepare for my engagement, saying that it will happen soon.

He's even taking me with him to parties organized by the *Bratva* and its allies.

Like today. He threw a party out of nowhere to celebrate the rekindling of our relationship with the Italians. Something that Adrian, the cunning wolf, made happen.

Needless to say, our house is overflowing with guests from all different factions and even businessmen that the *Bratva* considers friends. Most of them are Russian, but there are all types of nationalities here. The brotherhood believes in making global allies since that gets them what they want faster.

The overflowing of people makes my head hurt, especially since they only see me as stock. A bride to be married to the best man.

A prize.

I was with Rai a while ago, but she has shareholders to greet and rounds to make, and I'll just be a hindrance. Even though her stomach is growing noticeably, she doesn't let that stop her from being a kickass businesswoman. Kyle is by her side every step of the way, though.

As I stand in the corner, clutching a drink, I can't help watching how he gently yet firmly places a hand at the small of her back. How he strokes her over her clothes and gives her water to drink.

A shiver goes through me at the scene, and a pit of loneliness stabs me in the stomach. My heart aches and splinters at the memory of Knox holding me to him and stroking my skin as if he got pleasure from it.

And the thought that I might never get that again clogs my throat until I can no longer breathe.

Papa meant what he said that day a week ago in his office and he kept his part of the deal.

He left Knox alone and now, I have to do the same or Papa's answer will be written in blood.

I know what he's doing with these parties and by making sure to introduce me alongside Damien. He's getting everyone to see me with my "future husband," as he calls him.

Something that Abe, the father of Damien's supposed bride-to-be, took extreme offense to. And there might be a fight behind the scenes between him and Papa as we speak. I could tell when Vlad, Kirill, and Adrian followed Papa, Abe, and the higher-ups of the *Yakuza* upstairs.

"Shouldn't you be up there, too?" I ask Aleksander, who's standing not far from me, beside the balcony window.

He has one hand over the other, and despite his generally calm demeanor, his forefinger is twitching, which might be the only sign of distress he's ever shown.

"Boss told me to stay here," he says without looking at me.

"I'm not going to run away with so many guards in here. If you're so worried about him, just go up there."

He presses his lips in a line. "I won't defy his order."

"Good luck with the guilt when he gets hurt then."

Aleksander flashes me a deadly stare, as if I murdered his children and ate them for breakfast. "He's not going to get hurt. He can take care of himself."

"You don't sound so convincing. You're thinking it, aren't you? That something will go south and there will be no one to protect your precious boss."

"Miss…" There's a warning in his tone.

"What?"

"Are you enjoying this?"

I take a sip of my drink and revel in the burn of the vodka. "Maybe. I'm bored because you guys decided it was a good idea to track me, so forgive me if I choose to enjoy your misery a little."

"Your father is up there, too."

"He'll be fine. If anything happens, everyone will take the bullet for him, starting with Kirill."

I can hear the grinding of Aleksander's teeth, but before he can say anything, Damien waltzes in, carrying a glass of vodka and making a show of drinking it with leisurely calm.

"If it isn't my future wife." he speaks in an unusually cheerful tone. "And the pretty boy Sasha. And here I thought you were Kirill's shadow."

"He decided not to watch when he actually gets shot." I mean it as a joke, but Aleksander goes rigid, then storms in the direction of the stairs without a word.

"What's up with that crazy motherfucker?" Damien watches him for a while before he dismisses him and focuses on me. "Were you a naughty girl or a good girl with him?"

"I don't see why that should concern you."

A manic smirk lifts his lips. "Hmm…and here I thought you were a docile lamb, my Nastyusha. See, I prefer the fight, the running and clawing, it makes the chasing and breaking process thrilling."

I swallow, my heart jackhammering in my throat, but I refuse to show it. I refuse to show that he scares the shit out of me, that whenever I see his face, it's not his handsome looks that greet me, it's a devil in disguise.

So I inhale for a few more seconds. "Shouldn't you be with them? This whole fight is about you."

"Nah. It's not a real fight, so I'm not interested. Sergei started this mess and he can sort it out himself."

"I thought you wanted to marry the Japanese girl," I try in a softer tone.

"Nope, Rai and that fucker Kirill arranged it for some diplomatic *Yakuza-Bratva* shit. I couldn't care less."

"Won't she be sad that you're breaking off the engagement?"

"Why the fuck would she? We haven't even met."

Damn it.

I foolishly hoped there would be some form of attachment between them, that I could get in touch with her and come up with a plan to break off this engagement, but if they're strangers, I have no hope there.

What was I thinking, anyway? This brute is not the type to get attached to anyone or anything.

"Besides, I'm allergic to anyone who doesn't drink vodka." He grins, clinking his glass against mine. "At least you do."

"I don't love you, Damien," I murmur slowly. "I don't want to marry you."

"Love?" He appears genuinely perplexed. "What the fuck does that mean?"

"What Rai and Kyle have." I motion at them, then at Adrian's wife, who's talking with her husband's guard, but her attention is firmly on where he disappeared to with Papa and the others. "What Adrian and Lia have."

"You mean marriage."

"No. Love and marriage are different. Love is when you can't breathe when the other isn't there. It's when living becomes a chore, and waking up every day is an accomplishment. It's when you can't stop thinking about them and need them close so you can finally exist."

"Sounds like a fucking hindrance."

"It's not. Damien…please…I want to be with the man I love."

"Fine."

I pause, my lips parting. "R-really?"

"I told you, Nastyusha, you have time to ruin this marriage before it happens."

"But if you tell Papa you don't want to marry me…"

"No."

"Why not?"

"I'm not going to get on the *Pakhan*'s bad side for this. It's your mess. Clean it up yourself."

"Do *you* want to marry me?"

"Not particularly. I keep saying that I'm not husband material, but everyone refuses to believe me, so if I have to go through with this, it'll be with the *Pakhan*'s blessings. And also…"

He trails off, his gaze getting lost, and for a second, a fraction even, I see a spark in his usually dead eyes. It's a fire so hot that it nearly burns me, and it's not even directed at me.

I follow his field of vision and catch a glimpse of a petite Asian girl who's probably my age or younger.

She's wearing a simple black dress and heels that match her hair and eyes and contrast against her pale skin. Two Asian men in suits stand on either side of her as she carries a plate of pastries.

The moment her gaze meets Damien's, she freezes, as if the fire in his eyes could burn her from this distance.

Then she places the plate on the table, turns around, and leaves with a feather-like grace. The men follow after her, clicking their earpieces.

Are they from the Chinese triads? Or maybe the *Yakuza*?

I don't get a chance to think about it further, because Damien pushes his glass of vodka into my free hand. The fire that ignited in his eyes a moment ago is now pitch-black and seems darker than I've ever seen.

Even more than when he kills people.

"Hold this for me," he says in a calm yet charged tone, then he strides in the direction where the Asian girl just disappeared to.

Oh, well.

Is it wrong to hope that she's Abe's daughter and he changed his mind? I feel bad for the girl, but I also can't marry Damien.

I feel like I might die.

Opting to get some air, I abandon the two glasses of vodka on the nearest table and go out to the balcony.

I let the cold night air wash over me. Goosebumps pop up on my bare arms and I welcome the shiver.

I tried to avoid getting dolled up today, but all I have are cocktail dresses and beautiful flowery ones, so that wasn't really possible. I opted for a knee-length one that matches the eyes I've been continuously dreaming about.

Blowing out a puff of air, I retrieve my phone from my dress pocket. It's a new one Papa got for me, where only his, Rai's, Vladimir's, and Damien's numbers are saved.

It doesn't matter, though, because I memorized not only his number but also two others I probably shouldn't have.

I type one of them. No clue if it's the stress of the inevitable or the longing I've felt for the week and a half I haven't seen Knox. Not directly, at least, because I keep stalking him all over the media.

But I don't think about it as I hit Call. My heart thumps loudly in my ears as I listen to it ring. Is it too late to hang up and pretend this call never happened?

As I'm about to do that, the distinctive sound of someone picking up greets me, followed by a serious female, "Hello?"

"Hi. It's me, Teal. Jane."

There's a long silence at the other end of the line, so long that my breathing thickens. I expected this reaction, but ever since Papa laid out her and Knox's past in front of me, I couldn't help feeling the need to talk to her.

Maybe I sensed this all along, which is why I memorized her and Elsa's phone numbers. We exchanged them that one time we met, and Elsa might have forced Teal to do it. Before I changed phone numbers, Elsa used to send me good mornings and hellos and we chatted sometimes, but this is my first contact with Teal.

"This isn't your number," she says finally.

"I changed it."

"Okay."

I gulp again. If there's one thing I've noticed about Teal, it's her no-nonsense personality, so she'd expect me to get to the point soon.

"Listen, Teal…I…I'm sorry."

"About what?"

"Everything."

"He told you?" There's a tiny softness in her voice.

"Not exactly…"

"I knew he would."

"You did?"

"Yeah. He looks at you differently. Almost like the way Ronan looks at me, and let's just say I never expected to see that expression on my aimless brother's face."

"Teal…"

"So, what now? You feel sorry for us?"

"No. Of course…I…understand, or I hope I do. My childhood wasn't a colorful one either since I was raised by an abusive father." I pause, then blurt, "That doesn't mean that I'm downplaying what you went through. I know it's much more serious, and you guys are way more stronger than me. I called my biological father for help, but you found it on your own, and I guess what I'm trying to say is that I respect that. So much."

There's a pause before she says in a less defensive tone, "So you don't pity us?"

"Absolutely not. I just…just want to hug him and you…and I'm not much of a hugger. Besides, I have a feeling you're not either. But yeah, I don't pity you."

"Good, because I wouldn't let anyone make my brother feel less than what he is. He deserves better." Her voice lowers, and I think it breaks when she says, "He deserves the world for how he stood up for both of us."

"I know."

"No, you don't know. And even if you did, it's only his side of the story in which he must've made his role seem miniscule."

"There's another side?"

"Yes. Mine. What happened to us back then was…bad. It was so bad that we both consider it our lives' black holes. But I was able to escape it at a younger age. Knox hasn't. He buried it inside and thought it would magically heal, which is never the case. If anything, it will fester and become worse as the years go by. But do you know when the first time he allowed himself to be open, even a little, was? It was with you, and I could feel it, even if he doesn't talk about it, even if he still considers himself my protector and wants to shield me from pain. I know I haven't really been welcoming of you, but it takes me some time to warm up to people, so if you want, if you can, maybe we can meet sometimes?"

"I'm sorry, Teal." My voice is brittle, wrong.

"Whatever for?"

"I don't think it's possible anymore. He and I…we belong to different worlds."

"I thought that, too, when I first met my husband, but he's the most precious gift I've ever received."

"It's not the same…I…my father is the leader of the Russian mafia," I whisper the words, and feel so much shame, it heats my ears.

"So what?" Teal says.

"Huh?"

"I don't see why that should be a problem if the two of you are fine with it."

"Did you hear a word I said? My life is a disaster waiting to happen. There's always danger everywhere."

"It can't be worse than how pained you sound right now, or how down Knox has sounded over the phone lately."

My heart skips at the mention of his name and I tighten my hold on the phone. "He has?"

"He's been perfectly miserable and I finally figured out why."

"I…didn't mean to. I just wanted to protect him."

"You don't have to."

"You don't understand…"

"It's you who doesn't understand. If he wants you, *really* wants you, he'll shed blood for it, because that's who he is. A fighter. He's definitely not a coward who'll run the other way at the first obstacle. So give each other a chance, okay?"

Her words draw the tears that I've kept at bay and I sniff. "But it's too late. I'm engaged to be married."

Teal says something, but I don't hear her, because a violent rush goes through my limbs and goosebumps cover my skin.

And then I hear it.

The voice I'll never forget for as long as I live.

"Like fuck you are."

THIRTY-EIGHT

Knox

THE BLOOD IN MY VEINS BOILS AND THREATENS TO SPILL over.

Partly because I'm seeing Anastasia after a long time of living with her ghost and imagining her in every corner.

So seeing her right in front of me is no different than crashing into the wall created by my shadows.

Ever since I was young, they've tried everything to confine me within forts no one has access to.

But then Anastasia came along and she didn't even search for the keys. She went for the walls themselves, demolishing them one by each and every one.

Then she had the audacity to leave as if she hadn't inflicted that much damage.

As if she has no hold on my fucking soul.

My gaze rakes over her appearance, getting caught in her elegant dress and the way it fits her delicate curves.

She's not hiding behind glasses or a different hair color. I almost forgot how blonde her hair is—icy, bordering on white, framing her face in a halo. She's like an angel with her soft features, pale skin, and those blue, blue eyes.

Back then at the bar, they resembled a bright morning sky, but they're gloomy right now, filled with moisture and a somber edge that stabs my gut.

It's part of why I can't contain my rage, why it's treading on the edge of my control, about to snap it and wreak havoc on everything in its path.

But the biggest part is what I just overheard her say over the phone.

I'm engaged to be married.

As in, another fucker is calling her "fiancée" and he'll put a ring on her finger and make her his wife.

A pressing weight perches on my chest at the thought and it's hard to breathe properly. It's even more difficult to keep myself in check and not destroy everything in my path.

Starting with him.

The fucker who thinks he could take Anastasia away from me.

"K-Knox…?" she stammers, her soft voice unsure, as if she doesn't believe I'm standing here.

I wouldn't have believed it either a week ago. But ever since Daniel confirmed my doubts about her and I put all the pieces of the puzzle together, I had to find her again.

I had to rectify things.

"You were expecting someone else?" I can't control the venom in my tone. "Your *fiancé* perhaps?"

"Oh my God, you're really here…" I expected anything from her reaction—the initial shock, shame, maybe even anger, but when she starts shaking and her grip releases her phone, letting it clatter to the floor, the last emotion I expected takes refuge in her eyes.

Fear.

Deep, raw, and absolutely gutting. It's like she's seeing her worst nightmare coming true.

Or maybe the scariest ghost from her childhood nightmares.

She lunges at me, grabbing my arm with her unsteady one. "You have to go. You can't be here…"

I effortlessly pull free of her hold. "This is exactly where I'm supposed to be."

"No…" She's shaking her head, her frantic gaze searching behind me for something or someone, I'm not sure.

"On the contrary, it's a fucking yes, beautiful."

"You don't understand…"

I grab her by her slim shoulders, shaking her. "It's you who doesn't seem to understand the reality of things. Did you really think pulling that stunt with Daniel and disappearing on me would mean I'd let you go? You can run to the other side of the world, invent a new fucking identity and name and life, and I would still find you. You're mine, fucking mine, and that means there's no fucking escaping me. There's no escaping *us*."

A tear slides down her cheek and clings to her upper lip. I don't think as I lean over and lick it, my tongue clinging to her skin as I taste the saltiness. Then I drag my tongue up her cheek, licking the tear, and when I reach her eyes, I kiss the closed lid. I kiss those ethereally blue eyes that I haven't stopped thinking about since the first time I saw them.

Her nails sink into my forearms and she digs them in deeply, but nothing is deep enough to push me off her, so I continue kissing her tears and feasting on her taste.

"I lied to you," she murmurs, her voice barely audible.

I pull back but don't let her go. "About what?"

"About who I am. Where I come from. My family. All of it."

"You didn't lie. You just hid it. I knew all along there was more to the birth of Jane's identity."

"It's because…I'm…I'm…"

"The daughter of the New York *Bratva's Pakhan*. I know."

"And you still came?" She stares incredulously, some of her earlier fear slipping back into her eyes. "What is wrong with you?"

"You." I breathe out the word, leaning my forehead against

hers. "You are everything that's wrong with me, beautiful. You took something of mine and I need it back."

"Stop saying things like that…Knox…please, listen to me, you have to go. If Papa or any of the others see you—"

"I'm not scared of them."

She pushes at my chest with her fists, but there's no energy behind it, as if she doesn't want to be doing it. "Any person in their right mind would be. They kill in the blink of an eye and without any remorse. You'll just be another nameless person on their list."

"I'm not in my right fucking mind, Anastasia. I told you just now, you took something of mine. My fucking sanity included."

She clutches my hand, her grip clammy and still shaking, then guides me in from the balcony, her gaze watching every nook and cranny like a hawk.

"Where are you taking me, beautiful?"

"Shh." She shakes her head at me, then leads me to some stairs that are hidden from the main staircase.

I've been in mafia leaders' houses before when I was either investigating something or on a case. But the Russian *Bratva's* compound, aka Sergei Sokolov's mansion, is more like a billionaire's home that you could easily get lost in.

That's Anastasia's real last name. Sokolov. I finally have a full profile of the mysterious girl with the bright eyes and soft smile.

She basically drags me up the stairs, down a hall, and then pushes me into a room. The moment she closes the door, she releases a breath, but she doesn't relax her hold on my hand.

I throw a quick glance at the room and it doesn't take me long to realize it's hers.

There's a giant desk on the corner with three monitors, but the rest of it is girly. The bedsheets have a butterfly motif and the creamy wallpaper has flowers on it.

She's always been a conundrum of opposing things, but they still fit her character so well.

They still speak so much of her and who she is.

A soft woman with a secret wild side.

"So this is where you lived all this time."

She gives me the stink eye. "That's not what should be important right now."

"Then what is?" I step to her and she visibly swallows. "I think it's hot to see where you sleep every night in nothing but shorts. Maybe even naked?"

"S-stop it." Her voice is breathy, but arousal coats it.

My hand reaches forward and I wrap it around her throat, squeezing the sides a little. She briefly closes her eyes, releasing a chopped exhale, and I tighten my hold. I need to feel her, to be able to breathe again, but the fact that she's relieved as well? That when she opens her eyes, they're filled with a wave of longing that's as strong as mine? Those facts nearly make me go crazy.

And I have to grip her harder, to sink my fingers into her flesh and make sure she's here.

She's right here.

"Knox...I..."

"Shhh." I place a finger to her mouth and push her back with my hold on her throat.

A yelp echoes in the air as she trips on the edge of the bed and falls on her back. I follow with her, my free hand gripping her hip.

She slams her hands on my chest. "D-don't."

"Don't?"

"Don't turn me onto my stomach. I want to look at you," she whispers, her tone as vulnerable as the look on her face.

My fingers dig into her hips and I'm about to refuse that, I'm about to do as I'm used to, but something stops me.

The pleading in her eyes, the vulnerability in them.

Also, a part of me is fighting it, too. It's the same part that couldn't survive without her and has turned my life into a living hell since she's been gone.

Her palms flatten on my chest and she softens her voice. "I know, Knox...I know about your past and why you find it hard to get close and I understand, I—"

"Stop talking." The rage from earlier resurfaces again and this time, it's for entirely different reasons.

The shadows swirl around my head in a thick fog with the need to hurt her.

To shut up the woman who shouldn't have seen them in the first place.

But I clamp that need down, my fingers flexing so I don't hurt her. "How the fuck do you know?"

"P-Papa…he can find out everything about anyone."

"Fuck." My fist clenches and I realize it's on her throat. She's wheezing, her face reddening from the lack of air, and I release her with a jerk and start to sit up, but she grabs my cheeks, pulling me back down.

I use my arms to keep from crushing her with my weight, but Anastasia doesn't stop there, she doesn't stop with her fingers stroking my face or when her tits are inches from my heaving chest.

Her eyes trap mine and her voice trembles a little when she speaks, "It's okay, you don't have to hide from me. You don't have to look the other way or be ashamed of who you are."

"Even though I was a whore?"

"You weren't." The certainty and power in her voice stabs me in the fucking part of my chest I thought died twenty years ago. "You were an abused child and it wasn't your fault. It was theirs, your mother's and whoever she brought over. Just like it was my stepfather's fault that my mom was abused and beaten to death. It's never the victim's fault, no matter what anyone says."

I wipe the tears that have escaped her lids with my thumb. "Don't cry, not for this."

She shakes her head, her hold tightening on my cheeks. "Don't you get it? Ever since I learned about your past, I couldn't sleep at night. I wanted to run away again, to find you and just hold you close. If I could, I would take it all for myself so you wouldn't have to be shackled by it anymore. Your pain is mine, Knox. I feel it deep in my heart and I can't stop thinking about it."

"I have."

"No, you haven't. You just pretend you have, and I know it's a coping mechanism, but I just want you to know that it's okay if you're tired of holding the mask in place. It's okay if you want to drop it and just be you. I won't look the other way. I promise."

My hand finds her throat again, and I revel in the gulp and slight moan she releases. "You're a fucking nuisance, did you know that? You're not supposed to go digging in the darkest parts of me."

"They're still you and that's all I care about."

Well, fuck.

Just when I thought this woman couldn't engrave herself under my skin any deeper, she goes ahead and digs herself a cozier nook where I'll never be able to remove her.

And I want to shake her for it.

"You shouldn't like those parts of me, not when I hate them myself."

"You don't get to tell me what I like about you."

"Are you sure about that, Anastasia? Because there's a shitload of fucking skeletons in my closet that you didn't even know existed. I've been in bed with my demons for as long as I lived, ever since I was a clueless fucking child who still didn't know what the world is all about. Ever since I had strange men touch me inappropriately and was too weak to stop them and save myself or my sister."

"But you did." Her voice is low, but it's determined, as if she's making sure to drive a point home. "You ran away. You saved both yourself and your sister. When no one stepped up to be your hero, you became one yourself. So no, Knox, you won't scare me away. Those skeletons? I want to see them. And those demons? I will eventually chase them away."

My jaw aches from how much I'm clenching it. I want to tell her no, that she's not allowed near my fucking demons or else they will swallow her whole, but judging by the assertiveness written all over her delicate features, there's no way in fuck I would change her mind.

And it boggles the shit out of me. The fact that she wants me, that she won't shy away from any part of me.

Hell, she even wants to see me. *All* of me.

Not only the beautiful façade or the charming character, but also every fucked up side I've swept under the rug for decades.

Bloody *decades*.

And yet, she manages to drag everything out in no time.

"Besides," she continues. "Those who pick and choose what parts of you to keep and what to throw away should rot in the darkest pit of hell. Because those parts? Those are what made you the man you are. Those are what brought you to Jersey the day I decided to go against my upbringing and do one thing for me, not for my family or what's expected of me. *You* are that thing, Knox. That night might've been about sex, but it was so much more afterward. You showed me things I didn't know existed and opened my eyes to the world. You gave me the safety I didn't realize I was searching for."

"Then why did you leave?"

"I told you. It was to protect you."

I squeeze my fingers on the side of her neck, my voice tight. "Can't you fucking understand that what you've done is no different than stabbing me and letting me bleed to death? I got so used to your lively presence and nerdy talk, and now that you're gone, my flat feels like a tomb. I used to fall asleep listening to you narrate those long fantasy books in an awed tone, but now I can't sleep anymore. So I smell your orange shampoo like a damn junkie to get a whiff of you and still fail to fill the gap you fucking left behind. So if protecting me means I'll live without you, I don't fucking want it."

A lone tear slides down her cheek. "Knox…"

I cut her off with my lips on hers and I kiss her with a ferocity that hardens my dick and tightens my balls. I kiss her while holding her neck, and she continues to clutch my cheeks.

I kiss her until she's struggling for air and her tongue is so entangled with mine, I don't know where she starts and I end. But she kisses me back with the same heat, my Anastasia, as if she's waited as much as I have for a taste, for a fragment of what we have.

Still kissing her, I reach between us and lift her dress to her waist. She mindlessly clutches my belt and helps me unzip my trousers and free my hard cock.

It's been in a constant state of arousal ever since she left, and no amount of hand jobs could substitute for her warmth.

I move her panties to the side, groaning at how soaking wet she is, then I drive inside her without breaking the kiss.

Her body instantly welcomes me, opening up and arching in invitation. It's like she's been waiting for me as long as I've waited for her. Her back lifts off the bed and she shudders, her mouth parting from mine as she moans.

"Fuck, baby." I dig my fingers in her throat. "I missed you."

"I...I...missed you, too. I missed you so much, it hurt."

I lose control at the sound of her needy words, not that I have any when it comes to her.

She effortlessly turns me into a fucking animal who's unable to survive without her.

My pace picks up and I kiss her as hard as I fuck her until she's sliding off the bed and my hold on her neck is the only thing keeping her in place.

One thing doesn't change even as I fuck her hard and rough— the way she's looking into my eyes while holding my face.

I'm here for you, she says with those expressive blues. *I want you no matter what.*

And it drives me wild. Looking at her while being inside her, looking at her while her channel tightens around me, strangling me, drives me fucking insane.

But instead of upping my rhythm, I take it slow for the first time ever. I roll my hips and drive deep into her until she's shuddering again and her walls close around me like a vise.

My kiss becomes more passionate than frantic, my tongue toying with hers as my dick pounds her tight little cunt with measured thrusts. She pulls her legs wider apart, raising one up a little to allow me more access and I take it, going to lengths I've never imagined.

And when she starts shaking, her walls clenching around me, and she's moaning loudly, I'm right there with her. My spine tingles and I shoot my cum inside her in long spurts until my balls are spent.

I'm about to crush her with my weight, so I maneuver us so that she's on top of me, her icy blonde hair at my chin. But I remain deep inside her. My dick twitching, slowly but surely readying for another round.

We remain like that for a while, until her breathing evens out and I think she's fallen asleep. It's a habit of hers after sex.

Still wrapping a hand around her back, I reach into my trouser pocket and retrieve the butterfly pendant. I've kept it ever since she forgot it in the hotel room that day.

Every time I've looked at it, I recalled how the black wings flattened against her pale back when I first saw her that night.

The memory seems far away, but I can never forget it. If anything, I might have become obsessed with her since then.

I gently fasten the chain around her throat. The other one was ruined so I got her a golden chain to go along with it.

She stirs when the weight of the necklace—or its coldness—rests against her skin. At first, her gaze is confused, but when she looks down, her eyes widen. "My butterfly."

"You mentioned it has value to you, so I thought I'd bring it. I put it on a chain so you can have it on you all the time."

"Thank you." A soft smile lifts her lips. "It's the only thing I have left of Mom and it means so much to me."

"I'm glad I was the one who found it then."

"Me, too." She runs her fingers over the black wings. "You know, back then, I used to think of myself as the fairy of the forest and used this as my magic wand to order trees and small animals around."

A smile breaks on my lips. "I can clearly imagine you as a naughty fairy."

"I...wasn't naughty."

"Uh-huh. Did you wear skimpy clothes, too?"

"Stop, you pervert!"

"What? If you have a role-play kink, I'd be happy to oblige."

"I do not." She clears her throat. "Anyway, how did you get here?"

"An acquaintance Nate knows is apparently a *Bratva* associate and she got me here as her plus-one."

She lifts her head, leaning her elbows on my chest to look me in the eye. "A woman?"

"Yeah."

A frown appears between her brows. "And do you know her intimately?"

"Hmm. Maybe."

"It's a yes or no question."

"My, my, beautiful, are you jealous?"

"No." She stares into space.

"You're so fucking adorable to think I would look at any other woman after I've been with you."

She hiccups and it's obviously involuntary, because her face and neck become a deep shade of red. "I…can't look at other men either."

My eyes narrow. "Is that why you have a *fiancé?*"

"Papa picked him because he's Russian and part of the *Bratva*. I had no say in it."

"That will change." I slowly pull out of her, then stand up.

Even though my dick is craving another round, I need to take care of the fucker standing between us.

Anastasia's face, however, loses the easygoing edge and goes back to that frightened stage. "W-what are you going to do?"

I go to her en-suite bathroom and wipe off my dick, then I return with wet towels, but she's already cleaned herself with tissues and straightened up her clothes, and is staring at me with that perturbed look, one that I'll erase from her face, once and for all.

"You need to leave, Knox. I'll show you a back entrance where there aren't many cameras…"

I grab her hand and interlink our fingers. "I'm going nowhere. It's time I meet your family."

Then I'm pulling her out of the room in the midst of her continuous protests. The moment we step out, she gasps, her hand trembling in mine, and I realize it's because we're face to face with an older white-haired man who has Anastasia's exact eyes but with no innocence in them.

Her relation to him is confirmed when she whispers in a horrified tone, "Papa."

THIRTY-NINE

Anastasia

A TREMOR JOLTS THROUGH MY LIMBS AND I FREEZE.

Ever since I saw Knox on the balcony, I knew this would happen.

I knew he'd get caught by someone. Anyone. I just didn't think it'd be Papa himself.

You don't get into the *Pakhan*'s house while he's surrounded by his leaders and guards and hope to leave unscathed.

But I thought we had more time with the way all of them were preoccupied with the *Yakuza* stuff. I thought I could make Knox leave before they found him.

I might have let my vulnerability take hold of me for a while. I might have missed him so much that I just wanted to touch him, to make sure this wasn't one of my cruel dreams that I'd soon wake up from.

I wasn't jolted awake this time. Everything was real, whether it's the way he kissed me, held me by the throat, or fucked me.

No, it wasn't all fucking. At some point, he was making love to me while staring into my eyes.

At some point, he brought his forts down and allowed me to see him. All of him. Not the put-together lawyer who can blind anyone with his charisma, but the boy he once was. The broken, wounded boy he refuses to let anyone see.

But he let me. Only me.

I swear something inside me melted and fused with him at that moment. No idea what, but he's holding it even now as we stare at Papa, Vladimir, and Adrian.

The most powerful men in the *Bratva*.

They're not looking at me, though. Their hawk-like attention is on Knox and his grip on my hand. I try to release him, but he just tightens his hold on my fingers, refusing to budge.

"What is this?" Papa asks in his firm tone that rattles me to my bones.

My throat is dry and the words are stuck, but the stern look in my father's gaze propels me to fumble for words. "I…I can explain, Papa…he…he's…"

"I'm the man who loves your daughter and I refuse to leave without her."

"Knox!" I hiss low, my wild gaze flying to my father's.

"Then you won't leave. Not alive, at least," he says, then motions with two fingers at his guards who charge forward at Knox.

The worst-case scenario materializes in front of me as Papa's buff guard reaches for him. I don't even think about it as I jump in front of Knox, trying to ward off their malicious intentions.

"Papa…please don't do this."

"I told you to cut off all ties with him, Anastasia, but you didn't. So we're doing this my way."

The guards push me aside and I trip, but Knox grips me by the arm to keep me standing.

I grab onto him as if he's a lifeline. If he's going to hurt Knox, he'll have to hurt both of us.

Knox, however, steps in front of me, partly shielding me from my father. His broad shoulders are the only thing I see and I find solace in that. Safety in the midst of the chaos that's whirling around me.

"Don't touch her," Knox tells the guards, his posture turning rigid and his voice holding a lethal edge.

"Or what?" It's Vlad who asks in his thick, scary accent. "Do you think you can do anything? Here, of all places? I can put a bullet in your head in the next second for your insolence alone."

Knox remains in his erect posture, not even a little fazed by Vladimir's threats. "Is that how you treat possible business associates?"

"Associate?" Adrian asks with a note of curiosity.

Knox stares at Papa. "I have an offer for you, but I'll not make it unless I'm given your word that Anastasia will be safe and free from any engagement you forced on her."

"You do not make demands in my own house." Papa's voice hardens and I know he's getting angry. I can taste the thickness of it in the air.

So I soften my voice. "Just…hear him out, Papa."

I have no clue what type of plan Knox came up with, but any plan is better than nothing at this point.

"What's your offer?" Adrian asks.

"I won't say anything until I'm given your word."

"Speak or I'll put that bullet between your eyes." Vlad doesn't reach for his waistband, but I don't have to see it to know there's a gun there.

I release a fractured breath and tighten my sweaty hand on Knox's, then whisper, "Just say whatever you came to say…please…"

If he doesn't, Papa won't hesitate to give the order to kill him. And if I witness that, I won't be able to survive.

I can tell Knox doesn't want to budge, but playing hotheadedness with the leaders of the brotherhood is the last thing he wants to do. These are men who are used to violence and wouldn't hesitate to use it on him.

When I squeeze his hand one more time, he says, "I heard

you're looking to legitimize more of your income through your legal front, V Corp, and I can help with that."

"How?" Adrian asks.

"I own a third of a multi-billion-dollar empire that's currently managed by my father and my sister. That's how."

"So you'll invest in V Corp." It's not a question. Adrian is grappling with details and forming his own theories. "How much are we talking about?"

"Every penny to my name."

I gasp, holding my hand to my mouth to hide the sound. Did he just say he'll give all his money to my family?

For me?

Papa watches Knox without a change of expression and Vladimir still has suspicion written all over his face.

It's Adrian who remains in his calm and continues his interrogation. "Wouldn't your father oppose such a step? I believe a successful businessman like him wouldn't want ties with us."

"I already spoke to him and he won't interfere with any decisions I make about my inheritance."

A brief silence falls in the hall and I fidget, my hands turning clammier in Knox's as I wait with bated breath. In theory, they should agree. Adrian of all people would because profit is his first aim, but Vlad and Papa are much more traditionalist and wouldn't look at it from that perspective.

He's still an outsider and definitely not Russian.

"Leave," Papa tells Knox.

"I said I won't until you give me your word—"

"Leave," Papa cuts him off, but he's not threatening him again. He's not telling him that if he doesn't leave he'll kill him.

Which means he's changed his mind about something, or maybe he's considering another option.

I can't help the hope that blossoms beneath my ribcage and spreads to my whole body.

Knox is about to say something, but I grab his arm and shake my head. I rise on my tiptoes and whisper to his ear, "This is the closest thing to a truce that he can offer, so just go… I'll call you."

"No."

"Knox, please…you won't get another chance to leave this house alive."

"I don't want it if it means separating from you."

A shadow falls over us and it's Vlad, glaring at both of us. "Are you going to leave with your head in place or should I sever it first?"

"He will," I say firmly and then nudge Knox, begging him with my eyes to make the smart choice.

His jaw tightens and those beautiful golden eyes darken. For a second, I think he'll say no and land himself in trouble, but he slowly relaxes his jaw.

"If she doesn't call me in a day," he tells my father, "I'll be back, and this time, you won't be able to kick me out."

Vlad steps forward, probably to smack him for the insolence of speaking to the *Pakhan* that way, but Papa shakes his head.

Knox pulls me to him, brushes his lips on the top of my head, then says, "I'll be back, beautiful."

And with that, he slowly releases me and walks between Papa and Adrian with sure confidence.

I release a large gulp of air when none of the guards follow him.

He should be safe.

For now.

"Adrian, Vladimir," Papa starts. "Wait for me in my office."

They comply with a nod, even though Vlad hesitates. Adrian gives me a knowing look, one I don't really understand, but for some reason, I want to believe it's a good sign.

Papa goes into my room and I take the cue to follow him, my body heavy and exhausted, which has nothing to do with the way Knox took me ruthlessly, then gently, worshipping my body in ways I've never felt before.

As much as I want to think of him, I force myself to shake those thoughts away. I really shouldn't be picturing Knox and sex when Papa's shoulders are crowding with tension. He stands by my desk and watches the monitors as if it's the first time he's seen them.

Well, he rarely comes into my room, but he was the one who bought me my setup when I first started getting hooked on coding and computers.

He's also the one who took it away when I came back by severing the power cables in my room.

"Maybe I shouldn't have let you go into computer engineering," he says with no animosity, running his long, meaty fingers across the mouse pad.

Papa might have gotten old, but nothing, absolutely nothing could erase the power that radiates off him. My uncle was more ruthless, louder, and a man not to be messed with. My papa seemed the more approachable one, the strategist of sorts, but everyone knows Papa has the type of power that simmers beneath the surface and only shows when it's necessary.

It's not by a stroke of luck that everyone in the *Bratva* respects him. Men like Adrian, Vlad, Kirill, and even Damien see him as their *Pakhan*, and those men don't bend the knee to just anyone.

Even Kyle, Rai's husband, a merciless hitman who has no allegiance to anyone but himself, considers Papa the leader. Rai's love and adoration for my father plays a role, but still.

"If you hadn't, maybe you wouldn't have left," he continues.

"I would've found a way to protect *Babushka* after you sent her back to Russia."

"She's no good for you. That woman only fills your head with flowery dreams that have no place in our world."

"Papa, please don't hurt her—"

"You think I'm heartless enough to hurt a dying woman?"

"I don't know. You really won't hurt her?"

"No."

"T-thank you, Papa."

"If you really want to thank me, then do as you're told and forget about the British lawyer."

My chest deflates. "It's not up to me. I…can't. He makes me feel special, like my existence has meaning. He doesn't see me as your daughter or the *Bratva*'s sheltered princess, he sees me as me. Just me. And I want that, Papa. I want to get out of yours and the brotherhood's shadow. I want to be me."

I gulp in air after my word vomit. I wouldn't have been able to say those words if he were facing me. Even though I'm grown now, he's still that god-like man who finished my stepfather's life in a blink.

Papa slowly turns around and I expect anger, but his expression remains unperturbed.

I wait for him to say something, but the door barges open and I startle. Damien waltzes inside with that black cat swagger of his.

"I'm sorry, Boss." My father's senior guard peeks in. "I'll escort him out."

Damien tilts his head in the guard's direction. "First of all, fuck you. Second of all, fuck off before I stab you."

Papa motions at his senior guard to leave and he snarls at Damien. "Wait in my office with the others, Orlov."

"I just want to say something and then I'll be out of your hair."

"What?" my father asks with a note of impatience.

"As much as I appreciate Nastyusha for being a vodka lover, I can't marry her."

My lips part and I stare at Damien with wide eyes. Never in my wildest dreams would I have expected him to back off. Not after he said he wouldn't get on my father's bad side for something he considers trivial—marriage.

"Why not?" Papa's voice hardens.

"Remember that word I gave to Abe about marrying his daughter? I'm keeping it, after all."

"You were fine with breaking it not too long ago."

A dark smile lifts Damien's lips and he looks like a fallen angel. "That was before I knew who my future wife-to-be is."

"That doesn't change anything, Orlov."

"Yes, it does, *Pakhan*."

"Are you choosing a Japanese over a Russian?"

"I'm choosing the Japanese for us. Believe me, you'll like what I do with this whole fucking thing. Besides, Nastyusha loves that lawyer and I'd rather not kill a citizen and have her slice my throat in my sleep." He grins at me. "You owe me one."

And with that, he turns around and leaves, humming a tune.

I keep staring at his back, but that only lasts for a second, until Papa's guard closes the door.

Before I can wrap my head around what Damien said, Papa's clipped voice reaches me. "You'll marry Kirill or Vladimir."

"Papa!"

"Pick one."

"Vlad is like my older brother."

"Kirill then."

"Papa, please, no. He's even worse than Damien. Not only is he cunning and manipulative, but he'll also only use me to become the *Pakhan*."

"So be it."

Tears slide down my face. "Is that all I've ever been to you? A pawn on a chessboard? A prize for the most suitable?"

He's silent for a beat before he lets out a long exhale. "I have lung cancer, Nastyusha."

"W-what?"

"I'm in remission, but the doctors say I could relapse at any time and I might have to start counting my days."

The room sways but I realize it's me as I grab onto the nearest chair and use it as support. The information he just revealed pricks my skin over and over.

Papa has cancer—or used to.

"Oh, God, is this why you wanted to marry me off that time, but Rai volunteered to do it? You wanted to pick a new *Pakhan*, too."

"Yes. Only Rai and Vladimir know about my illness and we've kept it a secret from everyone else on purpose. I wanted to choose someone suitable for you before my time is up."

I don't think about it as I approach him until I'm so close, I can see how pale his skin is. Now that I think about it, right before I left, there were times when he pulled away from me and even refused to see me. And that pained me more than I admitted. It hurt to be just a wallflower in his house.

"Why didn't you tell me, Papa?"

"Because I don't want to hurt you."

"But I'm your daughter. I'm supposed to take care of you."

"You've always seen me as strong and powerful. That day I shot that lowlife, you looked at me as if I were a god, and I selfishly needed you to continue looking at me as such. I don't want you to witness me weak and coughing up blood."

"I don't care…I just want to be there for you like you were there for me when I was young."

He offers me his hand and I take it, sniffling back the tears. "Nastyusha…listen to me. You have to marry within the brotherhood to remain protected."

"No, Papa, I can't. I just can't marry Kirill or anyone else when I'm in love with Knox. It'll kill me slowly."

"Nastyusha…"

"Please give him a chance, Papa. *Please*. You'd be surprised to see the lengths he'd go to protect me and be there for me."

"What if he doesn't succeed?"

"He will." I have no doubt.

Because I realized something today.

Knox and I might belong to different worlds, but we belong together, and once we both put our minds to it, nothing can stop us.

FORTY

Knox

MEANT WHAT I TOLD ANASTASIA. IF SHE DOESN'T CALL ME today, I'm going back there, to the men she fears and doesn't want to defy.

Her father will either have to give her back to me or he might as well shoot me. That's the only way I would ever give up on her.

Fucking death.

I try to work normally, to pretend I'm a functioning human being, even though every neuron is urging me to go and find her.

Ten more hours, I tell myself.

Just ten more hours and I'll go find her.

My desk has been crowded with cases since the Bell trials made me famous—more than before—so I have even more people wanting me to represent them. I'll have to go through the details and choose which ones I'll take on.

I know for sure they're going to be cases for people like me—abused, broken, and with shadows crowding their lives twenty-four-seven. I always thought such cases weren't good for me; they'd trigger me, which is why I turned them down.

I used to put myself first, not caring about the fate of others. But through Sandra's case, I realized just how wrong that is. Yes, I'm allowed to feel pain, but not at the expense of ignoring theirs. I can have shadows, but I'm not supposed to be blinded to theirs.

It might have taken me some time to come to this conclusion, but better late than never.

And all of it is because of her, the woman who told me I could be a voice for those who have no voice. A bit like her, a bit like her mother.

She didn't give up, even though she barely knew me at the beginning. She pushed on and on until I conceded.

She's resilient that way, my Anastasia.

And now, I'm back to thinking about her, about how she begged me to leave, how she implored and insisted with those eyes that I can't stop picturing.

It's not lack of work that keeps me sitting in my chair, hands crossed behind my head, and staring at the ceiling.

I should've probably taken the day off and stalked her house, hoping the armed guards wouldn't chop my head off.

And honestly? It'd be bloody worth it.

When I told Daniel about my plan for last night, he called me a crazy arsehole, so I might as well live up to the expectations.

The door opens and I resist the urge to roll my eyes.

Speak of the fucking devil.

He swings it shut with his foot and storms in my direction, holding his phone and grinning like a bloody fool.

He removes his AirPods and comes to my side, then holds the phone up. On the screen, there's everyone from back home. Well, not literally, but most of them.

They're gathered at a huge dinner table in the home of Jonathan King. Elsa's father-in-law and Aiden's father, who's even worse than the sorry cunt.

Jonathan is sitting with his much younger wife. There's Elsa and her shadow—sorry, husband—Aiden, and their son, Eli, who's, unfortunately, turning out to be more and more like his father instead of his mother. It's those destructive King genes, I swear.

Ronan and Teal are smiling at me while holding a giggling Remi, who keeps chanting, "Nokth…Nokth…"

There's also the rest of my group of friends from secondary school, Xander and his wife Kim, and their daughter, who's hiding her face in her father's shirt.

The silent motherfucker with serial killer vibes, Cole, and the woman who tamed that destructive side of him, Silver.

And last but not least, the reason behind this call and who's holding the phone, Astrid. She's Daniel's best friend and always includes him in everything that happens back home with live video calls.

Her husband, Levi, another one with the destructive Kings, keeps watching her while simultaneously holding their twin boys. It's their birthday, I realize, because of the huge cake with "Landon" and "Brandon" written on it.

"Say hi to my bug, Knox!" Daniel says in his cheerful tone.

"You're my bug, Dan!" Astrid protests.

"I agree to that. If anyone is a bug, then it's this one." I smile, waving at T and Ron and they wave back. My brother-in-law is making a show of it like the cheeky bastard he is and even making his son join in.

"That's your uncle, Remi. And while you can love him, you're not allowed to become as desperate as he is, mkay?"

"Says the one who sent a thousand clingy texts to his wife back in secondary school," Xan teases.

Ron glares at him. "Hey! You shut the fuck up before I expose you."

"I still have the screenshots," Xan continues taunting.

"Me, too." Aiden smirks, one hand playing with his son's hair and the other stroking Elsa's hand on the table. He always has to be touching her in some way.

"Me three," Cole says with a perfectly straight face, wrapping a hand around Silver's shoulder. "And I might have taken a picture of a recent clingy conversation as well."

"You fucking—"

"Language at my table, Astor," Jonathan says in his usual stern tone.

"Just let them be." Aurora laughs, entwining her fingers with his. "It's fun."

"Dear Aurora," Ron starts in his fake dramatic tone. "I'll show you what fun is when I burn Cole's next special edition book."

"Not if you still need your life," Cole says coolly.

"Hey." Teal stares at Cole. "Stop ganging up on him or you'll have me to answer to."

"What she said. I'll also sue you for emotional distress, and my beloved brother-in-law will win the case."

I raise a brow. "The same brother-in-law you're telling your son not to grow up to be?"

He laughs, but it's a bit forced. "I was just kidding... Listen, Remi, your uncle Knox is the best there is. You can definitely become like him." Then he whispers, "Not."

"I heard that." I glare. "And I might be thinking about representing Cole in this case."

"Nooo," Ron says dramatically. "Not you, too, Knox."

Laughter breaks out around the table, and Dan and I laugh as well before he shouts, "Happy birthday, Lan and Bran. Your favorite uncle sends you the best wishes."

Astrid brings the phone down so that she's occupying most of the picture. "You could've been here instead."

"I have work."

"More like, he doesn't want to run into a certain blondie."

"Shut the fuck up." He snatches the phone and continues talking to Astrid on his way out, subtly changing the subject.

But I follow after him. What? The best way to kill time is to get on Dan's nerves.

I wrap an arm around his shoulder and join in on the

conversation. "He's so traumatized that he's been having PTSD episodes whenever I send a blonde hooker to his place."

There's laughter from the other end, and Levi slides to his wife's side, still holding his boys. "I told you there was more to it, Princess, but you refused to believe me."

A frown appears on her forehead. "Is it true, bug?"

"They're all little fuckers who love instigating chaos. Don't listen to them." He tries to push me off him, but I tighten my hold as Levi and I egg him on while Astrid tries and fails to take his side.

He hangs up as soon as we're by the door and gives me the stink eye. "Can't you stop?"

"What?" I grin. "Talking about your trauma from a certain blonde?"

"If you don't quit the wanker behavior, I'm going to fuck with you as well."

"Pray tell, how will you do that?"

"I don't know for sure, but Anastasia and I are close. I'll figure something out."

"Like fuck you will."

"Then stop being a motherfucking dick." He pushes me away. "And don't send anymore hookers to my place."

"I'll decide that according to how you behave." I open the door to my office. "Now, let's go annoy Sebastian or Nate, because I'm bored."

"Now that's what I'm talking about…" he trails off, and all his words and movements come to a halt.

I follow his line of vision and smile when I find the reason behind his state, then squeeze his shoulder. "My, my, Dan. Isn't that the blonde who made you hate all blondes?"

Instead of the anger I expected, his lips pull in a dark smirk. "The one and only."

⚖

By the time I get to W&S's parking garage, I'm ready to go to the *Pakhan*'s house and kidnap Anastasia if I have to.

Yes, there are still a few hours until the deadline, but there hasn't been any news from her. Not even a peep.

And I don't have the patience to wait any longer.

My feet come to a halt when I approach my car. Two tall, muscular men in black suits are standing in front of me.

One of them lifts his jacket, subtly showing me his gun as he motions to a black car with tinted windows that's parked near mine.

I don't have to wonder who it is. It must be Anastasia's father or someone close to him.

One of the guards frisks me, confiscates my briefcase, then pushes me not-so-gently in the direction of the car and opens the door. Sure enough, Anastasia's father is sitting in the back seat with an erect posture and his vision focused ahead.

"If you'd told me you were coming, I would've made reservations at a nice restaurant," I speak calmly.

"Drop the sarcasm. I already have an English bastard who's excellent at that. I don't need another one."

I straighten, staring at him. Does that mean he's going to accept me as a member of his family? For some reason, I thought I'd have to prove myself to him some more.

"Why do you want to be with my daughter? Think carefully before you reply."

"I don't need to. Your daughter is the woman who added purpose to my life and I can't imagine it without her anymore—"

"That's a very selfish reason."

"That's because you didn't let me finish. Your daughter is the woman who makes me a complete man, with flaws and all, and I will protect her with my life if I have to."

"What if you can't?"

"I can." There's zero doubt in my mind and my tone.

"I'm the *Pakhan* of the Russian *Bratva*. Do you know what that means?"

"That you're trying to intimidate me."

"That she's under constant threat due to being my daughter.

That's why I want her to marry someone from the brotherhood, someone who wouldn't hesitate to pull a trigger to keep her safe."

"And you think I would if her life was in jeopardy?"

He raises a brow. "You're on the side of the law, not against it."

"Don't let stereotypes fool you. Most of us couldn't care less about the law. We just use it."

"What if I tell you the only way to be with her is if you completely become an outlaw."

"I would love to, but that would just keep Anastasia in the life she hates, so I can't do that."

He pauses, raising a brow. "Are you sure you want to be telling me that?"

"Yes, and you feel it, too. Deep down, you know that she needs to get away from your world, even if only partially."

"And if I refuse."

I lift a shoulder. "Then I'll just keep on convincing you until you either agree or...agree."

His lips twitch in a smile. It's small and almost unnoticeable, but I know I'm getting somewhere with him.

And I mean it.

Either he lets me be with her, or I'm kidnapping her the fuck out of this country.

FORTY-ONE

Anastasia

PAPA ISN'T BUDGING.

He still has me under house arrest and refuses to let me go out, except when I'm surrounded by a thousand and one guards. Vlad is on his side, too, so he's ratcheting the security up a notch.

Rai tried to talk some sense into them, but neither was listening. She told me to be patient and said ambiguous words about how things are not what I think.

But that hardly gave me any hope. The only one who's given me a sliver of it was Adrian when I overheard him tell Kirill he'll convince Papa to take Knox's offer for the *Bratva*'s and V Corp's sake.

If there's anyone I know who'd be able to change Papa's mind, it's him. However, he seems to be taking his sweet time with it and I'm not sure if I'll be able to handle it any longer.

It's been a week since Knox barged into our house as if he had every right to, as if he couldn't care less about the scary painting in the entrance or the more terrifying people within this mansion's walls.

If I were him, I would've run the other way as I'm used to. But Knox has never been the type to run away. He might have hidden for some time, but he didn't run away. Not really.

The following day, when I didn't contact him, I expected him to bulldoze through the door again and demand things from Papa.

But he didn't.

That's when the doubt started to creep in. Maybe he came to his senses and realized that he shouldn't get involved with someone like me.

Surely, a fuck isn't worth jeopardizing his life at the hands of the *Bratva*. Surely, anyone with logic would convince him that he shouldn't be with me.

And while that's all I've ever wanted since I left, a weight presses on my chest at the thought of losing him. And sometimes, like now, I can't breathe. It doesn't matter that ever since Papa gave me back access to my laptop, I've been creating more systems than should be healthy and spied on his and Dan's social media accounts.

I know the right thing to do is to give up, to let him live his life as the hotshot lawyer and not drag him down with my shady family business. I should watch from afar and abide by Papa's wishes, but the mere thought of another man besides Knox touching me brings nausea to my throat.

It's even worse imagining him with another woman. It would eat me alive.

A knock sounds on the door and I murmur a "Come in" without breaking eye contact with the screen.

"Ana!" Rai's uncharacteristically cheerful voice makes me stare at her.

She stands at the door with a hand on her growing belly and smiles so big, it would be contagious under any other circumstances.

"What it is, Rai?"

"Granduncle is asking for you in the dining room."

"No…Rai…please stop him. He's going to make me marry Kirill and you know how manipulative he is. He'll swallow me alive and I can't…I can't just marry him when I have someone else in my heart—"

"Hey." She's by my side in a second. "There will be no marrying that cunning fox Kirill, not if I have to reveal his secret to stop it."

"W-what secret?"

"You don't have to worry about it. Just know that it's not going to happen. Besides, I'm pretty sure that's not the reason Granduncle is asking for you."

I frown. "Then what is it?"

"You'll know when you get there." She gently yet firmly lifts me up, then smooths my hair that's gathered in a bun.

I must look like shit in my PJs and makeup-free face, but my appearance is the last thing on my mind these days.

Rai intertwines her hand with mine and leads me downstairs. Papa's guard stares at me funny and I chalk it up to my unflattering appearance.

When Rai opens the door, however, the reason behind everyone's reaction materializes in front of me.

On Papa's right, the place that's reserved for Vlad, sits the last person I expected to ever be invited to our dining table.

He's wearing a sharp brown suit that brings out the intense hazel color of his eyes with that golden ring I've been dreaming about lately.

It hasn't been long since I last saw him, but he looks a bit different—broader, sharper, and with a face that's oozing masculinity and charm.

Maturity, too, I realize. In the span of a week, he seems to have aged and become wiser. Or maybe I'm the one who has.

"Knox," I whisper, unable to believe my eyes.

His lips pull in that charismatic smile that I could never resist. "Hey, beautiful."

I stare between him and Papa, then at Rai, secretly blaming

her for not making me a bit more presentable when she knew who was here.

"What are you doing here?" I ask Knox but stare at Papa, a bit scared that he'll order his senior guard, who stands behind him like a wall, to off Knox.

"Sergei invited me."

I nearly choke on my own spit. Did he just say Papa invited him? Also, please tell me he didn't just call him by his first name. Only the leaders of the *Bratva* are allowed to do that and never to his face.

Jeez, even Rai's husband, a complete rebel, has never done it.

My attention flies to Papa, expecting him to shoot Knox, but he remains in his element, not even looking offended.

"You invited him?" I whisper.

"Yes. He's a business partner now."

I'm unable to process that, so I just stare, dumbfounded. Does this mean Papa accepts him?

"And?" Knox asks with a mischievous grin.

"A possible son-in-law," Papa says.

"Hey, not "possible." Definite. You're the one who said I'll have to marry into your family."

Papa clears his throat and Rai chuckles by my side.

They...didn't just say what I think they said, right?

I don't get a chance to process it further before Papa stands up and heads toward me, his guard in tow behind him.

When he's within touching distance, he reaches a hand out and pats my head. And for just a second, I feel like that little girl again, the one who came out from beneath the table when he killed my stepfather. He patted my head then, too, before offering me his hand, and even though it was bloody, I took it.

Because he's my father.

No matter how monstrous the world views him, he'll always be the god who saved me from a life of abuse.

"You deserve much more than I can offer you, Nastyusha,"

he tells me. "But if he hurts you in any way, I'll make a lesson out of him."

"Papa…" I choke on my tears, then take his free hand and kiss its back. "Thank you. Thank you."

He strokes my hair for a few more seconds, then releases me and leaves with his guard. Rai winks at me before she jogs after him. "Wait for me."

Papa grabs her by the arm. "No running or you'll hurt the baby."

She grins at that and I smile a little, but it soon falls when I feel hot breaths at my neck.

I abruptly turn around and my air gets caught in my throat when I'm face to face with those golden hazel eyes.

He reaches around me and closes the door. I swear I can hear its resounding sound in my chest.

"Miss me, beautiful?"

"What happened?" It's hard to breathe let alone speak when his body is a few inches from mine and his warmth is flooding me. "How come Papa agreed?"

"I've been meeting with him ever since the first time he caught me coming out of your room. It took a lot of convincing, but he was being difficult about something we both wanted. He knows you're better off away from his world and that I'm the one who can offer you that life. So he suggested we get married."

"Y-you don't have to do that just for Papa. I can speak to him—"

"What are you talking about? You think I wouldn't want to marry you?"

My lips part and I fumble for words. "You want to?"

"What type of question is that? Of course, I want to. We might have started with my fucking your brains out, but over time, you became the woman I can't imagine my life without. You became *my* woman, Anastasia, and I intend to keep you."

I sniffle, the onslaught of emotions ricocheting in my chest. "Even though I hid my identity from you?"

"Even then. That's when I knew you were mine, and there's no fucking changing that."

"But my family—"

"I couldn't give a fuck about your family. You're the only one I care about. Besides, I have a big family as well and they're more than ready to accept you as a member. We can be a little crazy, just so you're warned."

"Oh, Knox…I love you."

He pauses, a gleam shining deep in his eyes. "You do?"

"Yeah, I think I've been falling in love with you since the first time I saw you."

"I've been obsessed with you for just as long. I didn't realize the nature of these feelings growing inside me at first, but I do now. They're stronger than love, beautiful, they're even more powerful than anything I've ever experienced and I'd be a fool to ignore them. You taught me to not ignore the ugly parts of myself. Hell, you even liked them and made me the better version of myself."

"You made me the best version of myself, too. You helped me find my own strength and I can't imagine my life without you."

"You've always been strong. Just because it was simmering under the surface doesn't mean it wasn't there."

"And just because you had a traumatic past, doesn't mean you can't rise above it." I stroke his face. "I'll be with you every step of the way."

"I sure as fuck will."

"You'll really have me?"

"The real question should be, will *you* have me, beautiful?"

"For the rest of my life, Knox."

"Good, because I wasn't going to take no for an answer." He opens his arms and I dive right in.

I dive into the place that makes me feel wanted, safe, and alive.

The place I'll never leave.

EPILOGUE

Knox

Two years later

"I'M TELLING YOU, ANA, WE USED TO BEAT HIS ARSE," Ron says with his usual overdramatization and T shakes her head.

My wife, who's snuggled in my lap, laughs. She just loves it whenever Ron or Dan tell stories about the past, which is why she gets along with them very well and demands we visit the UK any chance we get.

And yes, she's my wife now. Anastasia Van Doren. I married her a few months after Sergei gave me the green light. I would've done it sooner, before he changed his mind, but there were a lot of things happening in the *Bratva*, so we had to wait.

Even though my beautiful wife keeps in touch with her great-cousin and the grumpy arsehole, Vladimir, we're actually isolated from their internal and external wars.

Sergei made sure to keep her away from everything, as per

her wishes, but she still visits him all the time, checking up on his health.

Anastasia doesn't know this, but she's a mafia princess through and through. Whenever the chance arises, she still helps the leaders when they need any hacking done and cares about whether or not they're in danger.

Just because she was out of the house doesn't mean she forgot where she came from, and I love that about her.

I love how she's loyal to a fault and stands up for her friends, namely Gwen, Sandra, and my sister.

Yes, the usually closed off T doesn't spend a day without asking about Anastasia. When she doesn't pick up the phone, Teal calls me and tells me to pass it to Ana—without asking about me. The traitor.

Needless to say, I usually hang up, because my wife is a busy woman and I'm not prepared to share her free time with anyone else. She started her own IT company that works closely with several corporations, including V Corp. She's an absolute genius, so I had no doubt that she'd do well, even if the beginning was a little hard.

It took some time to settle into the new routine, especially with my demanding job and the number of cases I was getting. At some point, I had to limit the number and forward many to Lauren.

She's an excellent lawyer and a dedicated activist, so I know any sexual or domestic abuse victim will be in good hands with her—if Sandra Bell is any indication.

The scared young woman with the haunted eyes is also a successful businesswoman and an activist now. She got together with Lauren a few months after the trial and they've been in a happy relationship ever since.

Anastasia and I still meet with them whenever possible. They're close friends and Sandra's company was my wife's first client when she was getting started.

It took her some time to get on her feet. But I was there for her every step of the way like she was there for me when I needed her. But she didn't need my help much, because she's brilliant that way.

Even though I'm not a fan of the idea of sharing her, I can't help stroking her stomach every chance I get. Even now.

Anastasia is four months pregnant and I've never seen her as ecstatic as when she announced the news to me. It was about a year after her *babushka* died peacefully in her sleep right after we visited her together.

Anastasia said this baby was a gift since she's always wanted to be a mother like her own and her surrogate grandmother.

Teal and Elsa flew over to New York the day they heard the news, accompanied by their husbands and children that time. It was wild and annoying since they stole all her attention and wouldn't bloody shut up.

Aiden, Ronan, and I might have sulked while the women were doing their own thing, to which Aiden told me, "This is all your fault, fucker. You just had to knock her up and announce it."

"As you did to Elsa, you mean."

"I didn't let anyone visit, did I?"

He had a point.

Now is another one of those times, but we're only with Ronan and T at their house. Aiden left his son with Dad and Agnus, then took Elsa somewhere none of us can reach.

"Are you going to shut up, Ron?" I ask when he continues his monologue.

"What?" He leans back on the sofa and takes a sip of his beer. "Afraid she'll find out how much of a loser you are?"

"The only loser around is someone who sent very clingy texts to my sister and got ignored."

"Really?" Remi asks, his eyes bugging out.

Ronan lifts him and sits him on his lap. "Now, champ, we don't believe everything your uncle Knox says, mkay?"

"It's true, though," Teal says with a poker face.

"*Ma belle!* You're supposed to take my side."

"Not when you're wrong, hon." She smiles this time and I can see the exact moment his expression softens, and he pulls her to his side, hugging both her and Remi.

I do the same, my hold tightening around Anastasia's middle until she squirms.

"Did I hurt you?" I whisper, immediately loosening my hold.

"No." She smiles in that bright way that stabs me straight in the gut.

No clue if it's the hormones or what, but she's gained an irresistible type of beauty ever since she became pregnant. Her blue eyes are brighter, her icy hair is shinier, and she has this glow I can't get enough of.

"Then what is it?" I frown when she continues squirming.

Her lips meet the shell of my ear and I become rock-fucking-hard due to her movements alone. "I need you."

Well, fuck.

I love it when she says things like that. Anastasia might have been shy in the beginning, but now, she doesn't hesitate to tell me what she wants from me, and it's the best fucking turn-on.

"Need me how?" I tease.

"Knox!"

"What, beautiful?"

"Fuck me," she murmurs, then gulps, casting a glance at T and Ron, who are busy playing with their son.

"Oh, I'll do more than fuck you." I grab a handful of her arse and she stifles a moan.

Then I'm lifting her in my arms and carrying her away from everyone else.

It's time I claim my wife again and again.

She's mine and I'm hers, till death do us part.

THE END

Next up is the standalone book that features Daniel Sterling, titled *Empire of Hate*.

Curious about Nathaniel and Gwyneth who were mentioned in this book? You can read their story in *Empire of Desire*.

For more stories about Anastasia's Russian mafia family, you can read Rai and her husband's story in *Throne of Power* & Adrian Volkov's story in *Vow of Deception*.

WHAT'S NEXT?

Thank you so much for reading *Empire of Sin*! If you liked it, please leave a review.
Your support means the world to me.

If you're thirsty for more discussions with other readers of the series, you can join the Facebook group, Rina Kent's Spoilers Room.

Next up is the angsty, revenge-themed book, *Empire of Hate*, that will feature Daniel Sterling who was a supporting character in *Empire of Sin* and *Cruel King*.

ALSO BY RINA KENT

For more books by the author and a reading order, please visit:

www.rinakent.com/books

ABOUT THE AUTHOR

Rina Kent is a *USA Today*, international, and #1 Amazon bestselling author of everything enemies to lovers romance.

She's known to write unapologetic anti-heroes and villains because she often fell in love with men no one roots for. Her books are sprinkled with a touch of darkness, a pinch of angst, and an unhealthy dose of intensity.

She spends her private days in London laughing like an evil mastermind about adding mayhem to her expanding universe. When she's not writing, Rina travels, hikes, and spoils cats in a pure Cat Lady fashion.

Find Rina Below:

Website: www.rinakent.com
Neswsletter: www.subscribepage.com/rinakent
BookBub: www.bookbub.com/profile/rina-kent
Amazon: www.amazon.com/Rina-Kent/e/B07MM54G22
Goodreads: www.goodreads.com/author/show/18697906.Rina_Kent
Instagram: www.instagram.com/author_rina
Facebook: www.facebook.com/rinaakent
Reader Group: www.facebook.com/groups/rinakent.club
Pinterest: www.pinterest.co.uk/AuthorRina/boards
Tiktok: www.tiktok.com/@rina.kent
Twitter: twitter.com/AuthorRina